Desperate to Survive

Book Two of the Survival Trilogy

F. D. BRANT

F. D. Brant

GRESHAM, OREGON

Copyright © 2017 by **F. D. Brant**

F. D. Brant
P O Box 522
Gresham, Or 97030
www.fdbrant.com

Publisher's Note: This is a work of fiction. Names, characters, places, and incidents are a product of the author's imagination. Locales and public names are sometimes used for atmospheric purposes. Any resemblance to actual people, living or dead, or to businesses, companies, events, institutions, or locales is completely coincidental.

Book Layout © 2017 BookDesignTemplates.com

Desperate to Survive/ F. D. Brant. – 2nd ed.
ISBN 978-1-946179-09-8

This story is dedicated to, as always, family, and to the Queens of Science Fiction. I've read their many stories over the years and have enjoyed their fictional worlds – Here's to Anne McCaffrey, and Andre Norton, both having passed to wherever such writers go. To all members of my family, who have supported and encouraged me to continue to the completion of this project, and especially to my wife Audrey who has to live with this writer.

"Leader, I really do not understand this at all." He paused for effect before continuing, "These new females that we have added to our herd, a good portion of them have been with us now for one cycle of the seasons, and not one is carrying offspring."

Looking down before answering K'jor said, "I know, but you must remember that it hasn't been for lack of trying. I know that most of the warriors have tried to breed with them, and once these new females realized that there would be no choice, they submitted. Of course there are a few that will fight it, but once these were made an example of, the rest allowed it. But you must remember that they are magicians. They have been able to hide unseen for who knows how long – I suspect generations if we really want to admit it. And I was hopeful that once we broke through and destroyed their magician lairs and ways that we would be able to reap riches that these must have had, and with the increase to our female herds it would mean that we would also have an increase in warriors to help us later to become the ones who would rule. And we surely ended up with enough females, even though most of the males are worthless as slaves. Once taken from those lairs of theirs, to work our fields and other places where we have need of their labor, they have died off quickly, and the ones that remain are almost not worth the effort or food to keep them around.

"Since the new females now understand has there been any further resistance from them when one of the males signals them for breeding?"

The second shook his head and said, "No, when any of our males gives the signal, then the female will stop what she is doing, undress and present herself, so that in itself is not an issue at all – especially when they have witnessed what happens when one of them refuses."

Nodding his head in agreement the leader said, "Yes, yes, that does usually bring the rest around. Once they realize that refusal will change nothing, and that it will lead to punishment. Well, all we can do is continue to try, but since they are of a magic race, maybe these females are able to prevent the carrying. And on that subject, have they gotten over the idea that they are allowed names? It is something that I really do not understand. They are just one of the herd, and as such they are not allowed that kind of individuality. I just don't know, and truthfully this whole thing has been much more complicated than I ever thought it would be. Just keeping the tribes and clans united for this fight, to locate, capture these magicians, and destroy their hidden lairs, has proven to be almost impossible. Especially since what we have found, in their cities, as they call them, there hasn't been the bounty we expected or had promised. And now it has been a while since our last successful campaign, and I can see that the tribes and clans in the alliance are starting to become quite restless, and might even want to bring up the old scars, hatreds, and such, and begin to fight among themselves again. We need to find another one of those hidden cities, again as the magicians' call them, or this may come apart."

"It's not for lack of trying, as in our attempt of successful breeding. We have patrols and scouting parties out, and now it appears that something has changed." He paused again, not quite sure how to state it. S'lon took a deep breath and then said, "Okay, look, something has changed. I don't know what. But somehow it appears that maybe they learned what's happening. It's the only explanation that I have."

Looking up from his working area K'jor asked, "Changed? How so? Did we not plan these attacks down to almost perfection, and yes, I know plans fail once one goes into battle. But from the ones we conquered I do not believe that any escaped. So there is no way that word could have reached the other hidden lairs as to what has transpired. We have completely eliminated anybody who could have possibly carried the alarm. Even that one group that had escaped was destroyed in the Sacred Mountains. So what could have changed?"

At loss as how to explain, S'lon shrugged, "Everything you have just stated is true. But I do not have any other way to explain it." He took a deep breath and let it out slowly before continuing, "These lairs that we've conquered were not close to each other, and while the population in any one of them was greater than any one of our clans, or tribes, it still wasn't large. So maybe there are only the few that we found." Shaking his head he continued. "I mean how do we know just how many of these lairs are out there? And maybe, just maybe we have cleaned them out, and there are no more."

Breathing deeply and loudly the leader said, "That is a possibility, but I have a gut feeling that there are more of these magicians out there, and until I have proof otherwise, we will continue to go after them." With that he waved his hand at his second to leave. He had much to think about, and needed to come up with something to keep this alliance together.

Seeing the dismissal he turned and left, frustrated, as he really got no satisfactory answers to his many questions. But K'jor was very busy, and while it had been pleasurable to breed with the new stock, it was also very frustrating to see that none of these females were now carrying. *Just what magic do they possess that they can prevent such a thing from happening anyway?*

CHAPTER ONE

Saige looked across the hidden meadowlands as the morning light crested the extinct volcanic walls that surrounded them. With the clouds that hung in the sky and the suns rising, the clouds took on many colors, from a deep gray, and as it lightened, to a brilliant orange. If the situation wasn't as desperate as it was, such a sight would be worth stopping and enjoying. But fall would be here and in the lowlands soon, and that would mean that the primitives once again should be looking towards winter and a possible break in the attacks on the cities. With the destruction of who knew how many cities since their desperate flight, when theirs had been one of cities lost to the primitives, they had been cut off, isolated ever since. And he knew that none of the surviving cities had any idea as to why the ones that had been attacked had gone dark – silent as if they had never been. Whoever this leader of the united force was, he had been smart enough to make sure that no one left the attacked cities to warn the others – except their scouting unit, of course. And as far as the primitives knew they had been destroyed on their desperate flight, and the few that may have escaped had died here in the Sacred Mountains.

He hoped that the team that he had left back at Point Alpha, the Alpha, or Alpha compound, complex, facility, or however else they had identified this place, had figured out enough so that when he and this group returned that they would finally be able to make contact with any of the surviving cities – if there were any. It was hell not knowing. Yet at the same time he did not know what his small group could do anyway. Sighing and taking one more look around he could see that the rest were beginning to stir. It was time to get moving, to find where their ancestors had left this meadow to do their research among these primitives. Looking at the size of this bowl he shuddered with the thought of how it must have been in this area when this volcano had been active. It was only one of many, and it explained why the primitives had considered these mountains sacred, a place of their gods. It had to have been a spectacular and awe inspiring sight when they had erupted. He was quite thankful that all signs pointed to these as being extinct. He walked away from camp and relieved himself, and then on the way back in smelled the smoke of their cooking fire. He realized that he was quite hungry and his stomach growled in agreement. *It needs to be today that we find the way in and out of this place. I truly did not realize the size of this hidden valley. Probably would have been smarter to have had everyone out here looking. But Stone and Sorrel had stated that it was huge, in fact around 10 kilometers around the perimeter from their estimation. Still until one actually sees it – well I just didn't realize it, that's all. It really makes it a very large area to explore and find that elusive point where one can leave this place, and find that other exit out of these mountains.*

On the previous day as they had worked their way across they had searched a number of likely places. But so far nothing had been found. There were a number of smaller cinder cones and many ridges and rises. With one area looking like a small town with the spires and blocks of broken lava, and another looked to be a small army in the distance. He had pictured in his mind a rolling meadow, not this broken rough land that surrounded them. Yet, he had to admit that what they were seeing made more sense than the images he had created in his mind. The history that they had been taught in their education centers had turned out to be false. It had been the discovery of this Alpha compound hidden deeply within the Sacred Mountains that had shattered that false history. Here they had learned that one of the strongest held beliefs that they were from this world dissolved away. This facility proved, for anyone who would doubt, that they were descendants of anthropologists, sociologists, scientists, geologists, the support staff, and the researchers – ones who had come here to study primitives, their societies, their interaction with one another, the planet, plant and animal life, and geology – they were from another world. But something had happened and they had become isolated. Their ancestors had decided to remain separate of the native population, and to *hide* from their sight, using the technology that they had to make their cities invisible, and to build them in inhospitable areas to make it even less likely that they would be discovered. It had worked for a few thousand annuals, but now something had changed and the cities were falling to these primitives.

Winter was a time, from their personal experience and study that the primitives stayed within their camps and shelters. But late spring was a time to search and prepare for battle and with it, he knew, this alliance would search for more of their cities. Yet looking at this camp he would never have guessed that all this had transpired, or was pending. Here, right now, everything looked so peaceful, so normal. "Hey Saige, how'd you sleep last night? Stone asked. "It was much colder than I expected. But I guess I can blame it on the fact that we have been sleeping indoors for quite a while."

He's right. Even though we spent half of the past winter in the caves on these mountains, the last portion, through late summer, had been spent in the Alpha so all of us have gotten used to being inside. "Okay, I guess, Stone." Then changing the subject, Saige said, "That food smells great. What is it about food cooked over an open fire that makes it seem that much more appetizing, anyway? Did you see that sunrise this morning, spectacular if you ask me? Look, once after everyone has gone off and taken care of nature and eaten, we'll get together and look at how we want to approach this day. We flat are running out of time, and I just did not expect that there would be so many places that could be an exit out of here. One thing for sure, we cannot allow the primitives to discover the Alpha compound. We do not have the strength to defend it. And I know from what we have deduced there is another way out of these mountains giving us other ways to protect these secrets."

"Yeah, it only makes sense. Compound Alpha's best security is for it to remain unknown, and hidden. Not that our ancestors didn't do a wonderful job of hiding it. After all if you hadn't literally stumbled upon it we wouldn't have found it."

Laughing at the comment Saige said, "Now that's an understatement, if I've ever heard of it, and thanks for being kind about that incident." Thinking back on what Stone had just mentioned he knew that he had been lucky that he hadn't been killed. He had literally stepped off a cliff and had fallen into the compound. So, "stumbled upon" was being kind. Looking around he could see most of the rest of the team were returning from taking care of the morning nature call, and gathering around the fire. They shared the cooking duties and this morning Staven and Starr were preparing the food. He could hear the friendly verbal sparring between the members of the team, which sent him back to where it had not been so friendly, and their group had literally fallen apart. Saige had to admit that much had happened in such a short time, and knew that so much more had to happen in even less time. But he did not even try to guess what the future might hold at this moment, and having any ideas on how to break the alliance, well, none at this moment. All he could do was shake his head, as what lay ahead appeared to be quite overwhelming, if not impossible for such a small group of people that they had. It saddened him to realize that in that desperate flight that they had lost almost all of their members, and the ten that were left were so small, so how could one then defeat the primitives?

* * *

It had been difficult to make this Keenan understand the severity of the situation and that they were the real thing, and not some prankster who was trying to pull something over on them. After all, the Alpha compound had been forgotten in time, like their true history. So it was of no surprise that there were problems. Saar with the help of Seirra, Sabryn and Seve were able to finally get the critical information that needed to be passed on to the remaining cities, about what had transpired with the ones that had gone silent, had gone dark, and why. After all, whoever led these primitives had made sure that the attacks would be, first, a complete surprise and there would be no alarms to alert not only the occupants of the city under siege, and second that none would ever escape to alert the other hidden cities. These primitives had complete success until their attack on Sequoyah, it was the only city that still maintained a trained group of individuals who could live in the wild, and possibly meet the primitives on their own terms, giving them the tools to survive. The rest of the cities had eliminated these elite teams, saying that it was too expensive, and "besides they were safe within their hidden cities so such a force was no longer necessary or needed". Out of the approximate 100 members that escaped from the city of Sequoyah only ten now remained. They had to fight for every foot of their flight, and the cost had been high.

It wasn't that Keenan was one who did not care, or just went through the motions; no he was just the opposite. In fact he had been questioning why, when the last city had gone dark, silent, and that the reaction from the ones in charge appeared to be much too nonchalant, and that it was "business as usual". It was because of his strength of character that it had been so difficult. He was not going to move anything further along until he knew that what he was receiving was authentic – yet, now that the word had gone out, now what? The small team at the Alpha facility felt their elation slowly diminish. *Now what?* Saar knew that they were supposed to be getting ready to make this attempt at contact, then wait until Saige and that group returned, and once back then the contact attempt was to be made. But once they had put the coordinates into the system, the system had taken over and automatically began transmitting. There was nothing they could do but to continue at that point, which they did. And now that the cities were aware of what had transpired, again now what? It was not known how the primitives found them, or how they penetrated the veil that had hidden the cities from sight. Nor was it understood how someone had gotten this many of the tribes and clans together to form an alliance. Yet from the evidence that they now had this is exactly what had happened – *Again, now what?* How were the remaining cities going to be able to keep the primitives from attacking their individual cities, and to defend them? And how did the primitives know where to look? Yes each city had a map and location of all, but these maps were not easy to find, as they were hidden to prevent someone who had no need of that knowledge from accessing them, plus it required power to reveal the maps, and power was the first thing to go when the primitives attacked.

So while there was an initial exaltation from making contact, there was also consternation from not having a solution available to prevent further attacks. Saar looking back at the other three standing in the security office just shrugged. "I guess there's really not much we can do right now. I'll hang here so why not the three of you set up some shifts while all of you go and eat something. Then one of you can come back and take over so I can go and eat. I think that we will be very busy here for quite a while. I also suspect that we are going to get very tired of having to explain over and over again where we are and why we are here." So shooing them out he said, "Now go. I know that you Sabryn probably need to look in on Shayne anyway to be sure he's okay." He watched them as they reluctantly left the office and he took a deep breath. After all the silence that they had endured, they knew that soon they would be looking forward to, yearning really, just for that – silence once again.

CHAPTER TWO

K'jor sighed deeply as he got up from his working area. *It seemed so easy once we had discovered these magicians. To be able to get the tribes and clans aligned, with promises of wealth, prestige, and increases. And yes while we have increased both in slaves and females, it hasn't been nearly as successful as either I or the alliance has expected.* Shaking his head as he paced the bare room, he had no answers. The alliance was very fragile, and as his second had just stated, things just were not going well. *Yes, we increased our herd with many additional females, and even though there have been problems, most of them now understand what their roles are. Yes it had taken a few examples, which isn't something that I wanted, but it was necessary. After all, our roles as males are to protect the herd, to protect the females. And from this protection these females are to allow breeding by any of the warrior males. Why do these new females demand names?*

It really made no sense to him at all. They were just that – females, and part of the herd. Yet these new ones to the herd had brought a restlessness to it, demanding things, that again, the ones most outspoken had been made examples, to show the rest what they were and what their true roles are. Yet with some of them being in the herd for at least a full cycle of seasons none of these were carrying – and he had to admit that it wasn't for the lack of trying. He knew that these females had bled in their cycles which spoke that they were fertile. So why were none of them carrying? Shaking his head once again, all he could attribute it to was some magic that they possessed that allowed them to keep it from happening. He thought that maybe if they made examples of a couple of the stronger ones that just maybe it could be made to happen. But, then again, it went against their ways. Yes, if there was an obvious problem, a series of obvious refusals to submit, then the punishment was proper, but this – this was something different, something that they never had faced before. These females, being in their obvious prime time for breeding, but nothing coming out of it, other than he and the warrior males leaving their seed inside of them.

Enough on this! He had other issues now. The restlessness of the tribes, and the tension that was almost permutable, could almost be tasted, as it arose around him. They had been successful through this season of heat, and the past couple of seasons, finding and destroying eight of these magicians' lairs. But with season of falling, and season of cold approaching, and no others located, and again, with much in these lairs that were untouchable, because it had the magicians taint and thusly dangerous, the promised loot and rewards had not materialized. And, while the capture of these lairs had been easy, and they had been very successful, with little loss of warriors, the results were underwhelming, leading to this infighting and this alliance on the verge of tearing itself apart. But at this moment what could he do?

So far all of these hidden lairs had been located by how they were hidden. It was the one consistent thing they could find. Always in desolate out of the way places, areas where no one should have been able to live, and yet, these magicians did. Then there was that shimmering *veil*, more like heat waves, that hid the lairs from sight. And when one attempted to go through this *veil*, there would be both pain, and illusions of the mind, bringing terror and unconsciousness to any who attempted it. It brought back tribal memories that were told in stories of such things happening deep in their past. And of ones who had been severely injured awaking in, what only could be described as a very strange place, to be healed, and then once again find themselves close to their tribe with no explanation of how they arrived there, let alone why they were healthy once more.

This whole thing, the destruction of the magician lairs, wouldn't have even happened if not for an accident. Smiling as he shook his head, his introspection continued. Yes, if not for that accident, then this alliance, fragile as it is, would not exist, and these lairs would still be hidden from us and unknown. He remembered he was in camp, when one of the hunting parties returned with much needed meat. This party had been led by his second, and this hunting party rarely failed. But this time he brought back much more than meat for their clan – a tale, and strange clothing. Taking him aside S'lon stated that he had something important to discuss with him and at this time for him alone. So they went back to his portable shelter at the summer camp and S'lon sat down and waved for K'jor to sit across from him.

Then S'lon began, "We were following one of the herd beasts that we had wounded, and it ran far ahead of us. There was an argument about how much of an injury it had since it was outdistancing us, and appeared to be only slightly injured. But I prevailed and we followed it deep into the wastes, a place of little value, no water, much dust, and very little vegetation, you know the areas we know as the desolation. The only thing we could figure is that with its panic the beast just ran in whatever convenient direction it saw, and this direction was deep into the desolation.

Eventually we could see faltering and spots of blood showing us that it was finally reaching the end, and then we could finish it, dress it out, and bring the meat back to our camp. Except when we arrived where the beast had fallen there were two strangers that were dressed in these clothes inspecting the downed beast – both young – one male and one female. This seemed strange to us, since females never accompany a male unless it is for breeding. They know their place, and it is with the other females of the herd, not like this. And if she was there for breeding purposes, then she should have been without clothes. We knew that the beast was going nowhere so we briefly studied these two from hiding in case this was a trap of some kind. But they seemed totally unaware that we were even close. It became even stranger, as it appeared that this female had a name – a name, can you believe it? We could see that she was well past the time of first bleeding, so she was easily in her time for breeding. As you know if she was not then she would not be touched – so are our laws.

Since these two were not of our clan, then we felt that we could consider them enemies, and as such, one of the many things we do with enemies is breed with their females who are of age, since if we can have her carry one of our offspring then it is a victory for us to have one of our own in their camp. So once we determined that it was only they we attacked them, tied up the male so he could observe how we had conquered both he and the female. As we began he fought his bindings screaming at us, until finally we just killed him. To our surprise this female had never been bred and she fought us as we became the first in her life. She ended up bleeding a lot from where we entered into her, and her screams were worse than the male had been, and she, as all of us bred with her, continued to fight until one of us hit her too hard and she succumbed.

If she had been one of our females then she would have ended on the rack for punishment, but here had given up her life instead." Then shaking his head S'lon continued. "It was a surprise to all of us that this female at a prime breeding age had never been touched. It is something unheard of, yet it was so. The only thing I regret out of this is that she succumbed. We do not kill females unless they break the laws, and even then rarely. So as proof we stripped both bodies, took the beast, dressed it out, and then returned. And I am filled with many questions, such as why only the two of them? And where were they from? We found no evidence of either a camp or clan home close by – and if there was one, why so deep into the desolation? There is nothing there to keep one alive, let alone a clan home. And if there was no clan home or camp close, then the logical conclusion is that they were lost. Yet they showed no sign of being lost. It was as if they belonged there, and it is a mystery."

"Listening until the tale was complete K'jor thought for a while and was silent. Looking at nothing he leaned forward from his sitting position and finally said, as he handled the bloodied clothing. "You are right, this clothing is strange. I have never seen anything so finely woven. We surely do not have the capability." Then pausing again, he came to a decision. "Can you take me to where you found these two strangers? I want to look at the bodies, and especially this female who had never been touched. She must have been ugly to have been shunned."

"That's the strange part about this; she was neither ugly or had anything physically wrong with her, so it is a mystery as to why she had never been touched."

Standing up and signaling S'lon to do the same K'jor said, "It is too late today to go, but early in the morning when the suns first touch the sky you will lead me back to this place so I can see for myself." And with that the two left the portable shelter and continued with the work the season of heat camp always required.

* * *

The suns were just touching the hills surrounding the camp when the two of them left. It would take half of the day to reach the hunting area, and from there S'lon would then lead K'jor through the chase of the wounded beast to the area where the strange ones were found, and subsequently killed. "The bodies should be undisturbed so that you can observe the remoteness of this place, and the very dryness. Nothing should be able to survive there. We saw no predator sign at all. In fact other than the beast that we tracked, there was nothing but the dust. It was a quiet desolate area with only the wind as company." Shaking his head S'lon continued. "That is why it was such a surprise to find these two here."

"Did they have anything such as travel packs and such things to survive in such an area as this?" K'jor asked.

Shaking his head as the continued their careful trek through the wilderness, and while they did not expect to be attacked by a rival clan or tribe, it was always a possibility. "No nothing at all. Just those clothes I showed you, and that was another part of this strangeness. This desolation covers days of travel, and while we were on the edge there were no other tracks. The way we entered is the only way from this side of this vast area. It made no sense." Then for a while both were silent lost in their own thoughts, studying the countryside, and moving with stealth through the land.

Looking up at the suns K'jor said, "I believe we will stop here as it is close to high point with the suns. There is water and shade here, and it is a place where we can stay out of sight of any who might approach." They ate a cold meal made of travel rations, relaxing and apart. By keeping distance, which was as natural as sleeping and waking, they could not be surprised or both taken if one of the enemies appeared. Then after a short period of time K'jor signaled that it was time to continue and for S'lon to lead. They were on the edge of the great herds, and it was here this very season that they would return to get the great supplies of meat to last out the long seasons of cold.

The area here was of mixed grasses and trees with the trees being sparse, and many small streams and one major river flowing through this vast plain. From the direction they had come from, it was heavily forested in areas and they lived hidden in the hills inside a natural rock fortress that their clan had captured and occupied for many generations. So many generations in fact, that the original owners were unknown and the mighty battle to take this fortress was more myth than fact. These mountains, which they lived within, were just foothills when comparing them to the sacred range that only the priests and a few brave hunters entered. Yet their seasons of cold were cold, bleak, and long. So it was necessary to store vast amounts of food for this. The season of greening was also short, the grains produced helped, and while they had tamed some of the wild beasts, there were too few to provide all the necessities from them – thusly the season of heat camp and the hunting of the wild herds.

The two continued their hike, both remaining silent using only hand signals, and the surrounding terrain to keep from sight. Again they kept distance between them, and hiked far apart creating more than one almost invisible trail. Stealth was critical since they were not the only ones who hunted the great herds. Yet these herds were so huge and covered such a great area, that very rarely did two tribes or clans ever meet. When this rarity happened it was more of high tension, and wariness as one group watching the other would back away, and then disappear. They were here for meat, not war, so during the hunting season there hung an uneasy truce between the hunters. That did not mean that if an individual could be isolated that a rival tribe would not either capture or kill that individual, as it was the way of things. To make one's enemies weaker if at all possible was the way of the world. It was also why any of the females who were brought along to take care of the meat were never allowed to leave the camp where they were always protected. Since the law that this clan lived by was as the world. If any of their females had strayed and been found by an enemy then like them, they would all have a turn at breeding her so that if by some chance it might lead to the carrying of one of their own. The females knew this, and as such had no desire to leave the camp to the point that a place within the camp had to be set so that they could take care of their natural needs.

S'lon signaled K'jor to join him and waited until he approached. Then pointing at the ground he said. "If you look here, you can see the spots of dried blood from the wounded beast, and the tracks are easy to follow as it bounded away. We were cursing at that moment, since it moved just as we had let the arrow fly just wounding it, we now knew that we had to track it down and finish it." He pointed in the direction the wounded beast ran, at which point both separated once again. Now until they reached to point where the beast finally dropped, and then the discovery of these strange ones, both would track separately with a great distance between them, again so that if one was found, the other could assist, or escape.

Soon they reached the edge of the desolation and here the tracks of the panicked and wounded beast was plain, as were the tracks of the hunting party as they followed it. It was obvious from the tracks of the wounded beast that it had nothing but flight in its mind, otherwise it would not have gone the way it did. For whatever the reason, at this moment, the winds were calm not stirring up the powdery dust that dominated the desolation. Once deep into this area and with no food or water available, the wounded beast would expire without any additional attacks from the hunters. K'jor was amazed at the stamina of the beast. From the signs, the amount of blood he was seeing, and the slight faltering of steps that the trail plainly showed him, it should have collapsed long before it got very deep into the desolation. He could see that even now one day later that the tracks were beginning to vanish as the winds stirred the powdery dust into small whirlwinds, with shifting and blowing dust clouds which abounded. This was a place utterly without life, and a place to stay away. So what were two young strangers doing in such a place? It truly was a mystery, and one that gnawed on his mind. Something just did not make sense. All these thoughts were in the background as to let one's mind wander here could easily lead to death.

He saw S'lon signal him that they were nearing the area where it all had taken place, and he looked around and only saw desolation. He, for one, would be glad when they left this place of dryness and death, a place of the spirit world and returned to a green place. Again he marveled at the strength of this herd beast. They now were deep inside the desolation, and as he joined S'lon he found ahead of him a large flat area surrounded by what he could only subscribe as something at one time that had to have been mud hills, but moisture had left them long ago. There were a number of small openings and a very small cave or two off the edge of this open area. The two of them were utterly alone, with only the sounds of the slight wind, and the beating down of the heat from both the suns, which were well on their way towards setting, and the ground, which radiated the suns heat back to them. They could feel the dust sticking to their damp sweaty skin; K'jor could see both a look of surprise, and consternation on the face of S'lon. "What is the problem?" K'jor asked.

Turning around and facing the leader directly S'lon stated. "I am sure that this is the area where it all happened. The tracks lead right here and the lay of the land is correct, but . . ." As he trailed off he shrugged before continuing, "This just doesn't make sense."

"What doesn't make sense?" K'jor asked.

"Look around, and what do you see? Nothing . . . Nothing at all. That is what doesn't make sense. Even though the tracks lead right up to this place, once we are inside of it here everything is gone, wiped out, as if it never happened – and we were here yesterday, that I am sure of." He then began to walk the area mumbling to himself, and pointing out things as if to get it straight in his own mind. Shaking his head and placing his hands on his hips S'lon said once again, "This just doesn't make any sense at all."

Walking up to him K'jor said, "Now look, from what I can see there must be at least six of these areas that look identical, so it could be just a mistake here, and you just came to the wrong one. We are running out of time and will need to be gone soon. I do not want to remain here overnight, even with the evidence of no predators. Let's take a quick look at a couple of others, and then wrap up here. You do not need to worry about your tale as false. You brought back the strange clothing from the two so you have your proof. So if you miss where it happened here in this desolation, well so be it. You are a great tracker, and I am fair at it also, and I have to agree that the tracks do lead here, and just end. That is not to say that these devil winds have not wiped out anything beyond this point, and that we have just stopped short of where it actually had taken place."

"No! No, I am sure it was here. But it is very strange. Without known predators or even tracks of such, the bodies, and the entrails from the herd beast all should be here – and if not that, at least the dried blood upon the ground, not only from the beast but from the two strangers that we killed. It is like someone came here after we had left the desolation and then returned to our camp, wiping out all traces. But then again, there is no evidence that anything like that, or what we were involved in, ever happened. How can that be?"

Shaking his head was all that K'jor could do as he said, "I don't have any answers, and I believe you. But then again, other than the missing bodies for which we cannot account for, it could have been these winds that wiped out any sign leaving it as if nothing happened. And who knows, since we shun these areas, there might be a predator or scavenger we know nothing about that prowls these areas, and if so they could be responsible for the missing evidence, or maybe it could have been the spirits of the ones who have passed over." Sighing he continued, "We've run out of time, and need to head back. But you've given me much to think about." Then looking over the area carefully once more, they headed back.

* * *

He had to admit it that even after returning to camp, it continued to worry his mind. He did not like this kind of puzzle. And it wasn't until that season of cold, back within the fortress with time to really think that the idea began to form that maybe it wasn't some unknown predator or such, but maybe a hidden people, magicians that could hide from sight, and chose to live in the areas of desolation. After all they would have to be magicians to be able to live in such areas. Again he had no proof, but promised himself that with the next season of heat camp that he would go back and do a much more thorough search.

CHAPTER THREE

Sighing, Saige was becoming a little frustrated. The six of them had just finished the circuit around the inside bowl, along the walls of the ancient extinct volcano, and while he had been confident that they would find the exit point that their ancestors had used, it hadn't happened. *I was so sure that it had to be along walls, but we did a thorough search, and nothing.* Turning to the rest that was with him he asked again. "Yes, I know, but are all of you sure? From the way we entered into this area, there is no way that these pack animals could be taken out of here. So what are we missing?"

Shaking her head Shellian said, "I don't think we really missed anything. With two of us going down the walls on opposite sides of this crater and two searching through the middle area, well admit it, we did a thorough search. We took it slow and studied every centimeter of this place, and we came up empty." Shrugging before continuing she said. "You've got to remember, not that you don't, that when our ancestors put this facility here, it was well planned, and well hidden. If you hadn't literally fallen into it I don't think we would've found it. So if the main facility is that well-hidden, it only makes sense that the exit or exits out of this large meadowland would be just as well."

Stone, picking up on the thread continued, "We all know that the primitives are much better at this than we are." Pausing as he saw the reactions from the rest, "I know, before all of this happened, we thought we were as good. But, I for one, have to admit that we were proved wrong, and it was just through luck and good leadership that we survived at all."

Both Saige and Shellian looked at each other, and then at the other four members who were with them and Saige said, "Yes, Shayne was a great leader, I cannot say that either Shell' or myself have been equal to his high standards."

"What?" Sorrel exclaimed, "What do you mean by that? I would not be here and alive if it wasn't for the leadership the two of you have provided. Yes, I know that I lost my daughter, and it still tears me up inside, and brings almost instant tears to my eyes every time I think of my unborn daughter that I'll never see, who will never have a chance at life. And before you two protest, remember it was Shayne who told the two of you to take over the leadership just before he died. And I trust his judgment, and especially one he made on his deathbed. And as far as I am concerned . . ." Pausing for a moment and sweeping her arms around to include the rest that was there before continuing. ". . . His choice was proper and right. Do you not remember all the fighting and skirmishes that we dealt with, and the only passage that led into these mountains that had been blocked by that large patrol of primitives? Who by the way, had been placed there to prevent our passage into these Sacred Mountains? And yet here we are, now knowing our true history, alive, healthy, and trying to come up with some type of solution to break this alliance that the primitives have forged – all because of the leadership from the two of you. Yes, looking back I'm sure that I could find some way to do something you did better, but isn't the final result all that is important anyway?"

"But Sorrel . . ." Shellian responded gently, ". . . at the end just before we found this place, we had lost our leadership to the conspiracy, and from that your very life had almost become forfeit, and not counting the loss of your unborn daughter, we lost five, count them, five members before it was finally over, taking our, oh around a hundred members down to just the ten we have now. Of course I'm not including the two new lives that have joined us now. So as far as we are concerned, that's my brother and I, we failed, and failed miserably. We should have seen it coming, and prevented it from happening. Then instead of just the ten we have now, at least it would have been five more, and maybe like the other two women here, you would be with your daughter now, *instead of having to lament over your loss.*"

"Now hold on one minute Shellian." Staven stated, "I was one of the ones who were in the middle of that conspiracy. And other than the ones we sent away, it was our fault not yours. With everything you had to do just to keep us alive it's no surprise that you didn't see it coming. And had the rest of us been honest we should have recognized that both Schylar and Storme were eager to take over the leadership, but really had no skills to do it. So if any fault or blame needs to be placed it should be on us. And when we realized the very big mistake that we made, and was able to leave, we held out little to no hope that firstly we would find you, and secondly that you would accept us. After all if you had rejected us, like you first did, then we would have gotten what we deserved, what any traitor would deserve, but you and Stone came back for us, and now we have a child that like Sorrel's could be dead right now, along with us. And since bringing us into the facility we have been thankful every day that the two of you are leading us." Then waving them off when he saw them about to protest, he continued, "Look we had a rare opportunity to have been led by one of the best in Shayne, and then one of the worst in Schylar. So don't you think that we would know when the right ones are in charge? And I am glad it is not me. I am sorry that it took so long for us, all of us to realize it. Had we, then we probably would have put Schylar and Storme in their place. But instead we listened and believed them. So if any blame needs to be given, then it should be on us, the ones involved, not the two of you."

Silence reigned as both Saige and Shellian absorbed the words Staven and Sorrel had spoken. This leadership position had never been something that they had aspired to attain, and had reluctantly taken when there had been no other choice. They felt, as the rest, that there would be no way Shayne would die and he would lead them through all their present troubles. But it just wasn't to be that way and they had been placed in charge. Both felt that they had made mistakes, and blunders. "I don't know how to respond to that, Staven." Saige replied. "I . . . we, have tried to do the best we can, but know that we, well that I'm still learning, and that many times, just like this search we are involved with today, I fail in my guesses and assumptions." Looking to his sister for support, he paused not knowing how to continue.

"Look." Shellian said, "It was a real surprise to us when Shayne called us in and passed on the leadership to us. We never saw it coming at all. Both of us as a team are good at what we had been trained for, but never realized until it happened that Shayne had seen us, and our skills, as a team for scouting, to take over the leadership. Believe me, it was the last thing on my mind, and I am sure it was the same with my brother. Yet, it was Shayne's dying order, or wish, however you want to look at it. It still brings tears to my eyes as I see Shayne lying there with desperation in his eyes as he realized that he was dying and that there was nothing to change it." Choking a moment on the words as she recalled that moment, and almost bringing the tears back, she took a deep breath, shook it off and then continued. "This road to here hasn't been easy on any of us, and all of us have lost too many friends and comrades. We are barely a tenth of what we were when this all began, and with all that we need to do, and all that needs to happen I feel very inadequate. So all I, and I am sure Saige can do, is take it one day at a time. And any time we have a failure like this one, well I'll let my brother continue." Then looking at him, she shrugged and was silent.

"I guess what she's trying to say is that any failure against the time that we have means that we may have had another one of our cities fall, with any of the remaining cities, still none the wiser, as to why. So an assumption like I had here, and I know I wasn't the only one, but it cost us two days of fruitless searching, obviously we are looking in the wrong places. I guess we just haven't learned how to think like our ancient ancestors. Somewhere we have missed the obvious, and none of us have come up with anything that we can use against this alliance, let alone where it might be headquartered. So when we miss, make mistakes like this, it feels like a failure. And when it feels like that, then we feel — her and me — that we have failed as your leaders, and it hurts."

Pausing once again and looking over the group before continuing. "Okay we've had our say, and now does anybody have any thoughts or ideas of where to look next?" Again there was silence as each considered the question asked.

"I guess", Stone said, "that like you, I thought it would be off one of the walls. But now it is obvious that it's not the place or if it is, then it's well hidden. So, I guess, even though Sorrel and I searched the meadowlands, as large as it is, it's the only place left. As it was stated earlier, there is no way that the exit is where we entered into this place. And not to change the subject but, I wonder if Seve, Sabryn, Seirra, and Saar has had better luck than we have? It would be nice to have at least one success out of this."

Smiling, Saige said. "I can't disagree with that. I would love to at least get some good news, and that would be the best. Especially if their research shows that we will be able to make contact. Then we can only hope that we can – well, the day is getting late let's head back to the facility, get cleaned up, find out what's been happening since we've been gone, and sleep in a real bed tonight. How's that sound?" He got the response he had been expecting as they all began to head towards the buildings that led back into the facility.

* * *

As they entered into the facility through the cavern, they began to smell food being prepared, and it made their stomachs rumble. The thought of a hot meal not prepared over an open fire really appealed to them now. And with the public showers just off the cafeteria they could clean up before eating, and that appealed very much to all of them –

something about a shower that made one feel great. They, as a group, entered the cafeteria through the double swinging doors only to find three of the four members left at the facility busy putting the food together. "What's this?" Stone asked.

Smiling at him, Seirra said. "Well, we just couldn't have all of you return from your little foray out into the meadows, and then come back late on this second day without having something ready for all of you."

"Besides," Saar said, "we continued to monitor the meadow area so we would know when you would be heading back here. And we decided that it would be a great way to welcome all of you back."

"So why don't all of you head for those showers. I can tell by your odor that you've been out and about this last two days, and I'm sure that you have already discussed it anyway."

Laughing Saige asked, "Now Seirra, are you telling us in a nice way that we stink?"

Smiling, she said. "Saige, you can take it any way you like. But we won't be finished with the food until all of you are out anyway. And before you ask, Sabryn is working the security office." She made a shooing motion and said. "Now off with you, and we'll see all of you back here shortly."

* * *

After the meal Saar stood up and said. "Since I have been in charge of the facility, and haven't officially handed it back to Saige and Shellian as of yet, I'm calling a meeting. And yes even Sabryn will be in on it since we discovered how to use the intercom system. Bring your drinks with you, and if any has to make use of the restrooms do it now. There is much that I need to discuss with all of you, and I am sure that it will be the same with you to us who remained here. Now go and we will start just as soon as everyone is there."

Shortly, once everyone had sat down, with Saar still standing he said. "I'll open this up and bring everyone up to date as to what has been happening while all of you were tramping across the wilderness." This brought slight laughter from the rest.

"You seem to be in a great mood, Saar." Sorrel said. "Why is that so? Then pausing a moment before continuing, she smiled a devilish smile and said. "I've figured it out. Shellian is back." Then looking over at Shellian she saw her turn red briefly. She laughed and said. "I thought so."

"Now Sorrel, I have to admit to have Shellian back here safe and sound is something for me to be very happy about, since we have been apart for the last two days. But while that is very important to me, and I am sure to her, that is not the only reason I am very happy right now." Then turning to Seirra he said. "I'll let you break the news to them." Immediately everyone at the table other than the ones who had remained at the facility looked both at Saige and then Seirra – which caused Seirra to blush bright red. Laughing once again Saar said. "No, no it's nothing like that. I know that I'm the doctor around here and am usually the second to know if any of the women here are carrying, and at this moment unless one of you women have been hiding something like that, none of you are. No, this has to do with what transpired while all of you were out and about trying to find the exit from what I was going to call the hidden valley, but realized that where this facility is located is known to us as the hidden valley, so maybe we can . . . ah . . . call it the hidden meadowlands? Anyway now that we've finished embarrassing each other, I turn the floor over to Seirra." He sat down and then Seirra stood, still feeling her face a little warm from the flush.

"At least I can see that we all seem to be in a good mood. And on the subject we just touched, I honestly would like to add a new life to our small group, but it hasn't happened yet . . . which is fine." She added hastily. "That's getting off the subject anyway, and before I both dig a deeper hole that I can't climb out of, and embarrass myself further let's just move on."

"If you say so Seirra," Staven said lightly.

Taking a deep breath before starting she said. "As you know our assignment was to research the emergency plans, and communications circuits so that once everyone was back together that we could then put them to use and communicate with the cities. Well, what happened was more than we planned, and our *time of isolation* is at an end. When we activated the emergency circuits with plans of making sure that after all this time that they still worked, well, it or they just automatically connected." While the rest listened, she then explained all that had transpired since they had been gone. Yes it had only been two days ago that first afternoon when they made contact. And yes the information had been received, first with doubt, and then, when everything was confirmed, the information had been distributed to the remaining cities. They had learned that three additional cities had gone dark, making the total eight. At this point she sat down, and for the team that had explored the meadow area, there was a quiet silence as they absorbed the good news along with the bad.

Saar then stood up once again, and said. "The communications traffic that we are receiving now is driving us crazy. That's why Sabryn hasn't said anything from the security office as the voice from there is turned off." Turning and facing the monitor he said. "She can hear us," at which point she waved, "but if we had the sound on from there we wouldn't be able to concentrate. So, this brings us and you all up to date. Will you now let us know how it went on your exploration?" He then sat down turning it over to the other team.

Saige stood briefly and said. "I'm going to allow Stone to bring the four of you up to date, since it was Sorrel and he that found it in the first place. But before I turn it over to Stone, I – we have to say it really is great news that contact has been made, and at least the other surviving cities now know what they are facing. I just hope that we can break up this alliance before it is too late for us. The only thing we have in our favor right now is this hidden compound. And since it is in their Sacred Mountains it has a good chance of staying that way. With what we have learned here, I really cannot say how much will be believed back in the cities, but what can we say but the truth. I know that until it was shoved in our faces by being here, that I would have held incredulous anything that came out of this place. But as we who are here know, the proof is overwhelming. Still for many, even when the truth is such they will not believe. Such is life, I guess. Yet, even with the knowledge out there we have no guarantees that we will prevent the fall of our remaining cities. The only factor we have had in our favor is the distance between our cities, how they are hidden, and the fact that once winter arrives that the searches and attacks will end until late spring. We are heading into fall very shortly, which has traditionally, for the primitives, been a time of gathering for the winter time. So both searches and the attacks should diminish. That means that we will have a very short respite before the searches and attacks once again intensify. Again we need to be ready.

"Did anybody that you talked to offer any help for us? You know with the size of this place ten of us are too little. And the winter time would be a time to get additional bodies here to help. Although for the life of me I don't know how to get them here. It was only because of the desperation of the flight that we ended here in these mountains, and it is not close to any of our remaining cities."

Saar thought a moment before answering and then said, "In truth we've only been in contact for less than the two days you were gone, and I guess you could say that we spent a good portion of the first convincing them that we were real, and not someone just trying to screw with their minds. So I guess there's a lot of work ahead of us, both on the circuits and as well as solving this. And I guess to answer you, no; there just hasn't been the time."

Nodding Saige replied. "I guess that makes perfect sense. Like when this place was discovered it took a while before we really knew and understood it. Okay Stone, bring them up to date if you would." Saige then sat down.

Stone got up and cleared his throat before speaking. "Well, this is the last thing I really expected, but here goes. The feeling from all of us was to concentrate the searching along the walls with only two of us going down through the meadows and eventually we would find where our ancestors left the meadowlands. After all it was something that made the most sense, at least to us. Sorrel and I, when we first found it, had hiked some of the middle area, but only found some outcroppings, a large lake and the huge meadow area. So when Saige and Shellian suggested that four of us search the rim, with only two going through the meadows and it made sense. But, I am sad to say that the search was unsuccessful. We did a thorough search in both directions, with teams switching sides to make sure we had done a complete search with different eyes." Shrugging before continuing, he said, "It was a surprise, we really expected to just walk up and find it, but we were wrong." Looking around before asking, "Does anybody want to add anything else?" Getting no response he sat back down. It was silent for a short while then Shellian stood.

"It is getting late, we all need to add notes to the files, and I mean all of us. We, each of us have their own perspective on everything that has happened in the last couple of days, and it's important that we get those views entered. Then we can, at our leisure, if we can find such a thing, go back over all the data, and maybe something that someone observed might help. Plus with all of us back here, we need to share the duties in the security room. From what I am seeing I believe that we will need two of us in there at all times now." Then looking over at both her brother and Saar she asked. "Do both of you concur?"

Saar just nodded his head. Saige spoke saying, "That makes sense. I'm sure that Sabryn is going crazy in there right now with all the traffic that must be coming over the circuits." He looked up at the monitor and saw her smile and nod confirming his statement. "So I think it is a reasonable request. But, we still need to go out into that large caldron and locate the exit. All of this is important. Plus we need to start working with the pack animals so that they are comfortable with us, and be patient with us, since none of us has ever seriously packed an animal before. Yes I know, that in some of the training sessions that we did back in the compound we tried it, but to be honest we never seriously thought we would even need to do it." This brought a laugh from all of them as they visualized any of them trying to be successful. It looked easy, but they knew from personal experience that "looks" can and are deceiving. Turning towards Saar, Saige said, "Since you've been kind of in charge of the security room while we were gone, I'll let you set up a schedule, which once completed, you can post on all of the terminals. We are in desperate times here, and while it has been busy around here since we found this place, I have the feeling that this time that has passed by us will seem like time off in comparison to what we will be facing from here on out." Looking around the room he finished, stating, "That's all I have to say, does anybody want to add anything?" Again with no response he continued, "Okay then, until tomorrow morning – have a good night." Standing where he was until everyone had filed out he signaled Shellian to remain behind.

"Shell', what is your thoughts on how you want to attack that caldron?"

Shrugging and shaking her head she said, "I really don't know. Like you and I, and I think the rest that were there, we thought that the exit had to be along one of the walls. So with the training and practice that we all need to do with those pack animals, maybe just like the security office we should send out teams of two to continue the search. Even doing it this way will reduce the size of our people to only six working in the facility. We really could use additional people. I wonder if some of the cities may have only recently ended the program that we were a part of. If so, maybe we could find some way of getting them here to help – the ex-scouts. With the winter approaching, and the reduction in the patrols of the primitives in that alliance it just might be possible to get some of them here unseen. And with their skills to live in the wilderness have a real chance to get to the mountains, where we could have someone from here meet them and lead them back here." Then taking a deep breath before continuing she said, "The only worry is that one of the ones who would join us here may decide that because they were in charge down there, that they believe that they should be up here, and that will cause unending grief for us, and might make it difficult to accomplish anything." Shaking her head, she continued, "I don't know Saige. This whole situation just seems to get more complicated, what are your thoughts?"

"We truly could use more help, but you could be absolutely correct when someone from below got here, that they would want to be in charge. And if there were more members that had worked under whoever it is, then they would have the strength behind them to enforce it. That would be a mistake. Well, if nothing else, you've given me a lot to think about. Let's call it a night. We can tackle this in the morning when we are fresh. Today has been both frustrating and exhilarating, but I have to admit that I'm tired and ready for some down time. See you at breakfast tomorrow in the cafeteria, and then we can see if anything might have come to us over night." At this point both then left the meeting room, and headed for their own apartments.

As Saige headed down the hallway to the apartment, deep in thought by what some of the worries were, he unconsciously reached the door and entered. *Shell' has made a valid point. What if we did bring others in, and then because of their greater numbers they would decide that it was only right that they run everything from here, leaving us out in the cold so to speak. This is a big problem. Right now because of the work we've done, the exploring, and the uncovering of our past, I feel that now we have intimate knowledge and of course, experience on this facility. So, do we continue to work here as understaffed as we are, do we invite additional workers in, or do we not and continue to work this place as if it is our own? It would be easy to consider this place as home, with the loss of our city, and I can see why we could easily consider it so. But, do we have the right? Or better yet have we earned the right to claim it as ours?*

He found that he was sitting on a couch, and presently was alone. Seirra had yet to enter, and he had to admit he was looking forward to some close work with her tonight. But these thoughts kept nagging at him. *Eight cities lost. That means that if we can recover any of those people that have been captured by the primitives that we would be easily able to fill any of the empty spots here. Actually if we were able to recover ten percent it would be way too many just for here. This place was never meant to have much more than a couple of hundred. And I suspect that we are looking at maybe a few thousand that are probably being used as slaves, and worse.* He shuddered when he realized what was probably happening to the women. From observations that they had made, most of the primitives had taken the view and lifestyle of the herds that they hunted. He guessed it made sense, because the herd animals dominated so much of their lives. But that meant that any of the women who were captured would then become part of their female herds, and have to submit to any male. *At least, now with the information we have, no pregnancies could come out of those unions. But even the thought of having the women forced into such a thing hurts. Yet, maybe, while very unpleasant, and undesirable, still it might be better than torture, and death. At least while still alive, they have hope.* He just did not know how much damage to these women mentally, let alone physically, would result from their captivity and abuse.

With his eyes closed he thought, as he mentally shook his head, *too much to think about, too much happening and no answers for any of it yet.* He had been looking down, and suddenly realized that he wasn't alone. Looking up he saw Seirra standing in front of him with a look of mischief, and nothing else. He smiled as he thought. *It's amazing the difference between a loving relationship and one that is forced.* Very surprised to see her standing in front of him naked, he first wondered when did she get here, and then since the obvious invitation was before him he no longer cared.

* * *

At the cafeteria the next morning, a place that had become an informal meeting area, he and Shellian picked up from where they had left it the previous night. With a steaming cup of coffee in his hand he sipped and enjoyed the warmth and taste. "So Shell', any thoughts about what we left it at last night? Or like me were you too distracted to think about it." He laughed lightly remembering back to last night. He suspected that there was a similar reunion with his sister and Saar.

Catching his drift, she just smiled and said nothing for a few moments as she savored her coffee. It was amazing how much better coffee was than *shick*, and they always considered it a great hot drink to keep things going. Well, she knew that she would not ever be going back to *shick* if there was coffee available. "Yes, oh brother of mine we had a wonderful evening catching up on things. But even though that was so, I still feel, as we discussed, that it would be better if, at least for now, we keep it as it is. We've worked together, not just you and me, but the others who are here, for many annuals. And yes with all the trouble, and the losses we are few, but now we work very well together. And bringing in anybody would immediately cause friction and trouble, which, I have to say, is not a good thing while we are trying to solve this other life threatening thing."

"Yeah, I thought about it and have to agree. But here's a thought . . . what if instead of inviting any from the cities that are still hidden and alive, that as we start recovering our people we bring a few on board here. After all, like our city, theirs is forever gone, and if it has to be reestablished, then it will be as a new city somewhere else. And starting a new city may be very difficult, since the primitives are now aware that we exist. So while it may have been easy in the beginning when they first established these cities, now it shall not be so. I really think in the end, that the remaining cities will have to absorb the refugees, overtaxing probably most of them, but at this time it is the best answer I can come up with." He had been concentrating so much on Shellian that it surprised him when another voice entered into the conversation.

"Not a bad suggestion, Saige." Stone replied. "But we have yet to locate this alliance and where it is staying."

Turning around he saw that the rest of the group was here minus the two who were manning the security office. "So how long", he asked, "have all of you been listening?"

"Oh long enough to get the gist of both sides and the conclusions", Starr said. "I know that we would normally discuss things like this in a formal meeting, but I have to agree with what was being said here also." Then turning to the rest of them Starr asked. "Don't you agree? I mean it sounds almost territorial when you just think about it; we not wanting any others here and we surely could use the help. But I think that your conclusions are right. What do you think Staven?"

"Yeah, at first I thought the idea of getting more people in here to help us was a great idea, but when it has been presented this way, I cannot help but to agree. But how are we going to keep this from coming up as we deal with the cities? I mean, well, I think that they will be asking, don't you think?"

Saar, standing behind Shellian said. "Okay, all of you, I know that this conversation is important. But Saige, Stone, and you Staven have the breakfast duty, and while coffee is great, it won't sustain us. So go fix the meal, and then while all of us are eating it, we can continue the conversation."

Laughing as he got up from the table, Saige said. "Okay boss, right away boss", which brought immediate laughter from all of them.

* * *

It had been decided by Saar, that the couples would man the security office. He reasoned that because of the growing strength in their relationships with one another, that they would just work together better as a team. Of course there had been the joking about each distracting the other, which had brought laughter. Yet all had to admit it was a great idea. So after breakfast Starr and Staven relieved Seve and Sabryn. Sabryn then collected her son Shayne who looked up at her through sleepy eyes. She knew that the babies complicated things, but would not have traded it for the world. She listened as Starr gave her last minute instructions on her daughter Sommer. Of course with both Shellian, and Seirra available, there never was a shortage of someone to watch the babies. Shaking her head she thought. *There's just something about women and babies. Always wanting to be around the babies, and always wanting to hold them.* Looking down into those loving, trusting eyes she would just melt. He yawned and stretched, then rolled over in his portable bed, and fell back into a contented sleep. She knew that shortly he would be waking and wanting to eat, so she and Seve grabbed some breakfast before retiring back to their apartment, where they would try to get some rest between the waking times of Shayne.

Fortunately it had been a quiet shift in the security office, but as day approached, it had begun to get much busier. And by the time the two of them were relieved there was much traffic on the circuits. Fortunately most of it was between the cities and not directed their way, and it was good to hear. It was a confirmation that many of the cities still existed. It made it feel like it was almost normal instead of what was really happening.

CHAPTER FOUR

It was late into the season of heat before K'jor had another opportunity to pursue his thoughts he had gathered from the previous winter. He told the clan to continue the necessary work, and that he would be gone several days. He told them that he needed to head into the desolation to talk with their gods, and he needed to do this alone. Yes he would take part of the hunters with him for protection against attack from a rival tribe or clan, but once the area of desolation had been reached he would go ahead on his own. He stressed that the same group should be back to the edge of the desolation on the morning of the fourth day. He would return then, meet the hunters, head back to camp and continue with the work to prepare for the coming of the season of cold and the returning to their hidden fortress.

That had been one day past and he was on his own, and while his memory of any area he had visited was good, it appeared that the winds, and what little moisture fell in these desolate areas had changed the land. At times he felt that he was headed in the right direction, expecting to see something familiar that he had locked into his mind, only to find the expected feature either wasn't there, or appeared to have moved. He knew that was impossible, after all only the gods or . . . That got him to thinking once again that maybe if indeed there was a hidden clan, that they had to be magicians, as magicians could cloud one's mind, make one believe one thing, and even change the lands. Stopping for a brief period of time, he looked around and once again saw nothing that was familiar. It was getting late on this first day, and he needed to find a place to camp, a place that would hide his presence. Yet, hide his presence from what? There had been only the dust and the winds. Not one flying creature, not any scurrying on the ground, no predator, or prey, just he, and the silence in what he could only call a dead world.

As he searched he knew that there wasn't even a dead bush or tree to get fuel for a fire, and he had hauled everything with him. As the suns began to set on this first day he finally found a small depression in one of the small hills, which he had to admit, to call them small hills was exaggerating greatly. Mounds would probably be more accurate. Still the selected camp would be out of sight, and protect him from the cool night breezes. He knew that there wasn't any water, so like his food, he brought it with him. The pack had started out quite heavy, but by the time he met up with the clan once again it would be empty. He built a small fire, just enough to heat some water. In this he added some herbs, and roots with a couple of pieces of fresh meat. This would be the only meal with the fresh meat, as it would become bad beyond this time. So the rest would consist of the dried and jerked meat that they would take back to the fortress.

As it became dark his doubts began to rise, putting down the strength of his conclusions that he had arrived at the winter before. *Why would any choose to live in such a place?* He began to feel foolish, yet he would stay to his plan. *Who knew, just maybe I'm right and somehow there is a people or clan hidden here. After all what better place to remain hidden; a place that all shun, as lifeless, without anything to draw one here, in other words, a perfect hiding place.* While this made sense, why hide in the first place? This did not make any sense. Yes all of the tribes and clans had a tendency to fight each other, but other than the skirmishes, no tribe or clan had completely wiped out another, at least to his knowledge. Yes, camps had been destroyed and the prisoners from these destroyed camps became either slaves or were added to the herds, but it rarely was the whole tribe. So maybe in the end this would lead to nothing but being alone. *Enough of this for now, my food is ready, and it's time to extinguish this fire.* Yet, he was reluctant to do so. This was a strange land, and who knew what gods, or spirits roamed it in the darkness. Still he was resolute, and he would need to stay at least for this night as this would be a moonless night.

* * *

As he continued to look back into the past at that first night he had to admit that he came close to just giving up. The destruction of the lairs, now in the present, had been successful, and he felt that there were more hidden deep within the desolation. Shaking his head and sighing, he knew that the combined tribes and clans of the alliance would be breaking up and heading back to their individual camps. It was time to prepare for the season of cold, and while it had been quite a sight to see the alliance attacking as one, he wondered if he would continue to have their support in the late season of greening when again he wanted to attack another lair of these magicians. Yet, after the eight they had been unsuccessful in locating any more. So maybe his second was right, right that they had wiped them out. Unable to keep sitting he began pacing, and even this was not enough. So he left the room and went outside to the fresh air and looked over what he now controlled and the many slaves and females that had been added not only to his clan but to all of the tribes and clans in the alliance.

In the next few days he would see less as the different groups headed back, until it would only be this one. He knew that they still needed to assist the hunters to finish the gathering for the season of cold. And now with additional mouths to feed it would require more. Again shaking his head, he just did not understand why these new females that had been added were not carrying. *Their magic must be powerful.* He knew that many of the females from his clan were carrying, so there had to be very powerful magic that protected these others. It surely couldn't be the males that they captured and used as slaves. They were next to worthless, and they did not appear to be much of magicians at all. He had asked them to perform some of their magic, but none could. Maybe the priests were right. The lairs themselves were responsible for their strength and skills in these arts – the reason that much of what lay in the lairs were declared untouchable. And once these were taken away from those lairs, their power was gone. Still . . . still, if that was how it was, why were none of the females from those lairs carrying?

He had bred with all who were of age, as had all of the warriors, so again it was not from lack of trying.

Taking a deep breath and again shaking his head, his thoughts drifted once again back to those four days in the desolation. Deep in thought he went back inside to continue to review those first days there and once again, to see if he had overlooked anything at all. He leaned against one of the walls as he slid down to the dirt floor. That first night he spent in the desolate area had been a restless sleepless night. And then when he realized that he was thinking of that first night he remembered that one of the newer females would be leaving with one of the tribes in the morning. Yes he had bred with her soon after her capture from one of the lairs, but he had considered her a very healthy female and one who should produce many strong warriors. So he decided that he would have her report to him for one last chance to have her carry his child.

Getting up from the floor he went back out, signaled one of the members of his own clan and told him to have that female report to him as is proper for breeding, turned around and went back inside. As he waited he went back to the first night. He couldn't explain why, but it was as if the ghosts of, who knew of what, were haunting his dreams, and while he could not place any particular sound, maybe it was just the silence. A silence he was uncomfortable with, as the night usually had its own sounds. The sound of winds blowing gently through the trees, the scurrying of the small beasts, the sounds of the Loki that the flying ones fed upon, none of that here with the stillness that just continued to feed on his soul. It was a lifeless place, and again he wondered why he was here.

His thoughts were interrupted when as ordered, the female arrived. As was required she arrived naked, but also subdued, with a look of total subjection in her very soul. One who understood that she had no choice, and would submit as required. Shaking his head as looked at her, he could see the healthy body and as such he felt that there was no reason that she could not produce strong healthy warriors. Smiling at her he signaled her to his sleeping mat, his loins aching for her. Yes, one last time to breed with this one before she was gone.

* * *

The morning came much too quick, and K'jor heard the sounds of breaking camp. He knew that all the tribes and clans would be heading out today including his. They needed to prepare for the season of cold and that meant heading to the migrating herds, and then back to their main camps wherever they might be. He packed his equipment, rolled his bedding, tying it to his pack, went outside and joined his second. There was much dust in the air as the different tribes and clans completed their preparations for departure. Then silent for a brief time K'jor spoke as they assembled before him. "We have had a successful season. We have increased our slaves, and our female herds. While we did these things, I know for many it did not produce everything one wanted. But for good reason, the priests have put off limits much of what these magicians own, but we are destroying them one lair at a time. I feel that our gods are pleased. So, all who want to join me . . . us . . . . this alliance, for next season's campaign will meet here again mid-way after the first signs of green. I feel that there are many more lairs out there and we need to destroy all of them." Then looking around silent for a moment before continuing, he said. "With the knowledge that we have gained this season we should be more successful with the next one. With time comes experience, and with experience comes knowledge, and so what was unknown is now known, and because it is known we will defeat this hidden enemy. Now go your ways and we will meet in the near future." At that last statement he signaled break camp, and all returned and began the long trek to what still lay ahead of them.

Thinking back to late yesterday afternoon he had the female lay on his mat for which he then bred with her. She had her face turned from him and did nothing to prevent it, and remained silent as was required. When he had finished breeding with her she got up without cleaning herself, which again was required. It was a sign to all of the warriors that she had performed her duty, and could not be touched again for another full day and night. It was their way. Without a female there could be no new warriors, so while the females were required to submit, they were also not abused, thusly the limitation on how often a female must submit for breeding. The laws governing breeding were absolute and would not be bent or broken. All females who had bled were of breeding age, and must submit. Any female who was before the time of first bleeding was untouchable. The females were to arrive naked, silent, and ready to receive the male. The warrior, since this was a requirement to be able to breed, would then treat the female right. There could be no violence, and no abuse. If such were learned, then the warrior or whoever would be turned over to the female herd to be treated as they pleased. Once the breeding session was finished, then she would leave without cleaning up. This way it was obvious that first she had bred as required, and second that the proof was there for all to see, making her off limits until the required time had passed before she would have to submit once again. There were only a couple of situations where a female could refuse a request for breeding, and one was her time of bleeding, which cycled regularly, she was ill to the point of being restricted to her sleeping mat, or she was late in the carrying, where breeding could threaten her and the child she was carrying. She was unavailable after she dropped the child, and until the child was weaned, she was to remain outside of the breeding herd.

Punishment for failure to submit had to be substantiated by three males. This was to prevent false witness against a female by a male who did not like her. If substantiated, then she would be confronted with these facts, and allowed to defend herself. So if any of the above circumstances existed then it was within her right to refuse. But, if not then she would have to submit to the one who had requested it. Again with refusal she would then be found to have refused, which was considered a crime again the clan, she would then be placed on the rack. The rack was designed to strap a female into it in such a way that she would not be harmed, but at the same time could not prevent any male from breeding with her. Her offenses were the determining factor as to how long she remained strapped on the rack. When a female was placed on the rack, then she was available to any male at any time and the required time between breeding was waved. A mark then would be branded on her neck signifying refusal. If she ended up with two marks, and then refused to submit after that, then she would be ejected from the clan, with nothing – no clothing, no tools, no food, and no protection from the clan. It was as if she was no more.

There were laws that applied to the male also. First to have the right to breed with a female a male must be a warrior or a priest of their gods. This way the resulting offspring would have the strength of the two. As a warrior he must spread his seed among the females. If a female from a rival tribe or clan is found alone then she must be bred by as many males that are in the group that has captured her, before releasing her back. This purpose is to lead the enemy female to carry one of their own and from this begin to weaken their enemies, by having one of their own within the enemy's camp. There will be no breeding or an attempt at breeding a female before the first bleeding. If one has been found to have attempted or performed such an act then there are no second or third opportunities to correct. The one who has violated this is immediately expelled from the clan in like manner as a female who has refused. And lastly, any female of the clan will not be physically abused. No violence is allowed as it is the female that adds to the tribe. As in refusal, any who are caught doing such against a female has three opportunities in which to correct his behavior. If the male refuses, or at a later time returns to his old ways he is sent away unarmed and naked again never allowed to return under threat of death. A female from an enemy who has been caught and is away from their tribe or clan can either submit, or if she fights have a physical response in cuffing her into submission, and this is the one and only exception.

The females of all the tribes and clans were aware of this, and rarely ventured away from the "season of heat" camps, when the hunting and stocking of meat for the winter time was upon them. As the law was for their clan, it was the same for most. These things he contemplated as he watched the many tribes and clans leaving. This was the first time, as far as he knew, that there had been this great of gathering of what normally would be rival tribes and clans, ones that would be fighting each other. And because of this unique situation, it made some of the absolute laws change with additions. In no time in the known history had there been so many females captured, or slaves added. It was a new thing and required new thinking. He had gotten together with the priests and not only the priests of his clan, but the head priests of the other clans to help him work out a solution to this dilemma. With the destruction of the magicians' lairs, these females would not be returning to their places, so the rules of encounter with an enemy female would have to be changed – changed, specifically, to deal with these magicians, and the destruction of their lairs, and to make it very clear that this was an exception, and the only exception that would be accepted, by all who were in the alliance.

After much thought, arguments, and discussions it was decided that in view of the change the alliance brought and the fact that these females would not be returning, that they, after the alliance broke for the time between the season of falling and of cold, that these females would be divided among them and would then become part of the tribe or clan to strengthen them each in their own way. But, until the division at the time of leaving, they would be placed in a central location, be treated as females of the tribes and clans, and as such have the same treatment, being under the same laws – thusly providing some protection that an enemy female would not receive. And it was because of this he was able to breed with this particular female who now was leaving with one of the smaller tribes as a member of their female herd. Until the moment of the breaking of camp, she and all the other captured females, were available for breeding by the alliance warriors. Once the breaking of camp, then these females was officially members of the tribes and clans that claimed them by right of capture or conquest. He turned, and went back inside, sighed, picked up his travel pack, and then left joining his clan as they headed for the herds to catch up with the few from their clan who were working them. It was going to be a very tough season of falling with time shorter than normal to get the meat they needed. Plus the new slaves and females would have to be taken to their clan home as they would be useless during the hunt. And with the increase in size of their clan because of the captured magicians they were going to need so much more than they had in the past. Shaking his head he knew that the detour that they had to take to deliver these new females and slaves to the fortress was going to add time before they could hunt, making it even more difficult. But he could see no way around it. These new females were next to useless, and had much learning to do to be able to contribute to the clan. So it would be a burden to have them in, what would normally have been, the season of falling, camp. Yes it was pleasant to have them around for breeding, but without any experience in preparing the hides and meat for winter they would simply be taking up space, and the additional warriors that would have to protect them.

* * *

Sara, taking a deep breath looked out over the scene that was before her. She had now been a captive for close to an annual, and it had not gotten any easier. In her sleep she still relived in her nightmares of when the city was attacked, with the primitives breaking down the door to her home, her mate fighting desperately to keep them away and who then was killed right before her eyes. Then her own desperate fight to keep them off of her, and the rape that followed by the four of them. And then with little clothes on her body to be tied and led out to be put with so many of the other women, girls, and children before being untied. She felt dirty, helpless, and beat down. She could see that of the men who had survived had just as shocked of looks on their faces that she suspected that she did, and all the females that were in the same holding area as she. From the condition of the women, it appeared that all of them had met the same fate as she. There were tears and crying coming from most and of the ones who were not, some appeared to be far away as if what was happening no longer concerned them.

So many had broken distant stares that told her that they had been destroyed by what had happened to them, and only their bodies were still here, with their minds gone. She knew that most likely that these who maybe mercifully had escaped this way would probably be dead soon. She had searched desperately for her two children, again mercifully both were boys, but she could find neither. Then she saw the size of the force of primitives that had attacked their city and was shocked at the number. She knew that had they been prepared, that the city would have still fallen. She wished that she could at least go back and get some clothes and clean up as she, and looking at the rest of the women, shivered in the cool morning air. Looking around at the primitives she could tell that even if any asked for such a thing that it would be denied. It was a surreal scene before her with most of the women half naked, trying to hide their nakedness, and across the square their men being heavily guarded, with failure in their posture being able to do nothing for their women. What was going to happen to them? Since it had been morning, before any were normally up and about, most had not had the opportunity to relieve themselves and so with the women surrounding them, each woman took care of the need hiding behind the circle of standing women who watched outward to keep prying eyes from watching – there was blood left in many of those puddles. What else could they do?

She wondered if her brother Shayne, the one who was in charge of the scouting teams had escaped. But she doubted it. This attack had been too well organized to allow any to escape. She suspected that he was dead. Growing up together they both had worked as scouts. She had learned the language of the primitives as part of that training. Eventually she decided not to continue, had coupled and with her mate they had two sons who now were in their very early teens – one looking much like Shayne when he had been a teenager. Now all she could do is try to survive, and hope, even if that hope was slight, that somehow they would either escape, or be rescued. Again what was to happen with them?

That answer had come shortly. They all were herded out of the city, through the desolation that had helped hide their city, and then out into the grasslands, followed by entering a narrow canyon that opened up into a valley with meadows, trees and a number of small streams. In any other circumstance the setting would have been beautiful. But they really had no time to appreciate the views. Once they had left the city they never saw the men again. So their fate was unknown. Here they were put with other women, separate from the women of the tribes and clans. Just before being herded into a large enclosure they saw a number of racks that had women strapped in them. It was shocking in that all were naked, and unable to protect themselves. As they passed them they could see that the primitive men had sex with them a number of times and while these racks were shaded, and the design was such that a woman strapped in it would not be hurt, she could do nothing to prevent any male from taking advantage of her. They also noticed a small mark branded on their necks. Shocked from such abuse, all they could do was turn their heads away from the scene. There was absolutely nothing they could do about it. It made them wonder if they too would find themselves in the same situation very soon. The women who were in those devices had come from another city, and like them had been captured. The future surely did not favor them at this moment.

All of this had transpired a long time ago, but both with those nightmares and memories it was like it happened yesterday. Of course they had learned why the racks and why the punishment. From the primitives' point of view, refusal was against the whole tribe or clan. Back when she had been part of the scouting teams, she had observed some of the tribes. She hadn't understood their social order, there did not appear to be any method to how they lived. Now she knew, and unfortunately she knew personally. The times that she had to submit to them had been too numerous to count. They were uncouth, they stank, and their breath was even worse. And they hurt, since they never considered what was necessary to help, as they called them, a female to make it work right. It literally was wham, bam, and no thank you ma'am included. Then not being allowed to clean up afterwards was even worse. Yet again now she understood why.

In many ways, she guessed, that while the way they went about procreation was similar to the way of the herds, that there were laws in place to protect the female. And one of those had to do with no cleaning up after the act. It showed the rest of the males that she had performed her duty, and now was untouchable for a period of time. She was fortunate in one sense, by being older; she had not been forced into having sex with as many as the younger women. She had learned about those racks also, and had passed on this information to all of the women who had been part of the group that had been from their city. That time, until they were split up and the tribes and clans returned to their own permanent or semi-permanent settlements, was literal hell. All of them were raped at least a dozen times. After all what else could you call it? If one did not submit, even if submitting was against your will, you had that rack staring you in the face, where it was much worse.

Some of the most difficult members to deal with were the women of the clans and tribes. They only considered themselves females, and were proud of the times they mated with the warriors. And if the warrior was one of high prestige, they proudly showed off the proof to the rest of the females that they had mated with him. They were tougher to deal with than the men, since the men left the female herd to its own means unless they were, as they stated it, looking to breed with one of the females. Of course with new stock, so to speak, these became popular with the males, and built restiveness against them from the primitive women. It was never open, but things would happen to let the women from the cities know who was in charge in these female herds. It was back to the pecking order, and because she was one of the older women this leadership role fell to her for her people. But that still meant that as far as the primitives were concerned that the least among the tribe or clan females were still greater than the highest among the females from the lairs. She never understood why they were continually called magicians, or why their city was called a lair.

It hurt her to her very soul as everyday she could see the graves of the women who did not survive the ordeal, and what all of them from the cities considered continuing abuse. Many had given into the hopelessness that such thoughts generated, and the ones with broken minds had eventually perished. Since they had looked to her, even though she had not asked for it, she felt responsible for their deaths. But there was nothing she could have done to change it, or the outcome. With all the copulation happening with the women, she wondered why nobody had turned up pregnant. It just did not make sense. But she was quite happy that it hadn't happened. She knew that none of these women wanted a child from these males. From overhearing conversations, she knew that it had been a topic of discussion between the warriors and even the leader. From what little she could discern they thought that because they considered their city a lair of magicians, that they, the women, had power to prevent the carrying, as they called it. All she could do was shake her head at such ignorance, but something was going on. You just couldn't submit as often as they had to and not have someone get pregnant – mathematically and biologically it was impossible.

Yet their fertile cycle continued, showing that both they were fertile, and that they were not pregnant. The other thing she learned was that the young girls were protected at least until they reached the age where, again as they called it, her first bleeding. At that point then she was fair game. And unfortunately a number of the girls that had been captured with them had reached that time and were unceremoniously introduced to the adult world, and not gently. Some of the graves she saw each day belonged to some of these young ones.

When the division came, once again there were hysterical crying, clinging and tears; all knew that they probably would never see each other again. And with the split they became weaker, not that they together had been a strong force. She found herself with the group that became part of the leader's clan, and they headed deep into hills. Where she hoped that at least for the time on the trail that the attempts at making them pregnant would stop, but such were wishes and not reality. Again, if the circumstances had been different then the area they were traversing would be considered beautiful. Eventually they reached their destination ten days later. Now within the fortress there could be no escape, and now with even more males and females around them, things for a while would become even more difficult.

* * *

Time had passed and now she was entering her second fall with winter just ahead. She truthfully could say that things hadn't gotten any easier, but at least there seemed to be an uneasy truce between her women and the primitive women.

All that had come with her and the ones who had survived had learned the skills that were required of them. They assisted the mothers with their toddlers, knowing that once these children reached a certain age that they would be taken from them, especially if male. Males had to be raised as warriors and were taught by males only. She never saw her sons again. Every time she thought about them or her mate it tore her up inside, sometimes enough that she thought that just dying and joining them would be the way to go. She found that she would wake up in the middle of the night crying hysterically with deep soul wrenching sobs that were uncontrollable, and eventually she would fall back into an exhausted, troubled sleep. She lamented for her lost mate, she cried for the unknown fate of her children, and knew that she probably would never know what happened to them and that like those graves of other women, that this would, in the end, probably be her fate – a fate that never allowed her, or any of them for that matter, to return home.

She continued to submit, as did the others who had survived, again what else could they do? She looked out each morning on twenty-six graves, a reminder of those who hadn't survived the ordeals. But even after all this time, routine, and understanding of what they were up against, it hadn't gotten any easier. In fact at times it had been much worse as one or another woman would crack and become hysterical, requiring all of them to help the woman get back in control. While the loss of their names by the primitive culture hurt, they kept them among themselves. It was almost the only part of who they were that allowed them to keep their sanity. Still they only whispered them to each other. If the primitive women heard them they would be cuffed for such stupidity. Was there even a slight chance for rescue, and again why were none of them pregnant?

CHAPTER FIVE

"Look here!" Seirra exclaimed. "Something's happening, and I can't quite figure it out." She had been monitoring the feeds from space, and one of them had shown a great movement of something – animal or tribes she couldn't tell yet. With quick deft movements from long practice, she zoomed closer to what she had witnessed. "Saige, it's the tribes and clans, and I suspect that finally all this searching may be paying off. This has got to be where they're gathering to plan, and then attack the cities." She turned around and wrote down the coordinates that the view had given her so that she could come back later and study the area. Looking up she saw that Saige was standing over her studying the screen with her.

"Finally! We need to get Stone and Saar in here now. Can you set up the other monitors to show this? We need to start following some of the tribes as they leave. We'll worry about the clans later. We can probably pick them up at the hunting grounds and follow them back to their permanent settlements. The tribes are nomadic and we need to follow their range of travel. And I think that one of the smaller tribes will have to be our first target. We are just not a big enough group to go after anything larger. Although we have yet to figure out how we are going to do this. Yet, somehow we must. And each time that we are successful, it will increase our size, and maybe make it easier to accomplish what is before us." He turned and over the PA system asked for the two to come and join them as quickly as they could. He wanted Saar to contact the pivot city and let the information go out that the primitives were on the move, and then the three of them Seirra, Saige, and Stone, would try and monitor the tribes as they left and spread out in all of the directions of the compass. This was not going to be easy.

He turned and faced the door as Stone arrived and then shortly thereafter Saar. "What's happening?" Stone asked.

Pointing at Seirra, Saige said, "She's pinpointed the location of the alliance's main camp. They're breaking up into their individual groups and heading away to wherever, to prepare for winter. Saar, call the pivot city and let them know what is happening, we'll update you as we can. Stone, take one of the other monitors, we need to follow the tribes, and by their dress we should be able to tell the difference between them and the clans – they will be smaller and mobile, and it is one of these that we need to attack and recover any of our people that they may have. I'll put out a general statement over the speakers shortly as this will take priority over anything we may have discussed or decided to do. Once we figure out which one of the tribes will be our target, we will have to continue to monitor them so that we know exactly their range and what their habits are. Saar, I hope you caught that." He turned back around and faced one of the monitors and continued. "Stone, take this one – this is one of the smaller tribes, I'll take a different tribe from that one over there, and Seirra will use the one she is using to follow a third tribe. "Somehow this winter we need someone to go to this location where they've met so that we can study it. Again I don't know how, but it is something that needs to be done." Shrugging and shaking his head he said, "We just don't have enough of anybody to do any of this."

"Very true," Saar responded, "And even with this crisis, the cities that are still standing are very slow in recovering the scouting programs. Yeah, I know, some of them have had them closed down for quite a few annuals, and this isn't something that can just be rebuilt in a day. But, this needed to be accomplished yesterday, and even yesterday is much too late. Okay I'm contacting Keahilani now."

* * *

For the next several days the team followed the three smallest tribes out from the alliance headquarters and began to track their home range. As luck would have it, two of the three moved further away from their location in the Sacred Mountains, and the third, while not directly in their direction, did not head away from them, but even though they more or less approached them, the angle they took kept the distance between the Alpha compound and the tribe from getting any closer. It was decided that this would be the one that they would concentrate on. They passed on to the existing cities that they needed to monitor the other two tribes since both were close to a couple of the hidden cities and it would be so much easier for them, even with the scouting program having to be restarted from scratch, and that these reconstituted scouting teams needed be careful. It was imperative that these tribes be monitored.

During this time Starr and Sabryn had been preparing the computer system to send the data from the educational center out over the network so that the cities could have the true facts. They hoped that the ones presently in charge of those cities would allow the information contained to be passed onto the citizens. It was not a time to suppress, yet government being what government is, it probably would try. Everybody needed to know, so that they realized what they were really fighting for. And while the information would be a shock to all, as it was to them when they learned of it, it would provide for them in the cities the impetus to push forward and try and protect what little they had. Again, while they could not prove it, they, their people, could easily be the last of their species – one born on another world, and not of this world. And even though the tribes and clans that surrounded them appeared to be similar, built similar, procreated in the same way, these were the only common factors. It had been determined that a similar environment had been responsible for the species, and why the Alpha Compound had been set up originally. One, to study and watch the development of this species, figuring that there could be some parallels to their own distant past, and to allow the sociologists, anthropologists, and other scientific fields to study what could have been early earth – but, at the same time, to stay out of sight, and just remain observers. And within the facility to have researchers and a large support staff, with all of this happening a couple of thousand annuals in the past.

"Doc, do you think that you could make up some more of that extract that we accidentally discovered would kill the primitives? And if so, is there a way to weaken it so that it either just makes them ill, or incapacitates them?" Pausing for a moment as Saige watched the monitors while Saar continued to monitor the audio channels. "I'm beginning to believe that this stuff may be our only way of at least incapacitating our first group – that small tribe that is southeast of us."

"I really haven't thought about it. I was shocked that, that was the outcome, since we have used it for as long as I can remember. Once processed its colorless, odorless, and has very little taste – as close as one can get to being tasteless. It has proven to be a great pain reliever in smaller doses, and in larger doses, to be able to knock someone out." Shaking his head before continuing Saar said, "I mean it was a shock to me, after all, my job is to save lives, and not take them."

Smiling Saige said, "And that's just what you did. You saved our lives. If the stuff had worked as you thought, we still would have escaped. And yes I know that this has bothered you. Shell' has told me a number of times." Laughing from the look on Saar's face he continued. "Now remember she is my sister, and one of the one's in charge here. We share all information that is necessary to keep us alive and healthy, and if you think about it, the health of our one and only doctor is kind of critical, don't you think?"

Nodding his head in agreement Saar said. "Yeah, I guess so. But I hope that's as far as it goes. There are many things between couples that should remain only between them."

Seeing the direction that Saar's thoughts were heading he laughed even harder. "Do you think that we share bedtime stories?"

Seirra who had been listening in on the conversation and saying nothing stated, "I hope not! After all that's not something that needs to be said publicly at all." Then looking directly at Saige, who was her mate, she asked. "The two of you aren't sharing stories are you?"

This brought even more laughter out of Saige who once he was able to stop asked, "Now are we starting rumors here? Do you really think that we share that kind of personal information, especially about our bedroom behavior? Now that's funny." Then turning back to Saar he continued. "Now wasn't it you and Stone that were discussing just that kind of thing back in the cave last winter?"

Saar flushed red briefly. "Ah, well, yes, but we weren't getting into any specifics. It was just conclusions from what we had observed, and knew that at the time that Sorrel had been sleeping around, and we did not know who the father of her child was." Pausing and shaking his head sadly before continuing he said. "And that became a tragedy in itself. But I guess it all worked out."

"True." Saige responded. "But were you not discussing, somewhat indirectly the very question you just asked me?" After asking he turned and faced Seirra also, showing that he was including her with the question. And as you and Stone discussed that situation in generalities, do you think it would be any different with Shellian and me?" He could see both of the nodding their heads. "Yes, we may discuss things on how the relationships are holding up. After all if we end up with couples fighting, and arguing, and with as small of a group as we are, such a thing could and would have an effect on everyone here.

"We've been together long enough now to know pretty much how all of us work. No I'm not speaking down deep on a personal level. Only each one and their mates can see that, but how we work together, and apart, and how we generally think and act. It's what makes things work well. As long as all of us stay within what we've become comfortable with, and no one steps outside of that, we function well. After all, all of us had been trained to work that way anyway. Shayne had always pushed the importance of that."

Smiling Saar said, "Well, that's a relief." And then glancing over at Seirra he continued. "And I'm sure that she feels the same way." He got a smile from Seirra who continued to study the monitors, showing that she was listening.

Then with a look of devilment Saige continued. "So you must be having some wild nights if that is a worry you have." Pausing with a large smile before speaking again, "I can always ask Shell' to confirm it. After all we have been a team since we were children, and as such we don't need anyone to say anything to know the answer." Getting the reaction he expected he again paused. "Okay, I know that works both ways, so enough of the teasing, and besides this getting off the subject."

"Subject? What were we talking about anyway? Oh yeah, the plant extract. What's going on in that mind of yours anyway?"

"Well, Shell' and I have been trying to come up with some way to be able to recover our people without killing off the tribes and clans that have taken them. You have to admit that we are terribly understaffed to do anything directly. In fact right now it looks like only four of us will go on this mission when we decide to move. That leaves six back here to monitor it. And no women will be going. I don't want to risk the few we have to be captured by the primitives. We already know what is happening to the ones who were captured, and I am not going to be responsible for sending another woman into the clutches of the primitives to abuse. So shortly Shell and I will be presenting our rough plan and we will need everybody to give us input to polish this thing. As you know, we cannot attack even the smallest tribe out there directly, so anything we do must be by stealth and misdirection. And at this moment that's all I am going to say. Other than I need you to start working on huge batches of that drug. And of course we now know why it killed that patrol, while the same doses would have only knocked us out. I know that you do not have any of the primitives to test, but we are probably going to have to test the only way we can and that is by using it in a real and dangerous situation. Until we can release some of our people and find out what is going on, then in many ways we are still in the dark. Of course any we can free will add to our numbers here, and maybe a few after a time of healing and recovery will be able to join us as we continue to go after, first the tribes in this alliance, and then, because they are much larger, the clans." Waving his hands when he saw that Saar was going to protest, "Yes, yes, I know that's all conjecture on my part and way into the future. But you may be surprised that it really isn't that far into the future. We have to at least raid one of these tribes this winter, and hopefully, more before spring. Remember eight of our cities are gone, and with them all of our people that lived in them."

* * *

They continued to monitor the tribes over the next several days with again the two larger heading directly away from the central command area of the alliance, and their location at the Alpha in the Sacred Mountains. There were others, but again because of their limitations, they decided to only monitor the three. If the two that were heading directly away camped close to one of the still operating and hidden cities, then this information would be updated and passed on so that the closest city could watch them. This, of course, forced all the remaining cities to reinstate their scouting units. Some have been gone long enough that there were none around who had worked and trained for this difficult job. And to find the hardy individuals necessary, let alone train them in the short time that was now available to them, seemed to be impossible.

During this time as the rotations continued through the security office, and the two women with children continued to work with the educational computers, the rest of the team, other than Saar, who was busy with the equipment, producing the drug they would need, was out working the meadows trying to find the hidden exit and entrance. So far with a very thorough search, a number of times over, they had come up empty. Then came the day when they discovered it, and it was completely by accident. All of them had walked by the entrance at least ten times and had not seen it. Between the plant growth that was thick at this point and the illusion that the wall was solid, it had been easy to overlook. By only being there at the right time of day for the shadows to reveal an anomaly did it finally show. When they walked through the small opening, and it was again Stone and Sorrel who found it, it took their collective breath away. It took a few minutes to walk down the narrow passage which took a sharp right near the end. In fact at first it looked as if this passage was just going to end against a solid wall, and disappoint them once again, but once there and the turn made, they found themselves in an area with many trees blocking their view.

Looking further to the right they could see the wall of the extinct volcano continue to form what they were beginning to assume was another natural and hidden valley, but until they pulled out of the trees there would be no way to confirm this. In the distance it sounded like there could be another of the many waterfalls that were everywhere in these mountains. Pushing forward, since the trees were thick enough to prevent penetration, they finally edged around them. And as all the indications showed, they found themselves in another valley and meadow complex similar to the one that they had just left, only this one being much smaller. "Wow!" Sorrel exclaimed. "This is beautiful. How could we have missed this?" Turning towards Stone she said. "I was guessing, when you and I first found the meadows out there that, that was all there was. I would never have guessed there could be a whole number of them."

"I agree with you, but I should have known better. After all geology is one of my specialties, and it is not unusual in an area where a volcano has been active to have many islands of untouched land, but it just did not occur to me that it would apply here." Then shaking his head he said. "Don't ask me why, 'cause I don't have an answer for you. I just assumed we were dealing with only one." Looking across this smaller area, he could see where the small falls were cascading over the side, across a number of outcroppings that broke it into many smaller falls and rivulets throwing small rainbows from the mists created by the water striking the rocks on its way down to a small lake. As captivated as he was with the sights around him, it took a second to realize that Sorrel was trying to get his attention. "Sorry, this just grabbed me." He stated as he turned to face her.

Smiling at him she said. "I can understand that, but look over there, isn't that a building?" Then getting a look of devilment in her eyes she asked mischievously. "Wouldn't this be a great place to couple?" Then she laughed as she began to disrobe. He couldn't disagree, and he had to admit having a hot woman as a mate had its benefits, shaking his head inwardly and smiling as he joined her.

* * *

Later after the passion had faded, they worked their way over to the building that was constructed out of the native rock. Once inside, it took a few moments for their eyes to adjust to the dim light. Here there appeared to be no artificial light, and looking up they could see what they assumed was sky lighting. But through the annuals of abandonment these were covered in layers of grime, and he suspected that there probably was a growth of moss also. "I think I'll climb up on the roof and see if I can clear the sky lights. You hang by this entrance and let me know how it works. Might have to figure out how to get some water up there and clean them further, but won't know until I get that growth off." He then turned and headed back outside and had to stop once again as the bright light temporarily blinded him, causing his eyes to water for a moment. Walking around the building, which was built against one of the canyon walls, he found handholds that had been carved into the rock, and he slowly, testing each foot and hand hold, worked his way up and onto the roof. Then gingerly, he walked across, not knowing how solid the surface was. But found that he didn't need to worry as it appeared to be solid. The whole roof area was covered in growth, and he only located the sky lights by guessing and doing a preliminary scrapping with one of the long knives that they carried with them. As he cleared the material he could hear Sorrel moving below him. After a few minutes he asked. "Is this improving the light?"

Even though the reply was muffled by the thickness of the walls and roof he heard her say, "Yes." There was a pause and she replied. "Yes, it's working really well. There's still a lot of shadow in here, but I'm being able to actually see things in here now. And I think that there is no power here at all. But I guess that makes sense, after all this pretty far away from the compound, and this building is all by itself, so why?"

"Just wanted to make sure that what I was doing was working. This stuff has been on here from the looks of it for a long time, and the material that the light is supposed to shine through is pretty cloudy. So I was guessing that one of us would have to go over to the small lake and get some water and wipe this down. But if this works well enough, I guess we can wait on the final cleaning."

"Well, I can't say it's perfect, but I'm beginning to see things well enough to recognize the layout now. I think that once you get a couple of them scraped . . . look I'll come up and help. That way it will be done faster and then we can look over the inside of the place together." Then laughing she said, with a bit of humor. "After all, it is always nicer when we do things together."

Shaking his head and smiling he thought. *Back when we were in the cave I would never have thought of loving this woman. In fact back there she was so much trouble that we were constantly figuring out how we could control the situation. She was the first of the women who was with child, and she would not identify who the father was. We suspected that she probably didn't know, because at the time she was sleeping around. But so much had happened since those desperate times, and she lost her child and almost lost her life.* Now he couldn't see his life without her, and he knew that she felt the same way about him. He continued to scrape away and heard her coming up to join him.

"Okay, now that I'm up here which one would you like me to work on?" She was standing up close to where the handholds were carved in the rock wall.

Smiling and looking down at his handiwork for a moment, he didn't say anything. *She is such a beautiful woman, healthy, and so full of life and joy. I really thought that she would have permanent scars from her experience. But if she does, she hides them so very well.*

Smiling at him, and with a questioning look she asked. "What?"

Again shaking his head, he said, "Oh just you. That's all." Then sighing he continued. "You know you're so beautiful to me that it hurts, but to answer your first question. I think I counted five panels for the sky lights, so if we clear three of them that should be plenty. So work the one that's closest to you and then we both can work the center one." Pausing for a moment before continuing he said, "To the second, well let's just say that I love you and leave it at that." He sat back down and began to scrape at the vegetative covering on the sky lights once again. Concentrating on clearing the stuff off, he heard her sit down and soon could hear the sounds of Sorrel scraping. A little time later something struck him, and he looked up and over to Sorrel, but she appeared to be working away, and not paying attention to him at all. *Must have been my imagination or something fell I guess.* He turned back and continued his work, only to be struck again. This time he heard a giggle, and knew that she had thrown something at him again. She surely knew how to distract him, and he had to admit it was working.

Looking at him with a large grin on her face, she said. "You looked so serious over there. And so *tempting* of a target – I just couldn't let a moment like that pass." She then laughed.

Since he had a greater pile of debris he grabbed a handful and chucked it her way, which she easily dodged. She once again laughed and then stuck out her tongue at him. "You missed, and you're supposed to be a warrior. Some warrior you are – can't even hit a helpless woman."

Standing up once again he said. "Helpless? You? Somehow I don't think so. You seem to control the situation pretty well if you ask me, and I know that you aren't – helpless that is – but I'll say it anyway." He grabbed another handful and this time spread it as he threw it, making sure that she would not be able to dodge all of it. This started a free for all, and led to another physical session on the roof and in the warm sun. Breathing hard, all he could say was, "You sure make it hard for a man to ignore what you have."

Laughing once again, she said. "And that's the way I like it."

"Like what?"

"Why, I like it hard. After all it works better that way." Again she laughed. "But I think that both of us had better take a dip in that lake so we don't smell like, you know what, when we head back with the news that we probably found the exit out of the meadows. That's, of course, after we confirm that there is a way through the wall where this building is constructed.

"Good suggestion. I suspect that we reek a little, or maybe a lot. But do you think that this is the place? It could be that this is just an offshoot and that's all."

"No, I think this is probably it. As the light increased, before I came up here to help, I could see stalls, and storage areas. Then against the wall there looked like another one of those sliding doors, again not as large as the ones that are on those really big buildings just outside of the compound, but large enough for one of the pack animals to easily fit through with it packed. So I think that this was a staging area where they could do what was necessary before leaving, and be out of the weather if they needed."

"Sounds good to me. Let's get this scraping done, and then check it out. Once we confirm it we'll take that quick dip, and say we had to because of all the crap we got on us from cleaning off the sky lights." At this point, he turned back to continue when he heard her laugh softly. "What?"

Shaking her head the only thing she said was, "Oh you, that's all," and turned back to continue her scraping.

* * *

Sara sat working a hide to help cure it for later use when one of the older warriors signaled her that she was to breed with him. She sighed, shuddered a little, and with the rack always in the back of her mind went to him, undressed, and looked away. She had to concentrate on not making a sound. Because when they performed the act they hurt. She couldn't flinch, or groan, or show any sign of the pain it caused her, having to lay there until he was finished. This one had never been gentle, and this time was no different. She suspected that there would be blood afterwards. When he was finished she got up carefully as it really had hurt, and now she was very tender. As was required she dressed, returned to the skin she had been working and said nothing. She hated them, she hated the mess that she was not allowed to touch, but knew that this still was better than the rack and the punishment it represented. Looking down, as she suspected, she saw blood mingled with everything else that was on her legs. Taking a deep breath she thought. *It would be so easy to join the ones who are in those graves, and leave all this behind. There were now forty of them, and it would be so easy to become forty one.* Yet in her heart she knew that she could not take her own life. So she continued to endure the pain and humiliation. There was such a difference between this and the loving relationship that she and her mate had. But he was gone, as were her children. With these thoughts she began to weep silently once again. *Oh to wake up and to find this was only a nightmare and not reality.* It was a hope, but that was all, since she knew that what was happening was quite real, real for her and all of the other women who had been captured.

Some of the women that had most recently perished had perished because of infection. From the rough treatment they were receiving none had time to heal, and since there appeared to be a desire to see any if not all of them carrying offspring, the pressure to breed by the primitives had increased. And these injuries caused by this, with no time to heal had become infected, and with nothing to fight the infections, with poor health, poor nutrition, and worse conditions, these infections increased in strength killing many. Again there was very little sympathy, let alone help from the primitive women. After all, these upstarts were taking the males away from them, and they did not like it. And so an uneasy and uncomfortable truce existed between the two groups, with the primitive women retaliating any time they felt they could get away with it. Sara was sure that some of the deaths of the city women were at the hands of the primitive women, especially when they were very ill. But she could never prove it. This meant that all of them were very alone, very scared, and depression ruled their lives.

* * *

"Look all; we are dealing with a very tough situation here." Saige said as he opened the meeting. "Not that any of us are unaware of that. Somehow we have to get something started that will start developing doubt with the primitives. So far they've had it their way, and I'm sure their confidence is riding very high. It was only through diligence that we've been able, finally, to locate their gathering place before heading out and attacking our cities. And we've been able to track one of the smaller tribes to just southeast of us here. Now we have to start changing the direction, and tide and make it begin to work for us." He turned to Shellian and said, "She's going to bring us up to date to what we know and what we face. Then I'll put out to you our basic plan for our first offensive." Stopping for a moment and looking at all of them, especially the women, he said. "None of you, and I am specifically speaking to the women here, but including all of us, will like what we are going to propose, but hear us out. And if any, and I mean any of you have something better we want to hear it, and hear it here in this meeting." He sat down and turned over the meeting at this point to Shellian.

"Now most of the history we are familiar with so I am not going to bore you with those facts. But what I need all of you to remember that we were a very active scouting unit until our city fell. And it is this I want to talk to you about. We all need to remember the ways of the primitives. It is so important that as we plan this offensive, at least initially, that we do not allow any of the tribes either within this alliance, or outside of it to realize that there is another player in this game. So I need all of you to remember your history of how the primitives act, how they fight, how they scout, and how they live. Because for us, with this small force we cannot let them know about us at all. When we are finished with an attack and withdraw it must appear to be a rival tribe or clan that is responsible, not us. That means when we do this that we *must*, and I mean there can be no variance here, we must act completely within character of the primitives. I'll let you think about that for a moment, and while I don't like it either, being a woman, I see no other way of doing this, at least until we know more, and we have more people to work with. Our goal on this foray is to rescue some of our people. And initially they must feel that we are a rival tribe attacking and taking bounty from the attacked tribe." She leaned on the table and again looked at each one that was seated before continuing. "I can see that some of you are beginning to realize what this will entail. So now we will take a brief break to give everyone time to think about what we've said so far and then Saige will give you the hard facts." Taking a deep breath she said. "Okay, see all of you back here in about fifteen minutes."

She looked across to her brother and asked. "Do you think that they will have figured out what the four of you are going to have to do?"

Shaking his head he said, "I don't know, but once I begin to cover what it is and what we need to act like, well, I know the women, the mates to us are not going to like it at all." Taking a deep breath before continuing he said. "Heck, I'm a guy, and I don't like it. But if we don't then there would be an immediate red flag raised saying something here is just not right, and we cannot have any hint left behind that says we are not the primitives." He then asked, "Like to get a snack and maybe a cup of coffee before we continue?"

"Sure, probably should bring back a couple of, what did they call them, oh yeah, carafes. That way we can have some of it sitting here to use during this next portion. I suspect we are going to be here for quite a while, and I can already see the protests. I mean, I'll be the fortunate woman here as my mate Saar will not be involved with this, so it will affect me the least. But we cannot put our one doctor in a dangerous situation. Otherwise he would be part of this team. I can only hope he understands that."

* * *

Standing again at the head of the table he waited until all of them had quieted down and was looking at him. "Now I am sure that we all discussed what has been said when we took the break, and tried to understand why it was important to bring up the primitives and their way of life." Stopping for a moment and looking over the gathering he continued, "Okay first off we have been studying the tribe we plan to attack, and looked around the area where they are staying to see what other tribes may be in the area. We found two, so from our aerial view we have determined these rival tribes' totems. So when we go in for this attack we will become one of these tribes. That way, quite naturally as far as this tribe goes, they will assume that the attack was from one of these and not us. And this is critical. It must appear to be one of them."

Again pausing he said. "Now before I continue on this, I want to point out that we cannot afford any losses. And we've found another way down through the mountains so that we will be just south of their camp. We will be using tactical headsets so that we can keep in contact with each other. These are so small that they are virtually invisible." Again he stopped, and looked at each one of them. "This will involve just four of us with Saar and all of the women remaining here. And before you object Saar, remember you are our only doctor, and as such irreplaceable, so you and the women will be monitoring the situation from here. I know that we have not figured out long distance communication between a ground force and here, and I don't know if our ancestors had such a thing – but if they did, and if it is still here and operational, we have yet to figure it out. So all this will do for all of you who are here is to know the situation, and give you time to prepare for our return, whether it is successful or not. So that means that I, Seve, Stone, and Staven are elected. It means that we have to get into those skins that we made when we were still in that cave, and it means that we will have to go out to the meadow area here and begin to practice for this task. It truly has to go as close to perfect as we can make it."

Again looking around the room before continuing he took a deep breath, letting it out slowly. "Okay, our plan is not to wipe out this tribe. With that drug that Saar has been producing we could just do that. But it again would look suspicious for such a small force to wipe out an entire camp. We will take out the guards, and with the dart guns and packets we can throw into the fires put the rest into what I hope is a drugged sleep." Pausing for effect he then asked, "With what we know of these people, what happens next?" There was silence, and then he could see the realization hit home. Smiling even though it was a bitter one he said. "That's right. We have to have sex with at least one of the primitive women in that camp. Otherwise something would be very out of place. At least we know that there would be no offspring created from the union. But honestly from what I have seen of these women, I really have no desire to copulate with one. And if any of you have any idea how we can avoid it I am all for it." The reaction was just about what he expected, but he had no other answers, and they needed to save both the men and women that were being held there." Again taking some time to let it soak in he said. "We begin our training this afternoon. We are to be a scouting team from one of those rival tribes who stumbled upon their camp and attack it, performing what they would do, and take captives back with us. That is how it must look. Okay now that you know what we've come up with we now have an open session to either accept what Shell' and I propose, or come up with something else that will work."

CHAPTER SIX

K'jor stood at the entrance to the clan home and thought. *It's good to be back. And while we did okay with this period of rooting out the magicians, and we've increased our female herd, and slaves to work, it isn't quite what I had hoped or planned.* Turning around he said. "We're here, let's get the captives inside and explain to them where they will live and what will be required of them." The laughing he continued. "Not that the females don't already understand what their role is." This brought general laughter from his warriors. Since they had demonstrated what was required. And even though a couple had been placed in the racks to reinforce their role, overall these new females had bowed to the demands of the clans and tribes in the alliance. After all they had no choice.

* * *

The season of falling was here in earnest and the need to work the herds were strong. Otherwise there would be no meat to get them through the tough season of cold ahead. Where they were located, in the foothills, was such, that snow was common. And while not deep as the Sacred Mountains, it at least prevented travel, and at times even one from leaving their abode. Whether this shelter was a warrior's space, a common area like the female herd, slaves, or the place where the offspring grew. This latter area had to be kept warm since all offspring to the age of two and finally at a point of controlling their body functions wore no clothing. Once that time had been reached then the males would be removed from the care of the female herd and begin their training to become a warrior or a contributing member of the clan or tribe. No additional contact was allowed by any male offspring after the separation until they had proven themselves a warrior or priest – then, and only then, would they have a right to breed with the female herd, and add their seed and strength to the clan or tribe. This had been the way for as long as any could remember, and that included the story tellers, the true keepers of their past.

This was also a time of deep thought and preparing for the season of green, and a time for the female herd to begin carrying the next generation. When it was cold, it was nice to have one of the herd to warm one's sleeping mat, even if it was only for a brief period of time.

The female herd was responsible for the care of those underage, until the separation, and the young females would then begin their learning in the ways of preparing the hides, and the making of garments that all wore. They also learned the way of preparing food, and the preservation of meat. Here they learned their place and the importance of submitting only to the warriors, and only after their first bleeding. It was then that they would pass into full fertility and be able to honor the clan or tribe by being available and to produce healthy strong offspring. In the herd they would learn their place, and whatever special skills they showed would be encouraged and strengthened – bringing honor to the herd, and to the clan or tribe. And most of the teaching, most of the real work, for the herd was performed during the harshness of the season of cold.

So with the season of cold approaching and with this late start, the warriors left to hunt the herd beasts that provided for their long term needs. K'jor led, as he led the alliance. A few of the females would accompany them to work the meat into something that would be safe and transportable, followed by doing an initial preparation of the hides. They would be gone one full moon cycle, and two minor moons cycle. This would bring them to the brink of the season of cold, and the hunting party would need to be back inside the safety of their walls by then. Sara, watching the preparation, was quite thrilled when she found that none of the women, that the hunting party chose to join them, were from the cities. She realized that this made sense, as the city women were not very good at preparation yet, and with this late start efficiency was the key. So she, like the rest, that were to remain behind, watched as the hunting party left. This meant that with fewer males around that that should reduce the pressure on all of them to have to submit. Maybe, just maybe, there would be enough time between so that many of them could heal, including she. She turned to leave only to see that older warrior, the one who seemed bent on getting her pregnant signal. Looking down and shaking her head slightly she went to him, and prepared to submit. Now if she could just prevent herself from flinching. After this she hoped that he would leave her alone long enough to heal. With as dirty as these people were, it would be so easy to catch something from them and then die from it. It had already happened to far too many of captive women. To be injured down there from the rough treatment, and then not given the time to heal, followed by an infection that entered the woman's body through the injury, and eventually she would succumb – not having the strength to fight off the infection.

* * *

As they worked the herds for their needs K'jor again would return back to that incident that had eventually brought the alliance together. That first night in the wastelands had been hell. He had sworn that the spirits of the dead warriors were haunting him. He had thought he heard voices a number of times, but was never able to locate the source. When the suns arose the next day he was beat, on edge, impatient, and short tempered – lack of sleep did that to him. So instead of building a fire, which would be difficult with his limited supply of fuel, and he did not feel like trying to locate any additional wood to make it work, he ate his travel rations. His original time table was to be up to four days away here in the desolation, but he could see that water would be an issue, or at least he thought it would be, so he would use as little as he could to extend his time. The mystery of those two strangers worked on him. There just wasn't any explanation as to why they were here, let alone where their bodies had disappeared to. Were they of a magic race, a race that once killed, that they would just evaporate? He didn't know, and he had no way of understanding – to figure it out. So the mystery just deepened.

Those voices in the quiet of the night seemed so real, so close, but he had seen nothing. So once he finished his small meal he began to search the area where he had slept to see if he could find anything to explain last night. And as the suns climbed in the sky, the area began to heat and the winds pick up. Spirit spirals danced across the barren wastes. And other than the winds it was a silent dead world. Shaking his head he thought. *What was I thinking? Nothing can live here. It is a place of ghosts and spirits, a place of death not life. Even the very grasses that cover the plains cannot survive here, and the grasses usually survive in the worst of areas. But, I will give it through today, and if I find nothing, I will just have to assume that it is one of the many unsolvable mysteries. Mysteries that may have been created by our gods to lead fools like me to their deaths in these wastes . . . Chasing wisps of nothing, nothing but the ghosts and spirits who protect this desolation, and lead the foolhardy into folly and death. And even with the proof that there were two here, they too may have been part of the illusion to draw us back here. Back here yes, and for what purpose?* Again, for what unknown purpose could there be? The only thing that came to his mind, since he was a warrior, was a trap, and a very subtle one that would eventually kill him or any who would follow him here. And that immediately made him feel that he should run from this place.

He, as the leader of his clan, was a very good tactician, and from what his thoughts had brought to the forefront, he knew that if his conclusions were correct that he was no more than a child in comparison. This was subtle, so much so that even the most experienced would not see this trap. He began to look around expecting at any moment to be attacked, to be consumed. But the silence, dust, and heat were all that met him. Eventually, he calmed down a little bit, but then another thought entered his mind. *What if it is the spirits of the dead warriors that roam this desolation? If so then by our mutilation of their dead bodies, they cannot attack, but only watch and wait. Watch and wait until I succumb to this place. Maybe to have my mind wonder and leave me, and then my body perish allowing my spirit to face them in their realm.* But even if this was so, he had no proof. As the day continued to pass and it became drier and hotter, with the breezes pushing the hot air and dust around, the silence remained. There just was nothing here, nothing at all here.

* * *

It was a time of hard work, and short days, and with the hunting and then dressing out of the beasts, and the few females that took care of the preparation, all by the end of the day were too tired to do more than sleep. Here, at these times, and while most of the tribes and clans were involved in the same thing, there were a few that used this time to attack. Feeling that with either, much of the warriors were involved with the hunt leaving the places where the clans and tribes lived vulnerable with a much smaller force to protect it, or because of the fatigue that the camps themselves would be easy targets. So guarding their camps and the places where they lived was paramount. Still they all knew that with their forces divided, it would be an easier task to destroy a rival, and since this was something that was required of all of them every late season of heat to the season of falling, it would be easy for a rival to know, to spy, to plan, and then successfully attack either the camps or the places where they lived. So as tired as they were, guards were always patrolling both the camps, and their home ground. Yet, what could they do, but what they were presently doing? If they did not hunt the herds then there would be starvation and death at home. If they were successful in the hunt, then they would be able to survive the season of cold's harshness, but at this time be a possible target for a successful attack.

So with each trip out to hunt the vast herds, each warrior knew that not only to be alert for the beasts they would bring down, but to be alert for the dangers others could provide. Most of the hunts, because of the vast herds kept all of them away from each other, and it was rare for one to be attacked. Rare yes, but not unheard of, and many of the ones that had been surprised were no longer around. So with the required alertness, the hunting and preparing of the beasts, the guarding of their camps, there was very little time for breeding, and little energy left. That time where the breeding would increase in intensity, would be the cold time ahead, where there was little to do other than repair or replace equipment that had fallen victim to the storms, winds, time, and usage. It was during this time that many of the females began their carrying. And with it, a hope for an increase to their clan, and as always, a hope for the increase in males to be raised as warriors, all to increase their size and importance in this world of theirs, yet many never survived the time of carrying. But that time was still ahead of them. Right now they were behind on the needs of the clan. With the late start on working the herds, they had to be a little more careless than he liked. That meant putting more of the hunters out to hunt and leaving the camp with too little protection. But he had no choice. With the increase, through capture, of their clan they had more that would need food, clothing and shelter. So with too little time, and with the increase, calculated risks had to be taken.

Back where the clan settlement was located, he knew that with the additional slaves, they were adding shelters for the increase. These new shelters would be very rough, but at least it would keep out the winds and snow. As time continued, then there could be some improvements made, but since these were for the slaves anyway, it did not really matter. Still not only would there need to be an increase in shelters, the amount of wood necessary, for both cooking and to keep one warm, would greatly increase. This meant, that this would, once again, reduce the amount of warriors that would be with the clan, and to protect it and the wood gatherers, while they were out gathering the wood and fuels for the season of cold. With a small guarding force he had the young females, who were learning, out collecting the dried dung of the herd beasts. These young females were before their first bleeding so were untouchable anyway. And while not a pleasant task, this dung was a great fire starter, and would reduce the need somewhat for tender. He felt good to know that where their clan was located, that it lay hidden from most, and so had a far less of a chance of being attacked. Less of a chance was great, but not perfect. It could still happen, and if it did, it would happen at such at time as this, where they were so spread out, and at their most vulnerable. After all they now had more of everything that some unknown rival would covet, and want for themselves. He hoped that the ones who had become part of the alliance would refrain from such a tradition, but he felt that once the alliance went it separate ways to prepare for the season of cold that all bets were off, and if they had felt slighted while working with the alliance, that once this break came that they would then take it out on another tribe or clan.

* * *

She lay on her sleeping mat racked with fever, and at the same time shaking from the chills. She drifted in and out of consciousness, never sure where she was. Sara felt weak and could keep nothing down. All she wanted to do was to roll up in a little ball and forget everything. What she saw, when she saw anything at all, was worried expressions on the women from the captured cities. The primitive females avoided her with a fear on their faces; saying that they worried that whatever she had could take them too. Even though it was difficult, this realization made her smile, even if this smile was inward. She just hurt too much to really care about anything. She could hear voices around her, but couldn't understand any of them at all. Every once in a while something cool would be placed on her forehead, and while this felt good, at the same time it chaffed her skin which was tender to the touch. Her teeth chattered from being so cold, and yet the fever burned deep in her soul.

When she dreamed it was a nightmare that continually repeated of the fall of the city, and the days of hell, and loss, her time since that fall, her life here at this clan's home, and the continued daily abuse. Even here in the fevered dreams she could not escape it. In some of the dreams she was fighting an unknown monster that was intent on consuming her very body and soul. She tried to push it away, tried to fight, but the monster's strength was too great. She felt herself pinned and then hard physical contact with every inch of her body. Again she fought but it was relentless. Finally the monster worked its way down to her private area and she screamed as the pain washed over her in great waves. Was this beast going to consume her from the inside? The scenes continued to replay any time she fell into a fevered sleep, and even during the brief times she had returned to the waking world, it was only for very brief periods of time, being more in the twilight than the real world. Maybe, just maybe, she was going to join her ancestors, and in many ways that would be a relief. Just to give up, to give in to the infection that was attacking her body. Yet, something deep within would not let her give up, give in, to leave. And while she bordered on the edge of death for many days, eventually the ones caring for her could see a change. Finally at some point, and they knew not when that point was reached, they could see that she was finally resting. And though the fever had yet to break, it was becoming obvious that the crisis was over for now, and even if it was slow, her recovery would be soon, but soon could mean months. Unless she relapsed, and without their medicines to help her fight, they knew that the infection could, and most likely would return.

She awoke coherent for the first time in sixteen days. She felt weak, shaky, and completely drawn out. There wasn't enough strength to even turn over to find a comfortable position. "Water." Was all she could croak, her voice barely audible and barely recognizable. One of the women, who had been keeping watch, helped her sit up, and Sara drank thirstily as the cool water penetrated her dry parched body. Then too weak she fell back to sleep and it was another two days before she again awakened. Breathing out heavily, she blinked several times and found as she continued to wake that she hurt just about everywhere, and in the darkness of the primitive shelter and with the light from the flickering fire she realized that it was night. Even though it was difficult to do she looked at her arms and the parts of her body that was uncovered, and was shocked. She looked more dead than alive, her skin pulled tight against her bones. She stank, and so did the sleeping mat and coverings she laid on and under. She was so weak that it scared her. Carefully and with difficulty she pulled back the covers and she was naked, and seeing the rest of her body scared her even more. She must have been close to death to look this bad. How long had the infection raged in her body? She had no answers, and no real memory of what she had just endured.

Turning carefully, she saw one of the young city women close to her. She could tell that it wasn't that long ago that she had submitted for *breeding* as the primitives called it. She could see both the tears and the pain on her face and longed to reach out and comfort her, but had no strength. She tried to speak but found it almost impossible. Trying to clear her throat she finally croaked out just above a whisper "Can I get some water please, and maybe, something to eat"?

The young girl jumped from the voice, as she was lost in her own misery, and world. And even though it was her time to watch over Sara, the abuse that she had just received tore her up. After all this was not the way it was supposed to be. But she had no power to change what was happening to her as any of the other captives. With their known world crushed and destroyed, and this new one harsh and unfriendly she did not know how she would be able to keep going. She had only been here a short time, and wondered how the other women who had been captured a long time in the past had survived as long as they had. Although looking at this Sara, she really did not look to be around much longer. She called out to the others softly, as it was nighttime, and many were asleep. But all knew that if Sara came around that the rest would be awakened so they could attend to her. After all she was their unofficial leader, the one that helped them through this hell they were living with and in.

* * *

Dusk had settled in a few hours ago, and the smaller moon would not be adding any light for a couple of hours. The four of them continued to monitor the tribe's hidden camp. They had been here in the area hidden for the last couple of days, waiting for the hunting party to leave and make it easier to get done what they needed to do. That had finally happened earlier today, and if everything held up, the hunting party would be gone two days and this one night, returning tomorrow at dusk. So it had to be tonight. As to hang around longer, waiting for the next chance risked discovery, and if discovered they were too small of a group to do anything but retreat, and disappear – losing their one and only chance at this. Once they were discovered the tribe would be on even a higher alert making it impossible, and all the planning and practice would be for naught. Because of the reduction in warriors and because of the hunt, there would only be two guards.

Back in the meadows outside of the Alpha complex Saige had worked and trained them relentlessly. They tried and worked a number of different scenarios trying to cover everything that might come up. Yet they all knew that when they finally arrived at the real camp that what training and practice they did would make them a better team, but not necessarily mean that what they were planning would be a success. After all battle plans only held up until first contact, and then were generally worthless. From the observations that they made with the eye-in-the-sky, as they were calling them now, they had figured out that there were eight captives from the cities. And that initially, if they pulled this off, these captives would think that things had just gotten worse, since it would appear that a rival tribe had just attacked this one, and took them as captives to who knew where. It would not be until later, once Saige knew that they were safely away, that the truth would be revealed. If the primitive encampment came out from under the effects of the drug too soon, then, if they had to abandon the captives, the illusion that it was a rival tribe would stand up. If they had revealed themselves too early, and the captives were recaptured by the tribe, then it would be known that there were others out here who were of the lairs, and that, under no circumstances, could be known.

Saar had come through with the darts that they would use to knock out the rest of the camp. But the ones who were on guard would have to be killed. Again everything had to be true to the methods used by an attacking scouting force. Nothing could be out of character, nothing at all. Saar also had come up with an innovation, so now they had two options to knock out the rest of the camp. He had developed a gas bomb. To use it, one only had to toss it into a fire or the burning coals of a fire. It would then release the gas, and the container would be consumed leaving no evidence behind. They had tested these a number of times, and with some small improvements got them to the point that even a fire that was down to its last few embers would be enough to set them off. So with these as an addition to their arsenal, it became the preferred method of knocking out the primitives. With the darts, which they would have to recover so as to leave nothing behind, and it being dark, it would just be too easy to miss during the recovery and exit portion of the plan.

Now all of them were keyed up as shortly it would all become a reality, and either in about twenty minutes it would be successful, or they would have failed and would be running for their very lives. Saige wished he could communicate with the facility, as last minute intel would have been nice. But one worked with what they had. He signaled the "move" sign. From this point everything would be silent until the final check before the coordinated attack. And these communications would be very brief, just enough to confirm, and then either get the "go or abort" signal. They had finally decided that even with just four of them that they would continue as they did back in the compound, working in teams of two. Fortunately with only two guards out and patrolling, this would work. The camp was settling down and getting quiet as the tribe went to sleep. They would give it another thirty minutes, move into position and then make their move.

* * *

With help Sara was able to sit up. She was close to the fire, but with no clothes, and just getting over the infection, she was cold. Two of the women from one of the cities brought her something she could put on, and then brought her some broth, and water. While over the infection, her system still rebelled to the food, which she threw up immediately. So for the moment she drank the water, and let that settle on an uneasy stomach before trying to get something down again. Finally with care she was able to hold it down, but found that the effort had completely drained her and she was falling asleep once again. The next thing she saw was the sun shining through the open doorway as the building was airing out. She still felt very weak but better than last night. Right now she was alone. Looking around she saw that water and what was probably more broth sitting close to her. With care, because of her weakness, she reached for the water and drank deeply, feeling the coolness enter her body. Anything she did was difficult and took a lot of effort to perform. She knew that soon, someone would have to help her to the trench where they took care of their nature calls. She just did not have the strength to do it on her own. With her own reserves used up to fight the infection she had no endurance at all, and she found once again that after drinking the water and eating some of the broth she was tired. She lay back down, covered up, and once again remembered nothing.

When she awoke again it was early evening and there was the chatter of the primitive women, and some quiet talk from the captured women. Looking over she asked in a weak voice, "Can one of you help me to the trench; I really do have to go." Immediately two of the women came over, smiled briefly at her, even though she could tell that the smiles were forced, they carefully helped her up, and with her leaning heavily on both went to take care of nature. This was something that at one time was a very private thing, but privacy did not exist in the primitive world, so again with them supporting her because of her lack of strength, she took care of her need, and once finished the two helped her back towards the shelter.

One had glanced over her shoulder, and then whispered to the other two saying, "That older warrior is following us. I hope he's not looking to have sex with one of us. He scares me, not that rest doesn't." Sara did not have the strength to even turn around and look, and the trip had just about exhausted her once again. It was going to be quite a while before she would be able to do anything on her own.

Before reaching the shelter she let the two that were helping her that she needed to sit for a moment as she just did not have enough left to make it all the way back. So they stopped and found a tree that she could sit and lean against to get some of her strength back. At this moment the older warrior caught up to them and signaled the two who were assisting to stand away from Sara. Sara looking at the two could see concern and fear. She had to admit that she had fear also. If he wanted to breed with her right now it probably would kill her. So she just waited, not knowing what her future would be.

He crouched in front of her and then began to speak. "I'm the one in charge of making sure all tasks are handled within the clan's home. I organize and put into action what the leader wants done. With age I can no longer join the other warriors in battles and skirmishes. So it is to me that the training of the new warriors falls. I know that you speak our words so that you understand what I am saying, while the rest from your lairs do not, as I do not understand them. It is obvious that the world you come from and ours is different, and the ones who passed into the spirit world since you have been brought here have weighed heavily. We do not take the loss of a female lightly. We know that it they and only they that bring new life and a new generation to our clan.

"There is much we do not understand, and part of this is why none of you are carrying. The only answer we have is that you have strong magic, or that the totem of your people is strong. So strong that we are not strong enough as warriors to overcome this protection and it protects you from carrying our offspring. It speaks that in some ways we must be weak. Our own females are carrying, showing us that we are strong, fertile, as is the land. But any who have bred with you and yours disprove this. We feel that we will continue to breed with, you and yours, until our totem is strong enough to overcome yours. Then when this happens, the warriors that will come from this breeding will be stronger than the rest. Yet it is very puzzling, very puzzling to us. We conquered you and your males with ease. And your males are no warriors, and are making poor slaves. So the strength cannot be with your males, but you and the other females are not warriors either."

He paused as if thinking and then changed the subject. "You almost left us for the spirit world. It is obvious to any that you are weak; still have much time until you have recovered. Because of this, and because we value our females, you and two of yours will remain outside of the herd for the next large moon cycle to give you time to heal. At that time we will see where you are, and then determine if you can be returned to the herd." When he finished what he wanted to say, he got up, went inside the female shelter and then left with one of the younger female primitives.

* * *

All of them were in position; they were giving it just a little more time. But they wanted to be done with this before the moon rise. Staven and Stone were on the far side of the encampment lying in a ravine that ran parallel to the camp. The guard on their side walked the edge of the same just outside of the camp. Where Saige and Seve was located had much more cover. The camp was placed against the hillside on the north with it facing the open range where Staven and Stone were. The placement of the camp was such that it could be easily defended, yet at the same time provided easy access to the grasslands where the wild herd beasts roamed. This area had been used by this tribe for many seasons of hunting. It was an area they knew well, and were comfortable with. If an overwhelming force were to attack, there were many exits to make pursuit more difficult. Other than the night fliers screeching their calls, it was quiet. Stone, looking over and getting Staven's attention, signaled that the guard was moving towards him, and be prepared to move away, if necessary. The guard moved past him stopped, spread his legs and began to relieve himself. Stone, shaking his head, gave the signal to move, and the two of them easily took out the guard who was in a very vulnerable position at that moment and unable to react to prevent his own death. Breathing hard, from the quick strike, both returned to the ravine to await the response from the team leader to move on to the next phase.

Shortly they heard a brief struggle and the silence, followed by Saige and Seve joining them. Saige signaled them to begin the next phase, and they silently spread through the camp, quietly opening the flaps and tossing the gas bombs into the fires that were in each one. They avoided both the slave and female tents. At this point, no more than four minutes had passed since they first attacked the guards. Within the female tent were the offspring of the tribe, and they had no desire to do any harm to them. But, to carry this off successfully, they would have to enter that tent, subdue all who were in there, perform the act, take their prizes, both the slaves and females, and leave.

Giving the gas time to work before moving on to the next portion of the mission, they planted the evidence that would be found in the morning when the tribe awoke and found that they were attacked. Once they had performed all that they had planned then the females would be drugged so as not to raise the alarm. But they still needed witnesses to this next portion, so this drugging of the female tent could not happen until afterwards. Taking a deep breath, Saige asked. "Are you ready for this?" He knew that for all of them that sex were a wonderful physical act between their mates and themselves, and that it could easily be a driving force for a guy. But none of them was looking forward to this encounter. Where they were crouched giving time to make sure that all of the camp was out, the odors drifting out from that tent were overpowering. The smell emanating was somewhere between too much sex, dirty bodies, and a heavy musk. It was so overpowering that it almost made them ill.

Gritting his teeth, Stone said. "I know that we have to go through with this, but that smell almost turns my stomach. How are we going to do this again?"

"I know that we need witnesses to the fact that we did, as they call it, breed with one of their females, so maybe if we open the flap and hold it in the open position, we can take one of them out in front into the better air, take our turns as they would and then get what we came for and just get out of here.

I almost feel like after this that I'm going to want to avoid sex for a long time."

"Know what you mean Seve. But we have to do this, and that's a great suggestion." Saige responded, "So I guess let's get this over with, get our people and get out of here. Remember that until we are safely away we have to maintain the illusion that we are a rival tribe stealing prizes from our enemy. Only when we are sure that we are safe can we reveal to our people that they are in good hands. Okay let's get this done so we can get out of here. And if these females have anything we could catch, let's again hope that the concoction of drugs that Saar gave us takes care of it."

* * *

Even after the older warrior had departed with the female he probably was going to breed with today, she had to remain at the tree trunk that she was leaning against. She just did not believe that she was so weak. She had much to think about, but now would not be the time, exhausted as she was from this little excursion she had the two women help her back up and by the time she was back to her sleeping mat she was almost asleep. When she woke up much later that night she found the same two women still with her. By whatever luck of the draw, these two would be able to remain outside of the breeding herd because they happened to assist her at that moment. She was at least thankful for that.

After drinking more water, and eating more broth, and feeling a little better she could see that one of the women wanted to talk to her, but was afraid to do so. Nodding in this one's direction, she asked. "Is there something you want to say?" She had to admit that at this moment she could not recall her name, and again in the end it wouldn't matter, since here, they had no names.

Nodding her head the young woman said. "Yes, but I wanted to be sure that you wanted to hear what happened to you while you were very sick."

With a perplexed look, Sara asked. "Happened to me, what do you mean?"

With a quick look out the open doorway she then looked back at her and said. "It's just that, that old warrior is probably the reason you are still alive.

"Look when you fell ill, none of us knew what to do, other than to try and keep you warm and comfortable. We could see that you had a high fever, and at the same time chills were racking your body. We thought that most likely you had an infection, but we had nothing to fight it here. Everything we knew was lost back in the city. The older warrior came in during the early part of your illness. I guess to confirm that you were sick and not faking it to avoid all this unpleasantness." Here she stopped for a short time.

"He came in to check on me?" Sara asked. She knew that he was generally in charge of making this clan home, work, so she suspected that he considered it his duty to make sure all was running as it should.

Nodding this woman continued, "Yes. He had us uncover you so that he could look at your body. He signaled us to cover you back up, and left. You were naked because of all the sweating you did; we couldn't leave anything on you. You looked terrible. I didn't know if you would live or die then. But you got worse and we all felt helpless. We knew that the infection was winning, and you are the only one that speaks their language, and while I know you never wanted it, you are kind of our unofficial leader. You helped us through this hell, and if you had died, then we, all of us, would have felt totally lost and without any hope." She paused again, and then taking a deep breath said, "You have helped all of us survive this, and we have so little hope of ever leaving here other than the way it appeared that you were heading."

"You don't know how many times I had wished for that very thing. I've seen too many of us die at the hands of these primitives. I shudder to think what happened to our elderly. If you didn't notice, there were none of them in any of the camps." She could see the shock at the faces of the other women as they realized what she had said was true. While it was still an effort to talk, let alone concentrate Sara asked for her to continue.

"A couple of days later he showed up again. I can't tell you how much we fear him. He signaled for us to uncover you again, and at this point you really looked bad, real bad. He got down on his knees and began to run his hands over your bare body. You began to fight him in your delirium. You could tell that it irritated him, because such a thing is not allowed. He signaled us to hold you down, and we thought he was going to rape you right here and we were going to be party to it. But we had no choice, so we held your arms down. Even when pinned like you were, you continued to fight. I really don't know where you got the strength to do it, but we had a very hard time keeping you down. He started at your head and with a thoroughness I haven't seen, completely worked over your upper body; it was almost gross, the way he did it.

Once satisfied that whatever he was looking for wasn't there, he then straddled you with his back towards your head.

He then did the same with both of your legs. It was like he was searching for something. Again you were desperately fighting him, and he signaled for two others to come over and hold down your legs and to spread them. We really thought that he was just about to begin the rape – especially when he started working your private areas. He did a very close inspection, and started touching you there, and you screamed. His searches became more intense until he found the spot that made you writhe in pain. At this point he had us turn you so that light from the outside would fall on you there. Again he kept at it until he found whatever it was that he wanted. Then he drew out this small knife. We were all very scared at that moment, because we now thought he was going to kill you. We were all shaking in fear.

"He then bent over resting his arms on your legs so that with his weight you couldn't move. He got real close so he could see whatever it was and then pricked something with the point which brought another scream from you. He repeated this a couple of times, and the ones who had been holding your legs could see what he had done, and appeared to be a little sick themselves. At this point he got up quickly and left. We all looked at what he did, and there between your legs from your private area was a growing pool of pus, and a sickly yellowish liquid that was oozing out from the wound he had created. Before we could do anything, he returned. He had someone else with him, who then looked at the wound. He left, and the older warrior pan mimed to us to clean you up. Then the other returned with some type of rough cloth that had crushed leaves of some type wrapped in it. The whole thing was wet. After we had cleaned you up, he went to work with this compress, and again signed us to repeat this and keep the wound open and draining until it no longer flowed, and to use this compress to keep it clean. And that's what we did. Both of the primitives continued to check in on you, and once that poison was out of your system, it became the turning point to your recovery."

With the story before her, at first she felt violated, once again, and then began to wonder why the primitive males had done this. With all the abuse that the women had suffered it just seemed so out of character to what they had experienced. Then she remembered what the old warrior had stated to her after her first trip to relieve herself after coming back to the world of the living. With the way they were being treated, and his statement to her, it just did not make any sense at all. *But how did he know? Or did he? Was he just guessing? Was he what they called a doctor? No, he's a warrior, so the one he brought had to be their doctor. So, again how'd he know what to do?* Then it came to her. In battle there would always be wounds, and she was sure that many over time would become infected, so he only was doing what they would have done when treating an infected battle wound – thusly the reason for the very intimate search of her body. He was attempting to find just that, an infection. Then looking up, after thinking all of this through, she asked, "Where exactly was this infection?" She could see the women who had assisted him turn red.

Quietly, the one who had relayed the story said, "Right where a man would enter you," and said nothing more.

It had been one of the worries, and with the conditions and requirements put on them, she really was not surprised. She knew that she had been injured there a number of times since the capture, and she was sure that when she was put back into the breeding herd that it could happen once again. That got her thinking about what he had related to her just a short time in the past, and while in their own way they cared for, again as they called them, the females, it still was a rough and painful way of life.

* * *

They entered the tent hoping that they looked fierce. With the strength of the stench inside it was difficult to do. The odor itself could have been a weapon. They threw some additional wood on a fire that was in the middle of the tent. This put additional light inside so that they could see what they were facing. In the far corner furthest away from the single exit huddled four women who were obviously from one of their cities. They were still somewhat dressed in the clothes of their culture, but most were no more than rags at this point and time and the condition of the clothes were so poor that it barely covered anything at all. The team knew that these women had been raped a number of times, and it explained the shocked distant expressions with hopelessness showing strongly in their bodies. Turning and facing the tribe females they chose a younger less filthy one and signaled the breeding sign. This consisted of partially closing the left hand and then taking the right thumb and placing it inside the left with a single motion. This represented penetration and breeding.

Two of them took her just outside of the tent, and while she put up a token fight, that was all it was. There just had been too many annuals of submitting for one of them to outright refuse. And they knew that if they fought too hard they would be cuffed into submission anyway. The other two guarded the tent and kept the rest under a watchful eye, and as each had their turn at the female they would rotate this guarding. Once finished they roughly grabbed the female and returned her to the tent and then signaled the four in the corner to come to them. They could see the fear in their eyes, and it hurt them that they could not reveal who they really were, but right now they were in the middle of an enemy's camp and had to maintain the illusion.

The women were slow to respond, and two of them had to go get them and encourage compliance. They could see the fear growing as they expected to have the same thing happen to them that they had just witnessed. Once outside and before leaving, Saige re-entered the tent and acted like he was building up the fire once again, at the same time giving the females a very stern stare, he placed another of the gas bombs in the fire and knew that shortly they would all be unconscious and would not be able to raise the alarm. When he saw the gas bomb about to release the gas he left. Then the four of them led the women into the ravine just outside of camp and Staven stayed with them and with weapons drawn and hand signals to let them know what would happen if they tried to escape. The other three returned to the camp and brought out the four men from the city that were in the slave tent. Then when they had all of them they laid a false trail leading away from the camp and deeper into the grasslands towards the camps of the rival tribe that they had left false evidence within the attacked camp identifying that tribe as the culprit.

CHAPTER SEVEN

For the first half of the night they pushed deeper into the grasslands. The direction was generally away from the Sacred Mountains and towards the rival tribe. Saige knew that the travel would be slower than they liked, but the eight prisoners that they had with them had been through hell before getting to the camp they had just been removed from, and now supposedly captured once again as prizes by another tribe. He knew that their spirits had to be close to rock bottom. Eventually they reached the stream that he had planned on using, and they, using the shallow stream as a way to hide their tracks, hiked in the cool water back and then into the Sacred Mountains where the stream flowed from. The four of them needed to push the eight hard, as the trek they had ahead of them would be all night, and then go until the zenith of the next day. They had to reach a hidden camp that they had set up. Once there he felt that they would be far enough away that they could take a couple of hours before moving on to the second camp. Once this second camp was reached they would be deep enough into the sacred mountains that they could reveal the truth. But until then they had to maintain the fear and the fatigue level to make sure these refugees from one of their cities did not try and escape.

* * *

It had been a tough trip with the exhausted members of the captured city. But Saige could see where the second camp was. It still would be a little while before the reached it, and with all of them taking turns watching their back trail they finally took a very brief break. Looking at the eight of them, he could see fear, almost panic in them, but he also could tell that they were so tired that they did not even have the energy to speak to each other. When they stopped, they just dropped and did not move. He was sorry for having to do this, but unfortunately it was necessary, and while they were scared to death, this would change shortly. He left Stone watching over them and went back to Seve and Staven and asked, "Anything at all?"

Both just shook their heads no. "I was able to look back at the camp, and there wasn't even any movement that first day until late in the morning, so by then we were already here in the mountains, and they were tracking our false trail out in the grasslands. But nobody has come this way. Staven, did you see anything different?"

Staven shaking his head said, "No, not at all. I think we were successful with our false evidence we left, and with our trail leading away from their camp. Saw no one at all coming this way."

Turning around and looking at Stone and the ones he was guarding Saige stated. "I'd like to tell them now, but I think we'll stay to our plan. We are just about to the second camp where we have all of our supplies and changes of clothes for them as well as us. I truly am quite ready to get out of this stuff." That brought a bit of laughter from the other two. They nodded their heads and agreed with him. "Okay let's get this last part done so we can quit scaring them and give them something positive since their city fell. By the way have any of you heard anybody mention a name of either the city or themselves?" None had so at this point they just did not know.

The three joined Stone and then with spear points they prodded the captives into moving. There was no fight in them at all, and it took all their energy just to get moving once again. Saige thought. *Oh boy, this is going to take a little longer than I thought. At least there's no fight in them to make this more difficult. In another day we'll be at the first of the caves and within a couple of more back at the Alpha complex. So far, so good, and may it continue that way. It looks like we convinced that tribe that it was one of their enemies that did this, and that is great news.*

By pushing and prodding the "prizes", as the captured ones would have been considered, they finally came around a rock face into a hidden bowl that had running water and a small natural cave. They led them to the cave, and then inside where they had their supplies hidden. Then Saige breathed out a large sigh and said, "Finally!" Looking at the shocked faces of the eight he smiled and paused before continuing. "Okay, all of you sit and relax. We will be spending the rest of this day here to give you a chance to recover at least a little before we have to continue. We'll get a fire going, and over there in those supplies are changes of clothes for all of you. And for you women, there's an area at the back that you can have a bit of privacy as you change out of those rags. Guys, we don't have that option, so we will just step outside to change while the women are in the back doing the same thing."

"Who are you?" Asked one of the women, who had just sat down and appeared to be on the verge of tears. "You're not any of those primitives that captured us?"

Quietly he answered, "No, our city was Sequoyah, and it was attacked and destroyed over an annual in the past. Of that city there were only ten of us who escaped. We are part of that ten."

One of the men then said, "But, but we thought, we thought that things had gone from bad to worse. We've seen what they had done to our women, and we could do nothing, and we were then forced to work for them, and when you raided their camp we thought, oh no not again. Why did you do it this way?"

Before any could speak another of the women asked, "And all of you raped that primitive woman, just as we had been, why would you do something like that? Are you no different than they?"

Shaking his head and again pausing before answering, Saige stated, "Look, we will try and explain everything. But I, and I know the rest of my team, want to get out of these skins and into something a little more comfortable. Then we will bring up some water from the stream, heat it and we all can clean up a little bit and feel better about it. We can eat a hot meal, and then we will introduce ourselves and you can do the same – you, not knowing who we are, and vice versa, makes this a little uncomfortable. Just know that for now you are safe, and tomorrow we will be heading out and getting closer to safety." Turning around he saw that the rest of the team had the change of clothes for them and the other men. "Okay all, let's get out of this stuff and into something that is in better shape and is clean." He signaled the men to follow them outside and pointed the women to the back of the cave.

A short time later when the men had all changed Stone yelled into the cave, "Hey all you women decent?" The heard a muffled voice saying to give them a few more minutes, and Stone shrugged, "It's something I'll never understand. It never takes us guys long to change but always seems to take twice as long for a woman. While we're waiting let's go get some of that water so we can heat it. We know that we could use some cleaning up, and know that all of you are worse off, so I guess we will need quite a bit of the stuff. Sorry no soap, but warm water and a couple of the rags we brought will get the worst of it."

Next to the cave entrance behind some of the brush that was there he grabbed a number of collapsible buckets and all of them went down to the stream and filled them, returned to the entrance where this time the women were standing. "You look much better now," Staven stated, "How are you feeling?" There were a few smiles, but they were more tentative than genuine. They could understand that, since the rescued really did not know if it was over or not. After all they were still in the wilderness with four men who still could be enemies and this was just an elaborate trap.

"I know that everything that has happened to you appears to be a horrible nightmare that you can't leave. With our fleeing from our city it was the same. We started out with a much larger force, and it was whittled down as we were harassed and attacked by the primitives almost the full distance we traveled." Stopping a moment before continuing, Saige looked them over and could see that they were almost afraid to believe that it was over for them, but at the same time if they could believe that they felt guilty because they were safe. Pointing to himself he said, "I'm Saige, and this is Stone, Seve, and Staven. When we get back to where we are taking you, you can meet the rest of us. Like I said earlier, our city was Sequoyah, and we learned that our city was the last city to have a scouting unit, and we are the remnants of the same. It is probably the only reason we survived. Now before I ask you your names I need to explain why we did what we did back in that camp." At this point he covered the why, and what they had to do to keep the suspicion from them and on the primitives themselves. He also stated that their mates did not like the idea any better, but there had been no other way to accomplish this misdirection. Once finished with the explanation he asked, "First any questions, and if not please give us your names?"

With no questions from them, he looked at the women first and they began to give them their names. Joci was the first, and seemed to be the youngest – pretty, but not beautiful, and probably in her late teens. Jas sat next to her and looked like a mother, probably somewhere in her thirties, if not pushing forty. Jeanna was the beautiful one of the group. Her looks naturally brought men's eyes to her. She appeared to be in her mid-twenties and the dirt that covered could not conceal her beauty. They all knew that once she was back to herself that she would outshine all of the other women. Yet, she did not appear to put on an air of superiority, but more towards just a normal everyday woman. Jessi from her build was more athletic. She could have easily been a member of one of the scouting teams, and she appeared to be in her early twenties.

The men as they went around and giving them their names were as follows; Jaiden who had to be in his forties looked more like a librarian than anything else. Jed was in his thirties and worked the hydroponics, a farmer at heart. In size his was close to Stone and had a similar build and complexion. Jarid, in his late twenties was the one that women probably would have naturally been drawn to. His looks were rugged and handsome with a natural body frame to compliment his looks. And the fourth of the men was Judd. From the looks of him they would have guessed he was in his early forties, but were surprised to learn he actually was in his early fifties. He ran his own business, and had helped many others get started in their own. After introductions were over, all of them now had names; the team began to prepare food for all, and to set up the sleeping arrangements.

"I'm sorry, but we aren't set up with places to take care of your nature calls, so we've kind of decided that when you exit the cave to take care of your needs that you women go down and to the right, as you leave the cave, and there's a copse of trees that will provide the privacy you need. We guys will go to the left and stay parallel to the rock wall. A little ways out there's a pile of rocks that will provide all the privacy that we need. As far as sleeping arrangements all eight of you will have the back of the cave with the women sleeping in the area that again provides them their privacy behind that hanging curtain where the supplies are stored." Saige looking at them could still see the trauma that they had endured. All he could do was shake his head. Thinking back, he suspected that before they found the complex, they probably would have looked much the same. "I suspect that all of you are quite tired, and once you eat we suspect that all of you will be falling asleep. Please do that. We have far to go and will be trying to push through, based on how well the eight of you do. The four of us will continue to guard and watch our back trail. We know that we can hide our trail, but the eight of you do not have the experience or skill to do that, so I know that there is sign out there that the primitives could easily locate and follow.

"And on that note, if we find that they are trailing us, *then,* be prepared to move, be quiet, and do as we say. It could save your life. Be prepared for a real surprise once we reach our destination. And just a warning, be prepared to unlearn all we have been taught about our history. It was a shock to us what we learned, but for now that's all I'm going to say. From the smells I think the food is ready, and from the sounds of the complaints from my stomach it thinks so too, so let's eat."

* * *

"This waiting is killing me," Seirra said. Looking around at the others she could see that she had already said this too many times, and she suspected that the others had felt this way. "Yeah I know, I keep repeating myself, but I can't help it if it is true. I know from the imagery that it appears to have been successful, but we really won't know until they're back, or, at least, to the cave system that our ancestors built. And it should be today sometime when they hit the first one. And until they are leaving the last one, and before they arrive, will be the first time that we will be able to talk with them, but this doesn't make the waiting any easier."

Nodding her head in agreement Sorrel said, "Very true. I think that we got lucky on this first attempt. Saige and Shell', with our input of course, put together a great plan, and it worked. I'm sure there were a few problems, there always is, but like you said, from what we could see they rescued all of our people from that tribe." Sighing Sorrel continued. "I just hate this inability to be able to talk to them, and to find out which city these people came from. To find out if it is one of the most recent to fall, or whether our people have been captives much longer." Then she laughed and starting teasing the other women when she asked, "You aren't jealous are you, because they had to get physical with one of the primitive women?"

That got the others to look at each other, and actually from the guilty looks on their faces Sorrel could see that she had hit the nail right on the head. She had to admit that it did bother her that Stone was one of the ones who were involved, but again it had to be done to keep it true. It didn't make it any easier when, in a way, your man was going to cheat on you, and it was being done in the open, but from what they knew of the primitives, if they hadn't then it would have led the attacked tribe to know something wasn't right, and probably look elsewhere for the attackers.

At the present Saar, the only man left at the facility, was in the security office monitoring everything. Soon Starr would join him to assist. Actually she would relieve him so he could come get something to eat, before rejoining her. The shifts were being split a little differently with four of the team gone. To keep it fresh they rotated a single member through on staggered shifts to keep at least one of them somewhat fresh. Any and all other work and research had stopped until the team returned, successful or not. So the four women sat around the table in the cafeteria, Starr with Sommer who was content and asleep, and Sabryn holding Shayne, who just seemed content to let his mother hold him. It was truly rare that the four of them ever had a chance to get together this way. With so few of them it usually was no more than one or two of them and most of the time the men would also be around. Not that this was a problem, but the women would have liked to have more just "girl time", where they could talk freely, or complain about their men and not be interrupted or have one of the opposite sex close by to overhear what they had to say.

It was quiet for the moment and Starr looking over lovingly at her sleeping daughter sighed and said. "I've got to go, if she wakes and wants to eat bring her to me and I'll get her fed." She got up and quietly left heading for the security office and part of her shift. Starr had to admit that she almost longed for the quieter days before they made contact with the cities. Since then the circuits between the cities and the Alpha complex, compound or whatever you wanted to call it was busy all the time.

* * *

Saige, looking over the newly released captives smiled inwardly. To him, it had almost seemed a lifetime that they were at this Alpha facility. With everything that was going on, it was difficult at times, to remember how he had found this place. It definitely had been the hard way, that's for sure. Turning around he said to the eight, "We are just about there now. And you will immediately recognize aspects of this place, and immediately see the similarities between our cities and here." The suns were setting and there were long shadows being cast by the mountains, and trees, lying across the valleys and depressions, allowing one to see the true scope of the broken lands. He had to admit that if it had been his choice this would have been the last place to put such a place, but it made total sense. As they climbed the path that he and Shell' had when they were exploring this area, all of what had happened, the history, the discovery, the confrontation, and the reuniting of the remnant of the scout team, all happened here.

He stood in front of the hidden entrance letting everybody catch their breath. "Okay all, we are here."

"Here?" Jaiden asked, "This doesn't look any different than any other place we've seen in these mountains. Are you joking with us? Because if you are, it's not very funny."

Smiling, although it was a sad smile, Saige replied. "No, Jaiden, I'm not, not at all. You see it is important that you see this as it is. Before us appears to be a solid rock face . . ." He reached out and his hand disappeared through that rock face, and then he withdrew it. "As you can see it is an illusion: An illusion just as our cities use to hide the entrances to our hidden cities." Again he stopped for a moment, looking them over, shrugged and asked. "Shall we?" He then disappeared from their sight as he entered into the facility, or to be more exact the entrance to the large cavern.

In a few moments the rest joined him on the platform that sat above the cavern floor, which was bathed in a dim soft light. He could see that it had the effect on the new members that he expected. They were quiet, and he could see the tension begin to flow out of them, when they realized that for them the nightmare was over. Saige sent Stone, Seve, and Staven on ahead at this point. He wanted to be sure that everything was prepared for their arrival. And knowing the women who were here, he suspected that they would be impatient to both see their men, and to help the new arrivals. As he watched the three of them cross the dirt floor of the cavern he pointed out to the eight what they were seeing from where they stood. "For the next few days we will want you to recover. Saar will give each of you a physical, and whatever medicines you need to help your bodies heal, and to help clear any infections that you may have gotten during your long captivity. Then, and only when the doc gives you a clean bill of health and all of you feel up to it, it will be time to learn the truth about us." Turning towards the women he said. "I know what you had to face. You were required to join their breeding herds and submit to their males. Your names were taken from you, and then all of you were raped over and over again by the warriors. While they do not see it that way, it is the truth as far as our society sees it. And I know that the question would have come up as to why none of you ever became pregnant. Yet, as often as you submitted none of you did. I need all of you here to remember this. It will be one of the critical pieces that will help you understand what will be presented later, and will help you come to terms with what we have learned since rediscovering this place." Again looking at them he said, "Enough for now, let's go join the rest. I'm sure that a hot shower will feel great, and a change of clothes, followed by a hot meal. Then after that we will show you where the rooms for single members are so you can claim a space of your own. There tomorrow Saar will come for each of you and get you checked out, and other than that you will have free reign of this place. The rest of us have assignments that we must get to. So until the time you are cleared and then integrated into our teams, the time will be your own." They climbed down the ladders to the two lower platforms before reaching the floor, and headed through the double swinging doors into the facility.

* * *

Jed, looking around the meadows, was in awe to what he had learned so far. They had only been here fourteen days so far, and while it had been very difficult to accept, what he and the rest of the group that Saige and his had rescued, the evidence was overwhelming. He remembered the statement about the women not becoming pregnant, and he had to admit that they should have with as often as they had to submit. Yet, even now, living in the very facility where their ancestors had worked and studied the races of this planet and similarities to their own city Jade, well, it just couldn't be denied. As he walked this enclosed meadowland and the animals that lazily gazed at him when he came too close, he could almost feel safe. But the time of being a slave under these tribes and clans had left its mark. At least he had work here to help him forget. After all he was a farmer, so to speak. He looked the part and had worked the hydroponics, and had studied husbandry – although there had been very few animals in the cities. So studying them was just about all it could have been. But now here they were, and thusly why he was out in this place.

Jas, looking over at Saar felt somewhat out of place. Heck he could almost be her son if she really thought about it, but instead he was the doctor, and she was now his nurse. Her specialty had been pediatrics, and with few children there was not a great need for her services. Smiling she thought. *Ah, but it won't be that way for long. I am surrounded by young people who have coupled, and that leads to new lives.* She loved babies, and with Shayne and Sommer, she had two to help her pass the time. She had to admit that Saar was competent. She suspected that the fighting and running that they had to do probably had honed his skills and built his confidence. And with her arrival he now had someone to help. When the information about their true origins was presented she at first was in shock. It was counter to everything she had learned, but again she had to admit that the evidence was overwhelming. She knew now why Saige had made that statement when they were outside before entering this place for the very first time. She had to admit at that moment when he had stated that they were here, and all she could see was just a rock face, she felt at that very moment that some cruel joke had been laid at their feet. And then he demonstrated that they were facing the same illusions that the cities used, she then understood.

Jaiden, looking at the mainframe shook his head. *Yes, in many ways it looks archaic, but for as old as it is it functions quite well.* He had been a computer tech when Jade had fallen to the primitives. He had to admit that the physical labor that he had been made to do as a slave almost killed him. He never had been one to enjoy outdoor activities, and loved reading and computers. Like the rest, when the data was presented, at first he wanted to deny it. But, he asked himself why would they lie? And while Saige, Shellian, and the rest had been here for an annual, they did not have the skills to make this kind of change. Plus he knew that out in this world somewhere was an

Alpha City or station. But its location was unknown. Who would have thought that it would have been hidden in the Sacred Mountains? Not he, that's for sure.

Joci didn't know what to think. She was young and had very little confidence in herself. She had dreamed, as all teenage girls, of meeting the right guy and then somewhere later becoming a couple and then having children. *After all, isn't that the way it's supposed to be?* She had never been physical with anybody, and when she had been captured, like all the women in the city; she was raped by five of the primitives. It had hurt, and she had bled quite a bit. In shock, she never, in her worst nightmares, imagined it would be like this. Then she was placed in the breeding herd and the abuse continued. It had torn her both physically and mentally. Now learning that at least she wouldn't carry any of the offspring of the primitives was a relief. But she hadn't reached the age where she knew what she really had wanted to do. So for now she just assisted all of them where she could. She had lost her family, and desperately wanted to fit in here – feeling that if she wasn't accepted that she would just die. So much had happened to her in such a short time, and none of it pleasant.

Judd was quite happy to be free of the primitives. At least he had been in some type of physical shape, so the work he had to perform did not kill him. He was sore for a while from muscles he hadn't used in a while, but at least he, even at his age, had fared better than many of the others. Quite a few were no longer around, having died or been killed for not doing what was demanded. And when the camp had been attacked, he was worried that he would have to learn all over again with new masters. This primitive world was definitely tough. And after being taken by the four, who he thought was from another tribe, and under threat of death and with weapons drawn, his thought of escape left. Besides he had nowhere to go, and really did not even know where they were at the time of the attack. He had heard from the women, that one of the primitive women had been raped by these four, which bothered him, but he was helpless at the time to do anything, as were the rest. Then, when they were safely away, to learn that it all had been a ruse, to place the blame on another tribe, and to learn that these four were their own people brought release that said, maybe this hell was finally over.

He had been in construction in one form or another all of his life. So he took over the industrial replicators, and the maintenance of this facility, although the auto systems had maintained the compound quite well. Still, as time continued to pass, and more were possibly rescued and brought here, space would have to be ready. So there was much to be done. Right now the dorms, as they began to call them, were very empty. Each probably could hold fifty people, and with only four in each it could easily feel that there was a lot of privacy. Like the others, he had lost his family. He did not know if any had even survived. Fortunately his mate had passed away earlier, and for this he was thankful, he knew the hell she would have been going through. But he had no way of knowing about any other members of his family, and because of this, it was something that continued to work on his mind. Yet, at this moment, there just wasn't anything he or anyone here could do.

Jeanna had been a teacher of the young. And history had been her major. So at first she had strong arguments against what was presented. Again she had to admit, that what Saige had stated before they entered the facility had hit home. As often as she had to submit to the males, she should have been carrying. And if not she, at least any of the other captured women from the cities. Yet, as far as she knew, not one had become pregnant from any of the too many unions they were required to perform. So after the facts were shown to her and the rest, she went back and studied the archives, and in the end, had to admit that everything was consistent and out in the open. Nothing was hidden, it was all there. Then, during her recovery, she had walked the cavern, saw the meeting area at the top of the stairs, she hadn't quite gotten brave enough to ride the moving room yet, and everywhere she went spoke of her city, and her people. Nothing was out of place, or jarring in a way that spoke of misdirection or lies.

With her skills she assisted Starr and Sabryn on gathering the information for dissemination to the remaining cities, and like them, hoped that the governments within those cities let the information out to all so that they could learn the truth about themselves. She really wondered what had transpired that left them stranded here on this world, a world that for quite some time they had been claiming as their own. Again she had to admit that it was a shock to learn that they had come from a different world and one that was hidden from them. Yes, as she worked the education computers, she had found images of that world, and had found it beautiful. But it was out of reach somewhere in the vastness of space.

Jarid had worked the public communications circuits — both the visual and audio. In the audio he had a popular DJ program that he worked every day, and once every five days a popular music program that went out over the visuals. Much of what was needed here at the Alpha was skills he did not have. But at least he could help man the communications in the security office, to take the load off of the others. With his verbal skills he could deal with the individual cities as they contacted "Point Alpha", as it was known in each of the cities. And of course he could and would assist anywhere else that they needed a warm body. It had been a shock to him when the city fell. It was early morning, and he had been at the studio preparing his audio program when the power failed. It shocked him at that point, since this had never happened before. Of course he didn't realize that it was the primitives that had shut it down, and that they were attacking their city at that very moment. By the time he had figured it out he was a prisoner and on his way to becoming a slave. And again he had no skills for the hard dirty work that he was *persuaded* to do. He had been threatened with death a number of times, but eventually had figured out what they wanted and after a very tough period of strengthening his muscles he had been able to maintain, but just barely. Food was poor, conditions worse, and like the rest he had little hope of surviving this, let alone be rescued.

When the camp, where he was a slave, was attacked his hopelessness rose. He had barely figured out how to survive here, and now, could he learn what his new masters wanted of him? It had been a good question. With the time he and the women had been with the tribe, they had picked up a word or two and learned what they could from observation. With the women placed with the other, as they were called – females, and he a slave, no contact was allowed. He and the other three rarely saw the four women from the city. And somehow, by luck he guessed, all of them were from the same city. Their annual had eighteen months, and without a way to track them, he had lost track. But he knew that it had to have been at least four or five. It seemed like it was summer when the city fell, and sometime in fall when the rival tribe's scouting force attacked the camp. Fear had invaded his soul once again when they were led out of their tent and he saw the bodies on the ground. The other tribe members looked fierce and looking around at the damage just these four had inflicted made him decide not to try and escape. He wanted to stay alive, desperately. Then came that trek into the Sacred Mountains and the revelation that they had been rescued.

"We would like everybody to report to the meeting area. There is much that we need to discuss, and we need to learn what we can from the eight of you who were captives so that we can plan on our next move", the voice over the PA system stated. "This meeting will be after the mid-day meal." He hadn't been here long enough to recognize voices yet, but that was coming along.

CHAPTER EIGHT

K'jor, with the others, was once again hunting the vast
herds, and the campsite that they had chosen was the same. It
lay untouched, with the ashes from the previous times cold,
dead and spread out. It was here that he had first been
introduced to the mystery. And as the preparations continued
for the hunts, his mind went back once again to those
moments he had spent in the desolation. He had become
seriously concerned that the spirits were observing him. He
could sense that he was being watched, but everywhere he had
looked there was nothing – nothing but the swirling dust, hot
winds, and the dry lands. Yet it seemed as if there were distant
voices on the wind. Voices that was unrecognizable, almost
just beyond hearing. He sensing them more than hearing, and
when he tried to discern a direction there was none. It was as
if these voices were coming from everywhere, and at the same
time nowhere. He tried to go in the direction of them, but
every time came away with nothing. *I don't understand this.*
Looking up he could see that the suns were heading to late
day, and soon it would be dusk, and at that time it would be
worse. It was the time of day where the gods fought to keep

the spirits at bay. And he was here in this desolation alone. Alone! It was a time when a warrior would be required to be his best, lest a spirit would inhabit him and take his body over for his own purposes. He knew that this would be his last night here and tomorrow he would return to join his warriors, and to return to camp.

All the areas he had been searching were completely devoid of life, and as the time continued to flow by him, he found that the areas all began to look alike. More proof that the spirit world had control of this area. *After all every place has its own look, its own feel. I know that there are always landmarks to identify, and special features that allow one to know a certain place is that place. But here all is the same. It confuses the mind. The heat cooks the body, and fogs the mind. The waves emanating from the ground obscure the true world, and allow the spirits to roam freely. It is a place of the dead. Again, why am I here?* Again he felt that now it had been for a foolish reason. But when one faces these lands of gods, he would always seem foolish. This was so opposite of the Sacred Mountains, and he guessed that it made sense. But he left this to the priests to figure out. He was a warrior and had enough to deal with in the real world. Once he left this place of death, and they returned to the clan's home he would discuss this with the priests – that's if he survived to do so.

He felt as if he was going crazy. What else could one call it? Something was here, just out of reach, just out of view, just beyond his understanding, but as to what it was he did not know. He could feel something vibrate, but heard nothing. It was as if the earth itself was about to open and swallow him whole. And why not, after all, all of his conclusions said that this belonged to the gods, to the spirits of those who have passed. So why not be swallowed. *Ah, I did not think of that. Maybe, just maybe this is exactly what happened here. It is so obvious to me now. When my warriors conquered the two, and the beast in this land the gods considered it a sacrifice to them and the very ground opened and swallowed the offerings – even though this was not our intent, or desire. We were only following the laws . . .* This gave him pause as he stood there thinking. *Maybe that's the answer. Yes the warriors were following the laws. So to the spirits and the gods of this land this was a proper tribute, and they then took this tribute.* With this line of reasoning he began to feel better. And right now the facts seemed to support his line of thought. *Well, I think that I am now satisfied, and I know what happened here. But it is too late to leave. So in the morning I will leave these lands to the spirits and the gods and know that we have upheld the laws, and our gods are pleased.*

He turned around and found that the winds had wiped out his tracks, and again where he was appeared to be no different than any other place he had explored in this desolation. Glancing once again at the suns he realized that more time had passed than he thought and dusk would be on him shortly. He needed to find a place for the night and have his fire going to be protected by the light from the fire. Without the fire, he could be attacked by the spirits he was sure that inhabited this desolate world.

* * *

He was snapped back from his thoughts as a courier from the alliance came into the camp escorted by some of K'jor's warriors. It had taken some time to arrange a method of moving messages within the alliance – then additional time to develop a method that would allow someone to approach a camp without being killed as an enemy. After much argument between the many tribes and clans he had melded together, it was decided that a spear with its point turned upside down and a piece of cloth attached just below this turned point would signal all that this individual was a courier moving messages from one tribe or clan to another. At this time the color of the cloth did not matter it was just a way to confirm to any that this one had safe passage and could go and see the leader of the individual clans or tribes. With a courier there could be one more warrior since the dangers of this world went beyond just the warring people.

Still he was curious as to why now. This method was generally used only during the times when the alliance had re-gathered, and was preparing for the next battle. Now with the season of falling, all were preparing for the long season of cold and had gone their separate ways. He could see that this courier was waiting patiently for some response from him to approach. He let him wait as he studied the individual. After a few moments he came to the conclusion that he was from one of the smaller tribes that roamed close to the Sacred Mountains, which was about as far as the wild herds traveled. He personally had never been very close to those mountains, or to the far south to see where the lands became perpetual white. He suspected that if one traveled beyond the Sacred Mountains, eventually the lands of perpetual white would be there also. But with so much required to keep one alive right here, he felt that to travel just to see these wonders were foolish. Life was too short.

Looking into the eyes of the courier he could see a bit of nervousness, and at the same time, an attempt to hide it. To show any weakness before any enemy was not good. Taking a deep breath he then signaled the courier to approach him, which the courier did. Written language was just being developed, and only a few of the clans had it. So he listened as the information was passed to him. The courier stated that, as he surmised, that he came from one of the smaller tribes, and that they had been attacked by a rival tribe, and their prizes, and reward for service to the alliance had been stolen. They had lost warriors to the fight, and the increase to their female herd had been taken along with the slaves. They had tracked the enemy deep into the grasslands, but the trail vanished and they were unable to locate where they had gone. Would there be anything that the leader of the great alliance could do to help?

He signaled the courier away and to wait. Shaking his head inwardly he thought. *When I first thought about trying to bring us together against these sorcerers and magicians, I thought this was going to be so easy. And as time continues to flow past me as the rivers, it just gets more and more difficult. If I felt in my soul that we have wiped out all the nests of these vermin then I would allow us to go back to the way we were. I have had enough of trying to keep these squabbling children from fighting each other, stealing from each other, and killing each other.* Shrugging, he came to a decision and signaled the courier to approach. When he arrived K'jor stated. "I can do nothing about your past, and the loss that you claim. The fighting between you and your rival is between the two of you, as well as the outcome from those fights. So if you lost your prizes from this season's campaigns, they are lost and we cannot, and will not, recover them for you. It is the season of final food gathering for the upcoming cold time. All of us of the alliance are pressed because of the late start to get enough food. So there are no free warriors to help you avenge your loss. While I cannot promise how next season's fighting will go with the alliance, I will offer you and your tribe first choice of the prizes we take, and that is the best that any of us can do. Now return and tell your tribe leader of this decision."

He could see that the hope had been for instant retribution on the tribe that dared attack one from the alliance, and the disappointment was obvious on the face of the courier. But he knew that his decision was the correct one. None of them had the time to go chasing a tribe at this time. And if they were stupid enough to have allowed themselves to be attacked, well, they got what they deserved. When the courier had left, with his second waiting outside of camp, and with the clan's warriors escorting them away, all he could do was shake his head. As he had stated to this courier, there was just too much to be done and too little time.

And it was these thoughts that brought back another curious incident that had taken place, after what had happened in the desolation. One of the warriors, who had been guarding the camp, said he had seen an apparition – a stranger, who was tall and in strange clothing, standing at the edge of their camp and staring. The warrior said he had to look twice to be sure. Yet this stranger *was* taller and did seem to be dressed strangely. He said that he stared at the stranger, and before he could approach the stranger faded away like the dust. And since this was soon after the death of the two in the desolation the warrior thought it had to have been the male they had killed who then crossed over into the spirit world.

* * *

It was great to see the gates once again. The time of hunting was over and the days of cold were close. As they had entered lands familiar to them they could feel their muscles beginning to relax, as well as their spirits soar. Still they had to remain alert for an attack, but did it ever feel good to be here. The hunting, as usual was successful, but brutal. They had to push harder than they ever remembered. K'jor thought that in the next cycle of seasons that he would end the campaigns earlier. This had been almost impossible this time to get the necessary meat, and skins, and to still be able to get all of that back home. And with the increase from their raids it had required more of everything. He had sent a runner ahead to let the clan know that they were arriving and it would be just before the setting of the suns – although the skies were becoming overcast with a promise of rain. Well, rain was important as it fed the rivers and streams, and allowed the grains they grew to reach to the skies. And it wouldn't be long until what they had would be stored for this time of the seasons. With the young ones and the slaves, the grains should have been cut, and now with the arrival of the warriors, the grains would be separated from the stalks, and then stored.

He knew that this was one of the major differences between the clans with their semi-permanent settlements, and the tribes. What grains the tribes gathered were wild and in the vast grasslands. Mostly they followed the migrations of the herd beasts, with most of what they needed coming from the same. And while part of the clothing of the clans was made from the same skins as the tribes, they had learned how to make clothing from other substances, including some of the hair of the beasts. The tribes overall were smaller than the clans. Although the fierceness of some of the tribes made them appear to be much larger. Their warriors were unmatched in battle, and most left them alone, including him. He had not approached any of these to join the alliance. Maybe if this alliance held that someday they, as the alliance, could go against these tribes and eliminate them. But who knew? There was a great chance that within a couple of full seasons the alliance would have become broken and no more. He found that with less than the promised loot, that many within the loose alliance were quite restless. He had to hold this thing together somehow, at least, until he felt that they had eliminated these magicians and their hidden lairs.

He didn't understand why he felt so strongly about destroying them, but he did. After all these magicians had remained hidden for again who knew how long. It seemed that they kept to themselves, choosing only the most desolate areas to maintain their lairs. They did not meddle in the affairs of any of the tribes and clans, and anything that he could surmise said that if one was lost and injured, that they may have actually healed and returned the lost ones. Yet, he just did not trust any of them or their hidden motives. And they had to have hidden motives to be living the way they were. Maybe they had some influence on their own gods, and maybe it could be that this influence could spill into the world of the living. He had to remember to have some discussions this season of cold with T'som. He was their head priest, and between the two of them they could come up with some answers to the many questions he had. While the males from these lairs appeared to be weak, the females, even though many had passed into the spirit world, were not. Their magic and totems were very strong. So much so that not one warrior had been successful when breeding with them to have these females carry. Their own females, many of them carrying, proved that the warrior's seed was strong, but not strong enough to be successful with the females from the lairs. What power they must wield to prevent such a thing.

Still it was a strange thing. Like their males, they did not appear strong. Maybe it was the lairs that gave them their strength. But they had destroyed their lairs as the found them, leaving them silent and dead as the areas of desolation they existed in. It was the continued failure of the warriors to bring these females to carrying that strengthened his belief that there were other lairs out there. These additional hidden lairs, still giving power to these females and giving them the ability to prevent the carrying, were proving that they and their totem were much stronger than any tribe or clan. With the cold time approaching there would be more time to try and change this. Yes, they would remain within the laws, but there would be an increase in the attempts, so that maybe soon they could overcome this strong totem that protected the magicians, making them stronger, and like the fierce tribes unconquerable. What warriors could be produced once they overcame the totem of the magicians? They could become the greatest of their clan, and of the surrounding clans. Still he knew that it was the thoughts of any that had been part of the alliance, since they all had their share of slaves and females. Whoever was the first to be successful in overcoming the totem would be unstoppable. The horns blew announcing their arrival, which brought him out of his revere, and at the same time in the distance the skies rumbled a deep rolling sound.

He smiled accepting this as a good sign that their gods approved. After all it seemed that the gods were also announcing their arrival home. What could be better than that?

* * *

"So, R'san, how'd it go while we were away? I know between the raids on the lairs, and then the gathering of meat for the cold time, we have been gone a long time. It placed a larger burden on you, not that you couldn't handle it, but you had much less to work with, with most of the warriors gone." K'jor had to admit that even after all this time he still respected the old warrior. This one had even trained him, and had told him that he, because of his natural skills and abilities, would probably become clan leader. He hadn't believed it at the time. Since this warrior who trained him, did everything with no effort at all, while, at the same time, he struggled through his lessons on combat, tactics and such. But here he was many seasons later the leader, just as R'san had predicted. Still, smiling inwardly, he had to admit the he had even exceeded the old warrior's expectations by creating and leading this alliance.

In his usual way R'san paused before commenting. It had always been his way, and K'jor knew not to become impatient. R'san hadn't stayed alive through all those battles and skirmishes by being slow. He had always been second, never wanting to lead the clan. It was something that K'jor never understood. He had always felt that the clan would have prospered under R'san's leadership. "It has taken longer to accomplish what was needed without the necessary bodies to work. The slaves, we have lost many to the spirit world, cannot produce as well as our own. Yet, the tasks that you left for me are accomplished, if only barely. And no, before you ask, none of the females from the lairs are carrying. While there has been less to be able to breed with the females, some of our own are carrying."

"I noticed that the older female from the lair was not around, has she passed into the spirit world also?" K'jor asked.

Shaking his head he said, "No."

"Maybe I just overlooked her, but it does seem that there is less."

"That is true there have been many of the males and females of the lairs that have passed on to the spirit world. And she almost did the same. She became very ill, and I looked in on her a couple of times, and each time she was worse. So I inspected her for a wound and found one that was very bad. I opened it and let out the poisons and had our healer continue to tend to her. She and two of the females are in the healing area for the females and are out of the breeding herd until the next large moon cycle to heal." He paused as in deep thought, and seeing this K'jor waited knowing not to interrupt. "As you know, the ones from the lairs do not speak our tongue. They possibly speak the tongues of the gods, but this I do not know. Only T'som would know if that is the way, but this older female, who I have bred with a number of times trying to break the totem, knows our tongue. When I spoke I could see that she understood me perfectly. It is a bothersome thing. If these magicians are part of our gods, then it may be that she is a priest, one of high power. And if that is so, then I or any here will not be successful on making her carry. Yet, she almost succumbed, and entered the spirit world. I have to admit it is beyond my understanding. I understand why it is important to destroy the magicians and their lairs, yet at the same time if they are representatives of our gods, we could be dooming ourselves to oblivion, and find our spirits walking forever in the places of desolation. Again, this is something only a priest can answer, and yes I know we do not allow any females to be priests, but their strength, their totem appears to be very powerful, and when we captured them, they were not in herds like our females. They lived with individual males and only carried with these special males. I have to admit this is something well beyond my understanding, and I always thought I understood most."

These points that R'san were making, well what could he say? It was something he hadn't thought about, at least in the direction R'san had just led him. *What if that rolling thunder they had heard on their arrival was not a sign of approval, but of just the opposite?* He definitely would have to talk long and hard with T'som. "You've left me with much to think about. Do we have the necessary wood and grains stored for the cold time, not that I need to ask – since I know you well enough that if that had not been the case you would have confronted me right after we returned. This older female, while it is unusual that we even converse with females, do you think it wise that we actually talk with her?"

Shocked by the question from K'jor, he hesitated before answering. "Why would we do that? If we speak to a female it is for them to do as we tell them. We do not discuss anything with them. After all their purpose is to bring us a new generation of warriors and females, and to help strengthen the clan, to work where they are skilled, and that is all."

"Yes, all that you stated is true. But you have to admit that we have never been in this situation before. When we have added females in the past, eventually they carried our offspring. Our tongue is the same throughout this land, and the only right a female has is to remain with her tribe or clan, or accept the attacking clan or tribe as her new home. If a tribe or clan had been wiped out in battle it was only right to add the females to one's own breeding herd. And we have wiped out these lairs so that they may not return, and we have added the females to our herds, but none of them spoke our tongue, none of them understood the consequences for refusal, and thusly why the racks – something that we have rarely needed. In fact I do not remember ever seeing one used in my lifetime, until now.

"All what you say is true." Again R'san paused, "But this is unprecedented! Are we going to weaken ourselves by submitting ourselves to the females? I cannot believe you are even thinking this way?"

Shaking his head, K'jor said. "No, no I'm not thinking that way at all. But if this one does understand our tongue, well, who knows she may be able to give us answers as to why."

R'san shaking his head said, "If she is indeed a priest or I guess priestess, since she is female, then how could we go against her power, or even believe what she would tell us? No, I do not think this is a good idea or direction. It will make us appear weak."

Smiling at the statement K'jor continued, "Appear weak. What does it look like to you when we, we as warriors cannot make any one of them carry? Does that not make us appear to be weak? That our seed cannot conquer them? Where have you ever seen it so? Yet, here it is right before us. So what would you have us do? After all you have much more experience in life than I do, but I can see that you don't have an answer either. Okay, I will go see our priest and talk with him, and when I have I will have you join us, and see what we all feel about this. I guess at this point, as far as these new females are concerned, we will keep trying. Somewhere one will have to weaken and begin the carrying."

* * *

The cold time struck early, and while snow was something they dealt with, it usually did not hang around more than a day or two after the storm had left. But this season was different. And if it was beginning this way, would it be that way throughout the cold time? While they had always planned their supplies for the harshest of times, with the additional bodies to feed and keep warm, K'jor was already worried that it would not be enough. This time the snows did not leave but began to pile as the winds tossed it around like a child's toy. Looking into the great fireplace and the roaring fire within its confines, K'jor wondered how it could still feel so cold. If one got just a short distance from that fire one could begin to feel the chill that seemed impenetrable, refusing to leave, or be overpowered by the flame.

It was the kind of day that it would have been wonderful to have a female here to help warm his sleeping mat and his spirits, but that was not to be. Shortly the priest T'som would arrive and later R'san would join them. While all that was happening was unprecedented, they had to decide whether these females and the males that they had made slaves were actually servants of their gods, and what was happening, and not happening was because of that. After all if these magicians and sorcerers were servants of their gods, then by attacking and destroying their lairs, they were attacking the gods themselves. And he truly did not want to bring down their wrath on his clan or any of the others within the alliance. He paced the room like a trapped beast, he hated being stuck inside. It was confining and at times seemed to close in on him. Better to be out in the grasslands where one could see and sense all. Not here where everything was hidden.

He heard the stomping of the feet just outside of the entrance and knew that T'som had arrived. So standing his ground and waiting, he watched as the flap opened and the priest entered. "Good day T'som, priestly leader of our clan, please enter and sit." He stated by rote, the standard phrase when a priest entered one's place of living.

"May our gods favor you and yours." T'som responded back with his required reply. He stood a moment and then said, "It is not a good day out. I do not remember it ever being this cold." Looking longingly at the fire, and then next to it, he saw that the chairs had been placed close so that they would at least be warm while they talked. He also saw the large container that held the warm drink made from the grains they gathered. It was just slightly alcoholic, just enough to warm the insides. Smiling and looking at K'jor he said, "Ah, I see that at least we will be warm." He immediately headed for the chair he normally sat in when the two of them were discussing anything, and shortly K'jor joined him sitting down across from him. Between sat a small table which had the large container, and the mugs.

"We will have some time to cover much before R'san will join us. I want him here because he has been around much longer, and yes while set in his ways, and the ways of the clan, I value his insights. And what we are facing now requires as much insight as I can get. It has been a while since I have been even able to talk with you T'som. I never realized that when I began this that it would involve so much of my time. In many ways I miss the old days when it was just our clan and the problems and issues I had to face were small in comparison to what I am seeing with this alliance. Although without this alliance we would not have been successful in bringing to an end many of the lairs. And this is why I wanted to talk, discuss these issues with you. Some thoughts have been entering my mind and I felt that it was a subject that you could probably have better answers to, than I."

"Since a few of these new females have become part of the breeding herd for the priests, as well as the males as slaves, I think I can understand the issues and the questions that have arisen. Do these magicians or sorcerers have a power we are unfamiliar with? Why is it that none of the females are carrying? What is their strength that they can prevent the carrying? Why are the words they speak not understandable? Are they servants of our gods? And if so, is this why they are hidden from us? And is this weather at the start of the season of cold, a retaliation against us for attacking their servants? Why are there no breeding herds in those lairs and the females appear to have power and live with a single male? Do I have it about right?"

"Yes, and I know you probably have more that you could have added to the list of questions, but what you have said is very much the gist of it. So what are your thoughts on all of this?"

"To be truthful, I don't know all of the answers, or even pretend to know even close to all of the answers. Our gods can be subtle and quiet making it difficult to determine what their feelings are. And right now it is that way. Many times I can easily discern what it is that they want from us, and other times, like now, it is almost impossible. Like you, when you first discovered their lairs, I thought it was a sign from our gods giving us permission to destroy them, and to take our bounty from them. Then we walked through the fallen lair and we realized that much of what was there we could not touch. It had to be of our gods, or if not our gods, then the gods of these magicians and sorcerers. That meant that our bounty would be much less than promised. So much less that the only thing of value that we could safely take was the females and males. And since we destroyed their lair, it gave us the right to add the females to our herds and the males as slaves. Up to that point it all seemed quite normal, exactly what we expected, minus other bounties. But who was I to complain? We found and destroyed a hidden enemy, and increased our future strength by adding their females to our own herds. We increased our workers by the adding of these slaves. At this point all I could see, as you, was the increase in size and strength of our clan. And with these females carrying our offspring to weaken any of the other hidden, what was the word you used, ah *cities*, or lairs as we know them. After all, with each new female taken from those hidden lairs that is carrying our own, takes away the strength of the enemy that these females were a part of."

"Everything you have said is true, and up until that point it was as it should be. Then it all changed. Do you think, first that they get their strength to prevent the carrying from other hidden lairs that we have yet to find, or second that they may actually be servants of the gods, and it is they who prevent this, or maybe it is their personal totem that we must overcome, and be stronger than theirs – what are your thoughts?"

Quiet for a short time T'som stared into the fire before looking back at K'jor. "You've asked some very hard questions, and at this moment I do not have a satisfactory answer for either you or me. But we, my priests and I, will talk with our gods and see what they tell us. But they can be fickle and not tell us anything, making us figure out what they want us to do. Yet, just maybe this stronger than normal season of cold is a sign from them that they are not happy with us or what we are doing. I cannot say. After all if they are not, is it because we've not done enough, or is it because we've done the wrong thing, or maybe we've been doing the right thing but we did not take out the specific lair that they wanted to see gone? Ah, this drink always hits the spot, especially when it is cold like now!"

Watching K'jor he could see the intensity in this leader. Thinking back, since he was a bit older than K'jor he remembered watching him work with R'san, and really couldn't see this one leading them some day. He knew that his path was different, and he was to be a priest. Yet his aspirations had never been to be the head priest, and yet here he was. As time had continued to pass by them he watched a change come over K'jor, and there he could see a sense of purpose and an intensity that no other in the clan had ever presented. Those doubts about this one leading the clan, and that is what had taken place quite some time ago, vanished. He was sure that the female, who was well beyond the age of breeding by now, if she was even alive, would have been proud that not only did she produce a great warrior, but a great leader. Of course with the way new lives were created within the structure no male could claim to be the one who fathered him, since all females of breeding age were bred by all of the warriors. Well except a small group who were part of the priests' breeding herd. But this was getting off the subject. Who would have thought that K'jor would have become greater than any and all previous leaders of the clan, and actually unite many of the warring tribes and clans? Not he for sure. And now K'jor was asking hard questions, and asking them of him, and he knew that at the moment he had no answers. And with R'san joining them shortly that it would become more difficult.

Yes, R'san, the mentor, to K'jor, the keeper of the old ways, and in a way the advisor also. Because, this old warrior was set in the old ways, he had originally advised against forming this alliance. And he was sure there were other things R'san had advised against that K'jor had over ruled to the benefit of all within the alliance that he had created. He also knew that there had been a meeting between R'san and K'jor before this one that would include the three of them. Inwardly and shrugging he could only advise and pass on what the gods had told him, and right now they were strangely silent. So all he could do is look at the very subtle signs and hope that he understood what was being shown to him and the rest of the priests. "This older female, the one that almost passed into the spirit world, one of the ones from the lairs, who is barely within the breeding time, it is rumored that you and R'san may have considered her of priestly caste, do I have it right?"

How is it that this stuff gets around? K'jor thought. *As far as I know only R'san and myself had discussed this, and I know that R'san wouldn't have said anything. And being I am the only other, and I know I didn't . . .* "Why are you bringing this up? It was only speculation on our part. Speculation because of the way the females live in those lairs."

Smiling inwardly T'som thought. *Ah confirmed! I wasn't sure that what had been passed to me was accurate, but now I know it is.* "Speculation or not, if she is, do you think it wise that she is kept with the regular breeding herd? Do you not think that she should be with her own kind? And where you would never discuss anything with her because she is a female, we could possibly discuss, from a position of power of course, this with her. And if you only wanted to make it temporary with her returning to the regular herd, that would be okay. It just may be a way of learning about their power and finding a way to overcome and defeat it."

"You've left me something to think about. But for now she is out of the breeding herd because she almost passed into the spirit world. So it will be a while before she is allowed to be bred once again. But R'san has made her his special project to attempt to overcome her strength, her magic, her totem and have her carry. And before you ask, no he like the rest of the warriors is spreading his seed among the herd. His thoughts on this have to do with his time that he has been alive. Figuring that his greater experience and cunning will be able to get past the defenses she has placed upon herself. And if he is successful, and again no, she, like the rest, is available to any of the warriors, so there is no special treatment. She like the rest must be available once a day if signaled. Look shortly R'san will be with us, very shortly really, then you can bring this up with him also. If he agrees, then I have no problem with a temporary assignment. And maybe you can learn what it is they are doing to prevent the carrying. I know that it is not us, or any of the warriors, as many of our own females are carrying right now, and I know by the end of the cold season most will be. Not that all of the offspring or females survive when they drop the offspring. We are not allowed to be around them at those times, but from the screams of pain and the length of time that passes before it is over, it is not an easy thing. But it is the way of life, pain that is, and so we enter this world from pain, and many times we leave the very same way."

"Those last few statements make you sound more like a priest than a warrior – so why that direction in your thoughts?"

But before any answer could be formulated, R'san entered, grabbed the only other chair in the room and sat down, at the same time grabbing a mug and filling it, and taking a large swig, sighing said, "Now that hits the spot. K'jor, I don't know how you end up with the best of this stuff since I know it all comes from the same place, but you do. Okay, I'm here, now what is it that you want to cover with me? While the season of cold is upon us, unfortunately there is always something that breaks, or happens that requires my time."

His entry and energy broke their train of thought and it was silent for a short period of time. All they could hear was the howling winds, and the snow as it struck the sides of the building as the winds tossed it about. "T'som has come up with a suggestion, but being that you have made this older female from the lairs your personal project, we need to ask you what your thoughts are." K'jor then related to R'san what the two of the had been discussing, and then fell silent to let him have time to absorb what he had been told."

Taking his time before answering R'san said, "It is something I have not even considered. But it does have some merit. Although I do not like the idea of taking her to the priest's herd. As you know I have concentrated on trying to overcome her totem, and while this poison had almost sent her to the spirit world, she or any of the females from the lairs aren't carrying." Pausing and thinking a moment, he continued, "Although because of that poison and how weak she is, for her own health she is outside of the breeding herd, and will be for a while yet." Sighing and looking down at the dirt floor before looking at the two of them, he said. "I can understand why you would want your chance at this female. After all if she is as we suspect then you as our head priest would want to learn what you could. But I have a problem, a real problem with relinquishing her to your custody."

Smiling at him K'jor stated, "If I didn't know you better, I'd think that you have feelings for this female."

Guffawing at the statement, he asked, "Me? You've got to be kidding. She's a female and her place in the clan is where she is; to be available to all warriors, and to be proud to carry, to help the clan to grow stronger. Why would I have feelings other than that?"

"Then to temporarily move her to the priest's herd should not be a problem then, right?"

"I'll tell you what. I'll allow it for the time of healing only. After all she is my special project. I feel that it will be my experience that will finally get past whatever barriers she has placed there. Looking at her, we all know that soon she will be past the age of breeding, and I do not want to waste what little time is left with this one to beat her at her own game. I guess then very soon you will make the transfer, but she must be back here by the rising of major moon, so our healer can determine if it is safe for her to return to the breeding herd. Now I have assigned two others from the lairs to help her healing, and they are also outside of the breeding herd. I will send them along with her under the same protection until they return. Then once the older female is cleared all of them will return to our breeding herd."

"Okay all," Shellian said, "I guess it's time to get moving here." Looking around the table, she had to admit that with eight new people the table where they were sitting did not appear to be as empty. It had been at least fifteen days since the rescue, and briefly looking out of the window she could see that winter had arrived. Now, like the primitives there would be little movement, especially here in the mountains. But that did not mean that preparations and such would stop. This next spring she as the rest were sure, the primitives would be gathering to continue to find, attack, and destroy their cities and their way of life. This was to be the second winter they had spent here in these Sacred Mountains, and remembering back to the first and those desperate times, she felt that even with the threats that lay before them they were much better off. "What this meeting is all about, not that you were not informed, is to gather what information that we can about the primitives, and do this while it is still fresh in your minds." Again she stopped and looked at the newest members to the Alpha complex before continuing. "The eight of you are the ones who will have to help here. And yes we know that the language of the primitives is very different than ours, but I suspect for the length of time that you were captives that you picked up a word or two, and if nothing else from what you have seen, have some ideas as to what changed. We know that your city, Jade, fell after ours – sometime late spring in this annual. So that means that you have been under the control of the primitives for close to half an annual. Now we know that it has only been a short time since you arrived here, and the scars that you have, visible and invisible, will make some of this difficult. But please understand that anything, anything at all; that you can remember will make the difference in our ability to end this alliance. I'm sure that you were as shocked as we were when you learned about this place, and what it originally represented to our ancestors. And for you women who had to endure the hell and worry of becoming pregnant under those really horrible circumstances, I know it is a relief to know that the primitives could not make that happen. Biologically it is impossible. This is not to minimize the abuse that you lived through, the worry, the pain, the not knowing, the overall brutal treatment that all of you received." She stopped here and Saige stood up.

"What Shellian spoke of is very true. She wanted to address you women to know that while we did not have to suffer like you did, we did suffer at the hands of the primitives. Our scouting unit was decimated by them as we tried to escape, and to eventually find this place, which was more by luck than skill. We thought that we were good at what we did, proud to be truthful. But we learned that our skills were no more than a child's when comparing ourselves to the primitives. I guess you could say we played at something that was serious, life and death serious, to the primitives." He looked at the men that they had rescued before continuing. "I know that what you had to witness, and the helplessness as you watched your women being raped is something that will always be with you. Then, going from free people able to do what you wanted, in your own cities, to slaves with no control over anything in your lives. Again watching from a distance as your women had to submit would have made it easy to give up, and fall into the depths of depression and hopelessness. Especially since the odds of rescue was virtually zero. All the cities were independent, and we have no armies, and no way to go and find our fallen.

The primitives did such a great job of bringing down our cities that not a word ever got out as to what was going on. In fact until we escaped, no one had. And from what little we can gather, the primitives have confidence that this is still the way it is. And until we found this place, and then again through more accidental discoveries, made contact with the hub city no one really did know what had happened to the cities that had gone silent. In a moment we are going to ask for as much information as you can recall. What we want to know, more than your life in the tribe that we rescued from, has to do with this alliance. We realize that, that time was nothing but shock, chaos, and disbelief, followed by much pain and suffering. You see, we need to bring down the alliance and have things go back to the way it was, or as close as possible, before it existed – where the primitives are more interested in each other than some hidden cities that do not bother them at all. Now in front of all of you are pads of paper and something to write with. We're going to ask a number of questions, and want you to both write your answers, and speak to us.

Because something you say may trigger other questions that will help us solve this, and solve this we must. Yours was the luck of the draw, so to speak, as the tribe that you had become a part of ranged closest to these mountains. Had they gone a different way, you would still be with them, having to do whatever they would have demanded of you. So let's help those who are still captives, those who still have to submit, those whose freedom have been destroyed, and are completely hopeless, and probably feel as you did, that this would be how their lives will end." Once again looking over the table Saige asked, "When was your city attacked? Here I am referring to the time of day, not time of the annual."

Jarid stood up and said, "I don't know if you want us to stand and speak, but I thought I would. I was working before dawn on my program for later in the day. I guess it was probably around dawn, maybe sunrise; I'm not sure, since I was inside. But I know it had to be close to that time since suddenly the power quit. It was a shock! Never had that ever happened before." He then sat down, and began to write it down.

Jas then spoke up, and said, "It must have been somewhere close to that time of day because I was still in bed, and I'm an early riser." The rest nodded their heads in agreement.

"Just to let you know, it was the same with Sequoyah. And now that you've confirmed that the attack was pretty much the same, it makes me wonder how they figured out that the power systems were the key to letting everybody in to do their dirty work? And I think that as we rescue others from some of the other cities we are probably going to find it consistent. I guess until it doesn't work, they'll continue. So while they are showing some innovations in their attacks, it overall, isn't that imaginative. And I guess why change when it has been completely successful. That is, until we escaped. And our feelings at this point since there have been no additional pursuit, that they believe they killed all of us and their secret is still safe."

Giving them time to write before continuing with the questions, Saige drank some of the coffee that remained in his cup. He knew that after finding out about coffee he could have never gone back to shick – just something about the taste that just seemed to appeal to all of them. Maybe it had to do with the fact that more generations than he could possibly count had been drinking this stuff and it had become part of their physical makeup. He liked his strong, black and bitter, while he noticed that the women liked to add different things to the coffee, experimenting with the flavors, and passing on to the other women what they thought of the concoctions. He reached for a carafe and refilled his cup grabbing a snack that also sat on the table. So far these eight new members hadn't asked why the two of them were in charge, and seemed to accept their leadership. As they became more successful in rescuing their people he hoped that it would remain so. But knew that there were always others who thought they would be better at leading. It brought a shudder to him since he, and the rest of the original team, here at the Alpha had direct experience.

"Okay, I'm guessing that your city fell sometime this annual, and the condition all of you were in suggests that it could have been late spring to early summer, so this may have given you some time to at least learn a word or two of their language. We are fortunate that it is the same, at least for now, for all the tribes and clans out there. There is some variance, but not much yet. I guess that comes from there only being this one large land mass. From our views from above this world we know that there are many small islands, but none seem to be populated. What I, we, are trying to figure out here is this, how are we being viewed? And here I mean other than slaves and baby makers. There must be some feeling that anyone or all of you got about how they are seeing us. I know that when we were taught our history lessons in our learning centers that we were all one people. But now, and I hope you've had a chance to confirm and believe it in your own minds, we know we are not even originally from here. And ladies, that are why, thankfully, you never got pregnant from all the attempts to make you that way. It is impossible. I'm not a doctor or a scientist, so the data that is in this system goes way above me in that respect. But it is obvious that our original ancestors who were scientists were comparing the differences in our genetic structure. From what I can gather there are similarities, but nothing that is compatible with either race. So their females cannot become pregnant by us as much as you cannot become pregnant by them.

I am sure that this has made it more difficult for all of our women who are still captives. Since, as the four of you know yourselves, the frequency of having to submit is such that all of you should have become pregnant, but by not, you would be both relieved, but not understanding why you weren't, and at the same time with both the primitive women not happy with you, and the increase in the attempts to make you pregnant, it could not have been anything but hell. And I know that this would be something that would become a very big deal to the primitives. The best I can compare their life style to is the herds they depend on for food, tools, clothing, and so on. Only in their case instead of one dominant male breeding the females, in their society it is the warriors and only they who have the right to pass on their genes. Although they probably do not know that is what they are doing. Their societies are very warrior, and male centered. Women have no say, no rights, and must obey a lawful order from a male. While she has some protection under their system, she still is subservient to the males. While I knew some of this from observing, the meat of this information exists right here. So as time continues to flow past us, please study it. We need to know all we can. Now after this long winded introduction and a general overview of the primitives, I am sure that they have a different view of us now that they have destroyed many of our cities, captured many of our women and men, and other than the destruction of the cities and the increase in slaves, the other . . ." He stopped briefly and looked at the four women to emphasize what he was about to say, "aspect of increasing their stature, the size of their clans and tribes, and their strength through increasing, as they call it, their breeding herds has not materialized. Yes their herds have increased from our women, but nothing will come from the unions, anything other than the pain and suffering that you have experienced.

"This has to have shocked them to their very core, and I am sure it is a major subject anywhere you go in their world. After all they are warriors, and as such they feel that their 'seed' is also of warrior caliber. So for a mere female to be able to defeat them and their seed, has to leave them wondering what is going on. Again with this background and what the eight of you observed what are you sensing?"

It was very quiet as the newest members absorbed all of what Saige had just passed on to them. By living in this hell day to day, they hadn't thought about anything but surviving. There originally have been twenty of them that had been turned over to the tribe as part of their reward. At the time of rescue they were down to eight, and felt that within an annual or so that the rest of them probably would perish as the other twelve had.

Saige looked around and could see at this moment that they did not have any answer for him. "I can see that you are going to need to think about this, and I can totally understand that, so we'll break at this point to give all of you some time to think about it, get together and talk about it, and then come up with some ideas of what you've observed. We have other questions, but for now I think they can wait. Getting an answer to this one I just presented to you is probably the most important one anyway. We'll meet here tomorrow morning after we eat so that will give all of you the rest of the day. Before breaking this up, do any of you have questions for us?" Seeing a negative response Saige said, "We are done here for today. Keep those pads with you and jot down anything that you think might help us. You eight are the first of what we hope is the beginning of rescuing more survivors from these raids. I know that we cannot save everyone, but we will try to get as many of our people as we can. And you can rest assured that you will be involved every step of the way." And with that he waved them out of the meeting room and waited until it cleared. Sitting back down and deep in thought he turned and faced his sister and asked, "What do you think? Will they be able to tell us anything? I know that when you are in the middle of surviving there is little time to see anything else."

Shaking her head, she said. "I really don't know. It's a tough call any way you look at it. I mean we can guess from what our ancestors have gathered over the time they were researching, and we can add what we personally have learned, but it also means by not actually being inside of that society we could guess wrong. And, dear brother, that is something we cannot afford to do. We've been successful this one time, but as you well know, it may be the only success for a long time. So we have to be so careful not to jump to or cling to half-truths and make them real. We really have to be sure, and in war, who can really be sure? I thought that you did a great job of presenting that information to them, and I could see that it did have an effect on them. I know that with all we have been taught, that to flip a hundred and eighty degrees is very difficult. Although once again I could see relief in the women's eyes, now knowing for sure that they will not be carrying any child from the primitives. I think that it would have been a reminder to them of these really horrible times that they went through. And I'm sure they are having enough nightmares as it is. I know for a fact that I would be. After all it's one thing to have a loving relationship and enjoy the physical side of that relationship, and the children that may come from it. While it is another to be raped all the time with no hope of escaping from it and then producing children that you really do not want, knowing that once you've done that, that it will continue that way through the rest of your life." She shuddered from both the comments she had made and the images that it had created in her mind. Taking a deep breath, she said. "And it is this, along with every other reason I can come up with that we have to end this, and end this once and for all."

* * *

It was early afternoon and all of them were in the enclosed meadowlands that were part of the complex, where Stone and Sorrel would be leading them to the passage that would take them to the building that they had discovered. This was a work party to clear off all of the moss and such that had grown over time, so that with the skylights cleared they would have better lighting inside, and be able to inspect the interior. With lighting existing almost virtually everywhere with in the facility, it just seemed odd that this place did not have lighting also. And this inspection, cleaning and exploring was to learn anything they could about it. Again the passage into this section of the meadowlands was wide enough to pass any of the pack animals through, but was so well hidden that they had missed it. After studying the entrance it became obvious that their ancestors had worked it to make it almost invisible, and when one actually looked at the entrance it just appeared to be shadow and a solid wall. No different than thousands of other places along the inner wall of the extinct volcano.

This location enclosed another smaller meadow area, and a spectacular waterfall and small lake. Again the lake had no apparent exit so the waters were probably exiting through some underground river. The beauty was enough to take one's breath away. And looking around they could see that there had been some tables and benches set up, along with what looked like a play area for children. So it was obvious that their ancestors saw it in much the same way as they. Pausing for a moment and just enjoying the serene images before them, they turned and headed for one of the far walls and the building they were to clean up. "How'd you find this place?" Jessi asked.

Turning around and smiling Sorrel said, "More luck than skill really. You had to be here at just the right time of the day to make the shadows dance in such a way that it made it look like something was wrong with what you were seeing, and then when Stone and I found it, and entered here for the first time it really caused us to stop and enjoy what we were seeing" At this point she stopped and smiled, since this only told part of the story. Since she knew that she and Stone had *really* enjoyed the view. "Then as we explored . . ." And then again thinking back, *Yes, we enjoyed and explored each other's bodies as much as what we were seeing here.* ". . . this whole area and found the building back against the wall. But even though it was there, since it had been built from the rock that is here it was hard to see." She pointed at it as they headed in that direction. "See, even though we know where it is you have to really stare at it to see that it is really there and not just another of the many rock formations that are around."

Looking hard in the direction that Sorrel had pointed, she couldn't pick it up yet. Some of the others from her city had been to this area and had described to the rest of them. But their descriptions fell short of the true beauty of the place, and it had sent chills down her spine. And she knew it wasn't because of the cold. There lay a thin covering of snow on the ground, with a promise of more to come. But today the suns were shining and it would be a rare day that they could get outside and do anything. And to speed things up Saige and Shellian had requested that everybody but the ones working the security office would join the work party. As they approached Jessi eventually began to discern the shape of the building, but it was difficult, due to the age and mosses that had become part of the structure. Again like the entrance to this place, this had been built to hide as much as to provide whatever service it was meant for.

Even with the suns shining they all could see their breath as it was cold. There was a soft breeze blowing and it had a bite to it that immediately made on catch their breath. Eventually they reached the building and where Stone and Sorrel led them around to the back side and then using the handholds climbed up on the roof. Followed by leaning over and grabbing the tools they had brought, with the rest of the team following them up. For the next several hours they cut, scraped, scrubbed, and removed the years of growth. Occasionally stopping to stomp their feet and rub their hands to help keep warm. Finally, with the roof cleared, they descended and entered the building. "Wow, what a difference." Stone exclaimed. "Everything was just shadow and darkness when Sorrel and I last visited this place. Now you can see everything."

The eight new arrivals were still coming to terms with all they had learned since being rescued. But as each new aspect was being revealed to them, the facts and the truth could not be denied. This place was the hidden, unknown city that all were taught about in the learning centers. But the reality was much different from what they had learned. And here nothing had been hidden from them. It was as their ancestors had left it – left it, with the hope that someday they would be rescued and returned to their home world, ending their *time of isolation*. And none of that had happened, and now if it did, would they be able to accept the changes that they themselves had made verses what their true home would be? Would they even be able to relate to their own people? Or because of this *time of isolation*, had they changed to the point that they would appear to be no different than the natives of this world? What they had learned and were still learning was almost as much of a shock as the falling of their city and then becoming captives, followed by the rescue and coming here. One thing for sure, nothing would ever be the same.

When Sorrel and Stone had reported finding this area and the building, the two had completed a brief survey of the interior. The sliding door would not budge so they were not able to confirm that this was indeed the exit from the meadowlands that the researchers used to interact with the primitives. Yet everything about this place said it was so. With all five skylights cleared, and even with the day waning, it was now a brightly lit interior. Gone were the shadows and darkness that had greeted the two. And now they could see why it had been impossible for them to slide the door open. It had the obvious latch that Stone and Sorrel had released, but on the back end was another that had been completely hidden in the shadows. And once this one was released, even though it complained at the treatment, the door slid easily on its tracks, which considering its age and lack of use was a surprise. Expecting it to be dark just beyond the building within the cave that they had exposed they were surprised by the bright light. Stone could see that like so many of the others that they had located since being here, that this was originally a lava tube or steam vent. But this showed extensive rework. There had been a lot of effort expended by their ancestors, and it was obvious that the plans had been for a long term study. Of course little did they know how *long term* it would be. "Stone," Saige said, "since you are our rock expert lead us on, if you would."

"Sure, no problem," then laughing he said, "Now you are sure you want me to do this. Because, if I remember right, it was me who fell through and into one of these vents sometime in the past – and truthfully, I don't want to repeat it." This brought a laugh from the original group leaving the newcomers wondering what that had been all about. Sorrel seeing the confusion on their faces pulled them aside and explained what had happened to Stone before they had discovered this place. Taking a deep breath and looking around at the rest Stone entered the tunnel. Looking down he could see that the floor had been smoothed and where the walls were narrowing down there had been work to keep the width consistent. "I think that we can only go a little ways down this right now. Once again time is against us and it won't be long before the suns set, and like this building there appears to be only skylights to light our way." He headed deeper into the tunnel where it took a sharp right and immediately opened into a large hidden room, again carved out of the living stone.

Here they found much of the gear that the teams would use when they posed as primitives. All covered with dust of the passing centuries, undisturbed, untouched, and unknown until now. Seeing all of this continued to confirm the original role their ancestors had performed, and in awe, silence, and reverence they quietly walked and stared at what was before them. Looking around there appeared to be no exit from this space which did not make sense. "Did anybody see a way out of here, other than the way we came in?" Shellian asked. She could see all of them looking around but also could see that once the question had been asked, followed by all of them searching, there just did not appear to be an exit.

"Okay," Stone said, "I'll backtrack a little and see what we missed. Go ahead and see what's here, this is really a very large room, something I wouldn't have expected at all. Anyway, be right back." He backtracked from the room to where the tunnel had made the sharp right, stopped, and studied the wall and like the entrance into the smaller meadow area there was a turn to the left that when one first looked it appeared to be a solid wall. Shaking his head at the illusion, he was beginning to appreciate his ancestors even more. Somehow they had figured out how to place things in such a way, that unless one really searched these openings, they would remain hidden. He marveled at the design. By placing the skylight where they had, the eyes were naturally drawn to the light and away from the shadows. And where the tunnel continued it was in the deeper shadows, almost invisible. As he walked into the shadowed entrance he was surprised at the very size of the opening. A pack animal could easily pass through this. Again shaking his head, he just could not believe they had missed it. He could tell that dusk was on its way and it was time for all of them to head back and follow these tunnels out to where they left the mountains. It was critical that they know all of these passages which lay before them. Still it seemed to him and he suspected the rest that what they were trying to accomplish was impossible, but what could they do? Just let it go? No, he already knew the answer to that. Too many innocent lives would be destroyed if this was allowed to continue. He could hear the voices of the rest as they approached his location. He remained where he was and watched as they passed his location unaware of this hidden entrance. The entrance seemed hidden no matter which direction one was going. Shrugging he fell in behind the last of them and left the tunnel system, joined Sorrel, reaching for her hand and together with the group headed back to the warmth of the facility.

* * *

Judd, had been elected, to speak, to pass on what they had gathered – information wise – from their meetings together from the previous day. As the eight sat around the table, with Saige and Shellian presiding, he stood up, clearing his throat he said, "I don't know how I ended up with this duty, but here goes. One of the things that we men have learned, and it doesn't make it any easier, since we were helpless to be able to help in any way, is that the women had it much tougher than we first imagined, at least for us, maybe not you and your scouting unit. Not only did they have to deal with the males, but there was almost as much abuse coming from the females. I guess these females were jealous that our women would be usurping them in their roles, since interest seemed to have increased towards our women by the males of the tribe. From where we were we could not see much of this. Yeah, we could see them having to submit, but not too often. We now know that it was very often, and now we know why pregnancy would have been a very real worry. With the conditions being as bad as they were, there was a good chance that if they had, and carried to full term that they would have died in child birth.

'For us, the men, we were beaten often and directed to whatever work they wanted us to do. While not fun by any means, when compared to what our women faced, while not easy, still did not compare. So now I, if not the other men who were captives, understand why we lost so many of our women. There had been twice as many captive women as men, and as you know from your rescue there was an equal number. While we lost close to half of the men, it was probably closer to three-quarters of the women. I suspect that if we could visit the other tribes and clans that have taken our people that the attrition rate would be much the same." Stopping for a moment and catching his breath, Judd leaned on the table, and then grabbed some water before continuing. "All of us were so busy trying to survive that all we can come up for you is just impressions, and by not really knowing their language, again what little of it we learned really doesn't help a lot.

"As expected, there seemed to be a flurry of interest in the women, fresh meat, I think the term is, while we were cuffed, not only by the men, but by the women. Any time we were slow to do what they wanted, we paid a price. When we were first gathered and placed in the large enclosures we were separated, men and boys in one, and the women and girls in the other. And the distance between the pens, I don't know what else you could've called them, were on opposite sides of their compound. We were surrounded by huge amounts of these primitives, and there was no way, and I mean, no way to escape. In the distance towards where the women were being held there seemed to be some type of contraption. In it, well, it looked like a couple of our women were in it." He pointed to the four around the table and said, "They confirmed it. While I know very little about it, it seems that it is a punishment device that they use for women who will not submit to their will. And that is all I'm going to say about that, other than the obvious that our women were continually raped, and that didn't change, even after we were separated and given to the different clans and tribes. I, for one, have to say that it really sucked not being able to help and comfort our women. All we could do was watch and pray that something would come along and get all of us out of that living nightmare, which, thankfully, you and your team did.

"Although I have to admit once again, that when you attacked their camp, and from what the women passed on to us, since we weren't there, had sex with that primitive, we thought and they too, that things had just gone from very bad, to much worse. To us it did look like we were prizes being stolen from the tribe that had become our lives. So we did not know what to expect. We now know why you had to do all of it, including maintaining the illusion until you knew that there was no pursuit, and that we would be free of them. Although how just four of you pulled this off we really don't know, but are quite happy that you did. Again I have to admit that as we were being led away as captives again, that our mood was very dark, and we thought about trying to escape. But again had to admit, we were lost, we had no idea even what direction to go, and we probably would have just been captured once again making things worse. We all witnessed at least one of our own beaten to death, and it was not pretty." He again paused, "Again at this moment it's the best we can do. I know that this isn't much help."

"Survival was paramount to all of you, so it is no surprise that you weren't looking at other things. Possibly, if you had survived long enough and had remained a captive long enough, any of you could have begun to see the subtleties of how they were reacting to you and begin to understand how they were seeing the cities other than a place to destroy." Shellian, looking over the eight continued, "We hoped for more, but even what you have passed on to us can help. Not one of us in the scouting units have ever lived with the primitives, and to have something, anything, about how it is inside of their world is important. We need all of you to keep thinking about this. Not necessarily the abuse, but we do understand that it is difficult to separate one from the other. We have to build as much information on the primitives as we can. As someone said, knowledge is power. And right now even with what is in these computers, the primitives seem to know more about us than we do them." Again looking around the table before continuing she said, "Okay, I guess that will cover it for now. Just keep what we need in the back of your minds, and maybe something will click and what you remember can help."

After the eight had left Saige turned to Shellian and said, "I surely was hoping for more. But I'm not really surprised. Somewhere along the line we are going to have to get lucky and recover one of our own. And what I mean by that is a captive that was part of one of the scouting units. All of us speak the primitive language."

* * *

Staven, Seve, and Stone had been assigned the duty of exploring the tunnel system and to determine where it came out lower on the mountainsides. They had planned on a couple of days of being away and had packed to be sure that they had enough to go beyond that time if necessary. "Wonder if they'll learn anything in that meeting today?" Seve asked.

"Probably not," Staven answered. "Simply because when one is trying to survive, you are just looking at ways to make it happen, and not looking at other things. Still anything they can give us will help, eventually." Turning to Stone he asked, "Why are you so quiet?"

Smiling and with a faraway look he said, "Sorrel informed me this morning that she's carrying, pregnant. It has been such a worry for her that she wouldn't be able to after almost losing her life, and losing her first child."

The other two were silent, as they knew that they had been partially responsible for her loss, but could see from Stone's reaction that he wasn't even thinking in that direction. "I guess that is great news." Seve said.

Again smiling, Stone nodded his head and said, "Yes, it really is, a surprise, not that we haven't been physical, but with a chance that she could never be a mother, I know it was something that had been weighing heavily on her. Now we have to worry and see if she can go full term. And it is a big concern, worry if you may, to her and of course, to me."

"That's quite understandable really. But I've heard that a woman can miss her cycle every once in a while and still not be carrying . . ." Staven stated, as he stopped and faced Stone, "and it would just crush her if this turned out to be the way."

Stone thought a moment, back to when she had announced it to him, and he had, had the same concerns. He remembered back to when she has lost her child, and almost lost her life. The many days of being with her to help her through it, and the resulting strong relationship that had developed. Shaking his head he knew deep down that he did not want to go through that again, and he was sure that she did not. "She's taken that into consideration, and actually waited ten days before going to the doc, and Jas, who now assists him. I guess in a way it is nice to have a woman who can work with the other women. After all I know that most women would prefer a female doctor or nurse. Anyway, that's getting off the subject; both of them ran separate tests, and confirmed that indeed she is pregnant. You know that term wasn't used a lot, I mean we generally used 'carrying' for a woman with child, but it is one that our ancestors used, and we've sort of just picked it up."

"Well, if she went to all that trouble to make sure it wasn't the other way then its wonderful news. I know from talking with Sabryn, that she and the other women were really worried that after her near death, and loss of her unborn daughter, that she would never be able to carry after that. So this will be great news to them." Pausing for a moment before continuing, Seve said, "But I suspect that they already know. It's something that seems to get around without anyone saying anything. Fatherhood is interesting. I mean you are seeing things very differently as you watch your child grow, try things, and see things for the first time. It brings the wonder back into your own life with each new discovery and milestone reached. And it is work – all day and all night work. But I wouldn't trade it for the world, this one or the one we came from."

"Truer words were never spoken," Staven replied, "Sommer is a handful, but ever since she came into this world she has me wrapped around her little finger." Shaking his head with a smile he said, "I don't know how she did it but she did, and I have known that I'm in trouble with that one. It makes it difficult to set the boundaries that are needed, but, oh well."

"Guess we should get to searching out this tunnel system. There's enough adventure right here, but from what you are telling me, it sounds like the real challenges in life are still ahead of me, when our child enters this world." Sweeping his arms out in the direction they needed to go, Stone asked, "Shall we?"

"Sounds great, but I will just pass on one other thing, and I know that Seve knows what I am speaking about, and the feeling of total love and devotion that you feel when you have your sleeping child in your arms. It's an unbelievable feeling."

They reached the split where if they went right they would enter the room, but followed the subtle shift to the left. Again the distance between the walls would allow a pack animal ease in passing along the corridors. It was obvious that there had been much work on both the walls and the floor to keep the floors somewhat even and the distances between the walls consistent. Periodically there had been skylights cut into the roof, so while in the areas where there were no skylights, it never was darker than dusk. The grade here was always downward, and again the drop was not so major to make it difficult for any of the animals or people who would use these passageways. Eventually at what they considered a reasonable time, they were about to stop and take a break when just ahead in the distance the tunnel appeared to be much brighter. So curious, they continued a little further and were rewarded with the tunnel opening up into a small room that had benches carved out of the native stone, and some troughs for watering the animals.

Shaking his head once again in awe, Stone said, "You know, our ancestors seem to have thought about everything. I mean, look at this." He swept the area with his arms, pointing out the work and effort that went into creating this. "It's very obvious to me that our ancestors were here for the long haul. Everything I see that they did speaks of permanence, planning, and hard work. I would never have thought to create a break room like this. But now that I see it, it absolutely makes sense."

The other two couldn't argue. This had been as much of a surprise to them as it had been to Stone. "You're right, Stone. But you have to admit it is consistent to what we've learned." Staven thought a moment before continuing, "Now if you think about those caves that are strategically placed going away from the facility, basically in all directions, then what we are seeing here is consistent, and very much so. I guess we haven't really begun to think like our ancestors yet, and that is no surprise. Too much time separates us from them. And in that separation we have changed, which I guess makes sense. I just hope the change has been good."

"Amen brother," Seve replied.

CHAPTER TEN

Two of the primitives showed up at the door of the shelter where she, and the two who were helping her, were living, and demanded that all of them follow them. Very weak and a long way from recovery, Sara still required the assistance of the other two women to move any distance at all. At least it appeared that these primitives were taking that in consideration as they slowly headed off in a different direction, towards part of the clan's home that she had never visited. Right now any curiosity that she might have had, took a backseat to the effort of just moving. This weakness scared her. She had always been strong, even through the hell of child birthing. And right now she knew that she still was very close to death. If she caught anything, as weak as she was, she felt that there would not be enough strength left in her body to fight it.

* * *

The winds were picking up and as they gusted, shaking the shelter he was in, with forces that spoke of wanting to destroy.

All K'jor could do was again wonder if maybe he had read things wrong, and now the gods were letting him know in no uncertain terms that he had been wrong. With these thoughts his mind drifted back once again to the beginning of all of this. He was spending his last night in the desolation, with nothing to show for it, other than, a growing belief that these areas were where the spirits lived. It looked, and felt that way. And he had seen nothing to change that opinion. It was full on dark, and even the fire he had burning in front of him appeared to give out a very dim light, with no warmth, and no protection. He could feel the spirits closing in on him, but other than the fire he had no defense. He could see that there would be little to no sleep tonight. He thought that if he did try to sleep that the ones of this spirit world would take him. And if a living person was taken by the spirit world his body would never have rest – living, but not living existing between the two worlds forever. To be tortured by the knowledge that one could not be a part of the living, and at the same time, not a part of the dead, forever roaming alone and apart from everything and everyone. He thought he had remembered a couple of people who had been touched this way. In his youth he watched as one of their very own become that way. And then he just disappeared, and no one knew when or how it had happened.

He remembered these thoughts weaving strongly through his mind as he got up and began to pace. The day had physically, mentally, and spiritually worn him down to where it took movement, any movement to remain awake. His imagination began to create beasts and spirits beyond the fire, and he did not know if they were real or just a creation of his mind. He was glad that he had at least the dried mud hill protecting his back, and so his vulnerability was only to the front. Picking another point on this hillside, he sat down, figuring from this place he could see and react faster if something out of the dark attacked him. He leaned back to allow the hill to support him, but to his surprise there was nothing there! Off balance he fell backwards, received a large shock, and lost consciousness. As consciousness faded his thoughts said that he had failed, and the spirits with their traps had caught another.

* * *

Sara looked out the door and shivered. With the infection mostly gone her body was completely wrung out, and the thought of going out in this weather scared her. But in this world she had no choice, none at all. Either she did as she was ordered or pay with some kind of punishment. Steeling herself for the ordeal, she nodded to the two other women, and followed the two primitives that had demanded that she and the others follow them. Even though these two had slowed their pace they still were outdistancing the three women, since the two had to heavily support Sara. There just was nothing she could do to help. In her present condition she couldn't even make the trips outside to take care of nature calls. She was as close as anyone could be to be totally bed bound and death. She found that she was shaking not just from the cold and the cutting winds, but from weakness. It winded her to just walk at all. This scared her even more. This weakness was a sure sign that she was in very serious trouble, but again what could she do? She was at the mercy of this clan and its laws and rules. So with determination, and a lot of help, they followed, with her head bowed both because of the winds, and her weakness.

Eventually they got on the lee of some of the buildings, and with the winds blocked, it actually felt warmer. Looking ahead she could see the impatience in the ones that they followed, but there was no way she could pick up the pace. In fact, she had to stop, and with help lean against one of the buildings to get enough strength to be able to continue. Finally she nodded to the two and they continued up to a wall within the clan grounds, through a gate, and inside a smaller compound. She, with the other two, were led to a small building and the hanging skins that acted as the covering for the door were pulled aside and she was directed inside with the two women. *First impressions – warm, cozy, and dark.* Once her eyes adjusted to the gloom, she could see three sleeping mats, a place to both cook and serve food, and in the far corner away from the entrance a few chairs and utensils. Then she realized that someone was sitting in one of those chairs, but at the moment could really care less. She needed to lay down now. Whatever strength she had was gone and if she did not lie down she would fall down, support or not.

She signaled the two to put her down on one of the mats. With this male inside this place she knew better than to speak. After all it was not allowed when a male was present. She was half expecting to see the sign for breeding and waited for the inevitable, but it was not forthcoming. At least it appeared that they were going to abide by what that older warrior had said. Once on the mat, she found that she could barely stay awake, but tried. There had to be a reason for this one to be in here. Eventually her ragged breathing became closer to normal, and still this one did not speak. She then wondered if he was some guard or something, but again that did not make sense, but again she, from her exhaustion, clearly couldn't think straight, so reasoning out this puzzle was well beyond her.

He stood and approached them and then spoke. "I am T'som." When he spoke this it was as one who was used to wielding authority. "I am the head priest, and you three have been placed in my care for the duration of your recovery. For now, that is all I will say, since it is quite obvious that you are still very close to the spirit world. I will be checking in every day." At that point he turned and left leaving the three alone. Sara wondered what this was all about, but not for long as she drifted into a deep and exhausted sleep. The two that helped Sara reach this new place, and had been ordered to care for her, looked at each other, and then down at Sara. She normally translated what had been spoken by the primitives, but they could see that there would be no translations today. Sara was already deep in an exhausted sleep. The only thing they could discern, from the tone of voice, was that this one was another leader of some kind. It was obvious from both his body language and his overall aura that he had power here. But at this moment what that power was and if he was the overall leader they did not know.

T'som, upon leaving the shelter, could see that this female was very close to the spirit world. The distance hadn't been that great from where she had been living to this shelter, and she had barely made that distance. From listening to her breathing when she had arrived, with major assistance from the other two females, he could tell that it had all but done her in. He made a decision, and instead of heading back inside his own shelter, he turned and went back outside their area and proceeded to the shelter of the leader K'jor. This was an unplanned visit, so when he reached the flap that covered the doorway, he waited a moment, and then announced his arrival. As he was about to enter a female pulled the flap back and exited. He at once entered and found K'jor dressing. "What brings you back here in this storm?" K'jor asked.

"It is that female that has been assigned to me to learn what we can." He replied.

After dressing, he came over and sat in one of the chairs and with a questioning look asked, "Have you already learned something about these? And if so that was really fast."

Shaking his head in response, T'som said, "No, nothing like that. But from my experience, this one is very ill. She will not recover by the next full major moon cycle, and I suspect that it will be more towards three. Even with the assistance of the other two females, the short walk to where she is now almost sent her to the spirit world."

Quiet for a moment K'jor asked, "Is there maybe another reason that you might want to keep this one there longer?" He paused pointedly, "Maybe some ulterior motive to this request?"

"And why would that be, or what would it be? She's just arrived, and other than informing her and the two that this would be where they would stay until they were returned to the herd, I only know of her condition, which is very poor indeed. If I had known that she was this bad, I would have waited for this storm to abate, and then have made the move. Just this short time out in this weather and the short distance she had to travel completely wiped her out. When I spoke, she barely acknowledged that I was there, and I could see that it was a struggle for her just to stay awake long enough for her to listen to what I had to say. And besides, why would I care?

I know the importance of the females to our clan, even better than you, but she is only one of the many. But, as we discussed, if I am to learn anything from her, and hers, then she must be healthy. I will continue to check in on the three of the females every day, and you can send both R'san and your healer any time you want, and if it is every day, it is your right. If you want to check, again just do it. I will be having our healer look in on this one also, so if the two healers want to get together and discuss this, I have no problem." Inwardly he thought. *What is this about? He has his place and I have mine. Yet, it is like he is seeing something that is not there. This I do not understand. Maybe because I interrupted him with a female, that this has set his mind in this direction, and he is angry about such a thing. Who really knows? But if we are to learn anything, anything at all about these females that we have added, then I will need the time to find the answers. And with this one so close to the spirit world there is no way to get any of the answers until she is healed, the gods willing.*

"Sorry, T'som. I'm not, well, I'm not mad at you. But this storm seems so fierce for this early in the season of cold. It has me worried that maybe I did error, and misread what the gods wanted. I know that you told me that you have received nothing from them, back at the time R'san was with us. Has that changed now that we are alone? All of this has been weighing heavily on my mind. I expected this storm to have already broken, but there seems to be no end in sight, and it feels colder than I can ever remember. Are you sure that this is not a sign from them?"

"I truly wish I could tell you. But as I said when R'san was here, they have been strangely silent. But maybe this isn't caused by our gods at all. Have you thought about that?"

With another questioning look K'jor asked, "What do you mean by that?"

"These magicians or sorcerers and their lairs are both hidden and strange to us. So maybe we have been looking at this wrong. What if, instead of being servants of our gods, they serve different gods? And if they serve different gods, who's to say that, this . . ." Stopping briefly and sweeping his arms around, he continued, "this storm that we are facing now is from their gods, rivals to our own. And the reason why I, or any of the other priests, cannot get anything from our gods could simply be that they have their hands full dealing with this threat in their spiritual realm. So while we fight the battles here in the physical world, they are fighting these rival gods in the spiritual world. I don't know if this is what's happening, but this is a possibility. I have no proof, but thought that maybe it would be something I would pass on to you."

Again silent as he thought about what the head priest had said, he had to admit it was something he had not even considered. After all, what did he or any of them know about their gods. Other than trying to keep them happy and on their side, what could any of them know about their spiritual world? Any who had passed over could never return to tell them what it was like serving the gods. So, why wouldn't there be rival gods who grow jealous, and have their own worshipers, ones like they found in those hidden lairs. "I must admit, this is something I never even considered. And if this storm is a response from different gods, where does that place ours? Are these other gods stronger, so much so that they can warn us in this way to leave their people alone?"

"Don't take this for fact. I have no proof. But I think it is important that you consider it a possibility. Again what is happening could be from our own gods, and these are the only gods that exist. But just a short time ago we thought that we were the only people that existed, the clans and tribes. And then you found these hidden lairs with strange people, strange clothes, and strange ways of existing – picking only the harshest of lands to live, places that will send any of us to the spirit world – a place of strange artifacts that could only be of the gods. So would it seem strange that they would worship different gods? And with us now attacking these lairs, would not also seem logical that their gods would retaliate?"

"I have to admit that you've given me plenty to think about. All of this I haven't considered, haven't thought about, or even put it as a reality. Yet, everything that you've said makes absolute sense. I'm surprised that I just did not see it, let alone consider it. Okay, with the season of cold upon us I will have much time to think and consider what you've left me with. And I, and I'm sure R'san with our healer, will check in on this female often, and if what you say is true, there will be no issue with her remaining there until she is healthy enough to be returned with the other two, to the breeding herd. After all, we still must defeat their individual as well as collective totems if we are to become stronger. And if R'san is correct, by defeating the totem of this older female, the rest should follow shortly."

* * *

How long had she been between living and dying? While she had known that the infection that had almost killed her had left her weak, she did not realize how weak until being moved during that storm. As in a dream, she barely remembered the comments made by that priest. She had learned that he, two healers, and that older warrior had been here every day checking on her condition. She remembered none of their visits, if she had even been conscious. After being close to death before the discovery of the infection, she had hovered there once again after the move. She had been shocked to learn that she had been this way for close to twenty days. Now she was happy she didn't have a mirror because she suspected that she would be quite pale, and quite drawn. Even with consciousness returning, to just sit up had led her to shaking from the lack of strength. She could see the worry in the eyes of the two women who had been with her, but did not have the strength to even speak.

To feel this way scared her to her very core – never had she ever been this frail, this weak, and having to totally depend on someone else. She had always been strong, prided herself in her strength, both mental and physical. After all those many annuals of training in the scouting unit had developed a deep disciplined core, a ruggedness of spirit and strength that at this moment were as if they never existed. At the present she was propped up against one of the walls as she once again received some thin broth to eat. Even though it was warm in this shelter she was shaking from being cold. Just the effort of eating this small amount drained what little strength that she had, and she knew that shortly that she would be asleep once again. And in one sense, she did not want to, as she was continually facing demons in her dreams. Seeing her dead mate just out of reach, and her missing children, continually reliving the moments after their door was broken down, and the hell that followed. At least awake she could avoid them, but once asleep they were always there. She wondered why they had been moved, but at this moment in time could care less. And as these thoughts crossed her mind, once again, she faded from consciousness, into the oblivion and the nightmares in her sleep.

* * *

"You're right T'som, this female is very sick. I have seen very little signs so far that even indicate that she will recover from this. Yet, there seems to be a fighting spirit within her, and I see little signs that she is slowly returning. And I now understand why, back when you approached me with your concerns, that you felt that it had been unwise to move her, even though we did. That move definitely set back her time of returning. And when you first said that you felt that three cycles of our major moon would be more realistic, I did not believe it. But now I am of the opinion, that three may not be enough. And while I am not a healer, my opinion now says that it will be after the end of the season of cold before she will have recovered, if the gods allow. Each day that passes I still see the opportunity for her to pass into the spirit world. And if she does that, we may never know, never have the answers we are looking for. And she could defeat us by doing just that. If she was to pass into the spirit world before her totem was broken, defeated, then we may never be able to do just that."

K'jor got up and started pacing the room, unable to remain sitting for long. Another storm had descended upon them and was now dumping its fury around them. This season of cold was absolutely the worst he could ever remember. Turning and facing T'som he continued, "I've come to no conclusions as of yet, even about this female. It may be this sickness that she has could be a result of her gods defending her, and our gods attacking her. And with her in the middle not having the strength to either defend or attack. She is mortal like all of us and the gods are always immortal. It seems that we are no more than playthings. But like you said, all of this may not be the way of it either, and it simply could be that whatever it is that attacked her body left her in such bad shape that it will take a very long time until she has recovered. At times I wish that you hadn't brought up these other possibilities, as it surely complicates things, and I've had enough of that with the alliance."

Keeping silent and listening to K'jor, T'som truly could not add anything to what was being said. Sometimes silence was the best response anyway. There was so much he just did not understand, and he fully understood the quandary that K'jor was in. Heck, he faced that as the head priest almost every day of his life. Things were so much more complicated when one dealt with the spirit world, and gods. After all how could a mere mortal understand, let alone carry out, what the gods, who lived forever, wanted of their subjects? With an inward smile he thought that finally K'jor had to face some of what he did, and maybe it was a good thing. After all, K'jor had always been direct; let's get this done, and who cares about what the complications might be. Those could be sorted out afterwards. And now he seemed to be second guessing himself all the time. Yet, even here it was from a position of strength, as one in command. T'som had to admit that he felt lucky to have such for a clan leader. *May it continue to be so.* "Now you enter my world, where nothing is simple, nothing is as you see it, nothing is as you expect. It is not an easy place to be."

"No truer words have been spoken. I grow restless to return to battle. At least there, while the situation can turn complicated, it is there in front of you and you can adjust. This, this is beyond that. You cannot see your enemy, you cannot predict his direction, and you do not know the battlefield on which you are fighting. No, this is not my kind of fight! Give long knives, bows, and such. These I understand! But this other, this other is so far beyond me, so I am glad that I have you to cover our flank. Although at times with what you leave with me, it makes me wonder if you are not just attacking also." Smiling before continuing, K'jor said, "Now don't take that wrong. You are one of my most trusted, and we've been friends long before either of us rose to our places among our people, and I want our friendship to always be there. Again, at the beginning, which now seems more unreal, than real, I never saw or understood the consequences or directions this would take. It appeared to be so simple then. Destroy an enemy, grow in strength and stature from our successes, increase our herds, and our clan, and become strong enough that none of the others out there would want to attack us.

"Yet, while much of that has happened, I guess most of it really, we, well I expected to see an increase through our breeding with the new females that have been added to the herds. But while the increase in the size of that herd has been realized, none of those that have been added are adding to our clan. And it is because of this we are now here trying to learn why this is so, and of all things, having to depend on one of these females to enlighten us. Who would have ever thought that? Not me, never in my lifetime would I have thought that we as warriors, would be unable to make a female carry our offspring. Yet, that's the very truth that is staring right back at us. We consider ourselves strong warriors, yet these females, yes; these females are showing us that we are not that strong. After all they are defeating us. And if females can do this, how long will it be before we are defeated in battle?"

CHAPTER ELEVEN

Looking out the windows from the meeting area Saige smiled. With both his mate Seirra, and his sister Shellian carrying their first child he knew that with what had happened with Sorrel, that it would be something that would have weighed heavily on her mind. After all she had been the first to become pregnant so very long ago. But fate had intervened and she had lost her daughter, while the other two who had become pregnant later now had children. There had been a worry, because of the way she had lost her unborn daughter; that there was a great possibility that she would never be able to have children of her own. So when Saar had informed he and Shellian, that Sorrel was pregnant, and just glowing, it was a relief – showing that even she had been worrying about this. So if all the women who were now with child could go full term that would mean that all of the women who had survived the falling of their city and the desperate run to the Sacred Mountains would bring new lives into this world – *so many changes, so much still to do, and still no answers.* Yet, he had to admit, even in these rough times, life continued to flourish, continued to grow, and refused to go quietly.

And with the two children now both walking, well running probably would be more accurate, they seemed to be everywhere. And who would have thought that they could create so much chaos, so much noise, and disappear in an instant on those short legs of theirs. Shayne and Sommer definitely kept their parents fully occupied with just trying to keep up with them. So he knew that in one sense he was seeing his future. Yet, he had to admit it; he looked forward to the time when he and Seirra would be taking care of their own child. Although the thought of seeing her go through the pain of childbirth, after Shell' had described it to him, was something he did not want to happen, still, it is the way of life. And to him, with Seirra in the middle of her second third, she was more beautiful than ever.

And while it was nice to let his mind drift in this direction, it truly was not the reason he had come in here. With winter upon them, they needed to rescue more of their people. But at the moment he had no idea how to do it. The distances were just too great, and if the tribe that they had rescued the eight from had not been close, it would have been impossible. He knew from the records that when it had been originally decided to establish the cities that their ancestors did this during the winter time to minimize the possibility of being discovered by the primitives, who pretty much just remained in their camps and clan homes. And that they used a kind of shuttle that flew through the air, and was large enough to move not only the people, but the equipment to build the cities. But while there had been a description of these shuttles, no one had found anything on how they looked, how they worked, how big they were, what they used for energy, and besides even if they did know, no one here could operate one.

So presently they were on foot. Even the machinery that they used when monitoring the primitives was slow, and housed the equipment they used to record, track, and keep in contact with the forward scouts. These machines had never been meant for fast or long distance travel.

* * *

"Well, Stone what do you think? After all you're the rock specialist." Seve asked.

"All I can say is from the amount of work that has been done on these tunnels that we are working our way through, our ancestors had planned on being here a long time. While I can see that they used some of the original steam vents and lava tubes, there are places where they have just worked through the solid rock to enter into another series of tubes. Look there and you can see where this tube turned away from the direction they wanted to go. The debris that is partially blocking it is from the waste when they added to the tunnel. And to keep opening up the roof often enough to let light in and keep the air fresh. This was well planned and executed." As they turned a slight curve they found another room like the one close to the beginning and entered into it. Looking around they could see that it was set up very much like the other one. This was the third, and they seemed to be spaced to give any who would be using the system an easy half day distance between. From the shadows they could see that this must have been one for overnight stays. Built into the rock walls were bunks that folded up and out of the way when not inuse. Again supply cabinets, and fodder for any of the animals, and a section built off to one side for taking care of one's bodily needs. Towards one side and away from where the animals would have been kept was a raised stone platform that had a fire pit and next to the pit a generous supply of wood.

"They must have used these pack animals to haul this stuff in here, unless they had another way of doing it." Staven commented, as he looked around the room, and as it continued to darken, and like the caves that they found before discovering the Alpha, the walls began to glow that same soft light. "I really wish I knew how they did that. It's been a mystery since Saige and Shellian found that first cave. And I'm noticing that like those it's warm here also – subtle, very subtle, so much so that it would be easy to not even realize it."

"I guess we've lost part of what we once knew," Seve said. "After all we know that these people were our people, which mean that when the cities were established, this again was common knowledge. Or at least the engineers knew how to do it. And from what we've observed, they used it everywhere. So why'd we lose it?"

"Don't have an answer for you." Stone responded, "But if we've lost the knowledge to build this, how much have we forgotten over time, just waiting for a rescue that has never arrived. Even the Alpha's location had been lost, although that may have been on purpose, since it was important to keep the knowledge away from the primitives. Still, its location had to be written somewhere in the cities, otherwise no one could ever return, and you know as I, that it was abandoned with the thought of returning someday. Everything had been mothballed, and all the maintenance bots functioning to maintain the place in working order – all speaking of us returning here someday. And yet, even our history changed from the true beginnings to the mythology that then became the truth. We've learned a lot since finding this place, but I really feel like there is much it isn't telling us, because it was common everyday stuff. So instead of trying to advance ourselves, we've stagnated, playing a waiting game, and probably have actually lost a great deal in the process." Looking at the other two, and around the room Stone yawned, and said, "I don't know about you two, but once we eat, I for one will be ready to call it a day, and get some sleep. Who knows how far we still have to go?"

* * *

"Can any of you tell me where either Saige or Shellian is?" Judd asked, as he entered the cafeteria.

Starr looking up from breast feeding Sommer thought. *It won't be long before this will be a thing of the past. But it just seems so right, so natural. But Sommer is now preferring solid foods, and wanting the breast milk less and less.* "I think that Shellian is in the medical section. She mentioned that she was due for a checkup, and Saige, I think he has the security office duty right now, why?"

"I've just learned something that I feel is very important, actually probably critical for all of us to do what we need to do. Guess I'll head for the security office then, thanks." He headed out the opposite double doors and was gone.

Looking down at Sommer Starr asked, "Now what was that all about?" Then quietly laughing she could see that her daughter could care less, and was on the verge of falling asleep, with a very contented look on her face, then she said softly, "My how I love you my little one."

* * *

"What do you think, Stone? Where do we go from here?" Staven was looking around at the huge meadow that lay before them. They had just emerged from the tunnel through another one of those sliding doors into a meadow similar to the one close to the complex.

"Very good question," Stone replied. He was a surprised as the other two when they came back into the open. He had figured that their ancient ancestors had used these natural tubes all the way down the mountainside, exiting who knew where somewhere at the base. Instead they found themselves here, and while not as large as the one on top, this one was not small. *I can only hope that the exit out of this place isn't as hard to find as the one by the complex.* Taking a deep breath he said, "Okay, with the time that has passed since anybody has used this system we're not going to find a ready trail leading us to the exit. So, like our searches up in that meadow let's spread out and see what we can find. Seve, you take the left side, Staven the right and I'll go up through the center. That way we all should be able to keep in sight of at least one of us. Hey it looks like there are some of the same types of animals grazing in this one." He said as he pointed into the distance where these animals were barely visible. "Now I wonder how wild these are or if they've been worked by bots like the other ones?" Then turning to the other two he said, "Be careful, we don't know if they've even seen anything like us, and may decide that we are a threat. Let's take our time and do a thorough search, meet both of you on the other side of this thing." And with that began to head out into the large open area. Looking around and breathing deeply the cold fresh air, it smelled and tasted great after the tunnels. But there was a thin blanket of snow, not deep enough to bury the dead grasses, but it was obvious that as winter deepened that this area would be buried in the white stuff.

He could see the other two heading for the walls, and again all he could do was shake his head. This area had been another large caldron, and when these giants had been active this would not have been a very nice place to be. Everything that he had viewed said that these mountains had been completely built from ancient volcanoes. Evidence also pointed to them being extinct for a very long time. He knew from a few minor discoveries since living on these mountains, that there were a few hot springs and geysers, giving testament to the violent past. But the results from this mountain building were rich volcanic soils, and lush growth of the grasses, plants, and trees. Now if it wasn't so cold in the winter it would be a great place to live, not that the fresh air and views weren't worth a little discomfort. This brought a smile as he thought that with cold nights it was always nice to get warm with one's mate.

He stopped a moment, looked to see if he could still see the other two, and found that he could, but again this one area was turning out wider than he thought. Then he realized that something had penetrated his subconscious, as he had been thinking, something that seemed out of place, not natural. Looking back he saw a pile of rocks, not much different than any of the many that lay on the ground here. But there was something different about this one, and he turned around and went back to it. Then he realized that even though it was faint and almost worn away, there was a splash of paint on the pile. *A marker of some kind? Maybe, just maybe they did mark a trail across this meadow.* Now with something to look for he slowed his pace down and studied the many piles that crossed his path. After some distance and not finding another, he ranged back and forth to see if maybe he had overlooked one because it did not lie in the direction he had been searching. On one of the swings to the right he found another one, stopped, and tried to get the attention of the two searching the walls. Because he had slowed down, both were now well ahead of him and all he could see was their backs as they searched. Whistling he caught the attention of Staven, and once he did he signaled for him to join him. Turning in the other direction he attempted to get Seve's attention. But the winds were blowing away from Seve's location so he probably hadn't heard the whistling. So all he could do was wait until Seve turned to make sure he could see him, and then catch his attention.

He could hear Staven approach and then ask, "What's going on?"

"Right now I'm trying to get Seve's attention. With the winds sounds are being taken away from him, so he didn't hear my whistling. Watch with me and one of us should be able to get him to see us. If not, then either you or I must go get him, while one of us stays right here. I think that I've found what our ancestors did to make it easy to cross this area and know where you need . . . look I think he's turned around." Both of them began waving to get Seve's attention. Eventually they received the acknowledgement signal, and at that point Stone signaled assembly. While waiting Stone continued, "I think I've found what they used to keep anyone on track if they were coming across this area alone. As usual it's an accidental discovery, and because of the amount of time that has passed I almost missed it because the markings are almost completely worn away." Turning around and leading Staven to the stone pile he pointed and said. "Here, look closely and you can see what looks like paint. I found another one just a short time ago, but had to range a bit to find this one. So now with three of us to look we should be able to find others."

"Yeah, I guess that would make sense to do something like this. So how far apart are these things anyway?"

"I'd guess at least a hundred paces, maybe more. After all I've only found two of them, and did not take a direct route between them. They probably did this on purpose just in case the primitives came this far into the mountains to hunt. You know the fewer markers the less of a chance for them to be discovered."

"What's going on guys?" Seve asked.

"Stone may have found the path through this place." Staven replied. "Well, sort of, anyway. It appears our ancestors marked piles of rocks to keep anyone on track, but there aren't a lot of them. Stone feels it would be that way to keep the primitives ignorant."

"Makes sense to me." Seve replied.

* * *

"This meeting has been called this morning because of what Judd related to me last night while I was in the security office. We've been trying to figure out how we could cover the vast distances that we need to, and he may have found the answer. I don't know quite how we'll be able to use this yet, but can make a difference." At this point Saige sat down and turned the meeting over to Judd saying, "All yours."

"As all of you know, I've been a private contractor within Jade for just about as long as I can remember. Much of the work I did involve keeping things working, and using and maintaining the replicators was a major part of that. Without them we wouldn't have been able to survive where our cities were built. What most of you do not realize is that the computing system that operates these units is not part of the network. I don't know why, but it has always been that way. Still the computing power it takes to make these things work is tremendous, and maybe that is why they have always been isolated. Now why am I introducing it this way? Simple really. By these systems being separate there would be no way that anyone who did not have access or understand the replicating computers would know what is on them, what they can produce, or what their true capabilities are. So it would be no one's fault if this information would have been missed. To be honest, until I ended up in this situation, I missed it myself.

"Look, like you when I saw our true past, and realized that we all originated here from this place, and before that some other planet in the vast universe, it was a shock. That got me to thinking that while there has been little advancements, and now I know why, there had to be more than what we are using. And one of the mandates had been no traveling between cities once they were established. Yet, there had to be more than just these flying shuttles to move equipment and people around. And it was this and the machines that the scouting units used that got me looking through the catalogs within the system. For the longest time I was frustrated, because I couldn't even locate the plans on those units. And from the descriptions you gave me, I knew that they were not very new, and probably after they had been created, the information was buried deeper within the systems or maybe even wiped, to keep it out of the hands of people like me. So, most likely in the cities, this information doesn't exist anymore. But this is the original system, and one that has lain untouched for a very long time. And I was seeing much here that did not exist in those other systems. It confirmed that indeed either the information was never included or somewhere in the past it was wiped."

Saar asked, "Are you telling us that there was a conscious effort to remove something that could be important, critical to our survival? And if that is the true facts here, what else has our city governments done, that could jeopardize our survival?"

"A good question, Saar," Saige answered, "and it leads one in many directions, including the changing of our true origins. And it always brings up the question as to why the emergency signal from this place failed to continue to transmit. From what can be discovered at this point, much of this happened in the past, and I know that, that is an obvious statement." Pausing for effect Saige then continued, "Unfortunately we have no way of proving it was deliberate, or because it was deemed important to keep travel, and I suspect communication between cities to the minimum, that this information was left out intentionally – there's just no way to know." Turning back to Judd, he said. "Continue, if you please."

"Well, let's just say that what I was looking for was buried very deep. In fact none of this was in the catalogs at all. There was a section dealing with maintenance of the shuttles, and here listed under a subcategory were the units you, as scouts, used. And a whole subcategory of transportation vehicles that worked on the same principles as your hovercraft. Some could haul up to fifty people all at once, others were small and fast, called skimmers, and some had the ability to transport large amounts of material, including animals, in an attachment called trailers. The small skimmers could reach speeds of a hundred kilometers an hour, although I wouldn't recommend it. But even the heavier units could cover at least fifty kilometers in the same time if needed. And the good news is that these replicators here in this complex can construct them. The bad news is that there is no way to get one of those units off these mountains. If we could discover a way of moving them down the mountains in parts and put them together once we reached the grasslands, then we would have the freedom to move great distances rather quick, and be in many places that would be beyond the primitives understanding.

I do believe that somehow our ancestors used these things to move between the tribes and clans. I know from the data here, that we've been here a long time, but to gather as much as they have would have meant that almost everybody that was here would have to be in the field. And that ladies and gentlemen is impossible. So the only explanation is that they were using this equipment a lot to move from place to place. Then when the lifeline was cut to our own world, this information was buried, and with the establishment of the cities, possibly eliminated. From the dimensions, schematics, if you will, they are much too large to fit into the tunnels, which are being explored right now. And the terrain is much too rough for them to travel here in these mountains. Yet all the evidence points to their use. So somewhere there is an answer, and I am sure if it is here that we will find it. I'll continue to work the replicator system, but now by knowing what to look for, the rest can look in the networked system here in the compound. And this is just about all I have for you right now." Judd then sat back down.

Shellian slowly got up, being quite uncomfortable this late into her pregnancy. She had to admit she felt like a big ball, and felt warm most of the time, and with this out in front of her she could no longer sleep like she wanted, and all those trips to the restroom, but still had to smile to herself. It was such a wonder to feel that new life move inside her. "With what Judd has given us, we, not that we didn't before, have much work ahead of us. We really do need to move, this winter, to rescuing others while the primitives are not moving because of the, as they call it, the season of cold. So shortly we will assign different schedules for all of us to search the records." She looked around the table before continuing, "That's all we have for you now, but this is very important. While we may not be officially at war, we might as well be, so anything and I mean anything that seems like it could help bring this conflict to an end, we need to know. Have a good day all."

* * *

The three continued across this meadowland following the almost invisible markers left by their ancestors. Again it led to a passage within the huge crater and again like the entrance above, this path let to a smaller meadow and another building built from native stone, a duplicate really. So it was easy to find the sliding door, even with the skylights covered. Once inside the next tunnel system, they slid the door shut and continued on down the mountains. This time the tunnel was short and they came back out into the sunlight which blinded them briefly. Around them was a broken landscape with no sign of the continuing tunnel system that they had just traversed. Instead they found themselves back into the trees with a barely visible trail going down the mountainside, and as the suns approached the zenith they found another one of those caves that their ancestors had built. Turning to the other two Stone said, "This is just unbelievable. There was so much work and effort that went into this whole project. And we still don't know how they were able to both heat and keep out animals. Guess we'll take a break. If everything holds to what we learned, about dark we'll find the next one."

"I wonder," Seve mused, "yeah, I really wonder if these are monitored just like the ones close to the Alpha, or because these are so far away they didn't worry about it."

"That's a good question," Staven said. "There's just so much we don't know, or have lost since we moved to the cities, and maybe because these are so far from the complex they felt it was unnecessary. After all, there has never been anything in them, so if the primitives just happened upon them, they might think they were strange, maybe even something their gods created, but other than that what could they conclude? As we've learned, these mountains are pockmarked with caves created by these extinct volcanoes, and while a little different; I doubt this would generate much curiosity anyway. Besides, only the priests would possibly be up this far and only on rare occasions, some brave hunter."

Stone got up and headed out, saying, "I'm going to gather some wood. A hot meal before we continue would be nice. I'd guess with our progress, that tomorrow morning we should be back into the grasslands. We all need to look the area over so that we can add to our knowledge, as so far nobody has found anything in the system back at Alpha marking out these trails. So we are rediscovering all of this."

* * *

That night they were at the second of the caves, and while the trail had been almost invisible, they congratulated themselves on being able to stick to it. In some places trees had grown over the trail, and they had to work their way around obstacles that time and nature had put there. Yet they could see that if they had a pack animal there still would be no problem. None of these obstacles were such to block the surefooted animals. "I wonder where this eventually comes out?" Staven asked.

Shaking his head, because not one of them really knew, Stone said. "Don't know. But we've been heading down one of the gentler slopes, and there have been less rockslides and such here. Suspect that's why it goes this way. But I know that what you meant is where in those vast grasslands does this come out? Guess tomorrow we'll learn that one. Now that we are this far down it's really hard to see where this is leading. And I'm glad that the snow here has been light, and there's just a thin layer. I really wouldn't want to have to find my way with heavy snows on the ground."

"Agreed!" Seve responded, "Very much so. We've had enough issues with that when we spent our first winter in that cave. With us presently being in month D, and still looking at about six until the end of this annual, I'm glad we are doing this exploring now instead of maybe month sixteen or seventeen, when it would really be cold and miserable."

They knew that the primitives looked at their annual more as what season they were in, but with the annual being 540 days, and having learned that the world that they had come from ran to about 365 days, a similar monthly system was adopted. But with quite a few more days it was decided to make the months thirty days long with five six-day weeks giving them eighteen months. The system their ancestors adopted turned out to be simplicity in itself. With twelve months being the norm from their home world, they adopted a system of using the first letter of the months, and if there were more than one that had the same letter, then a number was assigned. Thusly the first month of the new annual would be J1, and the last month of the annual would be 18. Seasons were much longer leaning towards five to six months in length. And this cold season appeared to be one of the fiercer that they could remember. All of them were quite happy that it was this annual and not the last when they were trying to survive in the cave. Snows had been deep enough then. From the views from the "eyes in the sky", the lowlands, foothills, and grasslands were faring no better. It would be miserable no matter where one lived.

* * *

The three who had been exploring the tunnel system and pathway out of the mountains, arrived back at the complex six days after leaving, but before they could even relax, compare notes, and put together a report to present to everyone, news spread throughout the complex like a wildfire. Shellian's water had broken! A new life was just about to enter the world, and everything now became secondary as the women gathered to help with the birthing. With the father being the doctor, he would be closely involved.   While not a requirement, all fathers were encouraged to be there and help their mates through this tough and difficult time. After all it wasn't called labor for fun. It was a long, tiring and painful road that would only end when the child and afterbirth had entered the world. And it wasn't uncommon for the first birth to take a full day and night, leaving the mother completely exhausted.

And while the men attempted to put on an air of normality, it was obvious that each one would be seen listening for some message from the infirmary, and something to come over the monitors to let them know that it was all right. They all knew that they had an important part in creating a new life, but it is the woman who really touches eternity. She is the one who must allow the new life to grow inside of her body, and then endure the pain of childbirth, feeling like you were being torn in half, when it was time for that new life to begin on their own. Saige, remembering back to the conversation he and Shellian had about this, wondered how she was doing. He could almost remember a wistfulness in her voice as she recalled other births from the past, and that someday it would be her turn. Again, all he could do was shake his head. He knew that in a few months Seirra would be in that same room bringing forth another new life that the two of them created. At this moment, he wasn't sure he wanted to be there to see her helpless against the contractions and helpless against the pain. But at the same time, wanted to be with her, supporting however he could. But what could he do, but watch helplessly?

It was evening meal time, and all of the women had taken shifts to eat, and would only pass on that everything was fine and normal, but that these things just take time. Then once finished with their meals, would immediately head back. Saige, turning towards Stone asked. "I know that with what's happening right now that it is hard to concentrate on anything else, but how'd it go?"

"Interesting, very interesting overall. I first thought that we'd be in those tunnels until we came out down in the grasslands, but if I'd really thought about it, that just wouldn't have made sense. I think why so much of the tunnels to start with, were to keep this place hidden. After all, except for the way we entered originally, there is no other way into this place. And the entrance that you found is in such a place that no one would expect it to be there. And there is no way anybody can observe someone going through that supposedly solid rock wall. So I give it to our ancestors, they were very careful to keep this place well hidden. Once you call a meeting, then we can go over it in more detail. Still, the whole way is easily traveled, and I know that's still very important. Besides, the three of us haven't had much of a chance to really finalize anything yet. I don't know, maybe because something has been distracting us all."

The last comment brought a smile to Saige, but he knew that at the moment that his sister probably wasn't in the smiling mood. It was something that he or any of the rest of the males for that matter would never experience, but he knew that if one cared deeply for his mate, then it was tough in its own way. "Yeah, that's true, and I guess I'll be the next in that room with Seirra since she is the next one who will be delivering soon. Even though Sorrel has had one child, she was unconscious throughout the whole ordeal, so I suspect that when it is hers and your turn, that like the rest of us it will be like the first time. Anyway thanks for the information. I want a meeting after the morning meal in two days to cover what you found. Of course neither Saar nor Shellian will be there, as there will be something else occupying their time. And I'm sure Shell' will need the recovery time, oh look it's time, got to report to the security office. At times, I almost yearn for the time before we contacted the cities. It was so much quieter then, but now we always need to have someone to man the communications system, and someone else to run down the answers to the too many questions we are getting." Getting up to leave he turned and said, "Go spend some time with Sorrel. She's missed you. And before you ask, no she did not make it known, but to any who knows her, and the rest of us do, then it was very obvious that she missed her man."

Stone had to admit that he really missed her also. They really had only been apart for six days, but it seemed so much longer. *How'd this attachment happen anyway?* He had to shrug, because it did not matter how, but now he couldn't see his life without her.

* * *

Sometime between the dark of the night and dawn the word came from the infirmary that the baby had arrived, and she was quite healthy, and looked much like her mother, which was appreciated. Not that Saar was a bad looker for a guy, but Shellian was truly a beautiful woman, in an athletic way. The daughter's name was Samantha, named after Shellian's, and Saige's mother. One who had passed away in their youth, and with a father that could not raise two children when they reminded him so much of his lost mate, they had become part of the scouting unit, and now here in charge at the alpha complex so many annuals later.

* * *

"I'm sure that all of us have looked in, on the new mother and daughter, and have personally seen that both are healthy, and all of you women ogling over that new one, wanting to hold her, and giving all of those suggestions to the new mother. And of course, she isn't here, and will be off any assignment for a while to give them time. Unfortunately for Saar he isn't quite so lucky, although he isn't here, since he is our only doctor. He has gone to an on call status so that he can help Shell' wherever he can." Smiling before continuing Saige said, "And the miracle of life continues. Not that the intimacy that led to this moment wasn't very enjoyable, the results still leave me in awe as to the creation of a new life. I know that for now, of the original group who was first here that Seirra and I will be almost the last, not quite, but almost the last to join the families that are being created here. But this is getting away from the reason for this gathering and that is for Stone to pass on to us what they have discovered." Saige sat down at this point and signaled for Stone to continue.

Standing up and looking over the group Stone began. "Now Seve and Staven, if I forget or leave something out then let me know." At this point he covered in a little more detail what he had related to Saige two nights ago. Then he began to describe what they found at the base. "What is interesting is where this came out, and what we found there. What I mean is this, the trail came into a hidden valley, and when I mean hidden I mean hidden. It's not large, but could sustain a few of the animals for a few days. There's water there with a small stream running through it. It took us a better part of half a day to find the exit out into the grasslands. It is surprisingly wide, but is such that it just doesn't appear to be anything but a dead end canyon. I don't know if it is natural or our ancestors constructed it, but however it is it works. Now all of this is interesting, but we found in one of the constructed caves, a large one by the way, a facility that again is well hidden, that can be powered by, well my guess would be solar. We didn't do a thorough search, but there seems to be no reason to need this capability, so it is a question as to why our ancestors built it. But there appears to be many small rooms, and areas to both bunk, and put supplies. So maybe it is a place where they could operate and be right at the edge of the grasslands. There is equipment there, mothballed like here when we arrived, and all of it appears to be maintained by the same type of bots. So as far as we could see, like here, once one pulls it out of the shutdown mode that it presently is in, everything should work."

"Did you get a chance to see what type of equipment was there?" Judd asked.

"Not really, we just did a quick explore, and confirmed that what we saw was in working order. After all, this entire trip was to learn about the route down from here, and finding this was a bonus, but we needed to return. So I am sure, now that we know about this, that we'll be heading back to do a more thorough inventory of what's there." Turning to Saige he asked, "Am I right?"

Nodding his head, Saige said, "Absolutely. Judd has discovered some interesting things while you are away, and I'm sure his question had to do with those discoveries. With the excitement that has been going around here in the last few days, I'm sure that no one has brought you up to speed on that. Let's just say he's made some discoveries that will definitely help, and later you can ask him. Now with this discovery, I'm also sure that he'll want to make the trip down and inspect that place, and if he discovers what I think he'll discover, then we will be moving our timetable ahead to possibly try and rescue more of our people this winter."

CHAPTER TWELVE

"Well Judd, your rescue seems to have been exactly what we needed to make much of what we have to do to go forward." They were standing in the meadows outside of the complex, before them sat one of the skimmers, a three passenger unit. And while snow had been building now for days, it had been sunny for the last couple giving time for the solar system in the skimmer to charge. "While we've all had training on our units that we used in the scouting section, this . . ." Saige paused as he pointed at the skimmer and smiled, "This is very different, and looks to steer differently also. Who'd of thought a round wheel to turn by? The support units that we would use, used levers and pedals to turn and stop." Then looking into the open cockpit he shook his head. "This is very different – two pedals and one lever. What did you say this lever was for anyway?"

"The best I could determine from the arrangement of the system is that the lever is attached to a device that is called a transmission. Even your support units had one. But it only provided one gear forward and one backwards. Because of the speeds this can obtain it changes the ratio to the drive system.

And the one button on the dash switches it between the air and wheeled drive system. But again unlike your units, these only have four instead of six. And because of the surface that these can travel, when in wheeled mode, they are not very fast. Although looking at some of the training videos that were on the system suggests that there are roads similar to what we have in our cities that travel across the countryside both in our homeworld and here, these skimmers or whatever it is they use, seems to use the wheeled system more – meaning more speed. Of course it is on those roads and not the open countryside like we face here."

Turning to the entire group that was standing out here, freezing, while waiting, for what was to be a demonstration, Judd shrugged. He had to admit that even with the suns shining as they were there seemed to be very little heat. Maybe it was because they were in the winter months, or maybe it was because of the height of this facility, he didn't know. But it was time to climb in and see if he could actually make this thing move. He motioned for Saige to climb into the passenger side and he got behind the wheel. He turned the switch which activated the motors, and the familiar sound of a hovercraft rose and the skimmer lifted slightly off the ground. Stepping on the break, he eased it into gear, released both the hand break and the foot break and slowly pressed the accelerator down and the skimmer moved easily forward. Smiling to himself, Judd hadn't been sure that it was going to work, but it was obvious now that it would. "Better put on that seatbelt." He admonished Saige, as he did the same. "I don't know how this is going to respond once we get up some speed."

Since he had never seen, let alone operated anything like this, Judd tentatively pressed the accelerator, and the skimmer responded immediately moving with a nimbleness that had been unexpected. This brought a large grin to his face. He picked up speed and while the winds that were striking them were quite chilly, the exhilaration from the speed they were traveling felt great. "How fast are we going, Judd?" He looked down and saw that they were moving, according to the dial at about twenty-five KPH. He never had been in something that moved that fast! Glancing over at Saige he responded saying, "Twenty-five, I'm going to go a little faster and see what it will do. We have pretty much a straight shot for quite a distance. But I do not want to turn it at these speeds – afraid I might upset the apple cart."

"Apple cart?" Saige asked.

"Sorry, an old phrase, that's been in my family for who knows how long." That stopped him for a moment, since at this time he could easily be the last member of his family. Taking a deep breath before continuing he said, "I really don't even know what that is, but saw some minor drawings in children's books a long time ago that supposedly was one of those things. Okay hold on, here we go!" He pressed down a little harder than he had planned and the skimmer literally leaped ahead gathering speed rapidly. And now with tears streaming down his face from the stinging cold air he glanced at the dial and saw they were now doing twice what they had been. It was unbelievable that something could move this fast across the ground like this. Looking over at Saige he could see a huge smile as well as tears from the cold on his face. He backed off and the skimmer slowed to a stop. Judd could feel his heart beating rapidly, and felt completely exhilarated from the experience. Turning towards Saige, he asked, "Well, what do you think?" He could tell that Saige was breathing hard, but the smile had yet to leave his face.

"And to think that we were traveling that fast!" Saige, looking back over his shoulder could see in the distance and almost out of their sight, the team still standing. "Wow, this thing is fantastic! I never in my wildest imagination thought one could travel this fast. And you are saying that we only were at about half of what this is capable of?"

"Actually once I looked over the specs on this thing I found that what I had stated in the meeting wasn't quite accurate. The hundred KPH that I gave you there was a suggested *safe* maximum speed for traveling in uneven terrain like this. They have the capability to go much faster, somewhere between hundred and fifty, to two hundred KPH. Although the higher speeds shorten the distance one can travel before having to recharge the batteries that this thing operates off of."

There was a brief period of silence, other than the sounds of the hover motors. "I did not think that there was any way that one could move that fast on the ground. This explains a lot, and surely will make moving around easier. Okay turn this thing around and take us back. I'm sure that the rest want their time riding along in this thing before the batteries die. How long will a charge last, and how long to recharge?"

"I can only go by what it says, since we have nothing to base it on, but with reasonable speeds it can go all day on a charge. And if it remains sunny, as you are traveling, then it continually recharges, plus it recovers some of the energy from the breaking system. There also seems to be some type of turbine that recaptures some of the air movement off the hover section to put energy back to use. And that's all I know, and as far as recharge, I guess that would be variable to how much sunlight there is at any given time."

* * *

"While I know that it is winter, we do not have time to sit and just wait it out as our people are suffering at the hands of the primitives." Saige looked over all of them as they sat around the meeting table. Looking at his sister he couldn't help but smile as she held her sleeping daughter. *It wouldn't be long before Seirra would be doing the same with their child.* He thought. "Judd has confirmed that there is a smaller version of the replicators down at the base of the mountains, and it was specifically placed there to produce and maintain the field operations of our ancestors. With this knowledge, he's been working overtime, with help of course, to get the equipment we need produced, and we've all been training in the skimmer up here in the meadows. Fortunately all of them work similarly so there will be no issue moving from one type to another. Sabryn, can you bring us up to date on that research project that you've been in charge of?"

Standing and facing the group Sabryn cleared her throat, and glanced briefly at the new life that was at the table with them and smiled briefly. "Since many of you have been helping me on this you know what it generally is all about, but with only pieces and not the whole thing. We really needed to know how our ancestors presented themselves to the primitives so that they could get up close and personal. They needed a way to establish a relationship with the primitives that would allow them to contact any and all of the tribes and clans. So they created the traveling merchants. Their front stated that their clan was from far beyond the Sacred Mountains, and that this was the first opportunity that they had to come this far south. Their goods were implements that were just a little better than the ones that the clans and tribes could create on their own. Plus they healed the very sick. By doing this they built a reputation that protected them from attack – so much so that they were almost given the status of traveling priests. And any who would attack them would be distained by all others."

She reached down and took a swallow of water before continuing. "Okay, that was all well and good, but once we spread out to the cities this practice was stopped, and unfortunately, to our loss. Had we continued this practice, then we would have had the necessary warnings to maybe prevent what has happened, and is continuing to happen." She could see the reaction through the small group as they understood that once again there had been a failure in the system that their ancestors had established. She could see this in their eyes, but like them, did not know if this had been caused by a decision at the time they broke up to move into the cities, or it was something that was decided later, like the elimination of the scouting units.

"I can't lay the blame for any of this on the present leadership, except maybe the closing of the scouting units. We have no way of knowing if any of our leaders in the cities were even aware that this existed. All of us knew that a city known as Alpha existed, but it was a hidden one, and that was all. Now all of us know the truth about it, and so many other things." Again pausing, she looked around the table once more and saw Saige nod to her to continue. "What I want to cover now but briefly, is how they set themselves up, and then Judd has something else that he's discovered that will make all of our lives in the field much easier."

With that statement the rest turned and looked at Judd who was leaning back in his chair. He smiled and signaled Sabryn to continue. "We found a whole section dealing with the role of the ones who play the part of the traveling merchants. After I go through this and after Judd have said his part, Saige will give you the cover story that we will use. Initially we will be putting out two teams, and now we will be able to monitor them individually, which is very important. Anyway, we've been working on the clothing that the ones who will be the traveling merchants must wear. Fortunately there were still some of those things existing in that room that was discovered, plus a data terminal set up specifically to keep track of the needs of the field researchers. From that we have all that we know. Besides the goods that we will carry, and in these initial forays it will be knives and bow strings, there is a frame that mounts on top of the packs that has bells attached to let all know that we are the merchants and we are neutral, and we are off limits to attack. I know that it's been a long time since the merchants traveled, but we need to reestablish them, and learn whatever we can – for now that's all I have, and with that I'll give it to Judd."

She sat down and waited as Judd stood up. One thing for sure, it had been fortuitous for them when Judd had been part of the first group they had rescued. So much had been learned since his arrival, and they were so much further ahead in their planning because of this. "My part in this meeting will be short. When I learned about the "eyes in the sky", first off I really wondered what they were. So curious I did some research and found that they really are known as satellites, but we've called them the other for so long it probably will just stick. That's neither here or there, but I found that any time that our people would prepare to explore a new world they would ring it with these things. They have much that they can do besides just giving us great images and these satellites are even better than the first ones they setup here. They have the ability to be linked, to be used for communications – I suspect that's how the cities keep in contact with each other, which means that with the proper equipment any, and I mean any, in the field can talk, update, and have a two-way conversation with us here at Alpha. I'm still learning about the rest, and there is so much more they can do, but for now this new knowledge is critical for our needs. I'm in the process of fabricating the necessary equipment for the two teams, and we'll do some testing soon. That's all for now, so I'll give it back to Saige." He then sat down and once again leaned back in his chair and turned and faced Saige.

Saige again stood up, took a deep breath and said, "With the traveling merchants being out of circulation for as long as they have, we have to be sure that when we reappear that we are consistent with what both their oral and in some cases written history will say about us. So before we actually go to the field we, the two teams and the rest who will support us, will learn this inside and out, we cannot afford to make a mistake here. And with the support staff having to be immediately available to access something from the records that the ones in the field may need to keep things in control. For example, say we contact a clan, and the clan leader asks us who the last clan leader we talked with was. Now something like that would exist in either their verbal records, or written records, so it is something that we must know."

Leaning on the table and looking hard at all of them before continuing he said, "We cannot screw any of this up. The cover story is simple. The history that has been established by our ancestors stated that we are a clan from the far north, well beyond the Sacred Mountains. Our story is this: Sometime in the great past a landslide blocked the only route around the mountains and we, even with our minor priestly status do not travel through the Sacred Mountains. It has taken us all this time to discover a new route and to be able to return to the south. And with our return, we are only sending two teams out, since we've no idea what has changed since we last visited this area. But with these two we are trying to establish what used to be, by our own records and traditions. With contact established, and our ability to keep in contact here at Alpha, any of the cases that require our "doctor skills", will be immediately referred back to Saar." Turning towards him Saige said, "Sorry about that Saar, but you and now Jas who assists will be on call for this. I can only hope that eventually we rescue another doctor to help relieve the burden. As we are able to recover more of our people, your job will only get harder." Then turning back to the rest he continued," We will be starting out for our first attempt in less than a month, so everything will be very intense around here. That's all I have for you now, do any of you have anything they want to add before we break up and get to it?" Looking around he saw most shaking their heads and the others remaining silent. "Okay then, we're done here."

* * *

"Problems, Judd?" Seve asked, as the small team worked at the field unit at the base of the mountains. Everything at this location was very minimal. Even the system to keep power to the equipment was barely enough to allow it to run for any length of time.

Shaking his head Judd said, "No, I guess not. I'm just used to working with the stuff from the cities, or now from Alpha, but I guess our ancestors had to cut somewhere, and again with as little space as there is here, you can see that they had to cut corners. And unfortunately it seems that they did, just about everywhere." Again pausing as he looked around he said, "Well, I guess I can understand it. This was never to be used other than to build and maintain the equipment they used during their research. So there was, in a sense, more leisure time to get things done. Time to let the solar system recharge, and time to make repairs – all the things that we don't have the luxury of, especially time. So it's frustrating when you're in the middle of something just to have it shut down because of the lack of power, or because that particular component wasn't included here. Truthfully, I was beginning to feel really good about our ancestors, as everything I had seen and worked appeared to be over engineered, and robust. So finally, I'm seeing the other side where things were skimped upon, and things barely operate." Shrugging he said, "But what can we do? All we can do is take the time to get these things built and tested, but know that it's going to take much more time than I would like to invest, that we can afford to invest really. I know that Saige is impatient to get moving on this, and I can't blame him. Every day that we delay there's another chance that we've lost another of our people to the primitives. And from personal experience, I don't want our people in the hands of the primitives any longer than necessary. So here we are against the clock so to speak, against this equipment, and against the limited time our people have to survive."

"Yeah, believe me we do know the feeling. When our city was attacked, and we were able to escape, the original plan was to work our way back to one of the other cities. But we were never allowed. And from the original size of our scouting team, in the end we ended with just the ten of us, and the frustration that we had the knowledge of what had happened but no way to let anybody know. And knowing that we couldn't and that other cities were falling in the very same way just tore at our very souls." Taking a deep breath before continuing Staven said, "But it really was worse than that. We lost our leader in one of the many skirmishes, and he put Saige and Shellian in charge and through their leadership they got us into these Sacred Mountains. Got us safely to a place where we could possibly survive the harsh winter, and then we rebelled, and kicked them out. So at that point we almost destroyed any chance for any of us to help. You don't hear either of them talking about it, and you won't. Yet in the end of all of this they took us back without reservations. And I, for one, am quite grateful that they did. We were very close to death at that point, and if they had sent us away, as they had the right to do, I or the rest of us who were involved wouldn't be here, and I suspect that you and the ones with you would still be with the primitive tribe since they wouldn't have had enough people to go and rescue you. I guess Shayne, he was our leader, was right in who he chose to lead us. And I know now that they never wanted it, and because of this none of us will ever go against them."

Thinking a moment, Judd said, "I know when we finally learned the truth, I at first thought that those two were pretty young to be in charge like this. But as I've watched them, they appear to have a maturity well beyond their years."

"Living through what we did can do that to a person." Looking over at the panel Staven said, "Oh well, looks like the light's gone green again, so I guess we can move on to the next step."

"Yes it has. At least the time between the recharge is somewhat quick, but it sure seems to drain faster. Too bad we couldn't do some of this back at Alpha, but it surely would be a bear to transport anything down here, and time consuming, and probably in the end, not much savings of time even with these quick cycles. Okay let's get that next piece replicated and move on. We have too much still to accomplish."

* * *

"From the 'eye-in-the-sky', imagery I think we're about to be hit with a strong storm. It looks like it has been pounding the grasslands, and as it is approaching these mountains seems to be getting stronger. I know it's frustrating right now, but we're not going to be able to do anything until after this one blows through. Guess everybody can continue to practice, and continue to work on learning the language of the primitives. I know that as we enter these different villages – especially the clans' home turf – and such that we'll be planting bugs to begin a serious monitoring of the tribes and clans. So knowing the language will be critical." Turning around to Jed, who was in the security office with Saige, Saige asked. "How's the manufacture of the trading goods going? Are we going to have enough to do this job?"

"From what I can gather, yes, it should be enough. But you know this is just a guess. We've never done this, and either you'll end up with too much or too little. It's just how things usually work out."

* * *

K'jor remained within his shelter as the storm raged. This season of cold definitely was the worst. Even the elders of the clan were commenting that they could never remember one so bad. The sounds of the winds descending on them were deafening, tearing loose anything not tied down, and propelling it with crashes across open spaces. The shelters shook under the force and threatened to come apart, but somehow remained standing. What heat they had from the roaring fires seemed to be sucked out, leaving the only places within that were warm was when one stood very close to these fires. This was the second day, and if anything was true of this storm it appeared to be stronger today than yesterday. If it continued or became even stronger there'd not be a shelter left standing when it finally moved on. While briefly looking into the fire, with this storm raging in the background, his thoughts drifted back once again.

He didn't know how long he had been unconscious, but when he awoke it was still dark. When he sat up he first wondered if somehow the spirits had found a way to get past the protection of the fire and the light it produced. After all he had leaned back against a solid, well what he thought was a solid hillside, but had instantly fallen through and into unconsciousness. Before him he still could see his fire, although now it was dying down because no additional fuel was being added. Why could he still see it? If indeed he was now in the spirit world, was the normal world, even in this place of desolation that visible? If so, then it explained why the spirits could do so much harm. After all, if they could see his world this easily, and he knew that the spirit world was a place that could not be seen by him or anybody else, how simple it would be to attack and destroy. But if he were in the world of the spirits, where were they? Like it was when he was by his fire, he was alone. He knew that he was supposed to meet his clan in the morning, but he wasn't sure that he could return, cross over to the world of the living. He thought that there was a good chance that he would roam these wastes in the realm of the spirits until they released him, returning him back as one neither dead nor alive forever to haunt the living.

He sat watching his fire die, unsure as to what he should do. If indeed he had somehow accidentally entered their realm, maybe they had not realized that this was so. It would behoove him to watch and wait. He did not want to give away his position. With the light of day things might give him some ideas, so he sat cross-legged, not moving, reaching out with all of his skills to remain hidden. Somewhere along the time that flowed past him, he fell asleep, and awoke with a sudden start to the full suns rising. As he tried to move he found his joints stiff from remaining in one position too long. He felt like an old one, and panicked briefly when he thought that this could be the results of being in the realm of the spirits, draining his strength and youth, leaving him a shadow of who he was. Still it was morning and he needed to relieve himself, so got up, albeit slow, and carefully, and after looking around took care of business.

At least his weapons and water skin had come with him when he had fallen. There was a gentle morning breeze blowing that presently was cool, but held a promise of heat later in the day. Turning away from where the ashes of his fire lay, he saw that there was a narrow ravine with high sides that twisted away into the distance. He decided that since he had yet to be discovered that he would explore this, and since this appeared to be the only way to go; he felt that it would be simple to return to this spot. *How would spirits look in their own realm?* He had to admit that he didn't know. Again so far as he could see, he was the only living thing around. That brought a rough laugh from him as he thought about it. *Yep, if this is indeed the spirit world, I would be the only living thing here. All others would be spirit.* With all the stealth he could muster he worked his way down this ravine, and wondered if this was necessary? After all if the spirits who lived here were unseen, they could be watching him right this moment, and laughing at his antics of trying to stay hidden. It left him undecided as to whether to continue in this way or just give up and hike it. In the end he decided to continue as he started. He had no idea if any of what he had been thinking was true or not, so he'd rather be safe and continue this way until something proved he should change his tactics.

Stopping briefly and taking a large swig from his water skin, he could neither sense nor see much change as this ravine wound and twisted through an unknown section of the desolation only giving him a close view of the trail, the sky, and the hillsides that bordered this wash. He found that slowly the wash was opening up, and the mud hills were slowly getting smaller. He made a sharp left jog followed by an immediate right. He stopped immediately and his jaw dropped, this had to be a mirage.

* * *

"K'jor! K'jor, this is T'som, just a word if you please."

It took a moment for K'jor to understand that someone was at his entryway. With the winds howling as they were, it was almost impossible to hear anyone speaking or yelling. "Come in! Come in; get out of that nasty weather. What brings you out in this?"

Looking down and shaking his head, he said, "I wish I didn't. The trip from where I live to here was just bad. Look, with the weather turning so bad, I checked in on that female that we have placed in the care of us priests. She's still hanging on, but barely. Whatever she had gained, she has now lost and is almost at the door of the spirit world right now. It almost makes me wish that those travelers would show once again."

"Travelers?" K'jor asked with a look of consternation on his face.

"Well, I've never seen one of them, but they are mentioned a number of times in our archives. A number of generations ago they were regular visitors to all of the tribes and clans. They took no sides, and always said that they lived far to the north of the Sacred Mountains – saying, that there was only one very torturous and very dangerous way through to us in the south. They said that they took no sides in whatever conflicts we had, and would trade freely with all, offering the same to all so that none would gain an advantage from their wares. But one of the services they offered was healing. The records speak of many who were very close to the spirit world only to recover after these travelers treated them."

"Why have I never heard of them, and better yet why haven't we seen them?"

Shaking his head T'som was silent for a moment, and then shrugged, "I have no answers for you. If the truth be told, I wouldn't have known anything about them either, except when this female took a turn for the worst, I felt that maybe somewhere in our written text there would be something that would help, and then came across this information. These travelers used pack beasts but on the back of them had bells that would ring as they moved, proclaiming who they were, and they were enemies to no one."

"I'm sure somewhere along the times that they were here that someone must have attacked them. I can't see it not happening." K'jor replied.

"That could very well be true, and maybe that is why they stopped coming, but there is nothing saying that this ever happened, and that any remains of such an attack were ever discovered. Whatever their gift, if we are to learn anything at all from this female, then we need whatever these travelers did or used. After reading and rereading everything I could find on them, I suspect that their way may have become blocked. The one consistent comment made was how dangerous the journey to our side was and that this path could disappear in a moment of time, isolating them once again from our side of the Sacred Mountains."

"This female is that weak? She is really losing the battle?"

Sighing, T'som said, "Yes." He then sat down heavily before continuing, "And I fear that if she does pass through to the spirit world our one chance to understand will be lost. Let's pray to our gods that maybe soon that these travelers do return, although I could see from our writings that, that wish had been put forth a large number of times. Did you know that there was a time in our past where our clan was almost wiped out? And it was not from attacks from others. It was as if an evil spirit had moved in and was sweeping through our people, killing them one at a time, and sometimes many would fall in a day. There was much prayer going out to our gods to purge whatever evil was causing this, and to grant the return of the travelers. But either the gods heard and gave us pity, because the travelers did not come, but eventually the deaths stopped, and for a very long time we were weak, and would have been easily conquered. Yet, somehow we survived. So while the chances of seeing one or two of the travelers are very slight, it would be a good time for them to show again. For this is beyond your or my healers."

"Are you sure that these travelers as you called them, are not myth? I remember nothing ever being mentioned about them at all, nothing."

"At first I would have thought that also. But, there's just too much confirming that they were real. There is even a discussion that some of our warriors, at the time the travelers had visited, decided that they would follow them back to their homes, their clan, and discover 'their secrets'. From the narration the best the clan had in trailing and hiding attempted, and that it was it, emphasis, *attempted*. The results were embarrassing to say the least. It was as if children were trying to track and follow these. Our people would keep a great distance, track them, and then feel that they were succeeding only to find the travelers turning the tables upon them and walking into their hidden camps, smiling, and with the gentleness of speech warn them that if they persisted in these attempts that they, the travelers, would no longer visit the clan, offer their wares, or provide help with the sick. Then as easily as they appeared to the ones who were following, they would disappear." T'som paused for a moment, deep in thought, "You don't think that these stories of them being from beyond the Sacred Mountains was just a misdirection and that these strange ones that we are calling sorcerers and magicians may be the descendants of the travelers?"

Silence followed as the questions that T'som had just presented left him without words. Shaking his head, K'jor had no idea how to answer. This was becoming more complicated by the moment, and he was learning more about their past and incidents that until a short time ago did not exist as far as he knew. Shaking his head in disbelief K'jor replied, "I don't know what it is about you T'som, but it seems like every time that you show up here that you pass on more information that continues to make everything more complicated, and more difficult for one to come up with some type of decision. It was so much simpler when I was ignorant of all of this. And misdirection would be something that any of us would do. But there is a problem with tying these travelers into the sorcerers and their lairs that we are attacking, and that is this, if these travelers were from these lairs, why did they stop? After all with them being so close it would have been easy to continue to do what they were doing. And from what you've just told me about these travelers, my guess from our attacks and observations on these lairs, I see no sign that they are even close to being as skilled as your research suggests. In fact I would say that very young here within the clan's walls are more skilled than any of them. So my first thoughts are no, these cannot be of the same as your travelers, but I know that time changes things. Still if they are one in the same, what was it that made them quit?"

"You know I have no answers to any of that, and you also know that it is my job to bring you anything that can affect us. And this turning for the worse by this female is, as I said at the beginning, the reason for turning to the old words. And the possible conclusion that these lairs and the travelers could be one in the same just came out of what little evidence I could find. And maybe there is no connection at all and what the travelers said was true. That they do truly come from beyond the Sacred Mountains, and that the one and only way to our side was destroyed and prevented them from returning. I don't know – it's all just speculation. The records just say that there was no tapering off of the visits, they just stopped suddenly, and no one heard or saw them anymore."

* * *

"Okay all; once again we're here in another meeting. I would never have thought so many of these would be necessary. After all when we were just a scouting unit, we'd be lucky if we met formally once a month, but now these things at times seem to be almost daily. I have to apologize for that, but as we get closer to the time of heading out into the field once again, we continue to have to work together and discuss as a group how we are going to accomplish all of this." Saige paused for a moment, looked around the table and then said, "We've established the camp at the base of the mountains, and using the historical data that was in the systems here, we've duplicated not only the setup, but the camp location. It seems that to be consistent our ancestors established a base camp that would be visible to all of the tribes and clans, but at the same time off limits. In that cave at the base of the mountains was much of the equipment they used. And with Judd there we were able to duplicate most of it. I suspect that soon it will be known that the, oh by the way, I learned that we have been calling them the traveling merchants, but to the primitives we will be known as the travelers. Right now we of the scouting unit are doing most of this work, but later as the rest learn you will be involved. Unfortunately because of the ways that the primitive societies are constructed you women will not be involved with the field work at all. Instead all of you will be here working the support side. There's absolutely nothing we can do about that. After all you women are very important, and we cannot afford to lose any of you. Starr will be presenting some important facts that have come out of the research that our ancestors did, and then we need to figure out how to perform the same things ourselves. They obviously were concerned with the safety of their people in the field, and had developed methods to watch and protect them, and this is one of the things we all need to concentrate on. Now we are not nearly the size of that staff so we've got to figure out ways that will work for us." He turned to Starr and said. "It's all yours.", and then sat down.

* * *

Sara knew that she was in trouble. She could feel herself getting weaker, and her times of being conscious of her surroundings were getting less and less. When she could see the two who were trying to nurse her back, all she could see on their faces was worry and fear. She could feel the fever returning, and chills were once again racking her body, while at the same time she burned deep inside. With all that had transpired she really did not know if she had enough inner strength to survive this bout. She had been wasted from the last episode and she had barely survived, she just did not know, but as these thoughts poured through her mind she felt herself drifting off once again, and then remembered nothing.

The two women watching over Sara looked at each other in silence. The fear was deepening for them. If she did not survive, they would be sent back and would have to submit once again, and without Sara there to help them through these horrible times, they were once again without hope. After all what could they do, and what could they hope for? With the direction things had progressed, all that they could see was their own graves sometime in the near future, and no comfort between now and when their time arrived.

* * *

Starr stood up and looked over the group. Sommer was sleeping, so for now there would be no interruptions, which was critical, as they were just about to embark for the first time something that their ancestors did routinely. "We're at the end of this work and the beginning as we try and emulate our ancestors' research, even with the storm as it is, we will be fielding only two teams and with the setting up of the base camp at the base of the mountains we've begun to establish our story. Thanks to Judd we now know much more of how our ancestors operated and protected the teams." Everyone at the meeting briefly glanced Judd's way, which he acknowledge with a curt nod. "Simply stated, these 'eyes-in-the-sky' have much more capability than we ever imagined. They even can peer through a storm and see the ground, and also with something else built into them one can actually remove the vegetation and see the bare earth – and darkness is not an issue either. Before you, in the paperwork that has been passed around, are the assignments, and these take priority over anything that we may have had going on. The two teams will need all day and all night monitoring and support. And while from here we can do little to actually protect them, we can keep them apprised of what is happening around them. You will see in narrations that are included, that our ancestors faced problems all the time when dealing with the primitives. We can expect no less. Also in this packet is very explicit instructions on operating the different aspects of these, well, I guess the proper name is satellites. All of us who are in the support role back here, and that will be we women, must become familiar with their operation. And now once again because of Judd, we can communicate to our field teams anywhere on this world. No more issues with only visuals, no more seeing something and panicking because we can't talk to the ones we are watching. And with this discovery we now know why there was nothing set up at the caves approaching this place for talking back and forth. As usual the solution was right in front of us, and we didn't see or know it. So study this packet and learn what is there. It could easily mean the difference between life and death to our field teams." She sat back down, and Saige stood up once again.

Leaning on the table and looking at each of them, it was coming down to the time of the beginning of this operation, and weather good or bad, would not, could not delay its start. "All of us are critical, very critical to the success of this, so let's make sure that the teams are as much protected as they can be, and with that, we are done here. This whole operation kicks off before the rise of the suns, even though with this storm we won't be able to see them, tomorrow. According to what this storm is doing will determine whether we leave the base camp or not, but the hope is that we can. Our people are suffering and we need to learn as much as we can, in the shortest amount of time."

* * *

"Why bring this up anyway?" K'jor asked. "If these travelers haven't been seen in many generations, why would you think that they would suddenly show now?" Looking hard at T'som, he could see that something was up, but knew that the priest would answer him in his own way and his own time. Sighing he asked, "You know something don't you?"

"Funny you should ask." T'som got up from the chair he had been sitting in, and headed over to the fire to warm his hands. Even with the roaring fire going this shelter was anything but warm. He turned and grabbed the chair he had been sitting in and dragged it closer to the fire. Shaking his head he said, "I'll never understand this, with a fire going like this one, that a shelter can be so cold." He sat back down and signaled for K'jor to do the same. "Look, I was out and about, checking in on the young ones, and the females who are responsible for them. After all for many of these young ones, this is their first season of cold, and you know that we do lose a few to the cold, and whatever weakness that seems to attack during this time. Did you know that we had a courier, a runner, stop here very briefly?"

"A runner, with the storm tearing through the grasslands like this? Why wasn't I informed, and at least have this one report to me? He is from the alliance, right?"

Smiling, T'som waved his hands, palms out saying, "Now one of the reasons I am here is to inform you that indeed we had a runner stop by. But since it was not an emergency or something that required it to be immediately brought to your attention, I told that gate guards that I will pass on the information to you. The runner did not even enter the compound, but was immediately away. As to why this couldn't wait until the storms were over I don't know. Because, you see, what he had to say would and could wait. So while, as I said earlier, that I have been researching our past in our writings, I did not know what to look for, at least until that runner showed up. He was announcing that the travelers had been seen at the base of the Sacred Mountains in a camp waiting out this storm. He was sure that they had to be the travelers as they were exactly as described, down to the pack beasts, and the bells to let all know that they were not enemies. So now after all this time they've returned."

"Don't you find it convenient that with everything that has been going on that they suddenly show up?"

Smiling T'som said, "No, not really. I suspect that any time that they would have shown up would bring questions. From what I could gather we are only looking at a very small group of travelers. It could be that they are here to be sure that they will be welcomed as they had been in the past. After all if we had become hostile to them, then the loss of just a small group in the overall scheme would be tolerable. I suspect that if they find that they will be welcomed that we will again begin to see more of the travelers. I don't even know if this first group will even look in on us. I surely hope so. I'm really curious as to why it ended, and now why they are back."

Smiling himself, but in K'jor's case it wasn't a pleasant smile. "Me too, I'm really curious as to why now? I guess once this storm leaves we can send out our own runner, and see if we can entice these travelers to come here. After all, as you've said, we can use their healing abilities. And I'm really curious as to the whys. You know – why they stopped, and why at this particular time they are back."

CHAPTER THIRTEEN

"Remember that now you must go by the name that you've been assigned, since our way of naming is so vastly different." He looked at the five who were in the camp with him before continuing. "Jed, you and Jarid will have to remain out of sight here, as well as the points where we disembark from the haulers. We have a lot of ground to cover and not enough of us to do it. So this is our first attempt at this, and we only plan on hitting about two groups of the primitives a piece. Then when that is accomplished, to return here and wait until both teams have returned, compare notes, and see if we need to modify anything we are doing." The winds were still howling and the tent that they were in at the base camp rocked dangerously in the winds, threatening to both lay flat on top of them and to fly away and join the winds. "Judd you will be responsible for Stone who we will know as L'sum, and Seve who is known as K'fah. Jarid you have me and I'm J'far, and Staven who is T'soh. From this point on that is who we are, and we cannot afford any slip ups, slips of the tongue, on any of this. We've been studying these primitives most of our lives, and now we get to see if what we've learned will pay off." Saige began pacing the tent. He had to admit that he was nervous as hell. All their work had always been from a distance, but now, like their distant ancestors, they were going to get up close and personal. And he hoped that they were ready. Their group was still too small to be able to afford any losses.

Looking outside, they could see that it was still quite dark, but in a short time the gray of dawn would be touching the horizon. It was hoped that the storm would abate today, or at least reduce in the intensity and fury that it was demonstrating right now. With the new equipment that Judd had provided, they felt that there was no way they could get lost, and one of the devices would lead them right back here. It was disguised as a heavy necklace, and the communications devices were placed in the ear, which transmitted back to the haulers, which had stronger equipment. The haulers then would relay the signal to the "eyes-in-the-skies", and then to the Alpha complex. Built into those necklaces were cameras so that both the visual and verbal could be recorded, and studied later. The clothing that they wore was actually modern materials, but appearing to be identical to the standard dress of the primitives. The advantage being that the modern materials would keep them both warm and cool no matter the variances in the temperatures. Because of this it gave the illusion that they, as the travelers, did not have issues or were affected by the weather.

In the bags that they carried were the almost microscopic bugs that they would leave behind to continue monitoring the primitives. They would last up to half an annual before running out of power, or breaking down and if in the sunlight would recharge. It was hoped that this would be enough, and by then they would no longer need them. But that was in the future, and the present was almost an unknown. On the pack animals in the many packs were their wares of bow strings, and knives, and the antibiotics that they would be using to help cure any that they were asked to see in the capacity of healers. Of course with the ability to communicate directly to Saar, it would greatly simplify their tasks. Here, again because of the differences between them and the primitives, they were depending on the formulas that their ancestors found successful. From what Saar said, there really was only a slight difference between what they themselves would use, and what appeared to work for the primitives. So it had been easy to get enough of the medicines made that both teams would have plenty, if in the end, all they did was play the role of healers, and not merchants. And while they appeared to be unarmed, other than one long knife that they carried sheathed and attached to the belt, there was a device that threw out in a circle radiating from them a shock field that would stun anyone, or any group that became hostile and tried to attack. They had to depend on the ones monitoring their progress to be informed of any of the primitives who might be either trailing them or setting up an ambush.

All of them had to smile, when they realized that it was this method that their ancestors had used, to foil many attempts by the primitives to learn more about the travelers. With the information and technology that they had available, their ancestors could see and hear a great distance from wherever they were and from the haulers could follow them and see vast areas around the ones actually doing the ground work. Yet from the reports that all of them had read, they knew both from personal observation and these reports, that even with the technology, it had been difficult to outwit the primitives. And that made perfect sense. After all they lived and fought most of their lives, surviving not only the environment, but the struggles with each other. It was a difficult existence, and it tended to winnow out the weak, leaving only the strong, and cunning to continue. "Ready Jarid, Ready T'soh", Saige, as J'far asked. Taking a deep breath while looking out, he could see the beginnings of gray in the east. It was time, and from this moment on they were travelers, not ones from the cities, not the ones from a different world. All they could hope is that all of the training, and preparation would be enough.

* * *

R'san, sitting in the shelter of K'jor stated, "Even I cannot remember such a severe season of cold, and I've lived through a few more than you." At this point he laughed. It wasn't like he could definitively say that there never had been any like this. After all he could only look back over his own life. And he knew that there could have been such a season of cold when he was young, but would have forgotten it over time.

Smiling K'jor looked at both R'san, and T'som, as the three of them sat close to the large fire. "I don't know about all of that, but T'som has pointed out that somewhere in those old words that there have been such seasons of cold in the past — although I don't know whether he's just saying that or whether it is actually true." It was a slight dig aimed at the head priest, since there were two warriors in the space, and only the one priest. But K'jor knew that T'som would take it as it was meant. K'jor knew that it took both of them to insure the security and wellbeing of the clan. And after all, T'som had gotten his shots in himself. There really was a strong friendship between the two, and this one-upmanship that both of them did was all in fun, and he had to admit that T'som got the best of him many times.

Smiling at the two of them, T'som replied, "Ganging up on me are you? And me just a lowly priest, how could you think that I would do such a thing? After all I have to face the gods every day, and I obviously cannot physically fight you, because you are both warriors. What chance would I have?" Not being able to hide it, he finally burst out laughing. "Sorry I couldn't carry it off this time. But back on the original subject here, it's really hard to determine if what I've read can be translated to what we are facing this season of cold. But a couple of the past priests actually took records of how deep that white stuff got, measuring it against a body. You know, to the ankles, to the knees, and so on. And it is the ones who did that that has showed me we've faced something similar in our past – although we are still early in this season. So, I don't know if, in the end, that this one will be the worst we've ever faced."

"I truly hope not." R'san stated, "Because with the increase, I do not know if what we have put away will be enough. The wood that we burn to both keep us warm and cook our food is being used at an alarming rate. And no, before you ask, we are not running short already. But if we get a few good days, I will be forming a few work parties to try and find additional supplies. Not to change the subject, but to change the subject, have either of you heard any more about the travelers?"

It was not a surprise question; it was something that had been on all of their minds. After the first report, no additional runners had stopped by to bring them up to date. But again, that was really not a surprise as the storm still raged, and gave no sign of breaking. And K'jor wasn't going to send a runner out in this weather to confirm what had been passed on to them. Both T'som and K'jor just shook their heads in the negative. "Being the leader of this clan, and of course the alliance, I would like to know if what we were told is true, but I'm still responsible enough that I'm not going to send anyone out in this storm to confirm the story. If they have returned, then they aren't going anywhere anyway. After all, if our old words are correct, then they are here to trade, and to offer their services, and again with the old words telling us where their base camp is located, we can send one to check when the weather or gods wants to cooperate." At that moment a particularly strong gust of wind struck the shelter, shaking it with a fury that said that it wanted to tear it down, and spread the shattered pieces across the lands. There was a deep roar in the wind, and while it was at its fury, the three inside were silent, listening to the wind, and hearing the creaking and groaning of the shelter as it withstood the onslaught. Shaking his head, K'jor asked, "Are you sure that somewhere along the way to now, that I haven't made our gods angry? I felt like the timing of that wind was such that they could have been giving us their opinion."

* * *

When the four of them exited the tent, and the two who would operate the haulers remained inside and out of sight, the winds hit them full force. It instantly took their breath away, and chilled them to the bone, even with the modern materials and insulation. Moving to the lee side of the tent to get out of the winds J'far yelled so that he could be heard, "Wow, this is nasty! We may have to wait until this thing breaks. At least by staying here and working on the routines that our ancestors established we can get more into these roles. And we know that the word is out that we are back. So maybe losing a day or two isn't going to change things too much. Let's walk the camp, check in on the animals, sorry, I meant beasts, look in on our supply shelter and get back to where it is warm. It's much too dangerous to be out in this for any length of time."

"I can't disagree with that at all!" L'sum replied. The other two just nodded their heads in agreement. It was obvious that they were cold and miserable, with their heads scrunched down, and their hands inside of the clothing. They quickly made the rounds to confirm that all was well, and returned to the warmth of the portable shelter.

"I really didn't expect it to be that cold out there. I don't know about the rest of you, but this appears to be colder than that winter we spent, ah, there I go again, season of cold we spent in that cave. Got to quit that! None of us can slip up on this, it would give us away. I know that with where we are supposed to be from, that there could be a little difference in words and accents, but it cannot be something that we would say, and not the primitives." Looking around at the two drivers he knew that they had a limited understanding of the primitive's language and of what had just been spoken. All of the field team was now using the language of the primitives. And while the two who would move them about had begun to pick up the language, they were a long way from being fluent. Seeing that, Saige as J'far, said, "Sorry about that, but we've got to stay within character, so most of the time we'll only be speaking the primitive tongue. While this time out will be a short one, keep practicing. It would be better if all of us could remain in character, and while you may never be located while we are out, we cannot guarantee that fully. The four of us will only be speaking it, and if you need to understand something we've been saying let us know. Again like when we came and rescued all of you, we cannot afford any mistakes, or any losses. So work hard on this. We're going to stay a little longer, it's dangerously cold out there, and if we end up dying from exposure, we would have failed. So now we wait once again."

* * *

It was another two days before the storm blew itself out, giving the drivers plenty of time to immerse themselves in the language of the primitives. The four who were to carry out the roles of the travelers, worked continually with them to sharpen and improve their understanding, and it had helped all of them. Before the sunrise on the third day they were heading out to their appointed locations, with a tentative plan to be back at the base camp in two days. There was some flexibility built into the schedule since there would be no way to know how the contacts were going to work out. And again, since they had never done any of this before, all they had to go on was what had been written by their ancestors. And Stone as L'sum, with Seve as K'fah returned on schedule, but as the second day waned and darkness approached and the other team hadn't reported in, they were becoming worried. Yet there was nothing from the Alpha that spoke of trouble. Not that they could go charging in and rescue them if they were in trouble. So they had to sit and wait, and count on the support team to do their job. And once they had started this operation, they had to continue it for the duration that they had set, before returning. "This is always a worry, when we run separate operations like this," L'sum said. "And with the variability that is always there, it changes things constantly." He was pacing the tent area out of sight of any of the primitives who may have been watching the camp. Once outside of the tent they had to immediately resume their roles of the peaceful travelers who appeared to have a strong confidence in their abilities, and had no fear or worry of the tribes and clans south of the sacred mountains.

K'fah, sitting cross legged and leaning forward just shook his head. "Look, we've been on similar operations, even though we never made contact with the primitives during those times. Heck, we didn't even know that it was something that our ancestors did routinely. And in our scouting and spying operations, very few stayed within the original times that had been set up. There was always something that came along and altered it, and I suspect that this is the same. So all this pacing that you're doing won't change a darn thing. So just relax, and if you can't do that, go out and check on the pack beasts and make sure they are okay. It's something we'd do anyway, and it would give you a chance to burn off some of that worry."

Shaking his head and waving him off L'sum said. "No, not now, maybe a little later, I think that I'm just a little too wound up right now to pull it off." Looking over at Jarid he could see that he, at least, understood a little of the conversation between the two. Taking a deep cleansing breath he asked. "So Jarid, first off have you really been able to follow our conversation, or should we be translating?"

"Most of it, although with the speed that the two of you are talking, I'm missing a lot simply because I have to translate each word, and try and then put it together. Then by the time I do that you both are somewhere else in what you're talking about. I kind of figured both from the way you are pacing this place that you are worried about the other team, and that Seve, excuse me, K'fah reminded you that the schedules are a loose affair, and with no alarm coming from the team responsible for monitoring us, then we really shouldn't be worrying either. Is that just about right?"

"Yeah. Not bad, guess you're getting it then. At least for us it turned out to be easy, since we made contact with those two tribes, both small, and only one had any of our people, and fortunately not many. I know that all of what we are doing will eventually allow most of the ones who survive their captivity a chance to return to us. But it is so frustrating to see them suffer like they are, and appear to be completely unconcerned, as if they are nothing. It really tears at the soul."

* * *

J'far and T'soh followed the runner as he led them back to the clan's location. "This is highly unusual; we have our own plans and direction, so I hope your clan realizes how much we are sacrificing by this change. There were no plans this time to go this deep into the grasslands and foothills. This first journey since the rediscovery of a way past the Sacred

Mountains, was to only confirm that first, we were still welcome, and second that as we last had been here, if trading was something that all of you here would still be interested in doing, Thirdly was to insure that the trails found would remain open throughout the season of cold, and thusly why we are here now."

The runner listened, shrugged and continued on his way. "I don't know of your plans, all I can do is as my leader asks. It is said that one of the skills that you and the rest of the travelers possess is of healing. And right now there is one of importance that is close to the spirit world that could use that skill. That is all I am allowed to say at this point. You will be meeting with both our leader, K'jor, and the head priest T'som. They've both had their healers taking care of the one who is close to the spirit world."

"And that is why, and the only reason that we agreed to come with you. By doing this we will have left the others who are at the camp worried, and if a certain period of time passes without our appearance, they will assume that we were attacked, and are no more. At this point we will leave the grasslands, head north and never return." Saige knew that he needed to keep the pressure on, to include this runner. Fortunately they were being monitored and all of this was being recorded. They had been heading for one of the tribes when the team that was monitoring him informed him that they were going to be approached shortly. It helped him feel a little safer than even back when they scouted the primitives. So with the pack beast, bells ringing with every step, they proceeded to follow the scout.

* * *

"Your runner informed us that you had need of our healing methods, and that one of your clan who is important is close to passing into the spirit world. Maybe it was fortuitous for us to have arrived here at this time. There has been much discussion, once a way was found around the Sacred Mountains, as to when we should attempt to make contact after all this time. Most thought that waiting until the beginning of the season of greening would be the best, but it was decided that if we were to be able to establish the old trade routes that the way through would need to be tested for use for all of the seasons – so only two small teams of travelers and healers were sent." J'far stopped and was silent waiting for a response from the three who were in the shelter other than him and T'soh.

Looking at the two travelers were K'jor, T'som, and R'san. All were standing and there was a feeling of tension in the air, of static, of fire barely contained. When Saige had entered the shelter he had leaned against the entrance frame and had placed a bug that would give the teams back at the facility the ability to monitor what went on in this leader's residence. With the two groups facing each other the silence dragged on and on. Finally K'jor said, "I am very curious as to why now?"

With a look that a parent would give a child who had done something wrong and had been caught J'far asked, "Why now, what? Have you brought us here under false needs, and have decided that we are common criminals and are to be interrogated? That the reason that we detoured and came here was to fulfill and answer some suspicion on your part? I'm afraid if that is all it is, then we will be leaving. There are other tribes and clans who are eager for our goods and services that we can provide. Apparently you and yours are not." He turned to leave with indignation showing in every step. "Come T'soh, we will be sure to place in the writings that this clan is not to be visited in the future by us."

They got almost to the flaps that led back outside and away when T'som spoke. "I'm sorry, about this, but you see we have been fighting a hidden enemy, and our leader is just very suspicious of events that just seem too good to be true, and I have to admit that your arrival in the grasslands does fill those thoughts."

Turning with a questioning look on his face J'far asked, "Hidden enemy, what hidden enemy? I know that in the many skirmishes that are common among all that one is hidden to either surprise or to protect. So why would this arrival bring such suspicion? After all fighting is the way it is."

Through all of this R'san had been silent, just observing. He could see that this J'far was made of the same stuff that K'jor was, and there was no give in either of them. Inwardly he shook his head. For once he was just going to continue to observe and watch the battle. He had to admit it was a strange place for him, since he was usually in the middle of these *discussions*, but sensed he needed to remain aloof as was the one who was with this J'far. At this point T'som continued speaking. "No, we did not get you here on false words. We have one who is very close to the spirit world and do want you to see if there is anything that you and, ah, T'soh can do to bring this one back."

"If this is true, where might we see this one who is so close to passing into the spirit world?"

"First, with the permission of our leader, let us sit a moment, and we can discuss this. With the two of you this close to being out of the shelter, I'd feel better to know that you are going to stay and hear us out."

Still with doubt showing in his posture, J'far turned, shrugged and said, "Why not. This will only cost us a little time, and in the end we can still leave."

"That is very true. Now please sit and hear us out." Turning towards K'jor, T'som swept his arms towards the beckoning roaring fire and all of them proceeded to the chairs that had been arranged close to the heat. Whispering to K'jor as they headed that way he said, "Look, you just about destroyed any chance of us being able to use whatever healing they can do. It's going to be tough enough to convince them to stay once they learn that the one we want them to look at is a female. So don't stir things up too much. This J'far seems to be one of little patience and does not deal with ones he considers fools. So let's not show him that we can be one of them."

Grunting a reply, K'jor remained quiet for the moment. At this point he still hadn't come to any conclusions about these travelers. And the one who seemed to be in charge had a strength that showed he had to be a leader. But if he was, why was he here? He was finding that he was ending up with more questions, and getting no answers from his original suspicions. So for now he would let T'som do the talking. What he said was very valid. By the way the need had been presented he was sure that these travelers would be of the impression that one of the important males would be the one who needed the care. While healers looked in on the females, they did not get the same care as the warriors, or the priests, for that matter. And with the way this J'far had reacted to his question, there was just as good of chance that once he learned that they wanted him to heal a female, he could still turn and leave, leaving them without a solution, and practically guaranteeing this female would pass into the spirit world. So for now he would allow his suspicions to wait and observe these two travelers and see what he could learn. Once they were seated, there was an uneasy silence as the travelers waited to hear what the clan truly wanted of them.

"Look, if our old words are correct, then part of what you do is trade, and the old words stated that your offerings were superior to what we could produce. Is this true?" T'som was watching J'far, but was surprised when T'soh responded.

"I'm the one in charge of our trading materials, and yes our old words spoke of the same thing. But much time has passed, so we, our clan, have no idea if this still holds true. If you will allow me, I will go to the samples that we have on our pack beast and bring inside what we are offering this time around." Without waiting, T'soh stood and headed out the doorway and was gone. The three of the clan looked at each other and then at J'far, who remained sitting, giving the appearance that this could be just another boring day, patiently waiting for an explanation of the needs that the runner had relayed to them, but letting them explain in their own way and time. *I've really got to be careful. I think that who we have here is probably the leader of not only this clan, but I suspect he easily could be the leader of this alliance. Still I have to put forth what I am as J'far, from a position of strength, and one that is not willing to give in to the simple demands of a clan. After all, we, as the travelers, are supposed to be neutral, favoring no one.* Watching the entrance expectantly, all in the shelter shifted in their chairs showing that they were uncomfortable with the situation as it now stood. There was a draft of cold air as T'soh re-entered the shelter carrying a small bag that was made of leather, headed for the area in the center of the circle of chairs, sat the bag down on the dirt floor, and proceeded to open it with a flourish.

"We've only brought a couple of items this trip, again because we have no idea of the needs. After all with the generations that have passed since we last traded much could have changed. But we do know one thing; there is always a need for bow strings and long knives. So I have here samples of what we can provide. After this foray we may know better what the needs truly are, and be able to provide other items." He reached into the bag and pulled out one long knife, and one bow string and looked at the one he figured was the leader, and the older one who he assumed was an advisor of some kind. To the leader he handed the bowstring and the advisor the long knife. "Please inspect these, and give me your honest opinion. If you like what I'm showing you then we can discuss amounts and costs. We have higher quality strings and knives, than what I am showing you presently. But as one should expect the value of the better items is much greater." At this point T'soh shut up, and let the two inspect the merchandise. He could see the surprised look on both as they realized that these items were indeed better than anything they presently used.

K'jor, looking at R'san said, "This string is very interesting; here let me look at that blade." At this point R'san and K'jor traded items, and again inspecting them minutely. Both looked up, and T'soh could see that first they been impressed, but now they were trying to make it appear that while these items may have been better, that they really weren't that much better. Smiling inwardly, T'soh thought. *Yup, here comes the attempt to make these appear to be less than what they are, so that they can try and talk us down. It's an old game, and one from our records, as well as observing these people, have been used for almost as long as there have been items to bargain for – time to drop the hammer, and surprise them.* "These two items are for you to use and test. We will not be bargaining on these this trip. After all they are untested in your eyes, and I cannot set a value on something that you've not tried. So when we return on our next trading journey you will then know whether or not you want more of these things, and like I said, we may have other items to present."

R'san and K'jor looked at each other and then at the travelers. So far even with his suspicions, these two travelers appeared to be no more than what they said they were. Maybe it was just coincidence that they showed up now. And their story to this point was consistent with what T'som suspected had happened. And they did not seem to be aware of what had been transpiring here in the grasslands. Still, he would hold judgment until such time as it could be proved one way or the other. "So you are going to leave this with us are you? If so why not give us another set, that way we have proof if both hold up under the work we would use them for."

Smiling at them T'soh said, "Trying to get something for nothing are we?" He paused for effect, tipped his head to the side and then continued. "Actually we always, in the beginning, give you two of each item, for that very reason. But do not ask for more as anything beyond this will cost you." He then handed them a second long knife and bowstring, closed the leather bag, got up and headed back outside to return the bag to the pack beast.

"So, now that you have examples of our goods, who is this one that you want us to look in on, this one who is close to the spirit world?" J'far asked.

K'jor remained silent and looked to T'som to be the spokesperson for this. He felt that the head priest would do a better job of putting into words in such a way as not to cause these travelers to just pack up and leave. T'som, seeing the look he received from K'jor, knew that it would be his responsibility to get these travelers to look at the female, and also explain why it was necessary.

Not sure how to begin, since the request would be an unusual one, as they rarely used to healers for treating the females. It was something that was the responsibility of the herd. And usually the breeding herd was larger than the warriors, and priests, so it was expected that there would be losses with the herd. It was that way with the wild beasts of the grasslands, and it was no different for them. T'som got up and put his back to the fire and said, "Now on a cold day like today this feels very good." He looked down at the floor before looking over at J'far. "This is an unusual request, and it is because the circumstance is so very different."

Intrigued J'far looked at T'som questioningly, "Please continue. There must be a reason for this, ah, long winded explanation. I personally would think that if this one you want me to see is as close to the spirit world as you have been saying, that you wouldn't want to delay."

"True and this one is so very close, but as I was saying, this request is unusual as it is a *female* that we want you to see."

"A female? Really! Why would that be so? Why would I waste my time on a female? Is your breeding herd so small that even a loss of one going to affect you in such a way that it will have a negative effect on your tribe's future?"

Shaking his head and shocked somewhat at the strength of the reaction from J'far on even the thought of treating a female was a surprise. But, in a way, he should have expected it. After all if R'san hadn't initiated it with this female when he first discovered the ugly wound, then she would have passed into the spirit world a long time ago. Then he required the healer to look in on her, which even for them was unusual. "No, our breeding herd is strong, and we have added many, and this particular one is almost past the time of breeding so that is not the issue."

"If she is almost past the time of breeding, why bother? It is the purpose of the female to bring forth offspring from the union of the warrior class, to make sure the clans and tribes have future warriors, to be sure that after the dropping that these new lives are taken care of, until they can join and become part of this world. So again why bother with this female? Everything you have told me says that she is past the time of her worth. So why not let her pass from the world of the living?"

Now what? Everything he has said is true, and normally that is exactly what would be allowed. But . . . oh, I don't know, somehow he has to understand the importance of trying to save this particular female. "Yes, yes, everything you've said is true. And normally we would allow just that to happen, since passing into the spirit world is just as much of what life is, as our arriving through the dropping. But you see we believe that this one may be a priest."

"A priest? A female in such a position is not something I have ever seen in any of my travels."

Taking a moment T'som approached K'jor and whispered, "How much can I tell him? After all his questions are valid, and I have a deep feeling that if we lie, especially to this one, that he will not have the patience to stay and see this female."

Shrugging, K'jor responded, "I don't have an issue. Just do it, but keep the alliance that we've created out of it. He just needs to know enough so that he will do as we want him to, and that's all."

Nodding he turned back to the fire and its warmth. We've discovered and conquered a hidden clan that lived in the desolation. They are strange, different in so many ways to any of the known tribes and clans. They do not speak the tongue of the people. They live where no one could live and survive, yet they do. We've determined that this place had to be a lair of magicians and sorcerers; after all there could be no other way for one to survive where they lived. As is the tradition, once a clan or tribe is destroyed, the females become part of the breeding stock of the clan or tribe that has destroyed their place."

Cocking his head, J'far, stated, "A hidden people, and ones who did not speak the tongue, this is unusual. Are you sure you are not trying to fool me? After all this could be just a story to pull one into a falsehood. But I would not expect something like that from you, T'som, and a head priest at that. So am I supposed to accept what you say, or am I just going to put it to fantasy?"

"Oh you can accept it as fact. We, other than the fact of where they were existing, wouldn't have thought it too strange, other than this other fact, and it simply stated, is that they appeared to have no warriors, and nothing to prevent their demise."

Laughing now J'far said, "Now I know you are passing on a fantasy. A clan with no warriors and no protection, come on, you really expect me to believe such a tale as this?"

Sighing before continuing T'som said, "Yes, yes I know it does sound like a tale, but it is not. The only thing that we can figure is that they depended on the desolation to protect them, and until the accidental discovery by K'jor, we can say that, that's exactly what had happened. Until they were found, no one knew that they even existed. If you do not believe then you may inspect some of our slaves and see for yourself."

"Okay, let me see if I have this right, you found a hidden clan, destroyed it, and added both slaves, and females to your breeding herd, is that just about right?"

Nodding T'som continued, "Yes, that is right up to that point. And if everything continued like it would have normally, then there would've been no worry. Now what I am about to tell you must be considered privileged knowledge, do I have your word that it will remain so?"

"So far anything you've said requires no such thing. I will reserve judgment as to whether what you pass on is worthy of such a request. After all we know very little about each other, so I cannot make promises in such a situation."

"Fair enough. I will let you judge then, and after you see this female you can then make the call. As expected, all the warriors bred with the new females expecting to see the carrying. There was some resistance initially, but when it was understood that there could be no refusal, there was no issue from then on. Yet, many passed from this world. They appeared to be much weaker than our own females, and the laws dealing with females were upheld. That is one of the reasons that this female we would have you visit is not with the herd, and is being cared for by two other females and our healers. Anyway, when none of these additions to the herd carried, it made no sense. After all, we were seeing our own carrying. So, within the law, the pressure was increased to bring these new females to carry, but to this time, none are. This has led to the belief that this clan is a magic one or that they were workers for our gods, but since we cannot speak their tongue we cannot get answers. The worry, obviously, is that we, as warriors, are being defeated by females . . . By females 'by our gods'! So if we are being defeated by these females how long can we remain strong? Their magic must be strong to be able to do this, and it makes us believe that they, yes these females could be warriors, but they fell so easily. And again, as I stated, it has not been from lack of trying to defeat their magic ways.

"This brings us back to the female who is close to the spirit world. She must be a priest, as not only does she speak the tongue of the clan we destroyed, but she speaks ours as well. She is probably the only one who can explain why we are failing as warriors. And to be defeated by females is unthinkable, and until it happened, unbelievable. So it is this reason that we must try and save this female. We feel it will be our only chance to learn what we need."

Hope rose in the heart of Saige as he heard these words. This meant that this woman had to have been a scout at one time. But he was at loss as to who it could be. He knew that there were no older women with them as they fled the city, and as they were whittled down through the numerous skirmishes and contacts with the primitives, he knew that they had left no one alive behind. So she could have been from one of the other fallen cities, who had, at one time, been a part of the scouting unit before it had been disbanded. Now he had to continue to play the role, and not seem too eager to see this mystery woman. "I have to admit that this story is very unusual, and" –, smiling deeply while shaking his head, J'far continued – "this could be a great and fantastic tale if someone else had spoken it. So, with this tall tale should I trust you, head priest, or should I place it where it needs to be, as a great tale?"

"Oh I guess if I was seeing this from your side, it would be almost impossible to believe. And we are the ones living this, and it is very difficult for us. So I've revealed most to you, and have left nothing of importance out. What say you? Are you willing to, at least, look in on this female?"

Taking a deep breath and shaking his head J'far looked as if he was trying to come to some decision. There was a deepening silence as T'som waited patiently for some type of response. Eventually J'far shrugged, looked directly at T'som, and said. "I guess that it wouldn't hurt for me to at least see this female. Once I do I can decide what I will do at that point."

Smiling and rubbing his hands together T'som responded, "Good! Would you like to go now?"

With a questioning look he asked, "Now? Hmmm, well, I guess, why not." Getting up and heading for the doorway he continued, "Lead the way. The sooner I can see and decide the better chance for the two of us to get back to our original destination."

* * *

He and T'soh were led through the camp into the priest's compound, and to a small building that was isolated from the rest. He assumed that this was isolated to prevent the spread of whatever it was that had made someone sick. Even though he knew that the primitives assigned disease and infection to the gods, evil spirits, or poison, they had learned that sometimes isolation would prevent someone else from getting what the sick person had. With no announcement T'som with the two healers from the clan entered the shelter and signaled for the two of them to follow. He knew that the women that were inside had no right to demand anything, but even still he had difficulty overcoming this courtesy, but knew that he had to act just as indifferent or give himself away. Once inside, they had to wait while their eyes adjusted to the semi gloom and slight haze from the smoky fire that warmed the place. The small room smelled of women and illness, and it was overpowering. Again he knew that these three were unable to bathe, to be able to deal with the normal hygiene that helped a woman. And that by itself could easily lead to infections.

When his eyes adjusted, the first thing he noticed was the fear and utter hopelessness that the two women projected as they cowered before them. His heart went out to them, but at this moment he could reveal nothing. It was probably one of the toughest things he faced in his entire life. He wanted to reach out and comfort them, but knew he had to stay aloof, and appear uncaring. After all, they were just females, and part of the breeding herd, and nothing more. Turning towards the corner he saw a sleeping mat and a woman apparently unconscious, covered, and looking very drawn and pale. Turning to T'som he asked, "Is this the one?" He then pointed to the one on the mat, even though he knew that answer had to be her.

Nodding, T'som appeared to be exasperated by the question. After all wasn't obvious? "Of course, of course it is. What did you think that it would be one of these others that are here?"

Smiling and shaking his head J'far stated, "Now don't start that with me. I can still just leave. As far as I know this whole story is still just that. And this female who is covered is just part of this whole charade to see if the stories about us are true. So I will confirm before I continue. And yes, I can see that this one appears to be in bad shape, but again since I'm not of this clan, nor do I live here, can I accept your story? For all I know, this one is a favorite and you are asking me to heal her just so you can have her back." And before you get angry, again look at it from my side, and you can see that there are many different answers to what I am seeing here, and any of them are quite different than the one you presented." While saying this he swung his arm out with the palms up, making his point.

T'som had to grudgingly agree to this one's conclusions. After all what did they know of their clan, or why this female was here, other than what they had been told. And again he was right, there really was no way for them to confirm anything that they had been told, and there easily could be many other reasons for this situation before them. But, what he had told him was the truth, yet he had to admit it would be easy to discount most of what he said. After all, there never had been anything in either the written or oral histories that spoke of this happening. A female defeating a male through the very basic level of breeding, it just did not happen. "Yes, she is the one, and you are so right, there could be many other explanations than the one I gave. But do you not think that if I was attempting to pass a tale by you that it would have been something more believable than what I said?"

"I guess I'll concede that. After all it is a fantastic tale. Okay, I will see what I can do. Uncover the female and let me inspect her body." The two healers then uncovered the woman who was lying on her side and faced towards the wall. When they uncovered her, first he could see that she was shaking with what appeared to be chills, and second the odor that permeated the area after the covers were removed spoke of old sweat, infection and uncleanness, and was quite overpowering. He bent down and turned her on her back, and she was quite naked and emaciated, barely more than skin and bones. He could see that with those chills that she was running a heavy fever, and that she was not far from death. He, not being a doctor, did not know if what he brought could save her or not. Then as he studied the face he was shocked as he realized who he was looking at. It was Sara, Shayne's sister. He had met her once a very long time in the past, and had been surprised how much they both looked like each other. They could have easily been fraternal twins, but there was an annual between them with Shayne being the older. No wonder she could speak the primitive tongue, she had been one of the scouts before leaving the team. Somehow he had to save her, he suspected that she may be the last of her family, but she looked so bad at this point he just didn't know if it would be possible.

He turned and faced the three primitives who were with T'som he said. "You are quite correct. This one is very close to the spirit world. First what she is lying on must be removed and replaced. It has become evil and must be burned. It is the same for what she is covered with. All must be new, and that needs to be completed as soon as it can be done." Looking back at her he could see that she was shaking, and it hurt him to see her so weak and ill. Looking at the healers he stated that they needed to find something to cover her now, otherwise she could pass as they spoke. Turning to T'som, he said, "I must pray to our gods, and see what can be done. I will try and save this one. But as I begin this I will need to be left alone. You or any of your clan can check in at any time that you feel the need. T'soh will be at the entrance so that you will know that I am inside at that time. If either he or I am not there, then we will not be here, but back at our camp. Now let's move on this!" He grabbed T'soh and they left, and headed back to their temporary camp.

T'som, observing all that the traveler had done, shrugged. He could almost see something in J'far's eyes that spoke of concern. *He really didn't do much other than a brief inspection of this female. Yet, hmmm, I just don't know. Guess we'll just have to wait and see if these travelers live up to their past reputation.* Okay, you heard what the traveler requested. Do it, and do it now! We will allow this one to work, but I expect both of you to check in regularly and be sure that these travelers are only doing what they are supposed to be."

At this point, both healers got to work removing the old sleeping mat and coverings. He had to admit that there was a strong bad odor emitting from the stuff. With the healers now doing as requested he left and returned to both K'jor and R'san who remained behind at the leader's shelter to bring them up to date as to what had transpired in this shelter.

* * *

"Look, I'm really worried. Neither Saige or Staven have returned yet . . . you're telling us not to worry?" Stone asked as he sat inside the tent with the others of his team. The other team was at least four days overdue, but there, as of yet, had been no alarm from the ones who were monitoring the teams from the Alpha. Jessi, and Seirra were on duty in the security office, and he knew that if there was a problem that it would surely have been in the voice of Saige's mate. But she appeared to be calm.

"You're about to have to go out again, Stone. We've been in contact with them and he and Staven both have confirmed that everything is okay. But, as it was to be expected, he's had to change the planned schedule, which means that most likely the other tribes he had plans to visit will have to wait. I've been told that to keep it brief, and to just let you know that they are okay." Seirra stopped briefly, and for what seemed like too long from Stone's perspective, she continued. "Believe me, if there was issues I would be a wreck right now. After all I'm close to bringing in another new life into our growing city, and I for one would want my mate to be here, and if not that, to know that he is okay. And from all that I can see in both the reports and watching as a guardian, they are fine at this moment. So do what you need to do and leave the worrying to us."

Stone had to admit that the final comment almost sounded like an admonishment to concentrate on what they needed to do, and he could understand that completely. This foray as travelers overall was going to be short. So instead of being distracted, he and Seve needed to do what they were supposed to do – knowing that the other team would be doing the same. *I just wish, well, I guess I'm just a worrier. After all when we were still in that cave before the Alpha was located, we thought we had lost both Saige and Shellian.* Shaking his head he could see his thoughts going in the same direction as they had back then. "Okay, Seirra, we'll do what we're supposed to, but it's so hard to remember that we are being closely monitored."

"You don't know how closely." There was a silence followed by Seirra laughing.

"And what do you mean by that?" Stone asked perplexed.

"Well, let's say as we get better with this equipment that we can even watch you go out and pee." Again she laughed before continuing, "I really never realized how good this stuff is. Our ancestors could produce some great stuff."

"You can actually watch us relieve ourselves? Now that could be embarrassing."

"Oh don't worry Stone, I said we could. That doesn't mean that we do."

"That's a relief, I guess. But I suspect that the temptation is still there."

"I guess so, but there's so much going on, why would we really be interested in such a thing anyway? With the six of you out of the complex there are just not enough hours in a day to get everything that needs to be done, done. And with me heading deep into my third, I'm anything but comfortable. This one inside of me is making it difficult to do anything."

This brought back to him that Sorrel was also pregnant. It was fascinating in some ways to know that soon he would be a father. But Sorrel's situation was so different than the rest, from being the first of the women to become pregnant, and the subsequently losing that child, to now being the last of the women to become pregnant. Of course the ones that they had recently rescued were not included in his thinking at this moment. Turning to the other two in the tent, he said, "I guess we will be heading out in the morning, and then if we can hold to the planned schedule, will return in two days."

* * *

As they headed to their encampment just outside the clan walls, Saige whispered to Staven and said, "I know that woman, but don't acknowledge me until we are back in our camp and it has been confirmed that we can't be overheard." It took a few more moments before they exited the permanent encampment and headed for their separate camp. Both remained silent, and both took their time to reach the tent and enter. Saige waited as he wanted a confirmation from the ones who were monitoring them, that it was all clear. In what seemed too long he finally was cleared. With the tent flap closed so that they couldn't be observed he faced Staven and said. "I'm almost completely positive that the woman who is close to death in that encampment is Sara, Shayne's sister. Somehow we've got to save her, but as you saw she is really in a very bad way. It looks like the infection has invaded most of her body and she's barely hanging on. We really need her to survive if for no other reason, than the fact that as a slave to these primitives she can keep us up updated. I don't know about you, but it got a little dicey in there as we butted heads with that leader."

"Yes, it did. I can't deny that at all. I thought there for a moment that you had pushed him too far, and when you got up to leave that first time I thought, okay how's this going to play out? But you guessed right. Sara, who'd of thought that. That means she's been here for a very long time", he looked down while shaking his head, "No, not a good thing at all. How'd she survive until now? Did you see those graves off to the one side when we entered this place? Way, way too many. I have a feeling that too many of them are our people. After all, living in the cities has gotten most of us soft, and unable to actually survive in the wilds. And yes, she looked like hell. I know with me standing by the entrance I didn't have the view you did, but what I saw was shocking enough. And the odor in that place was very overpowering. And when she was uncovered it became infinitely worse. You could smell the infection. Do you think that what we've brought is actually going to help?"

"I don't know, and we need to contact Saar, and see what he says. I planted a bug, actually a couple while we were in there. That way he can see her, and while he can't actually physically check her out, at least visually he should be able to give us some suggestions." He stopped a moment and with a faraway look he asked. "You guys get that? Get the doc or the nurse to contact us as soon as you can, make sure they see the recording so that one of them can give us a direction. And we need it now; I can't say how much longer Sara is going to live if we don't get her something very soon." Looking back at Staven Saige continued, "I can only hope that one of them has an answer. I know that we have everything that we brought, since we never made our first stop. And I think that this time out this will be our only one . . . what's that?" He could see that Staven had also gotten the warning. Someone was approaching their camp. Signaling Staven to sit on the opposite side of their small fire, he sat down on took on the pose of one praying to the gods for the answer to the saving the female, speaking words that a priest would have used.

"J'far, T'soh, I've been sent by T'som. He said that the sleeping mat and coverings have been replaced, and the ones removed are being burned as I speak to you. He wanted to know if there was anything else for he, or the healers to do." The runner remained outside of the closed portable shelter not wanting to disturb the travelers, and yet having been ordered to relay the message.

J'far paused in his prayers and addressed the runner saying, "You may relay back to your priest that he has interrupted our prayers to our gods, and that it may bid an ill wind for doing so. But I feel that the gods will understand, since what your priest has asked is from concern. If he has accomplished this, then this female must be kept warm. The changing of her sleeping mat and coverings will have strained her even further, and even this could be enough to push her into the spirit world. So go and tell T'som that we are praying to the gods to spare this female." Once he finished he could hear the runner leaving, and he waited until the sound of the steps disappeared into the distance, and once again the one monitoring them said that it was all clear. Before he could say anything he heard Saar's voice, and confirmed that he was now listening.

"Are you sure of who she is? Of course you are, I shouldn't have asked that. But from the recordings of her and the live feed that I'm getting now, I just don't know if we can save her or not. She's that bad. Actually worse than Sorrel, and you know how close Sorrel came to death. Look, most of what I sent with you is antibiotics, and enough to treat at least a dozen people. And it's a little stronger than the ones we'd normally use, since they are a little different than us. There's that one small bottle that is in with the rest, it's to be mixed with anything you would give our people. From what I can discern from here, you will need most of what you've brought with you to give her a fighting chance. And you will need to inject the first three over a day so that it goes directly into her system, and doesn't have to pass through the stomach. After that then the ones who are helping can get her to drink the concoction four times a day. So that means that you will have to remain there for at least another day to give her the injections, and then leave the instructions on the rest. I assume that you'll be leaving a complete package for her to use once and if she recovers."

"Yeah, that's the plan doc. It really bothers me to see the abuse our people are living through, and to turn a deaf shoulder and appear unconcerned is very difficult." Sighing deeply before continuing Saige said, "But, we must stay in our roles no matter what we are witnessing. We just are too few to be able to do much as of yet, and the surviving cities cannot do very much either."

It was silent for a moment, and then Saar answered, "I know, and it troubles me to see what's happening, and at the same time feeling so helpless at not being able to help. It makes me feel guilty that I can be here safe, and comfortable, with my family, and it is a family now, and yet see the suffering, see our people dying . . ." He kind of trailed off and didn't finish his thoughts. "I guess we can only do what we can and hope for the best. Bug the heck out of that place so that I can monitor her if you would please. So you now know the order in which to use the antibiotics, and let's pray it works."

"You're not going to get me to disagree with you doc. Okay then, we'll start the process right now, that way we can be out of here the same time tomorrow, and head back to our base camp."

CHAPTER FOURTEEN

It had now been a few days since the travelers had disappeared. And true to their word this first visit in generations was very short. Even though their base camp had been under constant observation by the alliance, it was as if their portable shelters, and all of the equipment that were visible was there one moment, and the within the blink of an eye, all of it was gone, as if it had never been there. Immediately on the discovery they ran to the camping area, and could find nothing. Nothing at all, no tracks, no signs of there ever having been anyone here let alone a base camp. No dropping from the beasts, no ashes or fire pit, not even a single track. It was like the earth had just swallowed them whole leaving no sign or proof that they had ever existed, let alone had been in this place – it was exactly as the stories said. While it was an oral history and in the case of the clans written, most believed that what had been spoken or written was myth. Just as they had thought the travelers were, but they were real, and now they knew that what they had thought was myth had just transpired before their very selves.

Little did the primitives know that it was advanced technology that had been responsible for this little bit of magic. Where the ones that they knew as travelers had been camping and working from wasn't where it appeared. Instead they were located in a hidden valley close by, and with both transmitters and receivers a 3D hologram of their camp had been projected from the actual location of their base camp to where the primitives believed it was located. And since they were not allowed anywhere close to the traveler's camp, the illusion would pass. It was another reason for the power being available in that cave at the base of the mountains. The receiving emitters were well hidden, and only the digging up of the surrounding hillsides would eventually expose them. But there would be no reason to do that, and their small size would, even then, make it nearly impossible to locate.

"I'd of liked to see their faces when we turned off the images." Saige said, as they made their way back up through the trails and tunnels to the Alpha. "I have to admit that our ancestors had set up a pretty elaborate system. I myself wouldn't know where even to begin to do something like this. It's very obvious that they had planned very well with the idea of protection for any who went into the field. I never realized how much we've lost over time, since we've only been sitting on our bottoms awaiting rescue, and not really trying to advance. I guess this undeclared war with the primitives has forced us to face the truth that we really have stagnated, and actually have regressed a bit from where we were when we were a science group. And that makes it all the worse because we were originally ones who supposedly were making the advances."

The other five that were with him as they headed back couldn't disagree. With Judd working the replicators, and he finding something new almost every day, they could deny it, but if they did, it would be as if they were putting their heads in the sand, ignoring the facts as each was presented. "Not to change the subject, but to change the subject, when the two of you *J'far, and T'soh,* didn't show back up our camp, you really had me worried. It reminded me of when you and Shellian didn't return on schedule back at the cave. It was hard to know that you were being monitored, and that everything was in control. I went so far as to contact the ones who were monitoring us, since nothing was being said, and I was told that everything was going well, although a change of plans had taken place. I more or less was told to do what I was supposed to be doing and to let them do their job, and of course they were right. But I couldn't stop worrying until they let me know." Stone paused, took a deep breath before continuing. "So you found more of our people at that clan's headquarters, and to find, of all people, Sara. That is a shock. I didn't know if any of our people had survived the fall of Sequoyah."

"Yeah, we found her, but she might be dead by now. She was so very close when we arrived. And even if she survives, there's nothing but hell in what is left of her life if we cannot come up with some way to end this now. Believe me; it was very difficult, almost impossible really, to put on the air of unconcern that permeates the primitive culture as far as their women are concerned. And while they are treated very poorly, our men fare no better, although their situation is still better than our women. I'm just happy that none of women can get pregnant by these, these primitives. With the appalling conditions, it's no wonder so many of the women die in childbirth. And infant mortality is very high also. If nothing else this trip into the camps have pushed me to a higher level of commitment to save our people."

"If it makes you feel any better, not that it should, the tribes that we visited were probably worse than where you went. There were some of our people with them, but none of them looked well, and I suspect that what was left was just a small remnant of what started out with these tribes. Our people are dying, and here we are. So I agree whole heartedly with you. We've got to end this." Seve looking around at the rest of the group could see the same feelings in their faces. What they had witnessed, and really what the people they had rescued who were from the city of Jade knew from personal experience, that they needed to find a solution, and it was something that couldn't wait.

* * *

Sara came out of the fog of a very deep sleep, close to unconsciousness really, slowly. She felt like she had been ran over by a stampede of, oh she didn't know what, but whatever it was she felt that there wasn't anything that didn't hurt. For the first time in well, she didn't know how long, she was coherent, and she was so weak that any movement made her shake. She felt warm and comfortable besides the pain she was experiencing. She looked around the space she was in and saw that the other two women were asleep. She took a deep breath and carefully turned on her side, and was asleep again. As she drifted off she had a few thoughts flit across her mind, but they seemed so unimportant at the moment, and then she was sleeping once more.

A few hours later she was once again awake, and found that she was very hungry, starving really. Glancing at her arms that were exposed from under the covering she could see that they were almost skin-and-bone. No wonder she was so weak. She could see that both of the women were now awake and were doing things around the area to tidy it up. Finally one noticed her and came over smiling. "You're finally awake. We've been really worried, so very worried. You almost died on us, so close that we thought that you had at least twice. Our captors were very worried about your condition, and they've been here continually. And I suspect that one of them will be here any time."

"How long?" Sara asked. "How long have I been here? I don't even remember coming to wherever this is?"

"Well, the trip to here almost killed you, so I'm not surprised that you don't remember, and it has been somewhere in the neighborhood of a month and a half, give or take a few, around forty five days that we've been here. Look we need to get some nourishment into you to help you recover. While you look really bad, there's definitely a change. This is the first time that you've been back to us in all of that time." Turning towards the other woman Barb' said, "Beth, bring something over so we can feed this starving woman."

Turning her head so she could watch Beth, Sara realized that she had a small pot that sat on a small open fire, and was ladling a broth of some kind in an earthen bowl. While she was watching this, Beth lifted her to a sitting position and propped her against the wall. At this point she realized that she was naked, and asked, "How long have I been this way?"

"Since you've been here," was the simple answer. "There was one point where your sleeping mat and coverings were removed, burned and replaced with new. And throughout that whole time you never moved or gave the appearance of knowing what was going on. I really thought that you were so very close to dying right then and there. And if those other two hadn't showed up, I think you would have."

"Other two? What other two?"

Barbara approached, and asked, "Do you want us to feed you, or are you strong enough to do it on your own?"

Lifting her arms she found that she was immediately shaking, and overall she could see that she had little strength to even do that much. Smiling, even though that was an effort she said. "I think that you had better do it. I just don't have it yet."

"I don't know who they were, since we don't know the language," Barbara said, "but it was obvious to us that they were unhappy with the conditions when they came in here to look in on you. There seemed to be a heated discussion, and immediately after that discussion all of your stuff was replaced. The one who seemed to be in charge had inspected you, I don't know how else to call it, and then gave some type of instructions to the ones we are used to seeing in here. Then for the next day the one returned and did something to you, and continued to look over your body. And from what I could see, it wasn't in the way these primitives do when they want to mate with you. It was more like a doctor would. Then they were gone. We then were given something that needed to be put in your broth, and given to you whenever it could. And I know that when you look at yourself; you know that it wasn't a lot. Yet whatever this one did, it seemed to start you on road back to us. But it's going to a while before you'll even be able to get off this sleeping mat."

Puzzled, Sara couldn't remember any of this. She must have been unconscious. She knew that she would have been removed from the mat, and to lie there in front of the world for all to see that way was something she would normally had not done. "Well, I guess I'm glad that I was oblivious to that impropriety."

"Yeah, we know," Beth said, "we were embarrassed for you. None of us like to expose our bodies that way. But there was nothing that could be done. At least through all of this none of these males have attempted to mate with any of us. I guess as long as we are here to help you all of us are safe from that problem until you heal."

Sara had to admit that the broth that she was eating tasted really good. But even for this short awakening she found that she was tiring rapidly. It was going to take a long time to get her strength back. She wondered idly who these two strangers were. It would have been nice if she had been conscious at that time so she could have understood what was going on, but she wasn't and she couldn't change that if she wanted. "I'm afraid that I'm on my way to falling back to sleep. I can't believe that just this little activity has wiped me out." She found that even saying that much had taken a lot of effort. So with help from Beth, she was lying back down on her mat and was almost instantly out.

* * *

"Saige! Shellian! Where are the two of you?" The voice over the PA system asked. Both of them rushed to the security office with Shellian reaching it just ahead of Saige and with both of the standing in the doorway Shellian asked, "What's going on?" Sam' was napping and was with the other children in the converted daycare center, which had been the classroom for the children of their ancestors.

Jessi turned and faced them and then said. "Look, I'm sorry if I sort of demanded that you get here, but both of you said that if there was any change in Sara, that you wanted to be informed immediately, and there has been."

Saige and Shellian looked at each other and then at Jessi, and Shellian asked, "Okay, so what has changed?"

Shaking her head Jessi said, "Oh, I'm sorry. It looks like she's going to get better. She just woke up for the first time that I can remember, and then with help sat up and ate a little, and is now back to sleep."

"That's very good news, Jessi, very good news indeed." Saige said. "Please keep us informed, and when you go off shift let the others know this, and let's continue to monitor her closely, and thank you very much for letting us know. And I guess what the doc gave us has saved her. That's really wonderful news. As bad as she was when I saw her I really didn't think there was anything short of being here in the medical section that would save her life. The images on the cameras really do not give justice to what she really looked like."

"Shell', your daughter just woke up, and I think that she's looking for a meal. Can you report back to the daycare?" Joci stated over the PA system.

Smiling, with a deep love in her eyes Shellian said to all of them there. "A mother's work is never done, and to have to be part of the leadership of this place too really does keep me quite busy." She then left and headed out to take care of her daughter's needs.

Smiling as his sister retreated Saige thought. *And it won't be long before Seirra and I are parents ourselves. She's due at any time now. But I won't have quite the responsibility that Shell' does since the feeding and such is something I will do, but I don't have the equipment to do it all the time. So it is easier for me to play the leader than Shell'. Yes I know that there will be breast milk set aside for me to feed our child, but most of it will fall to Seirra.* "See you later Shell' and you're right a mother's work is never done."

* * *

Another storm rolled in off the grasslands and K'jor once again could feel the cold clawing at the shelters. It was a time to sit by the warm roaring fire and refrain from going outside. There had been no updates on the female, and as close to the spirit world as she had been, he wasn't surprised. He suspected that if she passed he would be informed as soon as it became known. Right now they were about half way through the season of cold, and the brief meeting that he had with R'san left him wondering if they would have enough to get through this one. So far the storms and cold hadn't let up, and had remained the worst he could ever remember. Well, there was little he could do about it. Their time had been short when the alliance broke for the season of cold, and while they had packed much away, and with R'san working everyone here, there should have been plenty. Still none of them had planned for a season of cold like this one, so it was a great possibility that there would be shortages. Again only time would tell if that would be happening.

His mind drifted once again to that first discovery and when he turned that final corner in that wash. Before him were shelters just like the ones his clan or any for that matter, used. There were a few trees, and dead grasses all around. There was a still heavy silence, one that spoke of abandonment, but at the same time a sense of a deep vibration that could be more felt than heard. The area sloped slightly away from him towards the shelters. There was a soft warm breeze blowing raising a little dust into a spirit spiral. Was this where he would come after he passed to the spirit world? It was a valid question. Yet, something didn't feel right. *As if anything in the spirit world would feel right. Come on if I'm really here then nothing would be as I expect. Even this, these shelters would not be expected.* Taking a deep breath and with some trepidation, he approached the shelters and upon closer inspection appeared to be weathered, ancient and showing no signs that they had been occupied for a very long time. He could see that there was a small ravine that split the shelters, and again just past them he saw the portable shelters that the tribes used. *What is this place?*

He began to search one of the larger shelters, and found just like in his own, sleeping mats, and coverings. There was old abandoned clothing that when touched began to fall apart. *If this is a place of the spirits, why would they have need of clothing?* It was another valid question, and one for which again he had no answer. With no sign of life, he became less fearful, and began a thorough search and with each shelter he searched he became more and more puzzled. Everything that a clan home would need was here, except for the clan. It really looked like whoever had been here just left one day, and never took anything with them. If there had been an attack or the evil spirits had destroyed them, then there should be remains here, something. But there was nothing, but the silence and the ever warming breeze. He moved on through this encampment to the tribe shelters and found the very same puzzling answers. And why would there be both so close to each other? It was a rare thing in the grasslands for any two to be this close. One could not protect like this.

Then he noticed, more subconsciously, than consciously, that as he approached the tribe's shelters that the deep vibration had gotten stronger. *Now what is causing that?* Curious, he began to walk in a number of circles trying to judge where the vibrations got stronger, and where they started to wane. In the direction where it got stronger and in the distance he saw what appeared to be more trees and some type of brush between them forming what appeared to be a wall of vegetation. And as he walked towards this feature, the strength of the vibration increased to the point that he could almost hear it, but it seemed to be so low that it was just below what he could truly hear. Then as he pushed through the brush he found a solid wall that disappeared in the distance along this brush and tree line. He turned to the left and followed it until it ended against one of the hills, which could not be climbed. So he turned around and went in the other direction. And just past the point where he had entered and to the right the wall changed direction slightly as it headed for another hillside. He could see that like the other direction that this hill would make it impassible also. *Just what is this all about? Maybe, just maybe, the area beyond this wall is where the spirits actually reside. That this place where I am is a temporary location where we, once we become spirits, learn to adjust to this new way. Then when we are ready, a spirit or maybe one of our gods, admits us.*

He had to admit that it was one of the many conclusions, but if that were so, why no spirits now? He decided to continue down the wall even though he could see it turn back in the distance to meet that hillside. But not all of it was visible, and before returning he wanted to be able to say that he did all he could. As he continued, the wall turned inward to avoid an obstruction and just past this obstruction there was a closed entrance. He stood there and stared at it. It had to be an entrance or an exit, but it was blocked by something just as solid as the wall. No matter how he pushed or pried it did not move. Even his knife left no mark. Frustrated by being so close to maybe solving this mystery, he sat on the ground cross legged and stared at this obstruction trying to figure out its secret. While sitting there thinking, he realized that the deep vibration was stronger here. There just had to be a way beyond, but he was running out of time. He knew that he was to meet with the hunting party today, and today was leaving rapidly. It was time to leave, but he would remember, yes he would remember. Of course this would only matter if he could cross back into his own world.

* * *

"We've made about half way through the winter, and our time is short." Saige knew that he kept repeating this, but it was true. With each city that had been lost to the primitives their small population was shrinking. And the ones who had been captured and either turned into slaves, for the men, or to become part of the primitive's breeding herds for the women, the life had become a living hell. And with most not knowing the first thing about living, let alone surviving in the wilds, too many had died. He looked around the table and except for the few who were manning the security office, or watching the children everybody was here. "We're going to be having more of these as we brainstorm to both break this alliance, and to completely end these searches and attacks on our cities. We do not have any way, because of the distance between our cities, to be able to defend and support each other. We all know that when our ancestors set these cities up originally it was not supposed to be for the time that has passed, so defense wasn't something that they had even considered, other than hiding the cities in the most desolate places that they could, restrict travel, and just basically hide.

And when you look at it, this is something that has worked for a very long time. But if we want to be completely honest, what has happened to us eventually would have. One cannot remain hidden forever – although this facility has done a pretty good job of it. So good in fact that its location was unknown even to us. Oh it was always mentioned, but no one knew of its location. So, we still have a technological advantage over the primitives. But if you look at some of the history from our home world you will find that such a thing doesn't automatically guarantee anything. There are many examples of a primitive culture defeating one that was technologically ahead of them, and again we are seeing it play out once again right here. So to prevent becoming one of the defeated, we need to find a way to end this now. I know, as you, that the remaining cities are working hard on trying to strengthen their own defenses, and will be able to offer little to no help to us. The only advantage, if you want to call it that, is the fact that we no longer have cities to protect. In this I mean our own. Of course since we are all one people, our ultimate goal is to be sure that all are protected. But by not having to put forth our efforts and resources to protect an existing city, we can concentrate totally on how to stop this undeclared war.

"As all of you know, we have just returned from emulating our ancestors and the way they did their fieldwork. And I think that while it was a very dangerous thing to do, we needed information, and the 'eyes-in-the-sky' couldn't give it to us. I have to admit that with us now knowing what these things are capable of; we have vastly improved our surveillance, and understanding. But to really get what we need meant that we had to actually enter their camps, listen, and converse. And again, thanks to our ancestors, what they had left us was the very solution to be able to accomplish that. The fears, of course, were; would the primitives remember these travelers, and accept them now after all this time. Apparently, and again thank you ancestors, the answer is yes. Every place that we stopped welcomed us. Although where Staven and I went, the leader wasn't just going to accept our story. This one, this K'jor is highly intelligent, and while it was never directly mentioned, I suspect that not only is he the leader of that clan, but there's a good chance that he's also the leader of alliance. Throughout our time with his clan, he remained highly suspicious of us. Yet, again thanks to our ancestors, we knew how to defeat those suspicions, and while he still never fully accepted us, he allowed the two of us to look in on this female who as they stated it, was close to the spirit world. All of you know that the woman in question is Sara, one from our own city. First off let me say it was a shock to find one of our own. Again as you know, she was very close to death. Whatever the infection was it had almost claimed her. Thanks to Saar and the antibiotics that he sent with us, she is now recovering."

He could see the smiles on the faces that this news brought to all of them. He let everything that he had spoken to this point soak in before continuing. He took a sip of water, leaned on the table and continued. "Once she has recovered enough, we hope to use the two-way that we planted in the shelter to learn more. I would guess that she will be safe from any additional abuse until sometime in the spring. It's going to take that long for her to recover, which means that the other two will be safe also. Before you, in the papers that have been handed out, are the translations of the conversations, which were recorded, we had with the primitives that we interacted with. Simply stated, all of us must read this material, and again thanks to these satellites for allowing us to record absolutely everything, so that what you have is accurate. From this and what the videos show us we must come up with a strategy, and put it into effect before the end of winter, or as soon as we can. As you all know, the beginning of spring is a time that the primitives replenish diminished supplies, and until they have, they will not meet back at what we guess is the alliance gathering grounds in that hidden valley. With so few of us we have way too much work ahead of us, but the rest of our people are counting on us to stop this before we are no more than a memory. We truly do not know what has transpired on our home world, and for all we know, we could easily be the last of our kind. So we must, and I must emphasize that word, we've got to end these incursions now. We will be meeting again after the morning meal tomorrow. We won't be discussing any of this here at this meeting today. So take this, read it, study it, put down notes and ideas, we need anything and everything you can come up with. I know that what I've said here this morning places a heavy burden on all of us, but try and have a great day, and let those thoughts and ideas flow. And with that the meeting is done for now. Don't hesitate to ask questions of each other, discuss this, and in the morning let's find the answers, thank you." With that final comment Saige dismissed the assembly and stood and watched as a very silent group left the meeting area. Inwardly he shook his head. He knew what was in those papers, and at this moment he had no answers or solutions to the many unknowns and questions that lay before them. But a solution had to be found.

Everything that was in the paperwork that was disseminated among the people here at the Alpha had also been sent to the surviving cities, with hope that someone somewhere would be able to give them at least some suggestions. Once Sara became well enough to be able to help, albeit quietly and in the background, it would provide more data, and at least some relief for their women, when they learn that they cannot become pregnant under the continual assault of the primitives and their attempt to make it so. Once the meeting area had cleared, he stood and stared out the windows into the small hidden valley where the Alpha lay hidden. Snow lay on the ground and added a white frosting to the evergreens painting a scene of peace, something that was so far from the truth. Sighing and shaking his head, he grabbed the other stacks of paper to disseminate to the ones who were unable to actually attend. Of course they could and did watch it on the monitors that were located in all of the work areas. He felt older than the annuals said, but the weight of leadership, even shared, seemed to age anyone who took the job seriously. Just what were they going to do? With only eighteen members here at the Alpha they were supposed to bring down the whole alliance. This brought out a laugh, but not of humor as much as disbelief. So few, but their people, all of the remaining cities, were depending on what they did here. Could they, would they come up with a solution in time, or would each city fall one at a time until they were no more?

When their ancestors had originally set up the cities it had never been from the idea of defense and support. The planned defense was the isolation and the hiding of the cities in the desolation where the primitives would not go. After all there was no reason. Again originally they had expected to be rescued in short order, and so the type of defenses that they now needed were never considered, and until the discovery of the cities by the primitives, never an issue. Looking through the large databases at the Alpha showed just how much they had lost or forgotten over time. And with little to no travel between the cities, again to reduce the chance of being discovered, this had isolated them even further. In some ways Saige was surprised that the communications circuits had remained, but now was quite thankful that they had. In many ways it was funny how life was. Here in the midst of loss, destruction, and death, life continued to flourish. By not including the eight that they had recently rescued, their small group of ten had increased by three with two more to be added in the near future. Shaking his head all he could say was that life went on no matter what was happening.

* * *

T'som entered K'jor's shelter and said, "It looks like whatever those two travelers did saved the life of the female. It looks like she's turned for the better, but she is so weak that it's going to take a very long time before she's able to do anything more than eat and sleep."

Shaking his head K'jor said, "They continue to bother me. I can't get it out of my mind that there's more to them than what we saw. I still feel that there's just too much coincidence with the timing of their arrival."

"Well, you'll not have to worry anymore about them. They have returned to where they came from."

"Really? Did any attempt to follow them back?"

Shaking his head in answering T'som continued, "Yes, and no. Yes in the fact that we, the alliance, were watching their camp, with the idea that once the camp was broken that they would be trailed from a safe distance. And no because the winds picked up a large cloud of what was called dust, and when it cleared the camp was gone."

"Gone? Do you mean that they packed up that quickly and then left?"

"It's an unknown. Before the dust cloud they were there, and after they were just gone. The ones who were watching went to the camp location and searched it completely. They found nothing."

"Nothing? What do you mean nothing? There had to be something – ashes from the fire, pack beast droppings, tracks, marks where the portable shelters were located, anything."

"I agree with you, but the word is there was nothing. It was like they never were there at all. But we know that not to be true as our scouts witnessed their location and watched from a safe distance. No, it's like they never were."

Taking a deep breath, and sighing K'jor stated. "I've got to go and see this. It is not possible to disappear that way. There is always something left – always."

"Normally I would agree with you, but these who watched were not ones who were out on their first scout or their first raid, they were some of the most experienced. After all from what we know of the travelers it would have to be that way. But in the end these travelers just disappeared, and left nothing behind to say that they were ever here. Yet you have the long knife and the bow string as proof. If you did not have these, and the healing of the female, I would say that all would have been a dream, wishful thinking, but we have the hard evidence right here. And once this storm breaks, even though the distance is great, I say go ahead and check it out yourself. But by then this storm would have wiped out anything the scouts would have missed anyway. So in my opinion it would be a waste of time, and you know it."

He had to admit that what the priest just stated was fact. With another storm raging with the high winds, and blowing snow, anything that could have still been at the camp site would have been wiped out, and it would prove useless and a waste resources that they didn't have. So grudgingly he would have to accept what was being passed on to him. Sighing he said, "You're right, it would be a waste of my time. But nobody just disappears like that. And while what you've said is true, even the best can overlook something, make mistakes, or miss the obvious when they expect it to be different."

"I cannot deny anything that you've said, but there were more than one who were observing the travelers camp, and they were spread out and while it was close to dusk at the time of the large dust cloud or maybe blowing snow, it hadn't been the first one, so there was no reason to suspect that this one would be any different. It was a shock when the air finally cleared and the camp was gone."

* * *

Sara awoke once again and this time didn't quite feel like she had fallen off a cliff and lived to regret it. She found that she was lying on her side facing the wall. As usual the one room shelter that she and the other two women were in was bathed in shadows and gloom. With the only light coming from the fire, and then some light from the outside coming through the many cracks and crevices that allowed the winds into their space. As her eyes focused she could tell that it had to be daytime, and that another storm was raging, as bits of snow would pass through these openings in the walls periodically, and she could feel the breezes slightly at those times. While their situation was hopeless she felt thankful to be alive, well, at least she thought so at the moment. She really couldn't recall much of her time when she had been close to death. She was sure that it was locked somewhere in her mind, but thankfully at this moment in time she was blank.

She really wasn't looking at anything, being in that twilight where one is neither awake nor asleep – a point where one is deciding if they want to awake or just go back to sleep. Suddenly at her eye level she saw something that piqued her interest, but it had to be an illusion, just the way the light played with the eyes. She closed her eyes for a few moments and opened them again expecting it to be gone, but it wasn't. *How'd it get there?* Was the question that flashed through her mind. She slid closer to the wall and was expecting it to disappear knowing that the mind could create images from nothing but random lines and curves. But it did not. She took a deep breath, and let it out slowly, then reached out with her hand and traced it with her fingers. And hope flashed briefly in her soul. *It's real, it really is real.* But before she could do more than confirm what she had found, she drifted off once more into a deep healing sleep.

A few hours later she awoke once again, and for the first time that she could remember needed to go. She looked across the small room and saw that Beth and Barbara were awake and seemed to be talking quietly. She tried to grab their attention, but they, at the moment, were not looking in her direction. She cleared her throat to try and speak and found that her voice cracked as she tried. Seeing Beth face her she could see that it was a surprise to Beth to see that she was moving. Beth arose and came over to her and asked. "What do you need dear one?"

"I need to relieve myself; can the two of you help?"

"Oh my yes," turning back to Barbara, Beth could see that she was joining them. They helped her over to the opposite corner where a pot had been set up for that purpose. Once out from under the coverings she felt very cold. The two women placed some clothing on her and she found that she was shaking. *Isn't this ever going to end?* It took all of her strength to perform what she needed to do and to get back into bed, with the image she had seen earlier temporarily forgotten. They propped her up once again and she had some additional broth. With the warmth hitting her belly she could almost feel it go throughout her body. She found that this time she could eat more, but once again she found that as she finished what she could she was drifting off to sleep, and could do nothing to prevent it. She knew that she had a long way to go for her to heal, and that the time of being awake would slowly increase, but for now when she slept her body was repairing itself.

* * *

It had been Saige's shift when he had been going through the many feeds that had been added with their visits to the tribes and clans as the travelers, that he saw Sara stare at the wall, and hope sprung up inside of him. He had placed that symbol where only she would find it, and it was something that would be ignored by the primitives, but known to any who had been part of the scouting unit. To any who were outside of the unit, it would appear to be no more than a series of lines and curves, which easily could be just a random jumble of nothing. But when looked at it in the right way would appear to be one of the birds of prey that this world held. It was chosen as their symbol long before any of them had become members, and all were required to memorize its vague shape. They used it to mark areas when in the field. The bird had been chosen for its ability to see great distances and to be able to locate its prey with this method. The birds could ride the thermals all day, barely moving and would study the surrounding lands for its next meal. The scouting unit had been told that while they were not looking for prey, they needed to emulate what these birds could accomplish with their abilities, and to be able to scout out their intended tribes and clans and to remain invisible and yet gather the intelligence that they needed. Smiling as he saw the recording of Sara finding the sign, watching as she traced the image with her fingers, he knew that soon she would be healthy enough for them to be able to move onto the next phase.

It wouldn't be long until his shift would be over, and then it would be time to eat, followed by their next meeting. He hoped that soon this would be ending for all of them. But for now he had a shift to finish, and the circuits never were quiet, and he was glad that on this shift he had the monitoring shift and not the communications shift that Jed was presently stuck with. But next time around it would be his turn. After all no matter what the rank or position everybody shared in all of the duties. Later as more were to become part of the Alpha that would change, but for now with there being so few, all shared.

With his shift ending, Saige headed to the cafeteria to grab a quick meal before meeting with his mate Seirra at the infirmary. She was in her last third of her pregnancy and had suddenly gotten bigger than they had expected. So today Saar, with the help of Jas would be giving her and her unborn child a checkup, and he had been told that it was important that he be there. He knew that Seirra would probably arrive there just ahead of him. But with his shift ending when it did, there really was little he could do about it. Looking up, he saw Stone and Sorrel come into the cafeteria, both laughing at some inside joke between them. He couldn't remember the last time that the two of them were down at all. While it never had been planned that the two of them become a couple, it was obvious to any that they thrived together. And to see the growing stomach on her brought a smile. It really had been such a worry to her that she could never again become pregnant after the loss of her first child. And that incident now seemed to have been a life time ago. "You two look great this morning."

Smiling at him with that smile of devilment that Sorrel had, the one that could drive a man crazy, she just nodded her head. Stone, smiling himself said, "Yes, you could say that. Understand that you and Seirra have an appointment with the doc this morning. Is there a problem?"

"No, not that I know of – but, Seirra has gotten bigger than the doc thought, so he wanted to make sure everything's okay. In fact I'm just about to head over there now, once I finish this coffee. See you at the meeting later. We'll pass on anything we learn, of course. Besides I know how it works. If we tried to keep the results a secret everyone would know anyway."

Smiling, Sorrel replied, "Funny thing about that. Even with the size of this place and the very few people that are here, everyone seems to know. What is it about that?"

Shaking his head and thinking, *yes, what is it about that anyway?* "I guess it's the way things have always been." Shrugging before continuing, Saige said, "When Shellian and I were working as a team back in the compound, it appeared that she knew things ahead of the release to all of us. I just chalked it up to her ability. But I've learned that it was just something I was unaware of. Oh well, like to continue our conversation, but I'm already late. Catch both of you later."

He got up, placed his dishes in the recycler, and headed out the double doors, and down the hallway to the infirmary, entered the doorway, and then into the examination area. He could see Seirra lying on one of the exam tables with the curtain pulled partially back to protect her privacy. He could see two pairs of legs under the curtains and knew that both the doc and nurse were in the middle of their exam.

Seirra was watching and listening to them, so did not see Saige enter. Whatever the conversation, it had her full attention. He waited and watched from a distance, not wanting to interrupt. When it appeared that whatever they had been discussing ended he moved and tried to get her attention, but was frustrated as she wasn't looking his way. So he moved up to the curtain, and said. "Good morning, my lovely lady!"

"Saige!" She said as she saw him. She beckoned him over to join her.

He could see that she was covered in a sheet as he entered the space, and saw that Saar was on one side of the table with Jas on the other. Jas, looking over at Saar asked. "Do you want to tell them, or should I?"

Seirra and Saige looked at each other and then at the nurse and doctor, and Seirra asked with a slight alarm in her voice. "Tell us what? Is there a problem?"

Saar, laughing lightly said, "No, not a problem really." He turned back to Jas and said, "Go ahead, you can tell them."

"Saige, why don't you grab that chair, and sit beside your mate," She pointed to one that was just outside of the curtained area, which he grabbed, and set it next to Seirra. Once she saw that Saige was now seated she continued. "With this increase in the size of you, Seirra, it made us, well me more than Saar, since I've worked gynecology in my past, but

I suspected that either you were going to have a large baby, or maybe twins."

Saige and Seirra looked at each other and then back at Jas, and together asked, "Twins?"

Again smiling at the two of them she just affirmed it by nodding her head. "It's the reason that we wanted you, Seirra, to come in. Your sudden growth prompted me to think it could be, and now we've confirmed it. You, Seirra, are going to have twins. With the equipment that we have here, we've been able to confirm that you will have fraternal, and not identical twins, since the sex of yours are one of each. You're going to have a boy and a girl. So, this will complicate the delivery somewhat, but I suspect it will also complicate your lives also. Not to say that with everything that is going on that it isn't already."

Stunned, they looked at each other and then back at her. "And you're sure about this?" Saige asked.

"As sure as anybody can be," she smiled encouragingly, "So I think the two of you need to add another baby bed to your apartment and be prepared for what this is going to add in your lives."

Saar then broke in and said. "Here, listen to this, and I think it will prove it to the two of you." He turned on a monitor and they could definitely hear two hearts beating, confirming that indeed she was carrying twins. "Now, I don't know about you, but that is just about as close to proving it, as it is to be actually holding them in your arms."

* * *

"I'm sure, since the rumor mill is much faster than the official channels, that most of you already know that Seirra is carrying twins. It has been a shock to both of us. And until they explained that there could be two kinds of twins I thought there was only one. But with the ultrasound they showed us the unborn children. And one is definitely a boy, and one a girl, so now I know the difference." Looking over at Seirra with deep affection Saige continued. "While, from what I've observed from the members who have added children to their families, adding one seems to make things much more difficult, so I guess adding two will even complicate things more. But, while this is so, and I'm sure that we'll instantly fall in love with these new lives, Seirra and I, we still must find the answers to our problem dealing with the primitives. So after the births of our children, as with the other women, Seirra will be relieved of any duty until the doc says she can return. I know that during this early time, I'll be distracted, tired, and even be impatient, but that doesn't mean that we don't want to see our goals accomplished. At those times when I or Shell' cannot be here, either Stone, or Saar will take over the leadership, just like it was back in the cave where we spent our first winter. Now with that out of the way, let's get to what we are here for."

He glanced briefly at Seirra, and could almost see an end to a shy smile on her face. Inwardly he found that he loved her more with what had been announced. He wanted to reach out, wanted to protect her, and somehow wanted to be able to eliminate the pain that was in her future, but knew that it was something that women had been facing since the beginning of time. Yet, even with that knowledge, he really wished there was a way for her to avoid it. At least here at the Alpha they had the modern medicines to help minimize it. And, again thanks to modern medicine, there was a greater chance that both the mother and babies would survive the birthing. While in the world of the primitives both the infant and mother dying during child birth was very common.

Looking around the table now and making sure all were ready; he followed this up by glancing up at the monitors and confirmed that the ones who were on duty in the security office, and in the daycare areas were also listening. "All of us have had a chance to review both the images and the translations of what transpired while we were in the roles of the travelers. Now we need to know how we can take this information and make it work for us. So with that, do any of you have any impressions, ideas, direction we should go, or even anything that would allow us to end these attacks?" At first all he got was silence, and the ones attending the meeting looking at each other and at him. He knew that he hadn't come up with anything as of yet, but again had to admit that with the worry he had been harboring for his mate it did not surprise him.

"I don't know what to say," Judd responded, "I mean, well, at least for me this is the first time I've been up close and personal, even though I know it's just the recorded images and conversations that the four of you had when you were the travelers, and then the additional images and such with the devices that all of you planted, so it is taking me some time to just absorb the differences. So, until I understand their way, their thinking, just the way they live, it will be very difficult to come up with anything at all – at least for me."

Saige could see from at the least the members they had rescued from the tribes, the ones from the city of Jade, that there seemed to be a consensus. In a way it surprised him since they had been captives. But when he thought about it, it made sense. They were just trying to survive, trying to adjust, trying to come to terms with the unthinkable, and not try and learn about their captors. Taking a deep breath Saige said, "I guess I can understand that. I've found that even though we were watching the primitives, trying to learn anything we could when we were part of the scouting unit, I have to admit that until finding this place and reading the research notes left by our ancestors, we were a long way from understanding them ourselves." He stopped and looked over the entire group before continuing. Then he looked at the ones who had survived the flight from Sequoyah and could see that while they knew more at this moment they had no solutions either. "Look, I know how difficult this is. We're dealing with a culture very foreign to anything we know. I have to admit spending even that brief time in their camps was very eye opening. I probably learned more about them from our brief encounters then all the time we've scouted them in the past. Their society is much more complicated than I ever imagined, and as all of you know, and I keep repeating this, our time is short, so please, please concentrate on coming up with something to get us going in a direction that could lead to ending this. I guess that's all I have, so let's get to it."

Once again Joci had been stuck with daycare. But she didn't mind. She loved dealing with the young children. And she had to admit that her experience in other areas was next to none. Heck, at the time the city fell she hadn't decided what she was going to do with her life, or even the direction of her education. And truthfully she had very little confidence in what she could or couldn't do. Then the city fell and she, like the other women found themselves raped, treated poorly, and then having to submit to the sexual favors of the primitives. It was something that had torn her both physically and mentally, shaking her confidence even more, if that was even possible. She, like the rest, had watched the vids, and read the translations, and an inkling of an idea was forming, but would she be willing to submit it?

After her rescue, everybody had been kind, and absolutely all of them supported each other. Yet, even now her personal self-confidence was shattered. So she listened more than spoke, and still was more subservient, willing to defer to the older, wiser members, or the more outspoken ones. After all, to have come from their peaceful society, and have it destroyed as it was, and then to be treated as all them were, and to be at a point in one's life to where she hadn't really done anything, helped create what she was presently. Being the youngest adult didn't help either, so working with the young ones was for her very comforting. After all their demands were simple, and watching the antics during their time of play could, for a short time, take her away from her personal hell, and bring a smile. She so looked forward to those moments when, even for a brief time, she would forget. And knowing that there were many more sisters still in captivity, still having to live under that abuse, under that terror of not knowing, with no hope, probably would be the very thing that would make her brave enough to at least present it to someone, but no, never in one of those meetings. She'd be so embarrassed, and felt that the pressure would be just too great. But who would be the right one, which of the many who were here could she confide in? After all, that was the dilemma wasn't it?

CHAPTER FIFTEEN

K'jor stared outside as he stood in the entrance to his shelter. The storm had ended, but the suns held no heat, with the breeze that was blowing briskly, cutting one to pieces if touched by it. He needed to get out, get away from the enclosed feeling that the shelter brought him. Shaking his head he could only stare, not truly wanting to face that wind. It was cold enough right here where the winds would only touch him now and then. Looking around the compound there was absolutely no movement. He suspected that any who may have ventured out because of the promise that the suns gave, changed their minds very quickly and headed back in. He knew that he'd be doing the same thing shortly. Going back to the warmth of the roaring fire, he knew that his supply of firewood would have to be replenished. Sighing, and shrugging he turned and went back inside. Maybe later it would warm a little, and it would be a better time to venture out. Sitting once again in his chair his mind drifted back once again to the beginnings of all of this.

K'jor worked his way back to the point where he had fallen through the veil and could see the ashes of his cold fire pit. Standing around it were the others he was to meet. It had surprised him that so much time had passed. But it must have since the proof was right there in front of him. Knowing that they couldn't see him, he first smiled, and then called out to them. He saw them jump in surprise, and S'lon asked. "K'jor, is that you? Are you now a spirit? Has this land claimed you also?"

So he *was* invisible to them, but as far as he knew he had not passed into the spirit world. Nothing felt different, and even though when he had fallen . . . fallen, maybe that was the answer. Could it be that when he had fallen that he had passed into the spirit world? After all, when one normally did that, they did not come back and report what it was like. It could be that it was just like being alive. But, that didn't make sense to him. He hadn't eaten in a while and his body was beginning to complain. He had taken a couple of nature calls, so he had to be alive. "No S'lon, I'm quite alive and well." Because of the shock and unconsciousness when he had fallen through to where he presently was, he really wasn't sure if he wanted to try it again. But there was nothing to hold him here so gathering the courage he stepped towards the fire expecting to be laid out like he had been, but instead it was an easy passage, and he was before them. The four that had been looking for him jumped when he appeared out of a solid hillside. In fact he could see a little fear in their eyes.

"Is that really you, K'jor?" S'lon's voice quivered a little. "Or are you some spirit here to fool us into believing that you are and are planning to lead us to our deaths, to our passing into the spirit realm?"

Looking over himself, he could see nothing that would make his warriors think this, so he shrugged before speaking. "No, as far as I know I'm exactly as I appear before you."

"If that's so, have you now joined the priests and can touch beyond the veil? Because I, we have never seen anybody just appear out of a solid hillside, or in the air as you just did."

"Well, L'sum, it is me." He trailed off partially distracted. Why was it so easy to pass back to the campsite, while going the other way had knocked him out? Then he remembered what had started this whole investigation and wondered if beyond that wall lay the answers. He thought that the male and female that his warriors had killed here might be from beyond that wall. But why would they have been out where they were found? He was finding that he was developing more questions than answering them. Yet, if these two were out here, then they probably had a way to pass back through this veil and not be harmed.

S'lon could see that K'jor was deep in thought and signaled the rest not to speak, letting K'jor think through whatever it was. He saw him look at him with a smile and so S'lon asked, "What have you figured out?"

"Look, I'll tell you on the way back to camp. We need to mark a trail so that we can get back here, and the trail must be easily followed. I found that out here it, even for one as experienced as we, is easy to get turned around. We need to come back to this exact place. Let's go, and all of you remember this place well."

So, as he requested, they marked a trail well, one that would remain through the changing times. They had need of returning to the hunting, to the preparing of the meat and hides; the cold season was almost upon them.

* * *

Sara found that she finally was able to stay awake longer than just a few minutes, and that she wasn't shaking every time she tried to do anything. She knew that finally she was on the road to recovery, but as close to death, and for the length of time of her illness, her body would take a long time to completely heal, and it would probably be longer before she gained back the weight that she had lost. At least she was coherent, even though through the time of her illness she could really remember very little to none of it. But that marking left where only she would see it, only she would recognize, burned deeply in her soul. Someone from the scouting unit had survived and had escaped, had returned here, and probably was responsible for her recovery. And even though the hope she felt was very small, it was more than she had before this revelation. This meant that there was a possibility that her brother had survived, had escaped with the teams, and that further meant that they would be trying to find a way to defeat the primitives. She didn't know if she would live to see how it would end, but at least she now knew.

She still didn't have the strength to do more than sit, so other than the trips to the pot to take care of nature calls, she remained on her sleeping mat. One time while shifting to a more comfortable position she knocked something loose that fell between her and the wall. It had happened when one of the primitives, one of the healers she thought, had been in the shelter. He had had his back to her at the moment that whatever it was had fallen, so was unaware of the object. She quickly threw the covering over it, although from the brief glance that she had, it probably wouldn't have drawn any attention by the primitive anyway. It appeared to be a small leather pouch, and similar enough in construction to have been made by the primitives, in other words something very common to them, thusly unimportant. She watched and listened, but said nothing, and eventually he left, leaving the three of them alone once again. At this point she didn't want either Beth or Barbara to know anything about what she had discovered. She didn't know if they could be silent about it or not. So she had to keep it to herself for now. Later that might change. So she let the two know that she was going to lie down for a little while, and that they could continue to do whatever it was that they had been, that this visit by the healer had tired her once again.

There was some truth to her final statement, since it really had – but not to the point of needing to sleep again. To tell the truth, that would be happening very soon anyway. She had to admit that it was very frustrating to only last a very short time before she needed to sleep. So she lay down and turned her body towards the wall, slowly brought the bag up to where she could see its contents, and almost gasped when she saw what the items were. What was in here absolutely confirmed to her that someone from the scouting unit indeed had checked in.

* * *

As fate would have it, Shellian was on shift when Sara found the bag. She smiled, but remained silent. She knew that when Sara would have a chance she would check out the contents of that small insignificant ordinary bag and know, absolutely know where it came from. Soon now, very soon, they would be in communications with her, and with her knowledge, and abilities, maybe some additional insight could be found, and they would be able to find a solution that would lead to the end of this reign of terror that the primitives had brought down upon them. And, of course, update Sara on the truth and why the women of the cities that had been captured, could not become pregnant by the warriors. It would be a small consolation to what the women had to endure, but with the knowledge that they wouldn't be carrying the offspring of the warriors, they could at least eliminate one fear.

Saige was taking a break in the meeting room, staring out of the windows; he was so hoping that they would have something by now. Some inkling of an idea, something they could begin to work with, to plan, to be able to not only end this reign of terror and destruction, but to save the remaining captives. He knew that each day they delayed, more of their people died. It was much too cold to go and walk the small hidden valley, and he could see some light snow falling anyway. But watching it and sitting did not relieve his restlessness, his frustration. They were heading for the end of the second winter here in the Sacred Mountains, and he felt guilty that they were well and free when so many of their people were not. Turning when he heard someone enter the room he could see that Shellian must have just finished her shift. She was carrying her daughter who was just content to be in her mother's arms. Smiling a loving smile at the child, that just lit her up, Saige smiled. He knew that very shortly, anytime now, that he would be doing very much the same thing with their twins. Smiling, as he watched the interaction between the two of them he said. "Shell', how are the two of you doing today?"

Looking up at her brother, she said. "We are doing quite well, aren't we little Sam'." She reached down and tickled her daughter and got a giggle from her baby. "You know that conversation we had a long time ago."

"Which one? We've had so many."

"True. But where you were asking why a woman would go through what she does in child birth, and then most of the time repeats it – that one."

Nodding his head he took a deep breath, and let it out slowly. The first time that had come up was back last winter when they were still in the cave just trying to survive, before everything fell even farther apart. "Yes, I do remember, but why bring that up now? Of course I know that other than my mate Seirra, all of you have now gone through labor, and all of you have healthy children, well, except for Sorrel, but she was unconscious through her delivery, so I don't know if that counts. Although she's well on her way to a second child, and I hope this one survives. She at least deserves that."

"Yes, yes she does. We came so close to losing her, and what a double tragedy that would have been. Anyway, if you remember what I said then, it went something about being an observer and not a participant, so I could pass on only what I had observed. Well, I've been through it all now, and even with the drugs it wasn't easy. But I'd do it all over again to hold her and love her like I do. So I think I understand it so much more now. And, I think that's why women have more than one child. We all enjoy the closeness with our men, and the physicality of it all. And then when we get pregnant, it's all wonder and awe, as we feel that child growing inside of us.

Then we begin to want to know who this new person is. How will they look, will they be healthy, what will they be like, and so many other things. So I think that now it all makes so much more sense. Anyway, this really wasn't what I was going to talk to you about. I'm just about ready to head for my apartment for some down time, and to enjoy some time with her before I have to go back and continue on the many projects we have. I just want to let you know that Sara found and opened the leather pouch. So she knows. But from what I can see, she's much too weak to be of any assistance yet. But, at least she is aware, and we are one step closer to finding a solution."

"That's great news sis. I've been restless and a little down thinking about how long we've been here, and thinking about how little we've actually been able to move towards finding a solution to this, and thanks for that other update. With Seirra just about to go into labor, I have been worried sick. Especially when we found out she's carrying twins. So I guess, as you know, when she does, you'll have the leadership until afterwards."

"Yeah, I guess in some ways that's true. But you have to remember that we've actually accomplished a lot. Contacted the cities, rescued those eight from one of the tribes, reestablished the travelers, and learned about our true past. That, in my mind, is quite a lot. And yes I know that we've yet to come up with a solution on stopping the primitives and their alliance, but I'm sure in time we will. Anyway, that's all I have, so I'll catch you later, bro. I need some downtime and some mother time." She smiled at him, turned and left. He watched her leave and once again was alone with his thoughts.

Seirra was sitting in the cafeteria, being quite uncomfortable, and quite nervous. Her time was approaching rapidly, and she'd been having some Braxton-Hicks, false labor, and it seemed like her twins were having a boxing match inside of her. She had dropped recently also, another sign of her impending labor. This was no fun at all, and while she was ready for this to be over, she wasn't ready for this to be over. At this time the cafeteria was empty and she was by herself, and with her mood, not that it was bad, she was happy that it was that way. No, her mood was more introspective and nervous, and she just wasn't in the mood for company at this moment, even Saige's. She looked up when she heard the doors swing open, and watched as Joci entered, who then saw her sitting there, stopped for a moment undecided, and then turned to leave. Smiling Seirra said, "Joci, you don't have to go. If you wanted to get something in here, please do."

Turning around and looking at Seirra, Joci replied, "Are you sure? You looked like you wanted to be alone, and I, ah, I don't want to bother you or anyone really."

"No, no Joci, it's all right." Then waving her arms she continued, "I mean, look at all of this space. We probably could have everybody from the complex in here and all of us still could be alone. So, you won't be bothering me at all." Seirra could tell that Joci had, had a very hard time of it. In some ways she reminded her of herself back in the cave when she wasn't very sure of herself. Although she suspected that it was much worse for Joci, since she had gone through the nightmare, before she had a chance to learn who she was, and the results would be anything but positive.

Joci decided to go ahead and stay. She was both a little hungry and thirsty, and there were some juices here that she really liked. So heading into the kitchen area, she got a roll with some spread, and filled a glass with the juice. Once finished she came back out into the eating area and undecided stopped a moment. She could see that Seirra was having a hard time with her pregnancy at this moment, and she could sense the worry. Coming to a decision, she sat at the same table across from Seirra, but further down at this moment. She still wasn't sure if the idea that had been forming was worth telling anyone. So for a short time she was quiet and just ate the roll and sipped the juice, "Seirra?"

While not looking over at her Seirra answered, "Yes Joci?" She continued to concentrate on the sensations from her own body, and she felt that things were beginning to move rapidly to a conclusion that she couldn't stop.

Joci slid down closer so that she would be across from her before speaking. "You really don't look like this is any fun." She paused not quite knowing how to continue, and then briefly looked away before facing her again. "You know how Saige and Shellian said, that if anybody had an idea about how to get the advantage on the primitives, to let them know. Well, I've had . . ." But before she could say any more she saw a surprised look on Seirra and with slight alarm asked, "What's wrong?" She could see Seirra both staring out in the distance and then looking down.

"Oh no! No, not now! Oh my, I think my water broke."

Looking under the table quickly, Joci could see that the pants that Seirra was wearing appeared to be wet. Alarmed and not sure what to do she made a decision, got up and came around to help her. "Here, let me help you down to the infirmary, I think it's time." She could see the shocked look on her face as well as some fear. It was time and from now until she held the new lives, her body would take over, giving her no choice.

"Saige, Saige, please report to the infirmary, your mate has gone into labor." The intercom then repeated the message. He had still been in the meeting room, and at first because of his thoughts had missed the alert. When it finally penetrated he caught his breath, got up and headed for the infirmary at a rapid pace.

With the message going out over the intercom, everyone in the facility was aware that two new lives were about to enter the world. Sorrel, looking down at her growing abdomen, and being in her late second to early third-third, knew that soon she would be the next. Although, even though she had no memory of it, she had been the first. Sorrel knew that Shellian, with Stone's help, would keep things moving. She suspected that it would be at least eighteen hours before it would be over, and to have your first labor be twins, it had to be scaring Seirra to death.

Joci, after getting Seirra to the infirmary, slowly walked back to the cafeteria. Once there she sat back down, and finished her roll and now warm juice. *Darn, I was just about to tell her my idea. Now what can I do? I felt that she was the only one I could talk to.* She felt miserable and afraid to say anything at all, and her one chance was now gone. *Well, maybe, just maybe, my idea isn't that good anyway.* Sighing, she took her dirty dishes to the recycler, and headed back to the education and daycare area. Again she really enjoyed working here, at least for now.

* * *

K'jor continued his view into the past – "Where were you? And why is it that you want to return?" S'lon asked, as he paced by the campfire. It was evening and the day's hunting had been complete. It had been a very busy day, and the carcasses had been stripped and the meat was drying on racks over the smoky fire. The females were working the hides so that they could be cured and then prepared for the return trip back to the clan home.

"Look, I don't understand all of it yet, but those two had to have come from somewhere, and that somewhere had to be where I was – although I don't understand where I was at all. Like you, I swore that I had crossed over, and what I saw when I entered that canyon seemed to confirm it to me, but it just didn't seem right. If I had crossed over, then where were the ones who had passed before us? Although when seeing a clan home, and the tribe portable shelters, I felt that I had. Yet the place had a silence upon it, a feeling of long abandonment, and a place where there had been no one in a very long time. And if I indeed had passed over, there should have been no way for me to return to this world, yet I stand before you." Smiling as he stood he said, "I guess that even this could be an illusion, something to test me, to find where I truly belong. But I don't think so. There is something deeper going on, and I want to know what it is. I want to know the answers to these questions that are burning in my mind."

"I can understand that K'jor, but that is a place of desolation, there is nothing there for us, no way for any of us to live. We get nothing from it, and it leads us into the spirit world if we go there. So why not just let it lie. We have enough going on with keeping our people fed, and safe from attack."

"I cannot answer that specifically, but there is something that is drawing me there, a strength of purpose that says that there are some important answers hidden there in those desolate lands. And I'm being driven to find out what that is." Turning around and smiling at S'lon, K'jor continued, "Now I'm not going to put our duty behind me to seek this out. We will do what we are supposed to do here, return to our home, and then the next season come here a little earlier to pursue these riddles, and I promise you, old friend, that if there are no answers next time, I will let it go away as the dust disappears with the wind."

K'jor, as he continued to look back, wondered if he'd been wrong. These strangers were definitely not warriors, but there appeared to be something, and he couldn't quite figure it out. T'som had informed him that the one female they were all interested in, was slowly, very slowly mind you, healing. From what could be observed by the healers their best estimate for her recovery could easily fall to the middle of the season of greening. At least these "travelers" seemed to live up to the old records – but why so few? Yes, they had explained why, but ever suspicious, he wasn't sure, and the way they left, leaving no sign behind. It led one to believe that they could be sorcerers themselves. Yet he had spoken with them, and they appeared to be no different. A little smaller in build yes, but even within the clan he could find ones who were built similarly. And as the records stated their skills in healing were superior to their own. But when they were observed, it did not appear to be so. But the results were before their eyes. One who was close, so very close to passing over, was now recovering.

He found that he was going in circles, finding no answers, and actually developing more questions. *Guess I'd better just stay with what I know, and it's becoming obvious that, that's not a lot.* It had been an unbelievable three cycles of the seasons and with the season of cold ending soon, and the preparations for a new greening season he knew it wouldn't be long before they would be searching for more of the hidden lairs. Here in the northeastern foothills they were only a few days travel from the Sacred Mountains, and the point where the travelers had camped. Even though everything would have been wiped out since they had disappeared, supposedly going back to their homes beyond the mountains, he wanted to see for himself exactly where this place was. Again the way they left had made no sense, and the reports had stated that the only way into and out of the area of the campsite had been towards the ones who were watching. There was supposed to be no other way out of that area. And that bothered him also.

As a warrior you never camped where you had only one exit. It was dangerous to not leave yourself more than one way of escape – since one never knew when they would be attacked by a rival tribe or clan, and if the forces attacking could overwhelm their camp – so additional exits could easily be the difference between surviving or dying. Restless, and not just because of having to remain inside because of the severity of the season of cold, he paced his shelter, and every once in a while would stand just outside until the cold winds would force him back inside. This one, even with it being one of the worst, had been tough for him because of the events that seemed to be taking place, unseen, behind, and invisible, leading to a complete and unknown outcome. It was as if the gods were now playing games of chance, and they were the ones in the prize pot to be used as they pleased. Again had he done right to attack and destroy these lairs, these magicians and sorcerers? And why now, yes why had these travelers who had been gone for generations arrive while the united clans and tribes were seeking out and destroying these lairs? Was it all coincidence, or was there a greater plan? And if these lairs were of the gods, why did these not speak their tongue? Ah, but then that wasn't necessarily true, now was it. After all this female – a female of all things – spoke their tongue. So she had to have been someone of high importance . . . But a female?

All of it was becoming more complicated, and as time continued to move, the less he understood. At the beginning it had appeared to be so simple, locate the lairs, bring about their fall, and take slaves, and add to the breeding herds. And all of it was very easy to accomplish. These lairs fell easily, the people within were captured and spread among the alliance, as tradition, well, there never had been an alliance before, but even though that was so, they still abided by the traditions, and laws, and had not deviated. All felt good about their successes, and all felt that with the increase in both slaves, and the breeding herds that their strength and size would increase. Then these strange ones, these magicians began to die, and most did, and what followed could not be believed, let alone understood. In fact if any had suggested such a thing he would have been laughed at and told to go and create other fantasies for their pleasure. And the proof that this was true lay before him right here. Absolutely none of the females from these lairs were carrying. It was noted that they bled as their own females proving that they could carry, but any and all warriors who bred with these females, and he knew that all had tried, never were successful in getting any of these females to carry. They were being defeated by females. Were they that weak, or were these females that strong?

At first it was considered a fluke, and the attempts increased. Many of these new females, like the males perished, showing them that these were not a strong people. Again not a surprise, considering how easily they had been conquered, and their lairs destroyed, but to have the power to prevent the carrying showed a power and strength that was completely unknown, and beyond their comprehension.

He'd been standing at his entrance when the suns were briefly obscured by clouds. Looking up he could see that another storm was rolling in, and the winds had picked up considerably, and the temperatures were dropping rapidly. Shaking his head he thought, *another storm, when will they end? Already this season seems to be intolerable, too long, and much too cold.* He turned a reentered his shelter, and went over to the fire, and added another log. It was going to be another very long day.

* * *

"The last word that we've received from the infirmary is that Seirra is still in labor." It had been eighteen hours ago when it had started, and no recent word had come forth to update them. Shellian, who was the last to go through labor felt for her, but she knew that it was a part of life. She looked around the table and with Stone sitting on her right, was there as the second, "We'll be continuing these early day meetings, even if they are short, until either we come up with a viable plan, or we get something useful from the cities, and as you all know, so far that hasn't happened." She turned towards Joci, and said, "You usually don't get a chance to come to these too often. We seem to have you taking care of the children, and honestly that's not fair to you."

Embarrassed by being singled out, at first she mumbled something, kind of ducking her head. When she realized that she hadn't been understood she said quietly, "Thank you, but I really love taking care of the children, and being so young in comparison to all of you, what could I add?"

Smiling, Shellian said, "Now don't feel like you have nothing to contribute. You have seen, and experienced, and not all of it fun or nice, much of what the rest of your city experienced. You've suffered at the hands of the primitives as the other women did. And I'm sure for one as young as you are, a teenager, that to be treated that way had to be devastating, to say the least. But you're smart, and I've seen that you observe what is happening around you. So, no matter what you think, your opinion, your input is just as important as anybody else here. So if you have something to say, something to contribute, please do. Since you've monitored these meetings, and I'm sure with the children, that you were distracted many times, you know what we've got to accomplish. So if you do come up with something, please let one of us know."

Shellian, seems so strong, so in charge, how can I even say anything to her, I'd be so embarrassed. She's one of the leaders, and I'm nobody, just a kid taking care of their children. I thought about, so many times, how it would be to be a part of the grownup world, and I knew that I'd be there soon. I liked to pretend that I was. What can I say? She looked up at Shellian who was waiting patiently for a response, and could feel the pressure building, and felt her face flush, which just made things worse. Then nodding her head she said, "Okay, if I think of something, I'll pass it on." The rest of the meeting was a blur, and she barely remembered any of it. All of them were heading for the kitchen for the morning meal, and she had dragged her feet so that she would be the last to arrive. *Why didn't I say something?* She didn't have an answer for that. But why would anyone consider her idea worth anything at all?

As she entered the cafeteria, she could hear the chatter of the many voices, but felt that while the chatter sounded happy, how could it be that way? All of them had suffered so much, and others were still suffering. It just didn't seem right. With her head down she pushed through the double swinging doors, and tried to put on a smile, even if in her soul she didn't feel that way. Then over the PA system came the announcement that two new lives had entered the world, and that the mother and father were doing okay as were the babies. This brought a cheer from the ones there. It was always good news when the birthings were successful. There were so many things that could go wrong, and every one that avoided those complications was great news. Plus, with their numbers being so small, to lose any was unthinkable. Joci had to admit that this lifted her mood a little. She had been there at the beginning when labor was just starting, and had helped Seirra down the hall to the infirmary. So maybe she was worth something after all. She could hear the chatter now turning towards babies and motherhood, and the joys and challenges that this brings. Again all she could do was smile, even though the smile was a sad one. Once again she felt that she was on the outside, not part of what was going on. She almost turned around and left, and if her stomach hadn't complained she probably would have. She felt that at this moment, especially after that embarrassment in the meeting, that she wanted to be by herself, but knew that it would be impossible. So after pausing, and being unsure, she reached a decision and went on in, grabbed some food, sat down, and listened to the happy banter that filled the room.

Saige, looking down at a sleeping Seirra, smiled. It was a tired smile, as he hadn't slept through the time of her labor and the delivery of their son and daughter. The girl had been born first so was technically the older one, but that was only by a few minutes. But he could see that there would be a point where the daughter would be pointedly telling her brother that she was the oldest, and definitely the one in charge. They were beautiful, these wrinkled, small lives that were now sleeping contentedly in their small beds, wrapped tightly in the birthing blankets. He had to admit that it was almost impossible to take his eyes off of them. "I wonder what the future has in store for the two of you." He whispered softly. With the work that Seirra had done, and labor was a very good term for it, she needed to sleep as much as she could right now. Again he looked down on her with a deep love in his heart only wanting to protect her, and the two new lives with his entire being.

Saar and Jas, smiled at the scene. Both were tired even though they had worked shifts through Seirra's labor. It was always great when the outcome was positive. *Two new healthy lives, with the mother surviving, and no complications, not that Seirra isn't going to hurt for a while, because she is, it's always a great outcome,* Saar thought. "Saige," Saar said. "Look, there's an exam table right there.

So if you want to go ahead and use it to catch some sleep yourself, please do. I can tell by looking at you that you're about ready to drop, you're dead on your feet." He could see that Saige was about to say, that he was alright, but interrupted him before he could say anything. "Look I'm the doctor here, and while you and your sister may be in charge of everything else, I'm the one who's responsible for everybody's well-being, and health, so what I say overrides anything you might want to say here. Look, this place was built to handle more than all that we have here at this moment, so just take advantage of it, pull over that table, and get some rest. We'll pull the curtain and no one will be the wiser that the two of you are here."

Shrugging, Saige could find no arguments to counter, and he really hadn't wanted to leave Seirra here by herself. He knew from what his sister had told him that soon the new lives would be waking hungry looking for a meal, and he wanted to be there to help as much as he could. Taking a deep tired breath he said, "Okay doc, you've convinced me." The two of them rolled the exam table into the same space that Seirra occupied, and they made a bed, he climbed in, and with one last look closed his eyes, and was shortly out.

Turning to Jas, Saar said, "Look, you pulled that last shift, go get some sleep yourself. I was here at the end to help with the deliveries, so am in a little better shape that you. Besides, even here, we've got paperwork to keep up on." Then smiling he looked over at the two babies and said, "Welcome to this world Saharra and Seth."

* * *

"What's that sound?" Shellian asked. She was in the security office with Seve on their shift, and none of the rotating images included the long hallway at this moment. So she got up and headed out into the corridor to look. She froze for a moment, turned and motioned for Seve to join her. Perplexed, he got up and joined her and saw Judd going up and down the hallway on some type of two wheeled contraption. He came up to them and stopped. "What's this thing?" she asked.

Smiling at the two of them Judd stated, "It's what is called a personal glider, at least that's what it says it is. I have to admit that it's fun and it makes it so much easier to get from one place to another in this facility." Stepping off and letting go of the handle, it just stood there.

"How does it do that? I mean with just the two wheels, you'd expect it to fall over." Seve exclaimed.

"True, but it's in its construction, and before any of you ask, the plans for this were in the replicator computer. Thought I would try and make one and see how it worked. I can produce enough for all of the adults that are here. None of the children are old enough or big enough to use one anyway. And they're easy to use, and not much of a learning curve. It's almost natural. Of course, they can only be used on solid surfaces such as these hallways, and if there were roadways or sidewalks they'd be good there also. But it sure speeds up moving around."

Smiling and shaking her head, Shellian asked, "Okay Judd, what else is in that computer that we don't know about? I mean, you used to deal with these computers back in your city, are you sure these plans weren't there?"

"No, and that's surprising. I mean, something like this would've been great to move about the city. Yet, there was no mention of these, and some of that other stuff that we've begun to use. I really wonder why so much of this was excluded from the city computers. They must have had some reason for doing it." Tipping his head to one side before continuing, "Oh well, I guess we'll really never know why. These things will fit through the doors and can be charged right then and there. I'm trying to determine right now, how long a charge will last. So I'll be running up and down the hallways and different sections until this thing dies and needs a recharge." He climbed back up on the glider, grabbed the handle, flipped or pushed a switch, leaned forward a little, and off he went.

Seve and Shellian looked at each other, and went back into the security office. "You know that's a good question." Seve said.

"Good question? What do you mean Seve?"

"Oh the one that Judd just presented us with. The one about what wasn't in the computers at the cities. Why hold back information?"

"You're right, why hold back the information? I guess we could speculate, but so far there's been nothing in these computers on that subject, and maybe it's because we've not been looking. Hmmm, it's something to think about." She sighed and said, "I guess our fun is over, now back to monitoring everything."

* * *

"What's that?" Staven asked.

Laughing Sabryn replied, "That's music silly."

"Oh, I know its music, but we've had none of that since we were back in our own city. And it seems to be coming over the PA system. That's what I meant."

"I guess that's quite true, and I guess I wasn't quite thinking about it that way. I just thought it was nice to hear it again. And until it started playing, I hadn't realized how much I've missed it." She sighed as she watched the monitors, and listened to the chatter over the circuits. Fortunately today there had been very little traffic directed at the Alpha, so it was more just watching the monitors and recordings being made from the many sensors that had been planted by the two teams, plus continuing to search with the "eyes-in-the-skies", to watch for any new movement of the primitives. So it was enough to keep one very busy when they were on shift at the security office. "Now that I think about it, you're right. How come we hear it this way?"

"Ah, I bet Judd has something to do with it. We've had all sorts of gadgets and things we never knew existed until he discovered them in that replicator computer. Not that this music came from there. But none of us had been trained in that way. So I guess in many ways it really is nice that he happened to be with that tribe we raided. Think of the difficulty it would have been to move around like we did. Now I can't see how we can live without this stuff. Yet, the irony is, that we were doing just that, and doing just fine." Shaking his head and smiling, Staven continued, "I'll never understand us let alone the primitives. It seems like every new thing he discovers becomes something we can't do without. And now I think he figured this out, so I suspect that it will just be one more thing that we would miss if he shuts it down.

Although, I have to admit that it's something like I've never heard" Hearing someone at the door, he turned around and said, "And speak of the devil, so Judd, are you responsible for our entertainment?"

Smiling, as he leaned in the doorway, he said, "Yes, rather nice isn't it? I was doing a check on the system for the whole facility, and came across this routine, and decided to see what it would do. The neat thing about it is that it will play different music styles each day. I guess they knew that not everybody likes all kinds of music, so it's set to vary the music it plays, and if someone uses the intercom, then it will mute. Plus it has the ability to allow any specific room or area to change or mute it exclusive to them." He came further into the office, went over to the system computer, and said, "Here, let me show you. I think that the way it is set, that at night it plays soft slow moving music, but if one was on shift here, it probably would put you to sleep, thusly the variability built in so that you here could put on something more upbeat." With the two watching he demonstrated exactly how to do it. Staven and Sabryn looked at each other and then back at Judd.

Then together they said, "Wow! That's easy," they both laughed and Staven said, "I wonder why we didn't figure this out. When you just showed us, there is nothing to it."

"True, but until I activated it from the main, it wasn't available. Okay, I know it's over 2000 annuals old, but enjoy, and have fun with it. I've still a lot to figure out, and this is fun." With that he was back out the door and heading down the hallway out of sight.

Again they looked at each other and then back at the screen, "What a find," was all that Staven said. Sabryn just nodded her head in agreement. It really was nice to hear music again even if it was a bit ancient.

* * *

Sara could feel her strength slowing coming back. But it was so frustrating to be this weak. She was lucky if she remained awake and moving for more than an hour. She continued to hoard and hide that small leather bag, and in a sense was thankful for the illness that had almost taken her life. At least she and the two, who were with her, had avoided having sex with the primitive males. The treatment was rough and painful, and uncaring. But she regretted her condition when the scouts had shown up. *But how?* When she had been with the unit they had never approached a tribe or clan, let alone enter one. Yes, she had been away from it for quite a few annuals, but had, from time to time, checked in on her brother, and as far as she could see, their methods had changed very little. At least, she hoped that maybe her brother had been one of the lucky ones. Although from the way their city was attacked, she was very surprised by the little gift, and the placing of the symbol, that any had escaped.

At this point she wasn't sure if she really wanted to bring Beth and Barbara into the loop. Even though they couldn't speak the language of the primitives, there could always be some way that they could give up the information. So now she tried to come up with some method to begin to make contact and find out what had been happening – from no hope, to at least a glimmer. Anytime she felt the overwhelming depression and hopelessness strike her, she would lie down and stare at that symbol, knowing that it was real, and that it had been placed there for her eyes only. To let her know, and she knew that this knowledge was precious to her, and even though she wasn't letting it go beyond her, there was a good chance that it would be critical to the rest who were now spread among the primitives having to submit to their wills and whims. So how was she going to go about it? With it as quiet as it was in this shelter, anything she might say would be overheard. In the end, she might not have any choice, she, no matter what the possible outcome, may have to inform these two women. Were they strong enough? Inwardly she shuddered with the thought of informing them, only to have it revealed to their captors, and abusers. It was a dilemma she'd have to solve soon. But for now she'd bide her time, really study these two women, and hope that the answer would present itself to her soon.

* * *

Joci sat by herself in the cafeteria. She didn't want to go back to the dorm where she could possibly run into one of the other women, not that any of them would bother her. After all, they all respected the privacy of the others. It had been something that had become stronger after their capture and rescue. But at this moment the quiet and loneliness here was what she wanted, and felt that she needed. Taking a deep breath, she folded her arms on the table and placed her head down on them. She found that she was having real difficulty coming to terms with what had happened to her, and as each day passed, it weighed heavily on her. She felt helpless against this internal struggle, and the shame she felt for having to submit that way to the primitives. She realized logically, that she shouldn't feel this way, and she was far from alone from this abuse. But knowing that still didn't prevent what she was feeling. She truly felt worthless, and if the children hadn't cheered her, a number of times, she thought that she would have reached the point of total withdrawal into herself – not a good thing at all.

In a sense she could sense that she wanted revenge against all of the ones who had abused her, and maybe if she could get brave enough to, at least, confide in someone her idea, that it might actually help her heal, and she wanted so desperately to heal, to feel normal again. But at this moment she felt that this was something that was close to impossible. Yet, when she looked and listened to these other women who had suffered in exactly the same way, they seemed to be moving on, why couldn't she? Well, if she had an answer, then she probably would be healing, would be moving on. It could be that one of the reasons was her age. She was the youngest by many annuals, and truly had no peers to speak to, to confide in, and talk things out, and so far, other than Seirra, she felt no draw to any of them. Seirra, so close that day, to being able to pass along her idea, so close to finding someone to confide in and she went into labor, and hadn't been around since. She felt like crying, and could feel the tightness in her throat and chest as she fought back the tears just waiting to flow.

She felt someone lay a hand on her shoulder. It was a gentle touch and completely unexpected. At first because it was a surprise she tightened up and felt the reaction from the one who had touched her. She was almost afraid to look up for fear of the tears that lay just below the surface. So carefully she lifted her head and looked up to see Judd standing over her with a very concerned look on his face. He didn't say anything, just beckoned her to stand, which she slowly did. Again without a word he signaled her to come to him, and when she did he hugged her. At first she resisted, but as the moments passed relaxed, put her head on his shoulder and let the tears flow. With great sobs she just cried it out; with him remaining silent until he could tell that the tears were subsiding. Still he continued to hold her, and she knew that honestly, it was the right thing to do. Finally drained emotionally she pulled back slightly and wiped her red rimmed eyes. She now felt exhausted and completely drained, and again without a word he helped her down the hallway to the entrance of the women's dorm, saying, "I think that getting some rest right now will help tremendously, so please try. And if you need to talk about anything, I'm here. And while I'm not your grandfather, I'm old enough to be, so consider me as a substitute."

She was about to say something, but he put his fingers to her lips, and just shook his head. He pointed to the closed door, reached down, and opened it, and with a gentle push sent her in the direction that she needed to go.

As the door closed he stood there silently for a few moments, and headed back to the cafeteria to get that coffee, *yes, that coffee, probably the greatest discovery of this place.* He'd been watching Joci for quite a while, even back when they were still under the control of the primitives, and he had worried about her then. Heck, he had to admit that he had worried about all of them at that time. And he had to admit that what he felt and saw left him hopeless. After all they had been hidden from the primitives for such a long time, so long in fact that none of them ever considered the primitives a threat. Yet, with what had been transpiring it was very obvious that they had been wrong, very wrong. So for their over confidence and their under estimating of the primitives, they, all of them, were paying a heavy price. And it could see in Joci that it was something that she did not know how to handle, how to cope or deal with what had happened to her. He could tell that it was tearing her up inside, but she continued to put forth a front that everything was okay. But he knew better. But how to reach her, how to get beyond those barriers that she was throwing up?

He was a male, a man, and right now this could be a very real problem. So when he had entered that cafeteria, like he was doing now, and saw her there, he knew that he had to reach out to her, or she might just break down. So he had touched her, and invited her into his arms so that she could, as what had transpired, cry it out. And with this first break in her armor, could he continue to build from there? When he stated that he could substitute as her grandfather, he'd meant it. In a way it would be something that would help him also. He had had young grandchildren, three actually, and all of them had been boys, which he had to admit that he was grateful for at this moment. If they had been granddaughters he didn't know what he would have done, knowing what happened to the women once the primitives got them. His family had always produced more boys and girls, so he had to admit that while he loved his grandchildren, he had longed for a granddaughter. So maybe they could help each other.

Grabbing a cup of coffee, he sat at one of the tables and continued to think. *I've got to keep this going. What is it that young girls, well young in comparison to me anyway, like?* It was a good question. He knew that as they reached the age that Joci was at, they were trying to put childhood behind them. He knew that girls seemed to push leaving home much quicker than boys did. Why this was so, he really didn't know. But he did know that whatever was their favorite thing, that many times this would continue into adulthood, and for some all of their lives. Looking back in his mind's eye he tried to remember what he witnessed when he had been around little girls, and ones who were a bit older. He continued to sit and think, and realized that as he tried to drink his coffee, that the cup was empty, so he got up to refill it, stopped a moment, smiled, and then refilled his cup. He knew what he needed to do. It had come out of nowhere, but as he had looked back, he began to see one consistent thing in his mind. Taking the cup and as quickly as he could move and not spill the precious brown liquid, he headed down to what he considered his office and workspace. He had some work ahead of him.

* * *

Sara finally came to a decision. She realized that she would soon be able to communicate with their mysterious visitors by using sign language. So with care, and being sure that the primitives were not around, she joined the two by the small smoky fire, sat down cross legged, and leaned forward. She could see that the two were watching her intently and just waiting. She also knew that with the weakness that was in her body she had a very long way to go before she could even remain awake for more than a couple of hours, let alone recover. And when those couple of hours ended she could barely think, let alone move. *Well, this isn't solving anything.* Taking a deep breath, she still wasn't sure how to present what she knew, she looked at both of them and said, "I've got to get both of you to promise not to say anything if you see me doing something unusual, just ignore it as if nothing is happening. Because if the primitives even get any piece of this we will be in even more serious trouble than we are now, so when you see me do something out of the ordinary, just chalk it up to me being sick." She paused and looked closely at both of them. She knew that if this information, even as sketchy as it was, was passed on to the other captives that the primitives would eventually figure out what was happening and that would compromise not only her, but the teams that had entered the camps. "It is so important that if I don't get your promises, I can't help us survive. It will bring death down on all of us, not that this isn't a problem already, if the primitives even get a hint of this." Then shaking her head she thought, *not that there's been any way to avoid that since we've become captives to these people. Of course one could be closer than the other, but it can only happen once.* There had been way too much death as it was, and she was proof that this aspect was far from over. She suspected that others probably had died and had been added to the growing grave yard during the time of her illness.

She waited and said nothing, but watched the two. She'd rather remain silent if there was a chance that she wouldn't be able to trust either one or both. In a way she could tell that these women were frightened, and that while they had appreciated the respite from the breeding herds, and all by accident, it was obvious to Sara that they were beat down, defeated, and without hope. So could she trust them at all, but what choice did she have? After all, what did she have to offer other than a little hope, and little was better than none. It could be something they could grab onto, and maybe change their view of the future from none, being black without form, to maybe a little gray with a slight definition. She also knew that soon she would begin conversations with their head priest. Although what it could be about, she had no real idea. So she would, at least in the beginning, remain silent as is demanded of their females, and maybe slightly aloof, but not so much to bring discipline down upon her. Maybe she'd finally begin to understand some things, and again with as much sex that was going on with the primitives, why were none of the city women pregnant?

CHAPTER SIXTEEN

Even though he was drug out from too little sleep, and the constant demands of the twins, it was his shift in the security office. Seirra would be excused from any assignments for at least a month. He had to admit that when the two entered this world he was in awe of what he had witnessed. He hated to see his mate go through this, but knew that it is the way of life. He found that his love had deepened for her and had expanded to include their new children, ones that they now could put a face and personality to, which up to that time could only be anticipated and guessed. Yes, even though they were just babies, he had to admit that his daughter already had him wrapped around her little finger. He knew that he had heard that it was something common, but until he experienced himself, he truly did not believe it. Smiling, he had to admit that now he was one, a believer that is. If his shift remained quiet, it was going to be very hard to stay awake. As time had passed, and the Alpha was no longer new to the rest of the cities, the traffic had lessened considerably, and while they still maintained two in the security office, it was much simpler now. In fact at times it was almost leisurely.

His fellow companion on this shift was Jessi. They tried to rotate everybody through, continually mixing all of the members, so that all would have worked with each other. Jessi was lithe in build, and had naturally darker skin, with light brown to blonde hair that she kept in a ponytail which hung down past her shoulders. In many ways she reminded him of his sister, both being athletic, and both truly beautiful women. Yet, that was where the comparison ended. He figured some of what she was dealing with at this time had to do with what had happened to her during her time with the primitives. But, it could be that she was naturally quiet and reserved. It wasn't that she put herself above anyone, it just appeared that way. In fact, once one was around her for any length of time, they found that it was quite the opposite. He knew that the women they had rescued had not revealed much as of yet, and he understood that completely. After such a lengthy and traumatic experience, it would be only time that would help. She was only a little younger than he, and probably close to the same age as Seirra.

On this shift she ended up with the communications duty, with him monitoring the many cameras, and feeds, that were in place. This included the many small bugs that they had planted during their time as the travelers. Fortunately, for all of them, the cities included, it was still winter, and that meant that they were still safe from the primitives. Glancing briefly over he could see Jessi staring intently at the monitors that were on her side. "I just can't get over these views from above this world," she said to no one in particular.

"Yeah, know what you mean. We were quite shocked when we accidently discovered it. We had no idea at all that our ancestors could do this. And, as you know, that was only one of the many shocks and revelations this place had in store for us."

She turned towards him and asked, "Is it true that you fell into this valley and that's the way it was discovered?"

Laughing, and shaking his head in memory he replied, "Yup, it wasn't the best of ways to find something, but that's exactly what happened. I was fortunate that I lived to be able to tell the tale." One of the monitors caught his eye, and he caught his breath. It was the feed from inside that building where Sara was. And while he was the one who had planted a number of them throughout that clan, and a few within that particular building or shelter as the primitives called them, he had almost been embarrassed to realize that his placement was such that it allowed none of the women any privacy at all. Something that he had learned was very important to women. But there was no way to go back and change the positioning of the bugs. Sara was lying back down, but had opened the pouch and had placed the small transmitter-receiver in her ear. He knew, from an earlier recording that she had confronted the two women, but at this time had yet to get any answers or promises from them. So he knew that she would not be talking at this time, but instead be signing. He was sure that she was rusty, since it had been a very long time since she had need of it.

Taking a deep breath, he waited a moment, picked up the mic, and pressed the switch that would only activate that feed. He turned to Jessi, and said, "I'm about to talk with Sara, I need you to monitor all of this from your side. All of this is automatically recorded, but it's important to monitor it in real time." He keyed the mic and said, "Sara, if you can hear me, just nod your head. We've bugged the shelter, and are aware of what is transpiring." He waited and watched, and saw her nod slightly to confirm she had heard him. He could see that hope was beginning to show in her eyes, but she was trying to keep it from showing too much. "There's much we'd like to tell you, but there is much we need from you also. The images that we receive are sharp and clear, so if you don't get a positive answer from the two who are with you, then we'll deal with the use of signing from your part." He waited, and watched as she signed that she understood. It was done slowly, and with slight movements so as to not let them others know that she was in contact with anyone.

He could see as she did this that she did not appear to be rusty at all, and he asked why this was so. She signed back that it was a game that they had played in her household. It was something that her boys enjoyed doing, so it had become a household tradition that everybody would practice, and be very good at it, with games where one would try and fool another by subtle use of the signing. She then asked about her brother. Saige knew that eventually that question would arise, and he hoped it would have been later. Pausing, and not sure how to answer, he finally just gave up, and told her that he had died during their escape. He could see that this had hit her hard, but what else could he say? So before she asked the next obvious question he told her, that as far as her immediate family went, they knew nothing. He also passed on to her that the scouting unit had been decimated by the primitives, and only a small remnant survived. He could tell that as each of these facts were revealed to her, that it was as if she was being struck physically, and he could understand that reaction completely. He could tell that she was tiring rapidly, and said to her that until later after she had slept that they would talk again, saw the understanding in her eyes, and broke the connection. He watched her as she closed her eyes, and then saw as the tears began to flow as she wept for the knowledge that her brother had not survived.

She awoke with T'som standing over her. He squatted down, and said, "I have much that needs to be said. The travelers who saved your life said that it would be the middle of the season of greening before you would fully recover. But K'jor grows impatient, and is in need of answers that we suspect that only you can give us. Soon, these two females that are with you will be returned to the herd, but not yet. I will be outside of this shelter and expect you to meet me as soon as you've taken care of your needs." He got up and with a quick glance at the other two who were cowering in the corner as far away as they could get, left.

She was still groggy from being very deep in sleep when he had awakened her, and it alarmed her that they would be taking Beth and Barbara from her. She still depended on them heavily. Now what? She slowly got off of the sleeping mat, and carefully worked her way over to the pot to take care of her needs, finding that she was still unbelievably weak. She took a bowl of the soup that had been simmering on the small, smoky, open fire, and carefully ate. The food was really hot, and could have easily burned her tongue. But she needed this nourishment to help her keep her wits about her as she faced this primitive. Not wanting to tell the two women what had been related to her, she made sure that the ear piece was in place, and the tiny, almost invisible bug that would provide the visuals was placed on the clothing she wore, placed just above her breasts. Again the sorrow hit her, as she remembered what this Saige had told her. He, her brother, had not survived, and as far as she knew, she was the last of her family. She knew of no others – and what of her children? She already knew her mate was dead but her two sons were an unknown, and so she had to assume that they were no more also.

As she followed this T'som, she could feel that dreaded weakness returning with full force, making her shake, and feel like she was about to collapse. T'som turning and seeing this, went back and then supported her for the rest of the distance to the shelter of their gods, and helped her sit. Looking her over closely, he could see that she still was in very bad shape, and even though he had told her that they would be removing the other two, it was now obvious to him, that this order would have to be delayed. The distance from where this female was living to where they were presently, was only a very short walk, but before they were even close to half way here, she had almost collapsed. It was again obvious to him that they were moving too fast on this. He doubted that he would get much from her at this point. In fact as he watched her, he could see that she was barely awake, and that the trip here had exhausted her completely. Sometimes he felt that K'jor, through his impatience, pushed things much too quick, and this was one of those times. He understood why, but sometimes one had to wait, no matter what one tried to do, and he knew again, that this was one of those times.

There was going to be difficulties on both sides of this. Females were not allowed to speak around the males since their true purpose was to bring new lives into the clan. Yet, from all indications this female was equal to him, a priest. So they should be speaking as equals, if not for who she was. This was shocking, yet he had listened to the comments from the warriors who had attacked these lairs, and saw for himself that what they said was true. The females from these lairs were equal to the males, and in some places above them. Just how could this be? Looking down at her as he paced, he finally stood in front of her and said. "There are many things that we are not understanding, and one of these major points has to do with the females from your lairs. But before we even move in that direction, I must make you aware that you will be given some opportunities that have never been granted a female. This is being allowed so that we may begin to make sense of what makes no sense to us at all. From what I can see, this will not happen today, since you can barely keep your eyes open, and so I will speak and you will listen."

Even through the fog of exhaustion from the short trip she thought, *I can't believe these primitives. I'm just supposed to listen to your speech, and thank you because you allowed me this privilege?* She concentrated once again on what this one was saying.

"Much of what I'm saying you are aware of, but it is necessary so that there is a starting place. In our world when a tribe or clan is conquered and their place of living is destroyed, then the females must become part of that conquering clan or tribe, to become part of the breeding herds that allows us to strengthen through the new blood and future lives."

He paused a moment, and looked at her closely to make sure that she was paying attention. He could see that she was attempting to do so, and was fighting hard to stay awake. At least that was a good sign. "So, with the discovery of the lairs, our victory over you, and the destruction of your lairs, this made you and the other females bound to join our clan, and the others involved, to further our growth. Even though there was some resistance . . ." *Ha, resistance, that's putting it mildly,* she thought. He could see that what he had just said had brought a brief fire to her eyes, but it was only short lived, so he continued. "All of you were added. At this point it was as it should be." *As it should be? In who's book? Not mine or any of the other women that you have enslaved.*

"And it appeared that all was proceeding, but then with the breeding, nothing happened, no carrying, nothing. It was as if the females from your lairs, those lairs I might add, that fell easily to us, were greater warriors than our own warriors – somehow preventing the carrying and the strengthening of our clan. At first we thought it was just a fluke. After all, the females from the lairs had the bleeding as ours, showing us that you are fertile, so there was an increase in the attempt to overcome whatever magic, totem, or hidden strength, that all of you used to prevent the carrying. But we are still being defeated, and this is something that is unacceptable. If females are able to defeat us, how long will it be before we are defeated in battle?"

So this is what this is all about. But priest or whatever you call yourself, I haven't a clue. With as many times as we've been forced to have sex with your warriors, some of us should have become pregnant. I'm quite happy that it hasn't happened. Because the last thing I want to do as a woman is to bring another one of you bastards into this world. So, for whatever is the reason, may it just continue . . .

"So with this happening, that is why you are here, and as I stated earlier, you will be allowed something that is forbidden to the rest of the females. We will begin, soon, to talk, allowing you to speak. Enough for now, I will assist you back to your shelter, and let you recover additionally. We will talk on this later." With that he assisted her back to the shelter, and to her sleeping mat. She lay down gratefully, and was out almost as soon as she relaxed.

* * *

When Joci had been led back to the dorm by Judd, and with his gentle nudging, she did lie down, and found to her surprise, that she had slept – and when waking felt guilty about it. Still she had to admit that at this moment, even though she was still a bit out of it, and numb from waking from a deep sleep, some of the demons that had been haunting her were strangely silent. She had been so afraid to open up to anyone, let alone a man. Yet, he had been so gentle, so understanding, and it just seemed natural to cry it out on his shoulder. She could sense no judgment there, only compassion. And he said so little, but his eyes had spoken volumes, and she knew that she had found a friend, and maybe like her own grandfather, who she was sure had perished, he would listen to her, and help her, and she knew that she really needed that right now.

She had come so close to being destroyed by what had happened, and she had seen other women who had been, and were no longer alive. She wondered if some of them committed suicide, something she had contemplated a number of times, even after the rescue from the primitives. Looking around, once outside of her personal area, she found that the dorm was quite empty at the moment and she had it all to herself. Looking at the clock, that was hanging on the wall; she found that she had a few hours before she needed to report to the daycare center to help there. At first she thought that she would just go read something in the area that was set up like a living room, with comfortable chairs, couches, tables, and lamps that projected a soft comfortable light. The floor in the area was covered with rugs, making the area feel homey and comfortable. She had some serious thinking to do. Then her tummy rumbled and she realized that before that incident that she had gone to the cafeteria to get something to eat, and had become overwhelmed. So she changed her mind and instead opened the door only to find a large box sitting next to the doorway with her name on it. *What's this?* Now curious, she picked it up, and found that it wasn't very heavy for its size. She shook it slowly, in case there was something inside that could be broken, and something moved inside, but it didn't have that solid feel. Now, undecided, she didn't know if she wanted to take it to the cafeteria with her, or return to her area and open it there.

After another moment of indecision, she decided to take it back inside to the privacy of her space. She was really curious. There was nothing on the box to identify who it was from, let alone what the contents could be. And the movement and slight shaking didn't give her a hint. Well, she had to admit that this had taken her mind, even temporarily, off her problems. So she entered her space, placed the box on the bed, cut the tape and opened the box, and found a beautiful large stuffed toy bear with a smile on its face, and its arms opened wide. She laughed slightly at the sight. It was as if this stuffed bear wanted to be hugged by her, and she just couldn't resist. *Wow, what a great gift!* When she picked it up and hugged it, she found it to be very soft, and she felt like she didn't want to let it go. *Who?* Yes she wondered who had thought of this wonderful gift. Then looking at the bear she smiled and asked, "So mister bear, who are you, and where did you come from?" She laughed in delight, someone to confide in, someone who would never judge her, someone who would listen, and someone to comfort her in her nights of terror. He was perfect. Why did she decide that he was a he? That was a very good question, and looking the bear over there was nothing that identified it as either sex. So she looked closely at the face, and thought that it was more masculine, than feminine, so she had made him a male.

As she thought about this, she thought it was strange that she should do that, with all the horror she had faced at the hands of those primitive males. Because of her youth, she had become one of the ones most demanded by the primitives as they tried to get her pregnant. It had been nasty, humiliating, and a very painful experience. One she knew that she would never want to repeat any time in her short life. Well, all of that was behind her. She just didn't know now after all of that abuse and pain, whether she would ever be able to make love with whoever would be her mate some day in the future. She really worried that she would have a real fear, have those hidden scars that just wouldn't go away, and ruin her life even more than it had been already. At least with her new friend here she wouldn't have to face that. She knew that her experiences that she had would always color her life, and she knew that it was that way for all of them. Oh well, that was for the future, once again her tummy complained and she knew that she needed to finish that interrupted trip to the cafeteria and get some food. Looking at the bear she asked, "What do I do with you? Do I leave you here to warm my bed, and be my secret friend, or do I take you with me and if the cafeteria is empty you can sit next to me and we can talk." In the end, at least for now, she decided that she would leave him here, and told him that she'd be back shortly and headed out to get something to eat. As she headed down the hallway, she again wondered, *who is the person that gave me such a wonderful gift?*

* * *

Saige and Shellian studied the video and conversation, if one could call it such, that this priest had with Sara. Of course the conversation was more he talk, she listen, but that was the way the primitive culture lived. Both of them had to admit that giving Sara the right to speak, even though it wasn't this day, was something that never had happened. Women were just not allowed that privilege at all, and could be punished for speaking around the males. From the bugs that had been planted it was quite obvious that when the females were back with the herd, as it was called, they chattered all the time. No different than with theirs when women got together. Both of them wondered when the change would come where women would be considered more than property, and only there to bring both pleasure and new lives. Saige could see the anger in his sister's eyes, but she remained under control. "This is the fourth time we've looked at this, and while it has helped with understanding some of what they do, all this priest is doing is speculating about why our women haven't become pregnant by their men." Saige said. "There's really nothing here that can help us,"

Letting out a deep breath in frustration, Shellian couldn't disagree with what her brother had just said. In fact she was just about to say the very same thing. "We've got to be overlooking something. The clock keeps ticking, and our time is very rapidly running out. If we don't come up with something soon, then the alliance will be getting back together, and once again seek out another of our cities. And while there has been much work on the fortifying of the cities, and trying to come up with better fields, and holograms, there's just no guarantee that any of it will work. After all, somehow they've figured out that the belts and clothes that all of us wear allow us to pass through those fields unharmed. So with the amount of people that they've captured and killed, there are plenty of those to go around." She got up and paced the meeting room where the two of them were presently.

Looking down at the floor, he had to agree with her assessment. He had asked the ones in charge of the cities why they couldn't just change the code or something so that the belts and clothes wouldn't work anymore. They had said that they didn't know why, and had asked that very question themselves. And the answer they got back from their engineers made them somewhat angry with their ancestors. They had been told that it was something that had been hardwired into the defensive equipment, and no one knew where it was located within the complicated circuits, or what it was that activated the devices. So it would take time, and research to be able to figure out what it was within these units that were responsible, and then develop a change. And maybe since they were at the Alpha that there could be something there that would give them the answers they needed.

Well, there were no engineers here, and while Judd was good at what he was doing, he wasn't close to being an engineer. So the weaknesses in the system remained. They had placed a high priority for the teams here to search the records for any hint, and again because none of them had the training, it was like trying to find that proverbial needle in a pile of grass, which meant that in the end, the protection would have to come from them, and their small contingent. Shaking his head, he looked at her stating, "Somewhere we're really overlooking something. I know that it's right in front of us, but we're just not seeing it. And it's just as obvious that the rest of the people here haven't come up with anything either. All the morning meetings we've had and are continuing to have, have given us nothing but wasted time." He looked up at the monitor, and saw that Seirra was beckoning him, so getting up he said, "The boss is calling. I suspect she needs help with the twins. I'm sure you'd love to check in on Sam' anyway. So let's break for an hour and then meet back here and see if something has just magically appeared to help us."

Both of them headed out the door, with Shellian heading for the daycare area where her daughter was presently staying, and Saige for their apartment where Seirra and the twins were, with plans to meet later. The time of Seirra returning to help them was still a couple of weeks away. And Saige knew that one baby was a handful, but two could be overwhelming. So he made sure he was available to help as she needed it. He entered the apartment to two crying babies and a harrowed look on Seirra's face. "Okay, which one do you want me to take?" He asked.

Over the crying children she said, "Oh that's easy. It doesn't matter. I think that we have two hungry babies here, and both of them needs their pants changed. So whichever one you take to change, I'll feed the other, and then trade off.

Once fed and changed, we can see if we can't rock them to sleep. One of them has that tired type of crying, and I suspect that once both of them have full bellies they will want to sleep anyway. So let's get started, shall we?"

He went in and picked up the first one he came to, and it happened to be Saharra, and took her over to the changing table, while Seirra grabbed Seth and began to breast feed him. Saige commenting more to himself than to Saharra said, "Boy you girls have lots of places to have stuff go when you mess your pants." Yet, he couldn't help but smile, as his daughter had quit crying and was looking up at him and seemed to be smiling at him. It made his heart melt when he saw such things from her, and once again he knew that he was in trouble with this one. "There, all clean and fresh." He tossed the soiled one into the recycler and picked up his daughter and brought her over to Seirra who was just finishing the nursing of her son. He was almost asleep. So carefully they traded babies, and he went over and repeated the process with Seth, who had only wet pants. Although, as he had learned, with boys there were other dangers that one had to avoid when changing their diapers. Eventually with both fed and changed, and with some holding and rocking, they fell sound asleep. He was about to leave when smiling, Seirra pointed out that he'd better change his outfit as there was baby spit up on his shoulder. So before heading in to change, he hugged Seirra, gave her a lingering kiss, that from her side held promises for later, changed clothes, and headed back out to the meeting room.

He was the last to arrive, with his sister getting there ahead of him. Smiling at him she said, "Parenthood is a full time job, isn't it. And with us being in charge, we now have two full time jobs. Hey, when I went to the daycare center to see how Sam' was doing, and of course she was fine, she's such a happy baby, and so far has been easy to take care of, but I was surprised that all the children now have stuffed animals and some small blankets with a silky border that the children are just loving." Pausing for a moment and then smiling once again, "I guess that while it was a great thing to be able to save some of our people from the primitives, I think that we've benefited more than they. That Judd is just unbelievable. He keeps finding things in those replicator computers, and we find uses for them. Now he's come up with another miracle, not for us so much, but for the children. I ran into him briefly, on the way back here, and asked him about it. He said that there had been a reason for him to research part of the system and to find something for the children. He said that the items he created are called teddy bears. He doesn't know why, but whatever the reason, he said that in the notes that these 'teddy bears' had always been a favorite of children, so he replicated a batch, with the accompanying small blankets, and brought them to the daycare center. He said that the toddlers just went nuts over them, and I have to agree. They've latched on to these things and won't let go."

She was leaning against the table, turned around and grabbed something that was behind her, and handed it to him. It kind of looked like an animal, and sort of like the pictures that they had seen on the computers of the creatures from their own world. He could sort of see why it had been called a bear, but the "teddy" part eluded him. "You say that all the kids just love these things?" He felt it and found it soft, and probably the word that came to his mind was of all things "cuddly".

She then handed him a second one which was a different color, which he asked, "What's this for?"

She laughed and said, "These two are for your and Seirra's children. He suggested that you read up on childhood history of our people and what they used these things for. So, I'll let you figure that part out. I kind of find them enduring myself. I wonder what he'll come up with next?"

Shaking his head he stated, "Yeah, I wonder." Looking up at the clock, he put the two bears down, and continued, "We're running out of time here. We've got a meeting shortly, and while I know that so far, we've not figured out much, we still have to try. Do you have any new ideas on how to tackle this? I know that I've run out of ideas, and the conversations that we've had with Sara, as short as they've had to be, hasn't produced anything that we can use. And even watching the vids of all the planted bugs haven't given us a clue. I'm afraid that if we don't have some kind of breakthrough shortly that there will be another season of raids from that alliance, and we'll lose more cities, more lives, and more of our people will suffer."

"Unfortunately, nothing at all – I've seen what this has done to our people, and even in the eight that we rescued, I see lingering problems. It's more obvious in the women, but I can see it in the men also. And the one that has shown most of the damage has been Joci. She's tried to hide it, but with the way she's withdrawn, been more subservient, and wants to be alone or just with the children, all point to one having a very difficult time adjusting to what has happened to her. And no, before you ask, she is no trouble, causing no trouble, and has been very good at helping. What I'm seeing is subtle, and it is something that took me a while to realize. I'm sure part of the problem is her age, and the fact that there's no one else around that is that close. I'd guess that she's very early in her late teens, and that's a tough time if everything is normal. Anyway I've kind of been keeping an eye on her," she then laughed a little before continuing, "in my spare time."

Spare time, right, as if any of us have much of that. He knew that the two of them had even less. But what could they do, nothing really, nothing at all. "I guess, I'll take these, ah, teddy bears over to our apartment, and be right back." He grabbed the two stuffed animals and went out the door. Shellian turned around and once again went through the notes that she had studying, trying to find anything that they may have missed.

* * *

When Joci entered the daycare area it was a complete surprise to see all the children carrying much smaller versions of the gift she had found at the door. She laughed at the sight, and thought that it had been a very long time since she had done that twice in one day. These things surely had lifted her spirit. When she turned around she saw Judd standing there and smiling at her. So it had to have been him. With a great big smile on her face she turned around and went to him and gave him a big hug saying, "Thank you, thank you, thank you."

He looked down at this young woman that he was holding, smiling inwardly himself. The gift obviously had the effect that he hoped that it would. He put his finger under her chin and tipped her head up gently so that he could look her in the eyes and said, "It was the least I can do for you, who I consider my granddaughter. I can tell that this has been good for you. So please let's continue in this way." He kissed her lightly on the forehead before continuing, "Now, I know we're just starting out, but I think if both of us try we can make this grandfather-granddaughter thing work." He gently released her, and pushed her towards her assignment. "I think that the children are staring at us."

She turned around and blushed a little, because, as he had stated, the toddlers all were staring at the two of them, and were quiet. When she turned back around to Judd, he had already left, so looking back at the children she began to help. In a short time, she would be relieved as today she was to be at the meeting. Maybe with the way she was feeling that she could actually say something. Especially since that idea she had wouldn't go away, but continued to nag at her. And since there had been nothing else presented that could help; maybe hers was a good one after all.

But later after the meeting, she sat frustrated. While she thought that she could present her idea, she found that she was so nervous, scared really, that she just froze up and couldn't say anything. Why was she having so much a problem with this? After all, she had just as much right to add her thoughts as any of the others, and so far there had been nothing forthcoming from any of the others – so why not her? Before the end of the meeting, the new schedule for working the security office had been handed out, and for the first time she would be taking a shift, and the other person would be Jas. Jas was nice, showing some gray in her hair, but younger than Judd. In a sense she was just about the same age as her mother. Maybe she could open up to her, but then again, maybe not. She'd been locking things up inside of her for so long, that even with this new friendship with Judd, and the fact that he had made her feel better about herself, she just didn't know how to get beyond the barriers that she had hidden behind. Her second shift would be with Stone, and he seemed so strong, so able to accomplish anything, and his mate Sorrel, what a beautiful woman. She had to admit that they seemed perfect for each other. At least with the first shift she would have a chance to learn what they did there.

Judd came past the daycare center where Joci had gone after the meeting and saw her sitting down deep in thought. At the meeting he could tell that she had wanted to say something, but was too scared. Looking around he could see that the center was being taken care of by Jed and Sabryn, so at the moment was in good hands. He went over to Sabryn and asked, "Mind if I borrow Joci for a short time?"

Looking up from the changing table she shook her head. "No, she hasn't actually started back on her shift. The meeting broke a little early, and I'm not to be anywhere but here today. Jed will be returning to the hydroponics after she's officially back."

"Okay, we'll only be gone for a very short time. I'm taking her down to the cafeteria, and on that subject, would you like me to bring you something from there?"

"Yeah, honestly, we had a bad night with Shayne. He had some type of nightmare and it scared him, and as a result was up half the night. He ended up sleeping with us, and kept kicking both of us in his sleep, making what little we got not quality. So lots and lots of coffee, please. Oh, and I like sugar in mine, about a spoonful."

Smiling he said, "Your wish is my command, oh princess!" This brought out a laugh from Sabryn as he bowed to her. He turned around and headed over to where Joci was sitting deep in thought, and not seeing him approach until he grabbed her gently by the arm and said, "Come with me, we're going to the cafeteria, just for a short time." He could see that she was about to protest, and at that moment pointed over to Sabryn and stated, "Oh it's alright, besides we're getting her some coffee while we're there. Since I suspected that she's the one in charge today, I'd get permission from her, and she said go for it. So shall we?" Again he bowed down and with a sweep of his arms in the direction of the cafeteria and asked once again, "Shall we?"

Again she laughed a little. What could she do? He seemed so genuine, and caring, and right now she admitted, even if it was only to herself, this was something she really needed right now. She reached out her hands to him, and he assisted her up, and they proceeded to the cafeteria. Once there, they found a couple of others taking breaks and getting some snacks or drinks. He had her sit down, and he waited on her, bringing some of that fruit juice she loved, and he a cup of coffee. Again something she hadn't started drinking herself. She had tasted it, and found it not to her liking.

He made himself comfortable, sitting across from her and said, "I'm not sure quite how to ask or state this, but I could see in the meeting that you had something on your mind, and that you really wanted to say something – do I have it just about right?"

How'd he do that? Yes she did, but how'd he know? As far as she knew, she had kept her feelings hidden, but now could see that it wasn't so. And if he could figure it out, how many others had? This bothered her even more and almost drove her back into the depression that she had been fighting for so long. Was she an open book?

He could see the emotions playing across her face and in her eyes. He reached across and gently picked up her hands in his and said, "Look, nobody is judging you. All of us are trying to come to terms with what happened to us. That's including our two leaders. We all have our demons, all have our ghosts, and we will always have them. What matters is what we do about it. Everything that happens in life colors who we are. My mate, bless her soul, told me that I was always sensitive to her and her needs, and I'm finding that I can sense things in you in much the same way. You're young, and yes I know when one is, they hate hearing it, but it's true. You don't know who you are, or what you will be, and then in the middle of trying to discover this, well we all know what happened next. Right now nobody has come up with an idea, let alone a solution to the primitives. So if you have something, I'm willing to listen, and then together in the next meeting *we* can present it, and I'll give credit where credit's due. I know with the insecurities that one has at this time in your life that it is difficult to believe you have something to contribute, but you do."

"But . . ."

He interrupted her, and shook his head, smiling. "No, no ifs, ands, or buts, and so on from you – look I know how it is. So let's work on this together. If your idea is a good one I'll let you know. And if it isn't, well then, we can laugh about it. Remember this, and I know it's hard to believe, but I was your age once upon a time, and had all, well not all, since my mate told me that men don't have the insecurities of women, the same insecurities that you have right now. So what do you say, are you willing to confide in me?"

She was quiet for a moment as she absorbed all that he had told her, and asked of her. And she had to admit that she had never considered that Judd had been her age once. Again, if she had honestly thought about it, of course he had been. Otherwise he wouldn't be here now at his present age. Taking a deep breath and with a small voice she said, "Okay, but . . ."

Smiling he said, as he shook his head, "I said, no 'buts'."

Laughing now, because he had said that, she knew that she was just about to protest, and protect herself from embarrassment. "Look, I just don't want to be laughed at, because what I might say, that's all."

"I said that if there were to be laughter from this that it would be both of us, and I promise that it will not be directed at you personally, unless," and he paused a moment and had a look of devilment on his face, "you do something that deserves such a thing. Fair?"

Looking down at the table she noticed that she hadn't touched her drink, and his cup was empty. Sighing she looked up and into his eyes and said, "Okay, I guess so." He prompted her, at this point, to pass on her idea, and that he would give her an honest opinion, and together they could work on it. So she related, tentatively at first, what had come to her. And as she saw the enthusiasm show in Judd she finally got over her fear and told him the whole idea.

* * *

K'jor, looking at the dwindling supply of wood, cursed as another storm rolled in on them. There just seemed to be little or no respite between them this season of cold. It was enough to drive one crazy. But what could one do? It was much too cold and miserable to be out in these things. T'som had visited him a number of times, keeping him updated on the recovery of the female. And he had cautioned him that she was a very long way away from being healthy once again, and to take care of his impatience. They would not be able to move faster than what the gods were allowing. He couldn't argue with that, but he so desperately wanted answers. At least with this severe season of cold time really wouldn't be an issue. He could wait.

With time on his hands once again his mind drifted back to the destruction of the first of the lairs. At that time it was only their clan. When they had returned the following season of greening they had the clothing from the strange ones, and they found that with those clothes they were able to pass through the veil unharmed. They didn't know what was special about the clothing, but whatever it was it allowed them safe passage beyond. He showed the rest of the warriors what he had found on his previous unplanned visit. And it still was as it had been then. He led them to the hidden wall, and to the closed doorway. They waited out the daylight, and then late in the evening with ropes they scaled the barrier, and briefly stood on top. All of them were in awe to what they were seeing. There appeared to be a large clan hidden here – but none like they had ever seen before. They dropped down into the lair that lay before them and worked their way through a silent strange world. As they worked their way deeper they felt that deep vibration getting stronger, but the sounds that were creating it were just below the threshold of hearing.

Eventually they came upon a shelter where the vibrations appeared to be coming out of, and three of them found an entrance, and with stealth entered. They encountered no one as they went deeper into this magic place. Here they could hear and see lights that shouldn't be there. Fear permeated the air that they breathed. What they were seeing was beyond their experience and understanding. But all of them felt that this had to be evil. So they worked on destroying whatever it was. To kill this hidden being that pushed out the vibrations they were feeling and now hearing. Taking a couple of large stone hammers they began to break everything that they could. Eventually a soft high pitched sound assaulted their senses, and then everything went silent and stopped. The sounds, the vibrations were gone. They left quickly, and because they felt that this was a lair of magicians and sorcerers they needed to destroy and kill everybody. So they went to the far side and worked their way back, breaking into every shelter and slaughtering all they found. This lair had to be inhabited by ones who had to be against their gods. And by the morning light not a soul was left alive other than the clan.

It had been a good thing that this evil had been wiped out. So much of what they saw during their attack was unknown, was beyond their understanding. As they left that bloody morning they found that the blocked door was now open, and as they continued down the pathway, the veil that had hidden the entrance had disappeared. Behind them they left a silent dead world. It was later, when they returned to collect clothing and to allow the priests a chance to see the lair, that the idea entered his mind that there was a good chance there were others. And the idea of other lairs, all hidden in the areas of desolation worried him. It was from this he began to approach the other clans and tribes, showing them what they had found, and with this discovery had asked them to form an alliance – one that would hunt down and destroy each lair as they were discovered. In the three seasons of existence, the alliance had discovered many lairs. They had taken many slaves, and many females to add to their herds. All seemed as it should be. These lairs fell easily, who in the end would have thought that it would be the females, after their inclusion into the breeding herds that would defeat the warriors. If any had suggested such a thing, he would have scoffed at for bringing forth such a fantasy. Yet, before him at this very moment, it was exactly what was transpiring. And this brought him full circle, back to his impatience, back to waiting for this one female to become healthy enough to answer those burning questions. With the alliance he commanded a few thousand warriors, and they had been successful on bringing down every lair they had discovered. Yet, not one of the females taken from those lairs were carrying, no not one.

He found that while he thought through all of this he was pacing back and forth in his shelter. He truly was on edge. He needed to get out, but the winds were howling, throwing the snow around and striking the shelters. Even the two skins that covered the entrance were whipping, allowing the cold to penetrate deeply within. And when the skins whipped aside new snow would blow inside and pile by the entrance. No he would have to endure this additional time here inside, out of that storm, even though his nerves were definitely on edge. He shivered when one of the blasts of air hit him and he retreated deeper into the shelter, getting close to the fire, sat down, and stared. The gods were definitely showing their power this season of cold, and it again showed him how weak he was when comparing himself to them. He grabbed another layer of clothing, and wondered how it could be so cold inside the shelter. He shivered a little, and pulled his chair a little closer to the fire, and for a short time stared at the dancing flames as they consumed the wood stacked within its hungry grasp.

While staring his mind took him back once more –

They continued to be successful in rooting out these lairs, and destroying them, allowing no one to escape so that any warning could go out to any that continued to exist – at least until that one. They never did figure out where this small group had found a way past the attacking forces, the many patrols, and lookouts that had been posted. With the amount of warriors that he had at his disposal, it had been easy to cover any and all routes out of the lair, yet this one group had – further proof of their skills as sorcerers. It had taken some time, but eventually they had been located, and through a number of skirmishes, and attacks he had driven them towards the Sacred Mountains, and the trap he had waiting for them. But it had failed and they had escaped into the Sacred Mountains. It had been a complete surprise when word had come back that the patrol, which was guarding the only route was found dead, with no mark upon them, no sign that any had been in their camp. It spoke of deep sorcery.

The following season of greening, hunters who braved the lower areas of the Sacred Mountains reported on finding three bodies, two males and a female. One of the priests and a healer went to check on these reports, and like the patrol that had been guarding the only route into the mountains, these three had no marks upon them to even know why they had passed into the spirit world. The conclusion, simply stated, was that it had been the gods who had gotten revenge on these three. The female had been carrying and was late in that carrying. On closer inspection of the bodies, even though their dress was similar to the tribes, they came to the conclusion that these were the missing ones from the one lair that a small group had escaped. And there had been no way for such a small group to have wiped out that patrol, leaving it once again to sorcery. At least he knew that with this discovery that none had escaped, and his attacks would remain unknown to any lairs that still existed, and he felt that there were many more out there.

"Look", Judd stated, "there won't be another meeting until tomorrow. I know that you've got to go and help with the children, and you love just doing that. I've got a couple of things that I need to do also. So continue to think on what you've told me. I think it's a great idea, and truthfully I'm surprised that someone else didn't see it. I mean it's been staring us right in the face all this time and none of us saw it, but you."

"But Judd . . ."

Again smiling, he interrupted her and said, "Now remember I did say no buts."

Laughing now because once again he had reminded her that was exactly what he had said, and once again she had tried. "Okay, okay. It's just that . . . well, I just thought that since it was something that was there, that it had been looked at and ignored as not important. Are you sure that you're not just being nice?"

"Oh I don't have a problem being nice, and no, that isn't what I'm doing. I really think your idea has merit, and with a direction to work towards, we can probably come up with a way to end this, even with such a small group. But," he paused and smiled, "there I just used it."

With a questioning look on her face, Joci asked, "Did what?"

Laughing he said, "I just used the word I told you that you couldn't"

"Oh." Then she saw the small joke and began laughing herself.

Once both of them had finally settled back down he said, "We're probably going to need some help from one of the cities. After you passed on your idea, some thoughts have been flowing through my mind, and if the rest are up for it then we may be able to finally see an end to these attacks."

"Really?" She asked, not truly believing that her idea was something that any of them would have considered valuable.

Again smiling Judd said, "Yes, really." Looking up at the clock on the wall he got up and said, "Oh my time does just fly. Look I'll talk with you again tonight at our final meal, but I have to go and work on something for the leaders." He gave her one last encouraging smile and went out through the double swinging doors and was gone. But very shortly he returned through the double doors, looked at her and shrugged. "I forgot that I promised Sabryn coffee, and I can't just head off and forget. I've found that there's too much of that as I get older." He went over to the kitchen area grabbed a thermos of coffee, and the condiments that she had requested and once again was out the door.

She took her half-filled glass, got up, and headed back to the daycare center where she had just been before this conversation with Judd. Deep in thought as she headed back, she looked up in surprise when she found herself back, and hadn't even realized that she had walked the halls to get back to the center. Looking up she saw that Sorrel had joined the others in the center, and was looking quite happy that her pregnancy was continuing without any complications. Joci had to admit that Sorrel was still a beautiful woman, even if she was somewhere in her second, third.

"Hi Joci," Sorrel said lightly, "how's everything going with you?"

She had to admit that since she had allowed Judd in her life as a surrogate grandfather that everything seemed to be looking up. Now she would have at least two people to talk to, and maybe she could even begin to develop a friendship with Sorrel. She really hadn't had much contact with her, but there just seemed to be a slight draw towards this woman. Where she felt that Seirra was like an older sister, she sensed that Sorrel could be a girlfriend, something that she had desperately needed, but since the capture hadn't been available. Still a little shy she looked down and said, "Okay, I guess. This has been so hard." Suddenly she felt arms around her and looked up to find that Sorrel had come over and hugged her.

Sorrel laughed and said, I'd get closer but I seem to have something sticking out in front of me that prevent that."

Considering what she knew of what had happened to Sorrel, it really was surprising to her that Sorrel could be happy, and appear to be unconcerned, if only . . . yes if only she could learn, but the nightmares were there almost every night, and the fears that would continue to surface unbidden, how long would it take before she was finally able to get past them? Because she really wanted to be able to move on and just be herself once more. She looked up into Sorrel's eyes and asked, "Can we talk, you know, as we girls like to do? I really could use a friend to confide in now and then." She was quickly embarrassed by what she had just asked, and actually could feel her face heat up, telling her that she had just blushed.

Putting her hands on Joci's shoulders she replied, "Look, there's no reason to feel embarrassed by asking such a thing. Of course, I'd love to be your friend. I'm sure while our experiences are somewhat different, I'm sure that at the same time we have a lot in common." She smiled, patted Joci's shoulder and said, "I've got to go as I have the security office duty, but please come and see me any time."

"Oh, thank you. I've had no one to talk to, girl to girl, since Seirra went into labor, and I've missed those times, and all of the times my friends, back in the city, and I would get together and just talk." She'd heard from the other women what had happened to Sorrel. And while she knew that she could never be as free with her body as Sorrel had, what had happened to her later really showed Joci what a strong woman Sorrel was. So in some ways she really looked up to her. She had survived, had lost a daughter, and while, at times, she could see the sadness in her eyes, she'd appeared to have moved on in her life, and was very much looking forward to this new child that was growing inside of her. Maybe she could fit in after all.

* * *

She was sitting in one of those meetings once again. But this time she was as nervous as one could get. She was truly worried that once Judd presented her idea that she would be scoffed, and laughed at. And even with her growing circle of support, she really didn't know if she could handle it or not. It would just be so much easier not to be here at all, but Judd had insisted, and told her not to worry. She had given him a brave smile, but honestly even that had been hard. So here she sat not really listening to what was being said as the meeting was brought to order. It would have been so much easier to be watching this from the daycare center instead.

". . . Judd had informed me that a very good idea had been presented to him, and one he feels is our salvation. He told me about it, and once he did, it was obvious that he was right. So I'll let him pass on what was told, and if you react the same way that we, Shellian and I, did, then you'll hit yourself for missing the obvious. I mean it was right there all the time, but all of us overlooked it as trivial, and unimportant."

Judd stood up and then presented her idea to the group, and as he did, she shuddered inside just waiting for the proverbial hammer to fall, but it didn't. There was silence as the people around the table thought about what he presented, and she could see the light go on in their eyes as they saw it too. Judd looked over at her and smiled. He'd been right all along. He looked back at the group and said, "As you can see we have much ahead of us to make this work, and like we've been told all along, we will only get one chance at this. And even though she doesn't want to be mentioned, the person responsible for this is Joci."

At this point when he had mentioned her name she flushed hot, very embarrassed for having been singled out. She looked down for a moment to try and get her emotions back in control, looked up, and saw everyone smiling at her. They spontaneously gave her a round of applause, embarrassing her further. Judd came over and stood next to her, looked down at her, and then placed his arms around her and whispered. "See, I told you it's a great idea."

Shellian tapped the table for attention, and Judd returned to his seat. She looked directly at Joci and said, "Thank you. We were getting very desperate with no one coming up with anything at all." She turned to the rest and said, "The winter will be ending soon, and with spring we will be running out of time, since we know that for most of the spring the primitives are trying to recover from the winter months. It has been shown that they begin their campaigns, and while I'm sure they do not call them that it's what they are, late in the spring, and generally run through the summer, and into early fall, where once again they must prepare for the winter. With winter almost gone, as I said earlier, we are very short on time. Judd has suggested that we get the cities involved where we can, and I have to agree. The three of us, Judd, Saige, and myself, have been discussing this a lot, and we're going to put forth some of what we discussed, and expect all of you to contribute. We need *all* input", at which point she looked directly at Joci, "any and all ideas to make this work is welcome." Turning to Jarid, and while she didn't know if Jeanna had worked in the entertainment field as Jarid had, she had noticed that they worked well together. "You and Jeanna will need to team up and come up with a plan and a layout, and the roles that we must play to pull this off. Again we're very short on time, and the pressure is on. To prevent any more suffering and the attack of another of our cities this must work, and work perfectly the first time. So other than the work in the security office and obviously, the taking care of the children, our time will be involved with this project. Saige and Judd will be giving out assignments to everyone. Now if there are no questions let's get to it." She looked around the table, smiling, as she saw that there were many very lively conversations going on – so much different than most of the meetings where there would just be silence as they broke up – a good sign, a very good sign.

She walked down the side of the table to where Joci was sitting, still in silence, and obviously still in shock that her idea could have had such an impact. Looking down at her once she had gotten Joci's attention, she said, "See, we all have things to contribute, and I know that being so young, and again I know how you hate to hear that, but it's true, we feel that many times that what we have, ideas that may have come to us, things we see, aren't important. But as you just saw that's not even close to the truth. Look, why don't you come with me, I'm just about to make contact with Sara, and see if she agrees with this. After all, like you were, she's presently a captive, and in this case the sister to Shayne who was our leader, and as you know died on our flight to here. But she speaks the primitive tongue and has more insight into their lives right now than any of us. So while I feel that what you've stated is correct, and that's why we're running with it, she'll confirm it for us, and if you're right, we may be able to get our people back and end their suffering, all because of you."

Joci, once again could feel the heat in her face as she was praised once again. This was beyond anything she'd expected. So instead of speaking, she just nodded her head, got up and stood beside Shellian, Shellian for heaven's sake, one of the leaders who were responsible for everything, including their rescue. She just didn't feel worthy. She followed Shellian into the security office, which had also become the operations office since they were in constant contact with the many cities, and where they were monitoring all of the bugs that they had planted. With all this additional responsibility they now had three people in here constantly, only reducing it to two at the late night hours. Seve was monitoring the bugs and the views from the above, and Shellian signaled him that she needed his place. Seve exchanged locations and stood by Joci watching, as she, to see what Shellian planned.

With practiced ease, something that would have been foreign just a short time ago, she brought up the images of the shelter where Sara and the two women were residing, and waited as she could see that the primitive T'som was talking to Sara. From the one sided conversation it dealt more with how much she had recovered, and soon they would begin their discussions. From the body language of the two women, who did not understand the primitive language, she could see that there was a lot of fear as they more cowered in the corner, than observed. The two hid as much in the shadows as they could, being as far away from the primitive as the shelter allowed. All of them felt for these women, but at this moment there was very little that could be done other than observing. If this idea worked, it could very well be that soon theirs, and all the others who were suffering at the hands of the primitives, would end, and they would be released. At least that was the hope. Since nothing like this had ever been tried, the outcome was unknown. Seve, who spoke the language, followed the conversation closely, while Joci, who had been studying the language as well as the others who had been rescued, could only pick up a word or two. She suspected that if this primitive spoke much slower that she might catch more.

Eventually, it was obvious that this one was finished speaking as he looked over the three women and left the shelter.

They could see that Sara still had little strength, and once again, even this short session with the primitive had exhausted her. Sara turned to the other women in the shelter and told them that everything was still okay, and that she needed to rest once again. At this point Shellian spoke, knowing that Sara was wearing the almost invisible ear piece that provided both send and receive capabilities. From the hidden bugs she could tell that she had received the voice transmission, signaled slightly that she would continue once she was lying down, did so, faced the wall and signaled Shellian to continue. In a quick precise way she passed on what their conclusions were, and the three of them in the security office saw her eyes fly wide open, and then there was a pause as she considered what she had been told. Then slowly a smile came across her face, even though it was fleeting. They all could see a flare of hope in her eyes as she considered the facts as presented. She followed by carefully signing a very big confirmation. This had presented to her a number of times with different primitives, from R'san to T'som. One way or the other in the words spoken to her, they had specifically presented their suspicions. And like the rest of them it was something that hadn't even occurred to her. They could see her shake her head slightly as she considered the ramifications. She signed simply a question that stated, "How could I have missed something so obvious?"

Shellian replied, saying, "You're not alone on that one. We all did. It took someone who was young and unsure of herself to point it out to us." She smiled, even though she knew that Sara couldn't see them. With the small kit that Saige had left there had been no contacts so the visual was missing. Contacts had to be made for each individual, and without knowing who they might come across it was decided to leave the contacts out. "Okay, you've given us what we needed. Now all we can hope is that we can bring all of this to an end soon. How soon we're really not sure, but as we get closer to what we will try to do, then we'll keep you up to date." She paused a moment as emotion choked her up. It was obvious to Joci that Shellian cared for Sara, and she could understand it. Before signing off Shellian said, "It is hoped that before the end of summer that this will be over one way or the other. Good luck Sara, and get better please." When Shellian turned around both Seve and Joci could see tears in her eyes. Shellian just shook her head and didn't say anything for a short time. "Okay Seve, it's yours again, Joci let's go, we've a lot of work ahead of us, and thank you so very much."

"Why are you thanking me?" Joci asked, quite perplexed.

'Because, my young lady, nobody here had a clue as to what to do, and the clock was ticking. We flat were running out of time, and if nothing happened then other of our cities would have fallen to the primitives, and more of our people would die, become slaves, or have to join those dreaded herds of theirs, suffer, and die at their hands, and now we have something, a chance to prevent it from happening. A chance to rescue the remaining ones, like Sara, who are still alive and suffering, and it's all because of you and your idea, that's why."

A voice came over the PA, "Shellian, your daughter needs you."

Smiling, Shellian continued, "And because of such things as this. I've a family now, that if I lost, it would come close to destroying me. I love Saar and Sam' with all of me, and to lose them would be devastating to say the least, and all of those cities that have fallen have so many of those tragedies, let alone what has transpired since our people have become slaves. I guess in some ways we can say that all of this happened is truly our fault. We grew complacent, and allowed our pride to reach the point where we never considered the consequences for our inattention or lack of diligence. And as usually happens, a leader arose among the primitives that brought them together, and now we are the ones on the run, the ones *desperate to survive*. Now all we can hope is that we can end it, and have our survival assured." She looked up at the monitor and said, "I'm on my way." She turned back to Joci and said, "Guess I'd better go, the boss is demanding my time. Just one last thing, remember everyone here is just as important as any single member and that includes you. So if you have any more brilliant ideas, let someone know please. Now don't take this wrong, but from what Judd told us, you've had this one for a while but was afraid to say anything, and I can understand that completely, but by you delaying, we've lost precious time, and that's all I'm going to say on that subject. Okay then, catch you later, or sooner since I suspect that you're heading for the daycare center, eventually." At this point the two women separated, with Shellian going to her daughter, and Joci heading back to the dorms for a short time before she worked with the children in the daycare center.

Joci had been chastised by Shellian for not saying anything until now, and in a way the dressing down had been mild, reminding her that she was part of this small community and her input was just as important as either Shellian's or Saige's.

Part of her was elated that her idea had sparked the response that it had, but she still truly couldn't believe it. Sighing she shrugged and headed for the dorm to change before getting some food. For some reason she was always hungry, and wondered why she just didn't seem to change, weight wise, with everything she ate. She knew that the rest of the women here were always being careful as to what they ate – always talking about watching their weight or something.

* * *

"Judd said that he could get someone who he used to talk with all the time at the city of Catskill. Funny thing, from the images the city sits just outside of that valley where the primitives gather before they begin their campaigns. It's a wonder that it hasn't been discovered." As Saige leaned against one of the walls looking out through the large windows on their hidden valley, he paused a moment. "I only hope that this works. We've got Judd doing the heavy lifting here, and with the help of, ah, who'd he say that was, oh yeah, Charley. With the help of Charley, who appears to do much the same thing as Judd, he figures that they can have everything put together that we'll need."

Shellian, leaning on the table and with arms crossed, thought briefly before saying anything. "I can only hope that they're able to pull it off. I know that we have Jarid, and Jeanna trying to come up with a script, and that means that as Judd and this Charley works on things, there will be changes and they will have to be able to get those changes produced. I know that we've formed teams to work with both Judd, and Jarid, and any of the members of our scouting team will be there to translate what they come up with, and also let them know if what they are working on will fly with the primitives. After all, something that we think might work because of our society would make no sense to other societies. And thanks to Sara, we've learned so much more. Between what we've gathered from those planted bugs, and her carrying that camera, plus what she's been able to sign to us is irreplaceable. Without that knowledge and what is in these computers, we could have tried this and would have failed because we would have been so far off the mark."

"True, it's so surprising that after all that time of spying on the primitives, doing everything we did when we were still in the city, feeling that we really had a handle on how they lived, just how far off the mark we truly were." Looking at his sister, he had to smile inwardly. It was surprising to him to find that now she was a sister, a mate, and a mother, and yet she appeared to be no different to him. *So many roles we play in life. I'm her brother, mate to Seirra, and father to our twins, and other than feeling older because of the burden of leadership, I really don't feel any different – well that's not quite true but close.* "It just goes to show that from a distance things can be interpreted so wrong. I suspect that anytime anybody does research on a different society, or group, or anything that is different, that we must be careful to exclude our own prejudices, views and such when we make conclusions. But how does one do that? I suspect that it's got to be close to impossible." Stopping for a moment and looking down, he said, "It's so hard to believe what has happened to us, and that we are here. In many ways it still seems more a dream than reality. And time is just flying by so fast now I hardly remember what day it is or even what month. I used to think that our time in training, in the many exercises that we did, in our life in the compound, things were complicated, and the days just seemed to go by quick, but in comparison to now, those times were slow and idyllic, restful, and simple – funny how the perspective changes. Heck, it's the annual 3029, or at least I think it is. Although now that I know what we've learned since we've found the Alpha, I wonder what that date applies to."

What do you mean by that?" Shellian asked.

Looking into her eyes he stated, "Look, we know now that we're the interlopers here. That we came to this place to study this culture and to remain hidden, which until recently had been quite successful. And we know that we've been here a couple of thousand annuals, so it becomes obvious that this number doesn't compute. So was it something that our ancestors developed by approximating the time of the rise of a civilization here, or does it apply to when our people began space flight, or is it tied to something else? I know it's something that, in the end, really doesn't matter. But we've been surprised by so much from the discoveries of this place, and the relearning of our true past, it's just another one of those mysteries that we've yet to solve."

"You know, this is something I really never thought about. You know like how we track the day, by the hours, minutes, and seconds." She laughed and then continued, "Hey we have our hands full with the primitive issue. We don't need any more on our plate, thank you, and besides that's off the subject – something to solve later on, if there is to be a later on that is." Pushing herself off the table now that she was standing, she said, "Look I've got to look in on Sam', and I'm sure that Seirra could use some help with Saharra, and Seth.

So let's get back together just before the midday meal and go check out how's things are progressing. We've only got a month or so left of winter, and we are going to need to be on site and have most of what we need to accomplish by the end of winter, leaving only the minor details to wrap up after that. I've a feeling, that between children and this crushing schedule that there's not going to be much sleep for any of us until this is over, one way or the other. See you back here shortly, brother." She headed out the door and down the hallway out of his sight.

He had to admit that she was right. Sleep would be a precious commodity for all of them until this was over. And he knew that when one did not get enough sleep that tempers could be short, and frustration high. But, whatever the feelings, whatever the pressures, they could not let up, nor fall behind on the very tight schedules, and the too many things that still had to be accomplished. When they moved out to do the actual ground work, it would leave the Alpha with only enough to operate the security office, since the rest would be needed on site, and they would remain there no matter what the weather threw their way, until they had accomplished what they set out to do. And he hoped that there would be time to run through it and test the many parts to insure that there would be no failures. Murphy seemed to always raise his head at the most inopportune times, and this was one of those times where they could not afford interference from Murphy.

* * *

Looking over the script that was being put together Staven stated, "No, no, you don't understand. If we did it that way they'd know immediately that we aren't who we are saying we are." He pulled up some images on the screen and continued, as he pointed at the screen. "Look here and watch the priest. I'll translate so that you can understand. Remember, they haven't reached the point in their advancements yet to where they know any science at all. So we cannot reference anything that suggests such a thing. You have to look at it as if none of this exists. If nothing else, look back on the early history of our own people, and I'm not speaking of when we came to this planet but back when we were primitives. Study that and see how we reacted." Staven could see the frustration in Jarid's eyes, but if they had tried what he and Jeanna had put together it would have failed, and failed miserably. Looking at the two of them he smiled and said, "Look we're all under both a heavy time constraint and a lot of pressure, but if we do it wrong it won't matter in the end. Do you need someone to come in and help research this so that we can get it close to right?"

The two looked at each other, with Jeanna shaking her head and he doing the same, both giving the negative. Sighing Jarid said, "I've been doing this kind of stuff for as long as I've been in the business, and I have to admit that this is, by far, the toughest thing I've ever attempted. I truly thought that this one would have worked, but again what you just showed us, and translated for us, once again, proves that it isn't right. Okay, we'll take a break, and then the two of us will start over."

At this point Staven left and headed over to help Judd. While Jarid and Jeanna had the burden of providing the direction and words that they would use, Judd would be responsible, along with his counterpart in Catskill, in producing everything that they would need. And most of this was being designed and built at the base of the mountains, at the secondary area where the ancestors had worked during their field work. Stone was already down there, and he was heading down to replace him. But first he needed to inform Saige of the progress or lack thereof, on the script. Again this was something that needed to be complete ahead of almost everything else. Since the actors in this fiction would need to practice their individual parts. He headed down the hallway to the security office where Saige, with Shellian were studying the small valley where the primitives would gather. He heard Saige say, as he reached it, "Look, there's the waterfall, and it does look like it puts out a lot of water. That's favorable, hmmm, three entrances or exits, we've got to reduce that to just one, and look this one leads directly back into the grasslands, so this is the one we need to keep open."

When Staven touched his shoulder Saige turned and asked, "Yes? What is it Staven?"

With both Shellian and Saige looking at him he said, "I've had to reject the latest offering from our script writers. I suggested that they look back on our own time when we were primitives. I also ran a segment that we recorded when Sara was with the priest and translated it for them. And yes, I know that this is critical, but if it is wrong it won't matter. Anyway, heading on down to replace Stone, so he can come back here and help where he can. Unfortunately we have no one who can replace Judd. He's the only one who understands this stuff, and the list keeps getting longer. I'm glad that he's got a counterpart in one of the cities that is close to where we will be working."

Shellian took a deep breath, "Okay, I was hoping that there would have been more progress on the script. Maybe we picked the wrong people to do it. I know that this was his business, and Jeanna had acted some, so she was a good fit to help, but now I don't know. Did you ask if they needed help?"

Shaking his head he said, "Yes, exactly, but both of them declined. Oh well, I'm off, see both of you later."

Looking at her brother she said, "That's really not good news. It's something that we need now." Then looking back at her screen, she said, "Guess we'd better get back at it. Look here", as she pointed at the screen, "it looks like the entrance from the grasslands is just a narrow passage with cliffs that overlook the path. This looks like an excellent place to set up part of our play. So have you thought about the time of day that you want this to take place?"

"Actually, yes. At first I thought anytime during the day would work, but as I thought about it, I think pulling this off at night would have a greater effect on them. And it would make it easier to hide anything that could accidently be seen. Darkness can hide a lot, and with our narrow window of opportunity I'm sure that we'll not remember, or be able to check that everything is hidden from sight. The one factor in our favor at this moment is that the primitives don't have a clue that we know their gathering place, and at no time has anyone from the cities put their noses outside of one other than us, so I think that they will go there with no expectations of discovery at all – and I'm counting on it. Look while these images are nice, with the next major storm we need to take a trip and be on the ground in this valley so that we can get a true feel for the place. Images are nice, but they don't always give one a true perspective. We've even attempted to set up a holos in the meadow area, and while it gave us a rough idea, we just didn't have to power to drive the units so the image was a bit ghostly.

"The other problem that we face is that there will be a couple thousand warriors in there, so this is going to be a nightmare as far as monitoring the situation. We are going to be spread quite thin with constant monitoring from here, and the communications and coordination on the ground. I'm glad that the systems that ancestors have in place allow night vision. All of us on the ground and everybody who will be monitoring this will be using it. But it would be so easy to be distracted because of everything that will be going on. Once we have an overall workable plan we'll begin to practice and test things out with that holos, and some props. Then we'll know if an idea will really work or whether we need to change it. We'll set up in that side canyon where Sorrel and Stone located the pathway down the mountainside. While it's not close to the same size as the valley we'll be working, it has much of the same things so that we, at least, can see if this will work at all."

Nodding her head in agreement she said, "I guess then we had better do our part, and that this had better work. Look, I've got to go feed a hungry daughter, but we've so much more to accomplish than just this. I guess it has been decided that if this works that we will have the primitives deliver their captives back to the same valley. I know originally we thought about using the camping area of the travelers, but that would be just too much of a coincidence to use that site – kind of giving ourselves away."

"True, Seve and I will be heading out to test those emitters to see if they are waterproof, and if they will receive a signal once they're immersed in water. We have Jaiden and with Starr and Sabryn, they are looking through the archives and research that our ancestors did to make sure that what we are attempting is accurate. They will need to continually check in with Jarid and Jeanna to be sure that we remain true. These people are not stupid; in fact they are quite intelligent and adapt quickly. So everything we do must ring true." Looking at his sister all he could think was that they were moving in the right direction, now if time would only cooperate.

"That leaves Seirra and Joci. They seem to get along well. So as time is available to Seirra because of the demand of the twins, the two of them are looking at accommodations for those that we will be able to absorb into the Alpha, and others that will need to be placed into the remaining cities. Then we still must man the security, slash, operations office." She sighed before continuing, "Just not enough bodies and that ole clock keeps on a ticking. Oh yeah, Jed has been working to get the full hydroponic system up and operating so that if we do end up with a very large number of refugees that we will have enough food to feed them. And while Judd is just too busy with the demands of this project, he'll eventually need to break from that work and divert some of the resources to additional supplies, so that we can fill all the lockers and supply rooms. We really have no idea what we'll need or how much, but I'd rather have too much than too little."

"I guess that's it. Shall we get our part going, now that we're up to date on what has, is, and needs to be done?" They both headed out of the meeting room, down the hallway in opposite directions with a promise to meet again after the evening meal. Shellian had an appointment to go and talk with Sara. The recovery was very slow, baby steps really. Had she been in the facility with the medical care available she probably would have made a full recovery by now. But such things did not exist within the primitive world. Sara was still fragile, and could still succumb in her weakened state, and it had been a miracle that she had survived long enough to receive the antibiotics. Only the fact that she, and the other two women were left alone had probably kept her alive.

"Look Sara, I know that it's something that's hard to understand, but they've come to the conclusion that you must be a priest, well priestess, and that's why they want so desperately to talk to you. To find out what you and the rest of the women are doing to beat their warriors. I know that you haven't a clue, and I'm just going to let it remain there for now. Just be comfortable with this fact, and we've confirmed it here, you and the rest of our women cannot get pregnant from any of them, it's quite impossible. So while we cannot do anything as of yet to prevent having to submit to them, at least you can be comforted from the fact that they cannot get any of you pregnant. And this is why they have concluded that you and the rest of the women are warriors. But because you speak their tongue, and they don't understand ours you have been placed in the same class as their priests. It, from what we can discern from both the bugs, the conversations that we had, and the attitudes presented, has led us to a very difficult conclusion. Since, as you know, we women only have two purposes in life. Bringing into the world the next generation, and the raising of the same to an age where they begin to fulfill their roles.

"So as you are brought before that head priest, you must begin to put on the air of an equal, and that is as you can. I know that the infection that almost took your life has left you without strength and endurance, but all of us are running out of time, and the leader of that clan is running out of patience. This problem has him very worried. I really wish that we'd been able to get you the contacts so that we could pass on the images that we have to be able to let you see the whole situation where you are, not that you aren't aware anyway. We'll try and give you as much data as we can as you go into those meetings with T'som. We need to begin to make it look like that you can see beyond just your small room, to give the appearance that you have the sight, and can see beyond your small boundaries, to begin to build some awe and some fear into them. And if they confront you, you have the very reason that you cannot but on a limited basis show your true power. We have an operation now going that we hope will get all of you safely away from them. It is still months away, and I know that this has to be a disappointment, but where there was no hope before, at least now there might be an end to this suffering and death in sight."

She could see Sara absorbing everything she had just passed on to her and had nodded just enough to confirm that she had heard all of it. It was obvious to Shellian that she was still very weak, and even listening to this long winded explanation had tired her. It was also obvious that she had questions, and was thinking about everything that had been passed. Even though it was obvious that she could barely stay awake, Sara signed a question. "How can you be so sure about this, that none of us can become pregnant? As often as we have to submit, it just seems to be impossible to prevent, although none of have."

"I can understand your concern," Shellian responded, and paused a moment to be sure and word it right, "but from the research that we've done we can guarantee that it's quite impossible. I don't want to give you the reasons that we know this, because if this became known to the primitives I believe that it would increase their attempts at destroying us, and I don't know about you, but for me and the rest, and yes I know you too, we're all *desperate to survive* this, and hope to find a peaceful solution to this. But if not peaceful, even an uneasy truce right now would be better than nothing. When we were there, we planted bugs everywhere, so we know just about everything that can be known about the clan that you're part of. And we will absolutely let you know all of it. Since we have no idea what will be important or what you will be able to use to fulfill your new role. Good luck with it, and get as much rest as you can. And I really, truly hope that very soon that I can see you in the flesh instead of this way." At this point she saw the acknowledgment from Sara, broke the connection, took a deep breath, shuddered a little, left the security office and headed for the daycare center. She needed to spend some time with her daughter. Seeing Sara like that, and watching the other two women cower in fear, shook her to her very soul, and right now she felt somewhat down. She needed this time with her child to temporarily forget about this and just be a mother for a short time.

Sara wondered why Shellian knew that none of them could get pregnant by the primitives. But she had to admit that so far none had. Again why wouldn't she tell her why? Was Shellian afraid that she would somehow let it slip? Well, as sick as she was, she guessed it could be something that might happen. But what was the secret that Shellian couldn't reveal? It must have been something huge, if they felt that by revealing it could increase the primitives' animosity against them. But weren't they the same people? After all that is what they all had been taught. But what if it wasn't so, no, that truly didn't make any sense. Oh well, she found that once again that she was falling asleep and couldn't do anything about it.

* * *

Saige, shaking his hands trying to get some circulation going said, "Damn, this water is icy." He and Seve were at the pond outside of the complex, feeling the cold, very cold really, spray coming off the waterfall. Even though they had sunshine from the two suns this day, there was very little warmth. Snow lay thinly all around them. Again this was something they had yet to figure out. Outside of this small hidden valley the snow was piled high. In some places they could stand on each other's shoulders and still not reach the top. It was a tough strong winter. Had it been that way the first season they had spent on the mountains, none of them would be here today, and all would have been lost. Saige looked down in the cold clear water to see if the casing around the emitter leaked. So far it looked okay. Between Seve and himself they laid ten of them across the length of the pond, just off the shoreline. Both of them had wet clothes now, both from the falling mist from the falls, and from immersing the emitters into that icy water. Turning to Seve Saige said, "I don't know about you, but I'm now thoroughly cold. And these wet clothes aren't helping. Let's go change, get something hot to drink in the cafeteria, and then see if we can make these things work."

Nodding in agreement Seve said, "You'll get no argument out of me. I'm freezing, and that water is just unbelievably cold. It seems cold enough to freeze, so why isn't it?"

"You got me. Along with the lack of snow here, it's one of those mysteries that we have yet to solve. It's obvious that our ancestors knew what they were doing, and that over time we've forgotten much of what they took for granted. It's frustrating to know that we've lost so much, and what makes it even more troubling is that we really have no idea. We only find out as we rediscover something else that we knew nothing about."

They returned about an hour later, warm, and now carrying a thermos of coffee to help keep it that way. "Okay, let's check and see if they've stayed dry. No, we're not going to pull them back out and check, but just see if we can see if any water has seeped in while we were away." A breeze had picked up while they were gone, and had a familiar bite to it that promised that there was an approaching storm. Saige started at one end, while Seve started at the other and they met in the middle. "The five I saw seem water tight, how about yours?" The emitters were in clear plastic containers that had spikes on the bottom to anchor them to the bottom, and none had broken free to float to the surface, so at least that part appeared to be working.

Seve replied, "So far so good. Let's get out of this wind; it just cuts through everything we're wearing."

"No fools in my family, I agree." Looking around Saige could see that the greenhouse area would allow them to see the pond and with the portable unit, from there, they should still be in range to test and see if this would work. So leading off he and Seve headed there, stepped inside briefly to get warm, and the returned to the outside. "Here goes nothing." Saige said, as he pressed the switch. They were to get a 3D test signal if the emitters worked, but instead got nothing. Looking perplexed Saige mused, "I wonder what happened?" He walked a little closer to the pond and tried again, and once again, nothing.

"I wonder if maybe it could be the water blocking the signal." Seve suggested, "And if it is, how do we get a signal to them?"

"I don't know, but I know that they were tested before we placed them in the water and they functioned as they were supposed to do. Well, I guess we can just leave them there, at least by doing so we will see if those cases will remain watertight. We'll need to go talk with Judd and see what he thinks. But for now let's get out of this weather. Heck, in the short time we've been out here we've gone from a sunny day to one where the clouds are starting to build. It looks like that storm is getting here faster than we thought."

* * *

Several days later Saige was walking one of the many hall ways within the complex when he heard children screaming. Very concerned he picked up his pace, and actually began to run as he headed towards the daycare center. Turning the last corner he stopped in his tracks and stared. At this time of day the door into the center was kept open, and on the floor in the hallway was a layer of heavy fog, not much more than ankle high, but what was something like this doing in here? He could see that it had filtered into the open doorway, and was slowly drifting towards where he was standing. He saw Judd approaching from the opposite side walking through this stuff seemingly unconcerned. He had a smile on his face and as he came closer he asked, "Well, what do ya' think?" Seeing the concerned look on Saige's face, he continued, "Oh don't worry about it, this is completely harmless. But you have to admit it's quite an effect, don't you think?"

"You created this?" Saige asked.

"Of course, I was looking over some of the theatrical equipment that could be created, considering what we are trying to do is put on a show, I thought it would be a good place to look for special effects. After all we're going to need everything that we can find to pull this off."

It wasn't long until everyone who was in the facility had come because of the screaming of the children, only to find them now laughing as they ran through this ground fog. They were as perplexed as Saige when they had turned the corner to find a ground fog hugging the floors and drifting through doorways. Turning and facing them Saige said, "Quite an effect, and of course, Judd is responsible. He's assured me that it's harmless, and while at first it terrorized our children, at least the toddlers, you can now see that they are having a blast." Turning back to Judd he asked, "What's your plans for this stuff? Plus we are inside, so it would be easier to make it do this, can it work in a large area?"

"A good question, a very good question. I think it comes down to the size and number. But by looking at the history of these things they have been used in large areas. When we finally set up our mock-up, then we can try it and see. I'm counting on the fact that at night there is little wind, and that this stuff will hug the ground just like you are seeing it now. Remember that there's a full air recirculating system in here, and it still has remained on the floor, although you can see it being drawn into the floor vents. I was curious to see what the stuff looked like. The images I saw in the archives looked pretty spectacular, and as you could see, the initial effect was fear. And before you ask, no I didn't think it would get this far down the hallway, and drift into the daycare center, but no harm done, as you can see, the kids love it now."

"That may be so, but it surely panicked all the rest of us when we heard the children scream, so please warn us in the future if you are trying something that could put us on edge."

Laughing a little Judd said, "Ah, where's the fun in that? Yeah I know what you're saying, but look, at times it is better to surprise someone to get an honest reaction. If it surprises us, or for a brief time scares us, then we know that it could have a more devastating effect on the primitives who have no knowledge of this."

Saige had to admit that what he stated made sense, but at the same time with the pressure, and time restraints everybody was on edge. "Okay, I can see that, but just be careful. Look I know that at one time we were going to be setting up out in the meadows, but changed our minds since the small attaching valley, where the entrance to the trail to the secondary facility is located, has much the same structure as the valley where we will be doing this, so, as you know, we'll be using it. It has the waterfall, the cliffs, the narrow trail into the area and the steep walls. Yes, it's much smaller, but if we can get things to work there on the smaller scale, all we will have to do is scale it up to work in the larger space. So any time that you want to get started on placing everything into position for testing, grab who you need and do it. We need to begin testing all of this and see what we need to change, what works, what doesn't, and what fails miserably. You know like our initial attempts to make the emitters work underwater. That took some work to finally solve that issue, but I have to admit that the effects that can be created are unbelievable. If I didn't know that they were just created images, I'd swear that they were real."

"Yeah, once the problem was solved the results were rather nice." Judd stopped a moment and then said, "Look, I'm sorry about the interruption here, but now that I've seen this, I think that if we can make this work that I have a great idea of how to enhance this to make it even more frightening to the primitives."

"That's great, Judd, but just don't test it here. We really don't need a repeat thank you."

Laughing once again, Judd replied, "Oh, you don't need to worry about that. Did you know that back on our home world that there was a tradition that they did once an annual? It was where they celebrated the dark side of things. From what I could ascertain it originally had come about as a way to appease the dead spirits when we were primitives, but evolved over time as a celebration, more for kids, and that much of what we are attempting to create was common in households. Look come by when you have time and I'll bring up the information and you can watch some of the footage on it, in fact it probably would be a good idea that in the next meeting that we have that all of us watch it. After all, as you've reminded all of us, we need all the ideas we can get to pull this off, and this could get the mind going in the right direction."

"Okay, look we have our normal daily meetings every morning, so do you think you could bring it up on the monitors in the morning? I'll come by later this day and you can show me."

"Yes to both. Look Saige, if you have a moment now, it will only cost you about thirty minutes, so let me show you now. Then if you want everybody to see it then it will be a simple thing to do, and why not have your sister come along, so that we have both sides. I'll be down in what has become my work area, so when the two of you can get over there, soon, please do. I'll be waiting."

After about twenty minutes both Saige and Shellian showed up at the work area of Judd, with Shellian stating, "Okay, Judd we're here, and I must admit that I could use the break, this schedule is really tough. But you won't hear me complain, since we have it so much better than others."

Judd signaled them over to one of the larger monitors where he had some large rectangular boxes set up. When he saw the questioning looks he pointed at them and said, "Oh these things are speakers. It was kind of a hobby of mine back in Jade. These are a very old design, but the sound quality out of them I just love. Anyway, have a seat and enjoy the show."

What they saw, as the archives played, were children laughing and having fun, it was nighttime and they all were dressed in some sorts of costumes. As they approached the houses there were decorations that reflected the dark, and some had those fog generators, others had what looked to be grave yards in the front area. They could hear those children through those speakers, and the quality was unbelievable. When the children would get to the doors they would knock or push a button and the ones inside would then open their doors, at which point the children would yell "trick or treat", hold out a bag, and something would be placed into those bags, and the children would move on to the next one.

"What I want you to see is all the different ideas that were used to give the feeling of the dark. And you can see that our ancient ancestors had many ideas. And you can also see that the very young who are apparently going on this trek for the first time are a bit tentative, but it doesn't take them long to figure out what's going on. And it looks like, even for the adults, that all of them are having a good time. I think they called this Halloween."

The two of them were fascinated by what they saw. So many of the homes decorated in the macabre, so many ideas, who would have thought? They looked at each other and then Shellian asked, "Are you sure about this? I mean I never realized that we did this kind of thing, and made it fun?"

Smiling Judd replied, "Yeah really. Maybe it was one of the reasons for coming here in the first place. While I'm sure that there's going to be major differences, there's probably going to be things that are similar. And let's admit it; death is something that we all face. There's no way to avoid it. Although again if you look through history, many tried, but as far as I know nobody ever succeeded in cheating death. So what do you think? Should everybody see this?"

Together Shellian and Saige replied, "Yes.", and then laughed. Saige said, "Go ahead sis, I'll bow to your will on this one."

"Why thank you brother, Judd, yes I think you're quite right, everyone needs to see this. And on another subject, I know that my brother has let you know about the thoughts on the test area, but looking at the time, the major moon will be in the sky in another five days, and from what we can see it should be a cold clear night. Do you think that we can at least see some of your magic then, so that we can get an idea of its effects? Now we know that nothing is truly ready, but as you so amply proved today, seeing is believing."

Thinking for a moment before answering Judd replied, "I guess so. But don't expect much. There's so much that is untested, and we've really nothing set up as of yet, but I guess we can at least try."

"Good, tap whoever you need. We need to at least see something if for no other reason than to show everyone that we actually are accomplishing something."

* * *

It was late at night and everybody was chilled to the bone. After all, while it had been clear, it was still winter in the mountains. The major moon had lit the countryside in a soft eerie glow, and as they had waited for the show to begin, the cold began to work its way through the many layers of clothing, but now that the short show was over and they were sitting around the tables in the cafeteria, drinking lots of coffee and trying to get warm, there was a cautious euphoria that had permeated all of them that were present. The test, which only had very little of the total planned operations worked, and that was all they could hope. Now with the script almost finished and the translation in the process, it wouldn't be long before they began to film the people who would be in this play.

From this point on until they did this for real, there would be practice, practice, practice, followed by more of the same. Judd, with Stone as his assistant, continued to test and work out the problems as they used the small valley as a test bed, slowly bringing in the different elements, and solving the many unexpected or unknown problems that continued to rise. Winter was almost at an end, and soon they would need to be in the valley where the primitive alliance would gather. It would take time to get everything in place, followed by the hiding of anything that they had worked in the valley. There could be no sign left to make the primitives suspicious that other than another tribe or clan, which wasn't a part of the alliance, had been anywhere close to this area.

CHAPTER EIGHTEEN

"Charley, look you've got to provide that stuff. There's no way that we will want to transport it from here. It's just too far, and there are too many things that could happen. Again it must be ready. Storms about to end, or at least switch to rain, and we have to have everything on site before they end, and the primitives begin their annual foraging after the winter. Plus most of the heavy lifting needs to be complete before then also. We need that rain to help hide what we're doing." Judd looked down at the monitor where he saw his buddy Charley.

"Yeah, I know," Charley said, "But look, this stuff isn't something that's that easy to produce, let alone handle. And with everything else that you've requested, well let's just say, that while we have the cooperation of the council and everybody here, since we've learned how close the primitive headquarters is to us, it still has taxed our capacity. And since much of this was never in our replicators, it has taken time to get the software integrated, tested, and operating. We've found that back when these cities were set up, that for whatever reason, it was deemed that none of the replicators would have this stuff, and they added software to block its addition if someone, oh you know, like me tried to integrate it back into the system. Even with the help of the software engineers here at Catskill, it's been a nightmare, and as you once again so aptly pointed out, time is not our friend. So we are very far behind on the requests, the needs that you have laid out to us, and, to be honest, even the needs of the city.

"Heck, since we've learned that all the cities are vulnerable, and even changing the frequency to our protections has failed, most of the time and resources has gone into coming up with some solution. It is another one of those unanticipated problems from our ancestors. It seems that they wanted to be sure that at any time that it was necessary, any of the citizens would be able to pass through the veils, and not have to worry about them. So there is woven into every stitch of clothing "IR" tags that automatically adjust to the changes. And we now know that is what the primitives are using to pass unharmed through our protections. It makes it very simple for them, and it is obvious that it didn't take them very long to figure this one out. And on that subject are you sure this show that all of you are planning won't be figured out also?"

It was a question all of them had been asking, and as complicated as the plan was, the whole thing was more a timing thing, than anything else, and that was one of the many reasons all of them were practicing so hard. Most of the operations would be handled by the computers that they would have hidden on site, with redundancy in every system, including the many machines and equipment that would be playing a direct part in the play. After thinking about this Judd answered, "All we can hope is that they won't. We have one hole card at this moment, even though I haven't had a chance to talk with her, but in a sense she is our front person. It turns out she is known by the people who rescued us. She is a captive of the clan whose leader is the leader of the alliance."

"A woman? Charley exclaimed, "I understand that women are no more than baby generators, and have no rights, or even are allowed to speak in the presence of any male. At least that is what all of you have passed on to us."

"And that's very true. I know it from first-hand experience having to watch our captive women submit to their males, and not be able to do anything about it, other than vow that somehow we could end it, and now we have that chance."

"Okay, I guess you just confirmed it then, but how is this particular woman going to help?"

"I'm really not allowed to say a lot on that subject, but let's just say that she has left an impression on the clan that she is more than just a woman, or in their case, a female. Anyway, this is off the subject, how much time are we looking at? With this next approaching storm, which is going to be another strong one, we'll be hauling everything we have from here to the site, and after we cache it there, will be coming to pick up whatever you have ready, plus anybody that you have, that is going to do the grunt work, which is necessary to get this set up. Every male here will be on site, leaving the women to operate the Alpha, and to monitor everything. We're quite short here normally, but by cutting the staff literally in half, it will be a critical shortage, and the ones left here at the Alpha will be pushed to the very limit on monitoring the situation as things develops and at the same time keeping us informed as to what is transpiring. As you know we've been testing all of this stuff, but the area where we were working is very much smaller than that valley, so while we've scaled up everything, there's no guarantee that it will be enough. That's why we need it in place well before the time of need, so that we can test everything when it is in place, and modify or add as necessary. Remember this valley or rift is huge, and lies just outside of the desolation, making it a very convenient jumping off point for their attacks, since all of our cities are located in that desolation."

Taking a deep breath and exhaling it slowly, Charley shook his head, "I just wish that we had more time, but I guess if wishes came true we'd see a rescue shuttle from our home world." He paused a moment and then almost whispered, "Who'd of thought that we weren't from here but somewhere out there in the vast unknown. I've had a chance to look over what was sent from the Alpha, and it sure makes one yearn to see it. I mean the images of this world from space are spectacular, and the images of our world make this one pale in comparison." Sighing Charley said, "Okay, I know that the storm will hit us first and that I've got to have as much as we can ready for you. So, one way or the other, I guess we'll actually be seeing each other face to face for the very first time, instead of just over the circuits."

"Yeah, I guess that's very true. You know maybe the isolation between the cities isn't a good thing. I mean I understand why they did this, our ancestors, but nobody can support anybody, and right now that is something that is very necessary. We're being lucky that you're as close as you are to that valley. Okay then, see you very soon." At this point Judd signed off, stood a moment staring at nothing, shuddered a little, as another dark thought went briefly through his mind, left and headed back to his shop.

* * *

It was moving day, well, that's what they decided to call it anyway. It was the day that all the men would be leaving the facility and with the storm raging, head for the valley of the primitives, as they had begun to call it. Once there they would cache the materials out of the weather with some of the portable shelters they were carrying. They were more than just tents, and could for a while be temporary living quarters, workshops, or whatever they needed. These units used air bladders to form ribs that supported them; being double-walled they did a fair job insulating any from the outside elements. They had enough vehicles that everybody was driving and no one was a passenger. Once they were set up, and the equipment unloaded they would then head over to the City of Catskill, meet Charley and his crew, and return. Then no matter what the weather presented, they would be working from dawn to dusk, and Saige was sure, as was Judd, that at times they would be working deep into the night.

The night before all had bid their goodbyes and they had proceeded down the trail to the secondary site, checked all the equipment one last time, and had "batched" it, before heading out just before dawn. Even with the vehicles it was a couple days travel to reach the valley of the primitives. At least with the storm there would be no sign of their passing. Again like their surveillance vehicles that they used when they scouted, these had the capability to either hover, or move on wheels, all according to the terrain that they were traversing at that particular moment. And when they finally reached their destination, it was with gale force winds and snow blowing and dropping from the sky causing white out conditions. At least there truly would be nothing left of the trail they had made coming here.

All of them got out of the vehicles and went to the lee side of the biggest one to get out of the wind. Even still it was almost impossible to hear over the gale. "I don't know if these shelters are supposed to stand in conditions like this. Did anybody see the specs on these things?" Saige asked. All he got was blank stares as the wind whipped his words away. It was freezing, and even with the heavy protection the cold was penetrating making all of them shake from the cold. "Look, this reminds me of our first winter on the mountain. Our research suggests that this valley is a result of ancient volcanic action as it was part of what created those mountains. So let's spread out in teams of two and see if we can find a cave or caves for us to spend the night. At least with our portable heaters we won't be lacking for heat, but this is absolutely miserable. So let's do it. Use the vehicles to get close to the walls, and then use the headlights to illuminate the area to make it easier to see. Use your headsets to keep in contact, and if anybody finds one that is big enough to hold our team, and then let us know and then we can use it for tonight. If necessary, tomorrow we can attempt to find something better if we need to. "

It had taken a full two days to reach the valley, and even though it was difficult to tell, they had arrived just before dusk. The only way they could judge, other than by the time, was the slowly darkening sky and the subtle deepening of the shadows in the surrounding area. With care, and half the vehicles now circled close to the area where the leader of the alliance stayed when the alliance was in the valley, they headed out in teams of two in the remaining vehicles towards the perimeter of valley. The storm was even interfering with the headsets, setting up a continual static making it harder to hear anything at all. So between the sounds of the storm, the vehicles, and the static, it took them a while to recognize that there had been a cave found, smaller than the one that they had lived in that first winter, but big enough to hold the team, but it had taken until full darkness had fallen for it to be located. Eventually they moved just enough equipment inside so that they could heat the small space, have some hot food and lots of coffee, and have a place to bed down. Once inside and out of the wind it was like a pressure being lifted off of all of them, and the silence in comparison to the howling storm left their ears ringing. Nobody felt like talking as they were beat. So one by one they grabbed their food, ate it quietly and then turned in. Tomorrow would be soon enough to begin the setup. And with this storm raging there was little to no chance that any of the primitives would be out scouting. It was just too nasty. The last thing that Saige did before he retired was to contact the Alpha letting them know that they were here and safe, although with the fierceness of the storm they would be spending the night in a cave.

* * *

For the next three weeks, with the help of the team from Catskill, they worked putting together and testing the equipment. They found, about three quarters of the way up one of the cliff faces, a hidden cave that was invisible from below. It was from this cave that they put their control room, placing a hologram over the entrance to hide it completely from the eyes of the primitives. Again this was set up to allow them to peer out and monitor with their own eyes if one of the many cameras and monitors failed. They placed a robust solar power system that was installed on a couple of the inaccessible cliff tops, placing them in such a way to avoid detection. Again the cave that they chose for their control room confirmed that this area at one time had been volcanic. Here, because of the size, they were able to put the storage batteries, and once all the equipment was installed, the one very large cave seemed a bit cramped. Yet with everything planned they couldn't reduce the size or amount of equipment.

The storms were lessening, showing all of them that winter were running out of energy and spring wasn't far off. Time was very short, and it just seemed like there was just too much that still needed to be done, and not enough accomplished. All would be up before dawn, and work late into the night, and at times they would break into shifts and with the great beacons would work throughout the night. As each piece and section was completed, they would test it, and test it again. And in areas where it was critical, not that most of these weren't, redundancy was the order of the day. Pressure was on, and with each short test and failure, replacements had to be installed. Soon it would be time to return the team to Catskill and they would be on their own, continuing to test, and run through the timings.

Standing in the early morning light Judd said to Charley, "Well, this has been a lot of very hard work, but we surely couldn't have done this without you and your people. I can really say that now, looking back on what we did here. Now for the rest of us before we return to the Alpha it's just test, replace where necessary, clean up and get out of here ourselves until that time when we see the movements of the clans and tribes heading in this direction warning us that it will be show time. Remember the frequencies, not that it's important that you do that since they will be given to every city that still exists." He reached out and shook Charley's hand, at which point Charley just nodded, climbed into the crew section of the vehicle with his crew and the vehicle pulled away heading off into the direction of Catskill. Judd watched it until they were out of sight sighed, turned around and headed back to the base camp. He glanced back at the cliff face where the hidden cave was located. It surely looked different with the scaffolding removed, and just the rope ladders hanging down. These ladders would allow them access to the many areas that they would have to reach before pulling them up and hiding them. Once the primitives were here in this valley they would be staying within that upper cavern out of sight and out of harm's way. They still had much to do, and they hadn't tried running everything completely through the program to see if the system would hold up.

He had to admit that a very hot cup of coffee this morning would be just the thing he needed. He was finding that he just didn't have the reserves that he had in the past, and that his recovery from being tired took longer. His mind said let's go do this and finish it, and his body would argue back starting with the question, "You want me to do what?" Just where were those reserves he had in his youth? It seemed as the long days had passed that it had been more and more difficult to get moving in the mornings, and his mind remained in a fog much longer than he could remember. He was finding it was easier to make mistakes, and mistakes he would have never made if he had been fresh. It frustrated him to no end – admonishing himself continually to concentrate, to get with the program. *Oh well, we'll be done soon, and once done rest will be there.* As he entered back into the camp area it appeared to be so empty now. With him there were only nine of them now. Breathing out deeply he stared at their small fire went over to it and warmed his hands.

Saige looking up from where he was sitting said, "I guess we're back to just us now. I'm glad that you had that contact; I can tell that we really wouldn't have been able to do this on our own with this small of a crew. Thank you for this, and of course before they left I personally thanked each one of them." Looking around the campsite he said, "I must admit that this place looks a lot lonelier at this moment with only us. But it is a lot quieter now, and I admit that right now the quiet is very nice. With all the work going on at times it seemed like we were building a city right here in this valley instead of setting up a show. I must admit that this gives me a much better appreciation for the work that goes on behind the scenes of some of those stage shows we used to go see now and then when we still had a city."

"You did that? I was under the impression that the scouting unit never left your compound and came into the cities."

Laughing Saige replied, "Well for the most part you are quite correct. But as rewards for teams we would be able to go get something special in the city or most of the time go see some stage entertainment. There were competitions four times an annual and the winners were allowed half a day to do what they pleased, and were given passes to the plays, and to go to the markets to get some trinket or the like. It was fun, and it gave us something to look forward to now and then. And the competitions were always fun, even though there was always a serious side to them." He paused a moment with a serious faraway look in his eyes, "But I guess in the end, it was proven that we weren't as good as we thought we were. Had we, then so many more of us would have survived that flight from our city."

Judd thought a moment before saying anything. He hadn't been there, but from his time at the Alpha he could see that this was something that continued to weigh heavily on both of the leaders, and he could understand it. Nobody had seen what had transpired coming. "I don't know how to answer that Saige, but none of us were prepared for what happened. And how could you and your scouts know that your team was the last? If the rest had kept the program, then there's a slight possibility that we would have had some warning, but would it had made any difference? I have no answers, and I know that you and Shellian keep beating yourself over the past, something we cannot change. Yes I admit that like some of those games that are available on the systems and boards, it would be nice if we could either start a level over, or take a move back on a board. Life, unfortunately doesn't allow second chances that way. So we have to live with what happened to us, and learn from it or be doomed to repeat. I would say that the two of you, and yes the rest of the scout team there at the Alpha has definitely learned from it."

Waving his arms around in the direction of the whole valley he continued. "Look here's your proof. If you and yours hadn't gained something from that nightmare I really don't think we would be here doing what we are. I don't think that I and the rest from Jade would be there at the Alpha either, and the knowledge that has been passed on to the other cities would have been either. Yes I know that it's in our nature to keep bashing ourselves for some oversight or mistake that we made, but it's part of life and if you think about it, we make small mistakes all of our lives. It's what we learn from those mistakes that makes the difference. And from my humble point of view, you and the rest here and back at the Alpha have learned quite a bit. And none of you have sat back and just watched the grass grow. We are here just about, hopefully, to correct a very big mistake made by our leadership, by our people, and save many lives, much misery, and destruction. And why is this happening? Because you learned, and were then willing to apply what you learned."

Looking around the valley once more before looking back at Saige, Judd continued, "Look, none of us can predict the outcome from this little adventure. All of us are hoping that it works. But what if it doesn't? Does this mean that you'll give up and throw in the towel? From what I've seen the answer is obvious, out in the open, it's there for any to see. No, you and the rest will continue to try to come up with something else, and continue to press on until either all of us are dead, or you have succeeded. I can see why this Shayne passed on the leadership to the two of you. Your abilities have been proven in fire, and because of this the two of you have, if nothing else, gotten stronger, you've been tempered to a strength and resolution of a high quality stainless steel of unbelievable flexibility and strength. And if you cannot see this, the rest of us can, and that's why we follow you and Shellian. You've proven your right to lead us." Looking around he could see he now had an audience. He smiled briefly and to all of them he said, "Sorry about that. I didn't mean to get up on the box and say all of this – although I won't take any of it back." He could see that the rest completely agreed with him.

A final test and everything appeared to work. They spent the next week wiping out any trace of their work and occupation of the valley, and hoped that the early spring rains would bring new growth furthering the illusion that the valley lay untouched. Through much of their time snow lay on the ground, and they had set up camp in the areas where the tribes of the alliance had, so that any paths and such that they created would blend in with the existing ones. It was time to head back and let the lands recover and finish hiding what they may have missed.

* * *

The rains had come and gone in the grasslands and the new growth and lush grasses had pushed up through the soils that were being warmed by the twin suns providing food for the herds as the migrations from the warmer areas to these areas that were normally under snow. The primitives were out, knowing that the meat from these beasts would be thin, yet it still was needed. This last season of cold had been the worst that any could remember, and while there had been enough fuels for the fires, and food, what they had been eating towards the end barely fulfilled their physical needs. All needed to get out and begin the renewing so that they would be able to prepare for the next unknown season of cold. And once this was accomplished, then and only then, would it be time for the alliance to meet in the valley, send out scouting parties, and find more of those hidden lairs.

K'jor remained somewhat frustrated as the female had yet to recover enough to be able to answer the burning questions that he wanted to ask. Yet as this one healed it was becoming more obvious to both himself and T'som that this female was a priest. Yet what tribe or clan would place a female in such an important position? Still he had to admit that as they attacked these hidden lairs, it appeared that these females held important positions, and were not a part of a breeding herd. This was something that he couldn't understand. It made no sense at all. Females and their position within the clans and tribes were for producing young, to insure the next generation. And as in the herds, only the strong would breed with them insuring strength for the future. Yet what he had observed in these lairs was nothing like this at all. It was beyond his comprehension and understanding. This had to be an aberration, what he saw was not normal, and another reason to see the end to these lairs.

Sara was frustrated with her slow recovery, but at the same time was thankful. Because had she made a full recovery, she knew that she would be warming some warrior's sleeping mat, completely against her will, but that wouldn't change or prevent it from happening. So with the brief meetings that she had with the priest she began to build her character as one who was equal to him. With the help of the bugs and the team back at the Alpha she knew what was happening within the clan, and of course most of what was happening out in the wilds. This information she used to present herself as not only a priest but a seer, one who had visions and could see even the intimate details. She could see at first surprise and disbelief from T'som as she met him as an equal. This was unheard of and at first she could see that he was indignant wanting to put her, as a female, in her place. But at that very moment she used her inside knowledge and told him exactly what he had been doing, and who he had bred with in the last day. She smiled inwardly as she saw the shock on his face, confirming the information that the team had passed on to her. Maybe she could get a small amount of revenge and begin to make them fear her a little. But she knew that this was too much to hope for. But the thought was nice.

The best part of this whole episode was the hope she now felt – something that hadn't existed for so long. She only wished she could bring the other two inside with her and let them know, but she had realized long ago that with the fear these two had, it would have been too easy for them to become traitors and try and protect themselves by giving her away. Now instead of knowing in her heart that she would die here under the thumb of this clan, she had hope that soon this could be over and she would be free of them. The ones at the Alpha wouldn't let her know what was planned, but only that her role as a priest would help. She had been told that the reason for not informing her was the chance of what they were planning could get back to the primitives. At first she was hurt by this, but realized that the less that knew of these plans the better the chance at success. So she had to be comfortable with what they were asking of her and know this imprisonment could be over very soon.

* * *

Seirra was back in the rotation for the security office and she saw that the tribes and clans appeared to be preparing to move. It was time to get the team into place. Her mate Saige, Stone, Judd, and Staven would be the ones on the ground. It was almost show time, and they needed to be there well ahead of any early arrivals. Seve would drive them there and then return. She announced over the PA that it was time to get the next phase of the operation into motion. She could feel the electricity go throughout the facility. Shorty they would know if all this planning and work was worth it. In the cafeteria they had set up monitors that would allow all who remained at the facility to watch the many hidden cameras that had been placed in the valley. Joci would be given a front row seat to this, since it was her idea. But would it bring an end to the attacks? This was a question that was on everybody's mind. Not only the ones at the Alpha, but all the remaining cities. The pressure and fear that had permeated the cities was substantial. With no one knowing who would be next, and with the failure of finding a way around the system that their ancestors had put into place, there would be no defense against the primitives. What had seemed to be a good idea at the time of implementation had come back and left the cities wide open to attack. With the cities that had fallen, the primitive warriors had enough clothing to outfit twice the attacking force's size – allowing them to pass unharmed through the fields and into the unprotected cities. At this moment the only protection was the illusions created by the holograms, and the shock fields, this had worked in the past, but not now. Somehow, somewhere these primitives had figured out the difference. Now it was only the distance between them and their locations within the desolation that had given them any respite.

* * *

K'jor looked on with satisfaction. While it had been a tough season of cold, looking around he could see that most of the tribes and clans had returned to this meeting place of the alliance. Soon, very soon he would be leading the greatest force of warriors that had ever gathered in the history of this place. Instead of fighting each other they had found a common enemy to unite against, and somehow through this he was leading. Yet he knew that if they didn't find any more of the lairs that this alliance would fall apart, and the old ways would return. In the next few days the scouts would be sent to locate more of those hidden lairs, and once located they would continue as they had in the past, attacking, destroying, gathering more slaves, and adding to the breeding herds. While many of the ones who had been taken in the past had passed into the spirit world, it was of no consequence. There were others out there to replace them, this he felt deeply inside of him. And soon, the one female who was still recovering from being at the brink of the spirit world would be able to provide answers. Yes, answers to the questions that burned deep in his soul.

This night there would be a meeting of the tribe and clan leaders just outside of his shelter as they renewed vows to stay and be strong within the alliance, to find how all had fared over this last brutal season of cold. He felt that the clans with their permanent settlements probably fared better than the nomadic tribes. Still what the tribes gained from the alliance was a strength they never had individually. And even though there were fewer warriors in these tribes, they benefited from the slaves and increases to their herds in proportion to their size. As he walked the camp areas he could see the smoke rising from many fires that marked the center of the camps of the combined alliance. He couldn't help but smile, and feel pride rise up inside of him. He led this combined might. With it just maybe, after they had accomplished what they were trying to do, this alliance could be used to bring other troublesome tribes and clans in line, and if they would not cooperate then, with this force they could be removed as if they never had existed. Shaking his head in disbelief, what he was seeing before him was something that had never been accomplished before, and this would be at least the fourth season of fighting, or maybe it was five, he truly couldn't remember. But what he had accomplished was unheard of. Looking at both the oral and written history, the records spoke of only a couple of tribes or clans ever alliancing and for only a short time. Here and over the time of its existence, he had thousands of warriors to command. Turning around to his second he asked, "What do you think? I really held out little hope back after our first season that we could hold this alliance together, but now after all of this time it is still here and still strong."

S'lon looked around at the many fires, and back at K'jor nodded his head in agreement. Like K'jor he'd had doubts that this alliance could be held together, but so far there appeared to be no weakness in it, and he thought that as long as this one common enemy existed that it would remain that way. He could see the pride in K'jor, and why not? He had been the one who had the vision to approach these many tribes and clans to convince them to join together. He really had held out little hope that K'jor would be successful, yet here before his eyes was the very proof that he had been. "I must admit that at the beginning I held out little hope of success, but you proved me wrong, and the proof is right here. I have to admit that this is a very impressive sight. And to see that most are still with you speaks much for your leadership." So many of the ones who were within the alliance had been bitter enemies at one time, and to prevent a renewing of the hostilities, the camps were set on opposite sides of the valley. Sometimes old hatreds died a hard death.

The suns had set and as dusk turned to darkness with stars shining brightly and the many fires rivaling those stars for attention, soon the major moon would rise, changing the landscape to a ghostly, shadowy image. It was a time for the spirits to walk, but K'jor knew that the priests had asked that this valley be protected. For both the major and minor moons provided the lesser light where the spirits dwelled. He could see the leaders approaching the meeting place and anticipated this first gathering of war. His faith was strong and his strength could be no better, he felt deep within that these other hidden lairs would be his soon enough, and then all could return as it was before, secure in their minds that they were in control of their destinies. No hidden lairs to threaten who they were or the directions that they may want to travel. *Yes soon we will have destroyed all of these lairs, and who knows, maybe we can move on and use this hammer to bring the troublesome tribes and clans in line and maybe keep us united.* These thoughts brought a smile to his face as he saw the future that this alliance could bring to this world.

As the major moon began to rise above the cliffs shining its soft dim light into the valley shadows and illusions of movement began to manifest all around them. And with this rising a slight breeze more sensed than felt moved the small grasses, and then a deathly silence fell that was unusual. So unusual that even the noises from the camps stopped. Looking around for a cause K'jor could find nothing. He could see that the other leaders had stopped in their tracks and were doing the very same thing. There was electricity in the air, one of anticipation, but of what none of them knew. This was very strange indeed. He turned to make a comment to his second, but before he could even state anything the sounds of drums assailed him, and all who were in this valley. But these were like none they had ever heard. The very volume shook them. The drums seemed to be emanating from the cliffs where the waterfall fell into the valley. As one they all turned and faced the cliffs, and before them sitting on the ground cross-legged were giants, except they had never seen any giants this big. In front of them were the drums and they were beating out a constant rhythm with high points and softer measures leading them to anticipation of something else happening.

They didn't have long to wait because across the ground heading towards them at a rapid pace was a ground fog that began to take on a life of its own. Dancing and rippling, moving around all barriers and leaving nothing untouched. This brought a ripple of fear as at points it began to glow as if it was a living thing. Then the campfires in the all of the camps changed color, going completely blue, dancing higher and stronger. When one looked into these changed fires they could see sprites dancing among the flames, adding more fear. What was happening and what was this they were witnessing?

Had the very gods decided to visit them? A very valid question to be sure. Then in the middle of these blue flames that continued to increase in size, beings took form and began to point at the tribe and clan members bringing them close to panic. Never had any faced demons but before them now were such. Even though at this moment these demons appeared to be part of the fire, the primitives had no idea if these would remain so. Fear continued to build, but the worst was yet to come. K'jor stood there transfixed with what he was seeing and hearing. Maybe he was about to get his answers to those so many questions, but at this moment he wasn't quite sure that he would like these answers. Turning towards the priests that had accompanied him he asked harshly, "What is this? I was under the belief that this valley is protected. Does this look like it is to you?"

All the priests could do was shrug. One responded, "We have laid down our prayers and protections, and it has worked in the past."

Waving his arms around wildly and with some anger K'jor asked, "Does this look like your protection is working?" He could see from the fear in their eyes and that they had no answers. He decided to head towards these cliffs and face what was there. He wanted some answers as to why, and while he knew that he was mortal, as far as what he was facing at this moment could be no different. With a fast pace he headed towards these distance cliffs finding that he was able to only go a short distance and the fog suddenly jumped away and strong winds struck him pushing him back. When he stopped and retreated a little, the winds ceased and the fog returned boiling at his feet. Suddenly he jumped back. It had felt like something had grabbed at his feet, but with the fog could see nothing. Stomping, and striking the ground beneath this fog he found nothing to make contact with, and retreated further until he was back at the edge of the camp. It appeared that he or any of the ones gathered here would not be allowed to approach those cliffs. Looking over at others he could see that some others had tried exactly what he had and were now at the edge of their camps staring at the cliffs with others watching the demons that remained in the many fires.

Whatever was happening, or was going to happen, the line had been drawn and whatever it was definitely had their attention. Most of the warriors in the camps were now staring at the cliffs remaining quiet, waiting to see what would be shown to them next. The moving ground fog took on an eerie glow with shadows moving within it making it appear that there were creatures living within that fog. And as the shadows would approach a warrior, the warrior would feel something touch him and he would jump. Yes there was something there, something that could attack them, but how could they retaliate? All there were was shadows and nothing of substance. How did you fight something that wasn't there? All of them had considered themselves warriors, and had no real fear of fighting others, but this was different, so very different. They were being attacked, but could not return in favor. And the fires continued to dance with the demons still controlling them, the fog and its many shadow creatures continued to flow around them, and all they could do was watch and wait.

The drum beat changed and in one abrupt roll stopped, and silence once again reigned. Instead of lessening of the fear it only heightened it. These giants remained silent and motionless. For what seemed like forever the silence continued. Suddenly the waterfall began to glow in a soft light which continued to get stronger. As its strength grew the giants bowed and touched their mighty heads to the drums, lying prostrate across the drums swaying to the motion of the waterfall, rising back up and began to beat the drums once again, but this time it was a softer and slower beat. The warriors' attention was now directed completely on the waterfall which now glowed in a strong light, and in that light they could see a being forming, forming out of nothing but the mists, and as this was happening the skies above them lit with mighty fires and explosions, erupting in many colors, and in those eruptions another being was forming out of nothingness. If there had been fear before in the camps it was nothing to what they were feeling at this moment. It was obvious to all of them that the very gods that they worshiped were showing themselves to each and every warrior that was here. And if this was indeed what was transpiring how did one survive? After all a mortal could not fight and win against an immortal – a god.

But the gods weren't finished with them as the very ground, close to those cliffs, there began to form another being. The demons had been enough, the addition of this ground fog and the shadow creatures that dwelled within had made it worse, but now at least three of their gods were making an actual appearance, would there be more, and why were they doing this? Was it to show them their power over all things living and those who had passed into the world of the spirits? K'jor was at loss to explain any of this, and he knew that the priests, from their earlier reaction couldn't. So he would have to wait as the others. Yes he had to admit that he feared what he was seeing, but so far he wasn't frozen to inaction. He knew that a line had been drawn by whatever or whoever these beings were, and the warriors had been warned that they could be hurt or killed if they crossed that line. So he continued to wait, as they all did.

The god of the waters was now visible and had been looking down. He looked up and directly at them pointing with his mighty finger right at them, this was followed by the god that hung in the sky and he too pointed directly at them. Both had a stern disapproving, reproachful look on their mighty faces. The third had yet to form, the one of the earth. Then this one came into sharp focus, and they were shocked to learn that this god was female. The god of the earth was female, how could that be? Of the three she appeared to be the one whose look alone could send one to the spirit world. She, like the other two pointed at them. Absolutely all the primitives now stood in complete shock and fear frozen to their very cores by what they were witnessing. The three gods turned as one and pointed to the cliff top, a place completely inaccessible to any other than the gods. As they pointed the cliff top lit up as if it was daylight and where the light shown stood a single individual dressed in a hooded robe, looking a little like their own priests, but at the same time not.

This priest was looking down and his face completely hidden in shadow. He turned to the three gods and bowed to them each individually, and as he did each god acknowledged this homage. The god of the earth turned and faced the primitives and spoke directly to them. The voice was deep and full, and when she spoke it filled the valley with power. "I see that you are shocked that I am female. Yet it should not be so. After all as your mortal female bring forth your new generation it is I who brought forth all that live on this world.

It is I who gave your first people their lives, it is I who produced the herd beasts, the grasses that they eat, the plants, all that is living is because of my creation." At this point she ceased and was quiet.

The god of the sky took up the next statements. "I am of the sky. I am responsible for the rain, the snow, the winds, the clouds. It is I who will give and withhold the rains, make them light, make them heavy, allow your foods to prosper or to wither, to chase the beasts away with the winds or storms, I provide this." He fell silent.

The third picked up from there, "I am the god of the flowing waters, of the lakes and oceans, I change the rivers, bringing it close or taking it away, building great lakes where the fish dwell, move it close to the beasts so that they may fatten and provide meat, take away when I am unhappy." He fell silent.

Then to the warriors' surprise the demons that were dancing in the flames began to speak in unison. "We are of fire. We can create fire from the sky, burn off great areas of the grasslands, forests, we will not be controlled by such as you, but allow the use of fire to cook your food, to keep you warm in the season of cold, and we watch always."

All of these gods, once again turned towards the priest that stood on the cliff top, pointed and as they pointed the drummers chanted something that could not be translated. This single priest was raised into the air standing on nothing with his arms outstretched they could see blue sparks emitting from his fingertips. The god of the sky turned back to the shaking warriors and asked, "K'jor, why have you attacked and destroyed our servants, our priests? They were hidden from you in the desolation. They were intermediaries between us, the spirit world and were tasked with the responsibility to watch, from a distance, you and yours. Yet you have come into the very place that you are not to be, a place of the spirits, a place where you can only visit with no way to survive if you remain. Why have you done these things?"

The god of the waters picked up from there and said, "We have been watching and have been greatly troubled by your actions. We sent warnings, which you ignored, we sent a harsh season of cold, which you ignored, we have been patient waiting for your understanding that this was to stop. Yet, here you are, as are all these warriors, getting set to start another campaign against our servants, against us. How are we to interpret this, to see your actions? And finally how are we to respond? These were things that we have discussed among ourselves. In the end it was felt that we should reveal ourselves, not all obviously, but we three were chosen. It is here that we draw the line in the sand. We have passed on to our servant who now is before you some of our power, although it will be only here and only now. This ends here, and if you and your alliance of warriors continues in this vein, we will bring forth all the power that we have and destroy all of you, all of the clans, all of the tribes, and the god of the earth will begin again, creating new life to replace you and yours if necessary. We require that you return all that you have made slaves, all that you have added to your breeding herds, return them here or feel the wrath that we can bring down upon you. The time is short and we who are over you will now have our servant demonstrate."

Again the three gods turned and pointed at the priest who was suspended in the air. At the moment they pointed he glowed absorbing the power from the gods. This priest then spoke, "The time is short, by the end of the season of greening all that have survived your abuse will be placed here in the valley of the gods. They must be returned unharmed; we know that many have passed into the spirit world, for they have told us of the abuse they received from you. The females were protected and because of this protection could not carry any of your offspring. It would have been an affront for such to happen." At this point this priest swept his left arm out from his body and as he did lines of explosions traveled rapidly across the valley in front of the warriors, and everywhere these explosions took place warriors from the spirit world appeared standing in ranks looking both at the warriors and back to the priest who seemed to be commanding them. They stood in ranks keeping beat with the drums that had picked up the tempo once again. These warriors who had passed into the spirit world were now shouting in unison, tapping the spears that many carried in time with the drum beat.

Then this priest swept his right arm from his body and great explosions followed closing off the two exits into the desolation, forever blocking access from this valley. He spoke saying, "Let this be known, that with the closing of the routes to the desolation that this is a symbol, a warning that as the Sacred Mountains are only available to the priests, and yes we allow the hunters to hunt in the low areas, so shall the desolation become sacred. For it is there that we priests and servants of the gods live by their request. Return the priests and servants, and understand this – this will be your one and only warning. If these attacks continue then in short order all who will have participated will join the ones in the spirit world." At this point he brought his hands together in a single clap, and out of the sky fell a large fireball that struck in the middle of the warriors from the spirit world setting the area on fire, this was followed by a spectacular explosion and numerous smaller explosions in the night sky, drawing all of the warriors attention to the display. When the light had faded they looked back to the cliff top, but it was dark and empty, and as they looked around all was as it was before. The ground fog was gone, the drummers were gone, the gods and spirit warriors were gone, and all that remained was a deathly silence. The gods had spoken, and had put forth their displeasure, and demonstrated what would happen if they did not comply. For once K'jor, who had been singled out by the gods, was silent. He now had his answers, and felt fortunate that he was still among the living. It was obvious to him that the gods saw each and every individual and what they did with their lives. He had worried all of the season of cold if he had been wrong; he wondered why these females didn't carry, and why a female would be a priest. Now he had all his answers, and much more.

The gods had said that this was the valley of the gods, and so it would always be known. For it was here that they revealed themselves to mere mortals. No wonder the servants to the gods had female priests, since the god of the earth turned out to be female. That was a shock, but once explained made perfect sense. New life came from the female, so all life had come to be in the same way. He could deny it if he wanted, but the power demonstrated tonight was so beyond any he and all the others had ever witnessed, that he did not want it brought down upon them. He, and the rest, would comply with the demands of the gods, and the desolation would thusly become sacred as the mountains, and with the appearance of the gods here in this valley he knew that there would be a demand that this valley also become sacred and he wouldn't argue that at all. In the morning they would break camp, head back, and bring those slaves and additions to the herd back here unharmed, and then, other than the priests, leave this valley and the desolation to the gods.

* * *

Joci sat in awe of what she had just witnessed. If she hadn't known that all of this had been created by them she could have easily believed that it was all magic and sorcery, and that the gods had actually made an appearance, vented their displeasure, demonstrated their power, warned their creations, and returned to wherever they went. It was a spectacular display – just unbelievable. She felt the emotions rising in her and she began to cry, but through her tears she could hear cheering behind her. With tears running down her cheeks she turned and saw the rest of the Alpha crew cheering for the success of her idea. She was completely overwhelmed. At no point did she feel that her idea had any merit, but here was the proof that she had been wrong. Was it finally over? Had they succeeded in bringing an end to the threat? It would be known in the morning, but from what they could see the answer was yes.

Saige made his way silently in the dark back from the cliff top and with the assistance of the night goggles reached the entrance to the cave and entered. Seeing Judd leaning against one of the dimly lit walls he asked, "What happened? Got that message from you in the middle of the performance that we had to jump ahead and skip part of what we had planned and jump to the end."

"We were almost out of power. We tested each element of this darn thing a number of times to be sure it would all work. But we didn't run the thing clear through to see if we had enough battery storage to make it happen – we didn't. In fact I was worried that we wouldn't get that finale complete before everything just died, it was that close."

Shortly they were joined by the other two who had worked other operations, and other than the reduction of the one part they all felt good. So they waited out the night monitoring the camps with the remote cameras, through the portable unit that had a self-contained power supply, and as the dawn began to break they could see movement from the camped tribes and clans as they prepared to leave. Joci's idea, and the subsequent work, and planning had brought about the results that they had hoped. The attacks should now cease and the remaining cities be untouched. They still had much work ahead of them, but at least now it would be from a place of safety instead of war.

Yes they'd return back to Point Alpha and have a quiet celebration of a job well done. And with the returning of their people to this valley they knew it would take time. Then came the hard work of placing them, but all of that was for the future. Now for the first time since the first city fell they could feel safe. Safe with the knowledge of their true past, and be able to look to a real future.

Winter was upon them and with the primitives once again locked inside their homes it had been a time to travel. Saige with Seirra stood on top of a small rise inside the compound that had been their home since they had joined the scouting unit. It was a bittersweet moment. He was holding his daughter Saharra, and Seirra their son Seth. Time had flown as their twins were close to walking, and with this being a strange place to both they could see both the excitement and fear in the children. Saharra clung to him, and he hugged her smiling, although it was a sad smile, and introspection had set in. It seemed almost like another lifetime that they had been here, living, unconcerned, practicing and learning. The clouds above them were gray and sullen, full of moisture and a light rare mist was falling, chilling them as the soft breeze would caress them. He could see the rest of the original team with their children, yes Sorrel had successfully carried and delivered a daughter, and with the healthy baby, one could see the additional worry and fear melt from her, and she was very happy. And to break from tradition she named her daughter April, but was it really, after all her daughter was born in the Alpha.

They were exploring the many buildings that stood vacant and broken, the places that had been home to all of them. Here they could sense the ghosts of the past, in this once thriving city which was dead, that had fallen to the primitives so very long ago. Towards the entrance to the city they could see Sara, she still was weak, but Saar had given her a clean bill of health, and with the care at the Alpha, she had recovered. Saige couldn't help but smile when he saw her kneeling down and straightening something on one of her sons. She had been through hell, and fortunate that when it ended that she was reunited with her sons. So few had been returned when compared to the numbers that had been captured. So many had suffered at the hands of the primitives, and had died. How many families were no more? It was a question for which he knew that he would have no answer. This was now a lonely silent world, this city, and a world that was not truly home. Maybe someday, their ancestors would look upon their birth world, if it still existed, and return home from a world that was to be a temporary assignment, a temporary stop in their lives. But time had shown that one can never predict or plan for the outcome that hides in the future, and while it was unknown to them, as to any who existed in this universe, at least they knew that with what their past had presented to them, they could face whatever the future handed them.

Turning to Seirra Saige asked, "What do you think, should we go join the rest of them? I feel that this is the last time we'll ever see Sequoyah, and now the Alpha is home, at least for now."

Like Saige, Seirra smiled, but it too was a sad one. So much had happened, so much had changed, so much tragedy, and yet here they were. Looking down and then into his eyes she said, "Yeah, lets."

Names of Characters, Cities and Locations

Pt Alpha	Hidden complex in the Sacred Mountains
April	Daughter of Stone and Sorrel
Barbara	Unwilling member of female herd – assisting Sara
Beth	Unwilling member of female herd – assisting Sara
Catskill	City located in the desolation close to the Valley of the Gods
Charley	Late 40's – Occupation: Replicator operations, jack of all trades
Jade	One of the destroyed cities
Jaiden	Early 40's – Occupation: Librarian
Jarid	Late 20's – Occupation: Entertainer. Good looking and lady's man.
Jas	Late 30's to early 40's – Occupation: Pediatric Nurse
Jeanna	Mid 20's – Occupation: Teacher and history major. A very beautiful woman.

Jed	Early 30's – Occupation: Farmer, hydroponics. Build – similar to Stone.
Jessi	Early 20's – Occupation: Physical trainer, could have been member of scouting unit.
Joci	Mid to late teens – no occupation at this time, but works with the children.
Judd	Early 50's – Occupation: Independent business owner and jack of all trades.
Keahilani	Pivot city for the hidden cities in the desolation
Keenan	Mid 50's – Occupation: Shift supervisor in the communications center
Sequoyah	Destroyed city #5 – Home to the last scouting unit.
Saar	Late 20's – Occupation: Doctor for scouting unit
Sabryn	Mid 20's – Occupation: Field operative, scouting unit.
Saharra	Daughter of Saige and Seirra (twin to Seth)

Saige	Mid 20's – Occupation: Part of 2 person scouting team, Co-leader, (J'far)
Samantha	Daughter of Saar and Shellian. Also known as Sam
Sara	Sister to Shayne, deceased leader of scouting unit, unwilling member of female herd.
Seirra	Early to mid-20's – Occupation: Monitoring team of the scout unit
Seth	Son of Saige and Seirra (twin to Saharra)
Seve	Mid 20's – Occupation: Field scout (K'fah)
Shayne	Son of Staven and Starr (Named after the deceased leader)
Shellian	Early to mid-20's – Occupation: Part of 2 person scouting team, Co-leader
Sommer	Daughter of Seve and Sabryn
Sorrel	Mid 20's – Occupation: Forward scouting. Has a way with men.
Starr	Early 20's – Occupation: Support staff for scouting unit.

Staven   Mid 20's – Occupation: Field scout (T'soh)

Stone   Mid to late 20's – Occupation: Information specialist, geologist, horticulture, important member of the scouting unit. (L'sum)

Primitives

K'jor   Leader of both the clan and the alliance

R'san   Old warrior responsible for day to day operations, friend and mentor to K'jor

S'lon   2nd in command

T'som   Head Priest of the clan, advisor and friend of K'jor

Locations

The Desolation: A great desert lying west of the grasslands

The Grasslands: A vast plain that runs from the southern end to the Sacred Mountains

Sacred Mountains: Volcanic range located on the Northern end of continent

Northeast Foothills: Where the clan of K'jor lives

Valley of the Gods: Originally known as the alliance headquarters and borders the desolation

ABOUT THE AUTHOR

F.D. Brant always wanted to write, but life got in the way. Finally after retiring he got his chance.

Storytelling and writing has always been F.D. Brant's passion, but responsibilities took preference. And because of those responsibilities it took retiring to allow those passions to come to fruition. Since retiring he has written 9 books, and maintains a weekly eclectic blog, Words in the Wind.

Growing up in the backcountry he learned the appreciation of "doing things for yourself". Because it was impossible to call in someone to repair anything one either did it themselves or went without. This led to the appreciation of the natural world, and the daily struggles that one faced as nature threw problems at the family that had to be overcome, leading to confidence and self-sufficiency. This led to the strong characters that populate his stories and books. And his female protagonists are strong willed and confident – something that he saw in both in his mother and sister.

www.ingramcontent.com/pod-product-compliance
Lightning Source LLC
Chambersburg PA
CBHW050604170726
48283CB00001B/99